FOOL'S GOLD

Jennifer
Skully

HQN™

ISBN 0-373-77081-2

FOOL'S GOLD

www.HQNBooks.com

Printed in U.S.A.

To my Mom
For allowing my irreverence with your English
heritage. For your delicious trifle and numerous
tarts. And for just being you, Mom. I love you!

Acknowledgments

Thanks to all the special people in my life!
Laurel Jacobson, Linda Simi and Krystal Mignone
for listening to my dreams and helping me
to believe they'd become a reality.
Jenn Cummings, Terri Schaefer, Rose Lerma,
Lucienne Diver and Dee Knight for all their help
on this manuscript. And Kathy Coatney for
once again keeping me honest with
that daily page count.

Ann Leslie Tuttle and Tracy Farrell. For all your
support. My brother-in-law, Jonny, for being
such a wonderful storyteller. Thank you for
giving me the Twinkie idea and for explaining
the intricacies of outhouse excavation. I hope
you find many treasures in yours!

The people of the real town after which I
patterned Goldstone, for giving me endless food
for thought. And Mr. Dahlstrom, for inspiring
such a great character and for being such a
character himself. Rest in peace.

My sister, Janice, for being the best sister ever!

FOOL'S GOLD

CHAPTER ONE

"MAGGIE'S *YOUR* SISTER." Desperation crept into Carl Felman's voice. "You tell me what I'm supposed to say to her."

Tyler Braxton suppressed a shudder. What man truly knew how to talk to a woman? "Maybe if I understood the problem better, I could help." He had grave doubts that would be the case. Marital issues were not Brax's area of expertise. If Carl wanted advice on how to take down a fleeing suspect without firing a shot, he could help. But advice to the lovelorn, especially to his brother-in-law? A scary thought for any male.

Brax had arrived in Goldstone, Nevada, that morning with a mission. To answer Maggie's call for help. The tone of her e-mail had been dire enough to have him make arrangements for a visit. Because a short vacation fit neatly into his schedule for other reasons, he hadn't bothered asking Maggie for any specifics.

He hadn't figured he'd be entering a war zone.

Admittedly, it was a silent war, with both sides refusing to meet at the bargaining table, or, for that matter, even talk to their opponent. In other words, The Cold War all over again. Despite staying at ground zero, Brax didn't have a clue how to negotiate a peace settlement.

"I'm afraid she doesn't want me anymore." Carl's chin drooped close to the foam on his beer, and his usual goofy grin was nowhere to be seen. "I don't excite her."

"Please don't let this degenerate into the lowdown on your sex life." His *sister's* sex life. God forbid.

"This isn't about sex." Carl sighed long and hard. "It's about our marriage."

Country music strained through the worn-out speakers, barely making it over the ka-ching of a slot machine in the back of the bar. The once-padded chair he sat in had long since lost its resilience beneath too many butts. The tabletop was gummy with age, elbow grease and sweaty palms. Brax had thought going out for a friendly beer down at the Flood's End might ease the tension. He'd been wrong. Being county sheriff back in California was a cakewalk compared to this, but he would do his duty to his sister. Even if he'd rather be breaking up bar fights.

"How long have you and Maggie been married?" His question was rhetorical; Brax knew exactly how long. The Las Vegas wedding in Dr. Love's Chapel would forever live in his memory. Maybe the pink flamingos flanking the altar had something to do with that. Who in their right mind would want lawn ornaments at their wedding ceremony?

Carl took his time before replying, "Ten years."

"Well, things can get a bit routine after ten years." A wild guess, since Brax had gotten divorced after only five.

"That what happened to your marriage?" Carl asked.

Damn. He'd opened himself wide for that one.

Brax sat back and crossed his arms over his chest.

Then he gave it his best shot, because that's what his sister needed. "It's all about communication, Carl." Something he'd never been able to do worth a damn. At least not where women were concerned.

"We communicate. She says do something, and I do it." Carl shook his head as if he were totally mystified. "What more does she want?"

"Women don't want you to just agree with everything. They want you to…" What? Brax started over. "They want you to help them find the solution that works for both of you."

"But she always ends up with the same solution she started with, no matter what I suggest. It's like talking in circles. So why do we have to go over and over it for an hour?"

Damn. Brax didn't have an answer. He was out of his depth here. "It's the talking things through that makes them feel better." That sounded like a reasonable explanation to him.

"She just wants me to say, 'yeah, you're right, honey,' after she proves how I'm wrong."

Sometimes it did seem like that, but Brax was sure women didn't mean it that way. "When in doubt, just listen. Women want to be heard." Now that was his ex-wife almost verbatim. He'd never *heard*, and he took full responsibility for his lacking.

Carl leaned forward. "But if I'm supposed to listen and not say anything, then how is that communication? Doesn't it take two?"

Christ, he was digging himself a bigger hole with every word of advice. Best to stop while he was…well, he couldn't call it ahead. "You need to read that book."

"What book?"

Uhh… "One of those 'how to' books." How not to flush your marriage down the toilet. "It's got something about the planets in the title."

"Did you read it?"

Brax hadn't known of the book until after the divorce. "I've heard it's great." Though he didn't know any men who'd read it. "If I'm ever considering marriage again, I'll sure pick up that book." Not that he planned on taking that particular risk any time soon. "Read it, Carl. It'll help."

He wasn't ducking his responsibilities here. He was simply handing Carl over to a greater authority.

"I guess I'll give it a try."

"Atta boy." Thank God. His duty was done. On to less dangerous ground. "Not very crowded here tonight, is it?"

Carl's glance strayed over Brax's shoulder, and not for the first time that evening. No small wonder when one considered the woman seated at the far end of the bar. Brax shifted in his chair for a better look.

Surrounded by three books opened flat on the bar top, she tapped a pencil against full lips, then hunched over to write furiously in a spiral notebook. Her blond hair fell forward, caressing her shoulders. Flipping a page, she underlined something, scratched out a line in her notebook and began scribbling again.

"It's Sunday," was all the answer Carl supplied.

And Sunday in Goldstone meant what? The town's dusty streets had never been paved, the rusted hulks of dead cars outnumbered working vehicles two to one, and the only church Brax had seen was made of corrugated steel like the Quonset huts that cropped up

in the fifties. He'd thought it abandoned due to the weeds choking its garden, but maybe that was a false assumption.

"You boys need a refresher?" the white-haired bartender called. A good salesman always asks, even when he sees half-full beers. Obviously, he considered theirs half-empty.

"We're fine, Doodle," Carl said, once more sucking at the foam that hadn't yet dissipated.

"What about you, Whitey?" Doodle tipped his head toward the lone man seated at the bar.

Whitey's garbled, scratchy answer was incomprehensible, but the bartender grabbed his mug and held it beneath the tap. Half foam, half beer, he slammed it down on the scarred wooden bar without spilling a drop. Whitey tucked his long white beard to his chest, sipped, licked his mustache and sighed as he closed his eyes to savor the brew. When he spoke once more, his words were still indistinguishable, as though rocks filled his mouth.

"Whitey, I swear, you have *the* most amazing way with words," the blonde said, her answer giving no clue as to what the man had uttered. "I really think you should be a writer."

Whitey sat straighter, smoothed his beard, and Brax could see his face in the mirror behind the bar fairly glowing with her compliment. He mumbled something, maybe a thank-you, and the woman beamed back at him with a heart-flipping smile. Brax had the feeling she often paid the old man sweet, unsolicited compliments he soaked up like a sponge.

Slapping her books closed, she piled them up and hugged the stack to her chest. Climbing down from her

stool to land on spike-heeled shoes, she pivoted and headed straight for their table.

Brax lost his voice. Hell, he might have lost his mind. She moved with the graceful glide of a runway model. A short jean skirt showcased her long legs, and a white T-shirt highlighted her tanned skin. Gorgeous hair spread over her shoulders, bouncing with a riot of curls.

She stopped close enough for him to draw in her light perfume. Subtle, yet intoxicating.

Sliding into the chair beside Carl, she plopped the pile of reading material onto the table. "Did you get my e-mail?"

Red seeped into Carl's face, spread across his cheeks and rose to his receding hairline.

Glancing first at Brax, she touched Carl's rigid arm. "Oops, sorry, didn't meant to embarrass you in front of your friend."

Carl could do nothing more than nod his forgiveness. Any man would forgive her everything when she smiled like that.

She gave Carl's forearm another soothing pat. "Are you all right? You look a little flushed. Mr. Doodle," she called, "I think Carl needs a glass of water."

A mason jar filled with ice and water miraculously appeared at her elbow. She pushed it to Carl and curled his fingers around the glass.

Though his delivery was made, the bartender didn't leave the side of the table. "Did ya figure out a witty euphemism for tallywhacker, Simone?"

Simone, a very classy name. But a euphemism for tallywhacker? Brax wouldn't touch that one with a ten-foot pole.

A slight blush colored her flawless cheekbones. "Why no, Mr. Doodle, I didn't," she said, then politely added, "But thank you for being concerned."

"I call it the Doodle," the bartender continued. "I ask Mrs. Doodle if she wants to be diddled by the Doodle." He cackled. "Works every time."

Simone smiled. "Well, that's wonderful, Mr. Doodle, but I think our conversation is further embarrassing Carl, and his friend. My mother would be horrified. She always says a lady never talks about..." She nipped her lower lip. "Um...about tallywhackers in mixed company." She glanced at Brax. "Especially when we haven't been formally introduced."

Lush eyelashes framed her hazel eyes, and her nose tilted endearingly, but it was her smile that damn near knocked a man's socks off. Sweet and genuine, it was the same one she'd given Whitey as she praised him.

"I'll introduce ya," Doodle announced. "This is the brother-in-law we've all heard about." He tapped Brax's shoulder. "Sorry, son, I forgot your name."

"Tyler Braxton." He stuck out his hand. "But everyone calls me Brax."

She shook it with a firm grip of soft, warm flesh.

Leaning closer, she said softly, "Mr. Doodle didn't mean to embarrass you. He's really a sweet old pussycat."

"Oooh, she called me sweet," Doodle cooed. "I think I'm gonna faint." Then he waggled his bushy white eyebrows. "Now that you've been introduced, can we ask him what he calls *his* tallywhacker?"

Brax didn't know whether to laugh or get the hell out. He was the closest he'd been to blushing since

elementary school when he'd gotten caught sending Mary Alice Turner a love note.

Simone sat back and folded her arms beneath her full breasts. Ogling women wasn't one of his pastimes, but Brax couldn't help himself. He looked. Briefly, very briefly. But one look was enough to make him lose his voice again.

"Mr. Doodle," she chided. "You really have to stop that." She nodded at Carl and patted his hand still curled around the water glass. "Carl is apoplectic over what *I* said, and Brax," said with a gentle pucker of her lips, "is going to leave town thinking we have no manners here in Goldstone."

Brax wasn't sure he could think at all. The woman simply bowled him over. Beautiful and sexy, yes, but her smile, her sincere flattery of two old geezers, the way she said his name with that kiss-me pucker, those things held far more punch than the stunning package God had wrapped her in.

"Thank you for that delicious glass of wine, Mr. Doodle, but my mother always says a lady shouldn't overstay her welcome. So I'm off."

She stood and gathered her books in her arms before Brax could make a move to stop her. With a smile for the room at large, she sashayed out the door, leaving the bar in a dull vacuum.

Silence reigned in the small saloon at least a full minute before Brax found his voice. "Just who exactly was that woman?"

Carl busied himself with a slug of beer.

"Simone Chandler's our local porn queen," Doodle elucidated as he sidled back behind the bar.

Brax put his palm on the edge of the table and

pushed back to look at the man over his shoulder. "Porn queen?" She was the furthest thing from sleaze he'd ever seen. And being a cop, he'd seen a lot.

The bartender nodded and beamed a toothy smile.

"She doesn't write porn," Carl muttered.

"So she's a *writer*, not an actress." Though most didn't refer to porn stars as actresses.

"Yeah. It's called *erotica*." Carl's face flushed an even deeper red.

"Isn't that another name for housewife porn?" Brax had read the description somewhere. He couldn't imagine the beautiful Simone penning classless drivel.

"No. Her stuff is very—" Carl hesitated as if searching for the best descriptor "—tasteful."

Doodle snickered. "Oh, it's tasty, all right. The wife loves reading Simone's little stories. They get her pump primed, if you know what I mean."

Brax was sure he didn't want to know. The man was seventy if he was a day, and the idea of any pump priming involving the Doodles was as disturbing as advising Carl on how to communicate with Maggie.

It was Carl's reaction to Simone and the telltale stain on his face that unsettled the beer in Brax's stomach. Being a sheriff, Brax listened to what people didn't say in addition to what they did. He watched for more subtle nuances as he asked, "So, how do I get to read one of these 'little stories'?"

Carl slumped in his chair. Doodle answered the question. "She's got this really special Web site. You tell her your fantasy in simple terms, all the details you want her to be sure to include, then she writes a hot, hot story. The wife's always e-mailing her little snippets to work up."

Brax had never heard of anything like it. "She writes *custom* pornography?"

"It's *not* pornography," Carl snapped, still concentrating on his beer.

Why did it bother his brother-in-law so much when Brax described her writing that way? A man didn't blush like that around a pretty woman unless his thoughts about her weren't pure.

Damn. He did *not* want to believe Carl was having impure imaginings about Simone Chandler. Or worse, that he'd acted on them. Was Carl one of her customers?

Brax had used his sister's e-mail as a reason to head out of his hometown of Cottonmouth for a couple of weeks. To gain a little perspective. A good man, a friend, had been murdered; Brax blamed himself for not reading the warning signs. He should have been able to stop it. That was his job, his obligation, and his responsibility. One in which he'd failed. Miserably.

Now he'd landed himself in the middle of another mess. His sister's marriage was on the rocks, and he'd met the woman who might be responsible for Carl and Maggie's trouble.

Simone Chandler couldn't be more than thirty years old, and Carl was pushing fifty-five. Imagining her in bed with his brother-in-law was downright pornographic.

He had to prove it wasn't so. For his sister's sake. He owed Maggie an investigation.

He turned to Doodle. "What'd you say that Web address was?"

PEOPLE NOT IN THE KNOW thought the desert was unbearably hot in the summertime. But Goldstone was

high desert, and during the day, July was a comfortable ninety-five degrees in general. At night, the temperature dropped to a lovely mideighties. There was no finer place on earth. Okay, the winters could be bitingly cold, and the air so dry it hurt to breathe. Out in the icy wind, a person's bones creaked, but inside Simone's trailer, the pellet stove kept everything toasty warm. In the summer, you couldn't use an air conditioner because there wasn't a lick of moisture in the atmosphere with which to run it. But when the cacti bloomed in the spring, my oh my, the desert was heaven on earth.

A warm summer breeze fluttered up Simone's skirt, flirted with her hair and caressed her face like the lightest of fingers. Earlier, she'd walked the four short blocks to the Flood's End. Nothing was too far to walk to in Goldstone. She only drove the truck when she had to shop in Bullhead thirty miles to the north. Goldstone didn't have a grocery store, only the minimart on the highway at the edge of town.

The walk home gave her a quiet moment to think about euphemisms for tallywhacker. She needed something scintillating, not the same old tired phrases. Her thesaurus was completely useless. Of course, pondering tallywhackers renewed the slight blush that had heated her face when Mr. Doodle brought the subject up in front of Carl, and his brother-in-law, Tyler Braxton. Brax.

Maggie Felman had been a fountain of information about her brother. He was thirty-eight, divorced for five years, no kids, no girlfriend, a good steady job and a minor mortgage. Maggie, older by four years, used to beat him up when they were kids until he got big enough to hit back. Which he never did, Maggie had

added. All in all, he was a well-rounded guy, but Simone hadn't expected him to be such a hunk. With an
engaging smile, short, semi-unruly hair, piercing blue
eyes and bulging biceps the size of sand dunes, the
man set a woman's heart aflutter. He hadn't even gotten mad when Mr. Doodle embarrassed him with the
tallywhacker question.

Hunky Mr. Nice Guy with a sense of humor. His sister was definitely setting the matchmaking stage here.
Was she hoping they'd fall madly in love during his
short visit?

Not likely. Love took much longer to grow, and
even then, you couldn't count on your partner to completely accept everything about you. Nor to stick
around when the going got tough or your life imploded.

There was no question that Simone would ever leave
Goldstone. Though she'd only lived here a little over
three years, this town had become her haven. She'd
lived in a lot of places, but Goldstone was the first
she'd ever called home—much to her mother's complete and total horror when Simone told her about the
town. "Oh my heavens, you're trailer trash," she'd
gasped with shock, followed by a weird little sound that
might have been retching.

So, what about a short, casual fling? Simone liked
sex. Sometimes she was very noisy during it. Too
noisy. Andrew, her ex-fiancé, had found it a little off-
putting. All right, she'd embarrassed the heck out of
him. Men didn't like women who lost control of themselves. She should have listened to all her mother's lec-
tures about excess and exuberance. The breakup had
been a bit demoralizing. Okay, it had been devastating
and badly shaken her confidence in the sex depart-

ment. She'd learned that you had to know a man before you exposed that much of yourself, figuratively and literally. Short and casual was definitely out.

Still, she could fantasize. In fact, fantasizing was what she did best. What was the old saying? "Those who can, do, those who can't, teach." For Simone, it was "those who can't, write." She made a darn good living conjuring up fantasies in which her heroines enjoyed hot, noisy, screaming sex and weren't ashamed of it. And their men loved it. Tyler Braxton provided excellent hero material. She could always pretend he liked that sort of woman. Hmm, maybe she'd include him in a short vignette she could post on the Web site as a teaser.

A shadow shifted in the chair to her left as she stepped onto her sunporch.

"Hey there, pretty lady."

Simone jumped and dropped her armload of books, the screen door banging her butt.

"How did you get in here, Mr. Lafoote?" Darn. She should have noticed his car parked across the road in front of her neighbor's trailer, but she'd been too preoccupied.

"The door was unlocked," Jason answered reasonably.

No one locked their doors in Goldstone. But neither did anyone walk in uninvited. Not usually.

Jason Lafoote fancied himself a big-time developer, but in Simone's opinion, anyone who dreamed of turning the Goldstone Hotel into a gambling resort had to be small potatoes. Some of those baby potatoes with the yellow skins. In fact, Jason's skin was sort of jaundiced, and he was thin as a scarecrow. The comparison maligned scarecrows everywhere. Jason might have a brain, but it was definitely slimed.

"It's late." After nine o'clock. He'd killed that pleasant, sensual buzz she'd gotten thinking about Brax. "I'm ready to turn in for the night." She didn't mention the word bed. He might mistake it for an invitation.

He rose from the chair and glided across the green indoor-outdoor to stop directly in front of her. Moonlight gleamed in his eyes. "I could tuck you in."

Yuk. He'd taken her words for an invitation anyway. Simone gave him a proper set-down. "No thanks."

She'd sidestepped him and put a hand on the front doorknob before she remembered her books. They lay scattered at his feet, but no way was she bending down to retrieve them, not in her short skirt.

"Have you spoken with the judge about pushing those permits through for me?" he asked, half turning to face her.

That's what he really wanted from her. The awkward attempts at seduction were a disguise.

"I told you I wouldn't talk to Della about it."

"I thought perhaps you'd reconsider when you realized how much prosperity a renovated hotel could bring to this town. All it would take is a few words from you and those permits could materialize. The judge respects your opinion."

The judge was her friend, and Simone wouldn't abuse a friendship, even if she'd believed in Jason's dreams. She'd seen pictures of the old hotel in its heyday back in the early part of the century, before the gold ran out, before the flood and the fire destroyed most of Goldstone. She'd fallen in love with the stately winding staircase, the thick carpets covering the hardwood

and the graceful palms in huge pots. Turning it into a resort for gamblers wouldn't bring those days back. Besides, the people of Goldstone already had prosperity, of a different kind. A prosperity of the spirit.

"No one wants a resort here, Mr. Lafoote."

"Not even a beautiful young woman such as yourself?" He licked his thin lips, his gaze touching on her breasts, then lowering to her bare legs.

He had that eye-touching thing down to an art, but if he ever laid a finger on her, she'd belt him. His gaze creeped her out.

"Nope, not even me."

"A lot of wealthy men would suddenly be part of Goldstone's landscape. Powerful men who know how to take care of a lady."

Gross. The implication was clear. "Does that smarmy, rich playboy act work with most women?"

He laughed. It didn't reach his eyes. "Simone, you're the exception to the rule."

"Maybe it's because I really don't need a man to take care of me."

He looked left, then right, the length of her screened-in porch, and finally his eyes rested on the metal siding of her trailer. "You could do so much better than this. I could even see to it that you had a job at the hotel. Manager perhaps."

With a key to the executive suite? In which Jason would reside? Not on your life. "I like my trailer just fine."

"You're a jewel buried beneath Goldstone's dust. I can help you get out of this loserville."

The image of this man shining up her jewels was barfy. The slur on her beloved town just plain got her

blood boiling. "Goldstone didn't have any losers until you came to town."

It was a mean thing to say, but the people of Goldstone took her in when she hit rock bottom, and she'd never forget that.

His eyes gleamed. "I like a woman with sharp claws."

Ugh. More barfy rhetoric. Would nothing offend this man enough to make him go away? Obviously not. Simone took the direct approach. "I won't talk to the judge for you. I don't want a resort. No one wants it. Now I'd like you to leave."

He smiled, and the sallow flesh of his face stretched over his bones. "Some day soon, I think you'll change your mind. About everything. You have my card for when you do."

What did that mean? It brought to mind more yucky images. She'd thrown his card out almost as soon as he'd given it to her.

"I won't change my mind." Neither would the judge. Della would hold up those permits and licenses until Jason Lafoote expired. Or drove his shiny convertible sports car, which probably wasn't even paid for, out of town for good.

"We'll see. Till we meet again. Toodle-loo." He waggled his fingers as he stepped down onto the gravel path.

She wasn't sure about the man. There was something dark and reptilian in his eyes. Was he a fool or a predator?

Though she couldn't put her finger on what had changed, with Jason's arrival and his hard-sell attitude, something had started to smell a little off in Goldstone.

This time when she went in for the night, Simone locked her doors.

CHAPTER TWO

AN EARTHQUAKE SHOOK his shoulder, and a voice blasted his eardrums. "Wake up, Tyler."

Only his mother and his sister called him Tyler. Brax cracked one eyelid open. It wasn't even light yet, and he was on vacation. "What do you want?"

Maggie wafted a mug of coffee near his nose. "Carl left a little while ago. I need you to follow him. Get up."

He'd doubted his sister's sanity from the moment she'd married Carl, a man she met on a Las Vegas weekend junket. Living in Goldstone, where everybody was running away from something, had obviously pushed her round the bend. She wanted him to follow her husband?

"I'm making you bacon and eggs the way you like them," she singsonged, and now he could smell the irresistible aroma of frying bacon.

Crazy, but cunning. Like most women, she played on a man's weaknesses. Breakfast was the only worthwhile meal of the day. It was one thing when a wife or lover played you, but being played by your sister? That was downright pathetic.

Still, no sense in wasting a perfectly good breakfast.

Fifteen minutes later, showered and shaved, Brax pepper-and-salted his eggs. "How do you expect me to follow him if he's already left?"

"You're a cop, you know what to do. Besides, I've got an idea where he went."

He stopped, his fork halfway to his mouth. "Where?"

"The Chicken Coop."

An immediate surge of relief spread through his chest. She hadn't mentioned Simone Chandler. He finished his forkful of eggs before answering. "So now you've started worrying when your husband goes out to the local farmer to buy fresh eggs or poultry?"

Maggie rolled her eyes. "It's the brothel. Just outside of town. And he sure as hell isn't buying eggs there."

"A whorehouse named The Chicken Coop? You've gotta be kidding."

She shrugged and tucked into her crispy bacon. "All the good ranch names were taken."

For the first time since he'd arrived, Brax really looked at his sister. He should have done it before, but sometimes even a sheriff is a coward, and he hadn't wanted to see too much. She was older than him by four years, but today, it could have been eight. The flesh of her once-rounded face had drooped, thin lines radiating out from her eyes and her lips. Deep grooves etched her face, following the line of her nose. She'd visited Cottonmouth a little over a year ago, and those lines hadn't been there then. Maggie's strain was having a physical effect, and it was dereliction of brotherly duty that he hadn't paid more attention to the altered tone of her e-mails over the last few months.

"Why don't you tell me what's going on, Maggie." Brax steeled himself for another awkward conversation like the one with Carl.

"He's having an affair, and I'm sure he's going to leave me. He's been sneaking money out of the bank account and hiding the statements, and he won't let me into his office anymore, and we're either fighting or not talking at all, and I go crazy whenever he leaves the house because I'm sure he won't be back and he'll just leave me a note or worse, send me an e-mail saying *sayonara,* baby." Finally she took a breath and swiped at a tear that slipped down her cheek.

Oh man.

His ex-wife had been a crier. Brax had never felt so helpless as when she'd had one of her crying jags, mostly because he didn't understand them and he had a gut-gripping sense that they had more to do with her own past than anything he'd done. His tactic then had been retreat and regroup. Bad choice, but he still hadn't learned a better way. All he could do now for Maggie was pat her hand.

Which brought on a full-fledged watering pot.

He patted harder and decided his course of action. Maggie had invited him here for his detective skills. So he'd detect. "Buck up, kiddo. I'll help you figure it out. How much money are we talking?"

Everything always started and ended with money, and damn Carl for taking even a micron of the little savings Brax assumed they had. Carl hadn't worked in the entire time Brax had known him, and whenever the subject came up, Maggie always claimed he did "this and that," which sure as hell didn't sound like much of a profession. But then, in Goldstone, the prevailing occupation was "none."

Over the years, he'd gleaned enough through his sister's e-mails and phone calls, not to mention his

mother's frantic late-night calls after her twice yearly visits to the small town, to form a less than totally favorable opinion of either Goldstone or Carl. Still, he'd reserved judgment due to the fact that he was hearing a one-sided version.

Maggie pressed the heels of her hands to her eyes. Her lips twisted. "He's not taking much. But when I asked him about why he was taking money out at all, he hid the bank statements in his trailer and took away my key."

His sympathy for Carl was dying a quick and painless death. "So you don't really know for sure?"

She gave him a speaking glare. "Of course I know. I looked up the accounts online."

Of course. "So. Is he putting you in the poor house?" Hell, they were already there. They lived in a trailer. True, it had three bedrooms, a pushed-out kitchen nook, a Jacuzzi tub on the screened-in porch out back, and damn near rivaled the size of Brax's house in Cottonmouth, but it was still a trailer. Most of Goldstone's residents lived in trailers. Which smacked of nonpermanence and made the whole town a trailer park.

Maggie drew a pattern on the tablecloth with her fork. "We're still okay."

"What the hell does that mean, Maggie?"

"It means we're *okay*. He's been doing fairly well—" she shrugged "—so there's a little extra, you know."

"Fairly well at what?" He needed a spotlight in her eyes to get answers out of her.

"Well, he sort of like…uh…well…"

"Spit it out."

"He started doing really well with this outhouse

excavation thing, and now he's sort of like doing it full-time."

He jiggled his ear because he was sure he couldn't have heard correctly. "Outhouse excavation?"

"Yeah. You'd be surprised what they used to throw down the hole. You know the old saying. One man's trash is another man's treasure."

He realized his eggs had congealed and the bacon was cold. "We're not talking trash, here, Maggie, we're talking shit."

She flapped her hand at him. "That's all decomposed by now."

It would be a really nice thing if he were the kind of guy who could lay his head on the table and cry. She must have seen something of that in his face, because she rushed on. "And sometimes they'd lose stuff. Once he found this big fat diamond ring someone must have dropped in accidentally."

Guess the owner hadn't wanted to go fishing around for it. Brax drummed his fingers on the table. "You haven't told Mom about this, have you?"

"No. And you better not, either."

Mom had broken out in hives when she'd learned Maggie was marrying a guy she'd known less than three days. Who the hell knew what would happen to her if she found out Carl was a professional outhouse excavator?

"So, how many outhouses can there be?" Not enough for a full-time…job.

"Limitless," Maggie confided. "In its day, Goldstone had quite a thriving population. And you know, they couldn't keep using the same spot in the backyard for the outhouse. Had to move it around. But half the

town was lost in the great flood of 1923, and they'd hardly started rebuilding by the time the great fire hit in 1929. It sort of broke the town's back. They never did rebuild."

Brax had seen the evidence of that. The only buildings remaining were the crumbling old schoolhouse, the hotel, the Flood's End, and the county courthouse and jail facility, which looked to be the only structure that received regular maintenance. Hell, no one had even cleared away the rubble. Broken foundations tripped you up if you shortcut across an empty lot, and holes that had once been basements still yawned wide in the town's landscape. One trip to the Flood's End had shown him all that. Carl had guided him through as though it were a minefield.

Brax pulled them back on track. "So he's not taking *everything,* but he's salting away *something.* Or is he spending it?"

"Well, he's gotten into that splunking stuff, but he put the equipment on his credit card."

Carl had a credit card? "How do you know?"

"I looked that up online, too."

Boy, Maggie would have made a top-notch investigator. "What the hell is splunking?"

"You know, exploring caves."

"You mean spelunking."

"Whatever. I hate all that bat guano."

An outhouse excavator would be used to it, however. "Okay, let's hit the high points here." Again. "He's taking money, but not too much, and you don't know what he's doing with it, but he doesn't seem to be spending it."

"He's probably got some offshore account, and he's planning to run away with another woman."

Offshore account? Maggie obviously read too many mystery novels or watched too much TV. Or both. Brax dealt in facts, not speculation, so he continued as though she hadn't spoken. "He won't let you see the bank statements, and he locked you out of the trailer he uses as his office." Not to mention Carl's adamant refusal to let Brax use his computer last night. Which was in the small trailer out back. Carl had told him to use Maggie's, but Brax hadn't wanted to leave an Internet trail when he checked out Simone Chandler's Web site. At least not one that Maggie could follow. Not until he knew more about Carl's relationship with the woman. "When did this behavior start?"

"I don't know. Maybe three months ago. First it was the money thing. He got angry when I questioned him, and that's when he started locking up the trailer."

"And you think it's an affair be-cause?" He let his words fall off in a question.

"He disappears for hours."

"Maybe he's spelunking or excavating."

"Bat guano doesn't smell like department-store perfume."

Oh, so that's the way the wind blew. "And this is where The Chicken Coop comes into it?"

"Where else would he meet a woman? It's not like he's going to run off with Mrs. Killian. She's got seventeen children."

Brax almost shuddered. Seventeen children. The woman must have been changing diapers for almost twenty years. Twenty *years* of dirty diapers. It boggled the mind.

Of course the obvious woman to bring up was Simone Chandler. Brax didn't.

God, he was suddenly tired. The sun had only just risen from behind the hills visible through Maggie's kitchen nook window. Right now, he didn't want to be a cop. He didn't want to feel responsible for solving his sister's problems. Neither did he want to think about Cottonmouth or the murder that had occurred on *his* watch. He'd rather fantasize about Simone. Simone and him, not Simone and his brother-in-law.

Maggie picked up their plates and crossed to the sink. Her worries had taken a toll on her—less bounce in her step, less sparkle in her gaze. She'd aged. Just as a man didn't tell a woman her derriere had gotten a tad larger, he also didn't tell his sister he thought her husband might be doing a gorgeous blonde more than ten years her junior. Especially not if he wanted to live out the rest of the day.

"So you'll check out The Chicken Coop for me?" she asked as she ran water in the sink.

"Yeah." Maggie needed his help, and he was duty-bound to give it, no matter the weight of his own crap on his shoulders. "Where is the place?"

"Just south of town, right on the highway. You can't miss it."

"Good."

She shut off the tap and stood for a moment. "Thanks, Tyler."

"You're welcome, Maggie." He'd clear this whole thing up in an afternoon.

Picking up a towel, she dried her hands, then turned to lean against the counter.

"Carl said you met Simone Chandler last night. What'd you think?"

Busted. As if his thoughts comparing Maggie and

Simone had telegraphed themselves even while Maggie busied herself with dirty dishes. "Pretty," was all he said, remaining as noncommittal as possible.

"She's more than pretty, and you know it. I think you'd like her."

He cleared his throat. "You know her well?"

She gave him that sometimes-men-are-really-dense look again. "Goldstone is a small town, you know. Everybody knows everybody. She's a sweetheart. And she's smart. She's really made that Web site of hers grow."

Holy hell. Maggie knew about that, too. But did she know Carl might be a customer? "I heard all about the Web site. You ever read one of her stories?"

"No. I'd be embarrassed sharing my fantasies."

Brax would be embarrassed hearing them so he didn't press. Her answer did confirm one thing: Carl hadn't shared whatever was in that e-mail Simone had sent him. Brax's last hope died a fiery death.

Wouldn't that be just perfect? If the whole situation didn't involve his sister, he'd say it had the makings of a TV tabloid episode. The kind of thing that ended in an all-out bitch fight. Or murder.

IN THE END, he didn't make it to The Chicken Coop right away. Patrolling Goldstone's gravel streets—and there weren't many of them—he'd recognized Simone's blond curls in a white pickup as she passed in front of him heading out to the highway. Seeing her was no coincidence. It was divine intervention.

Or so he told himself as he followed her north out of town towards Bullhead, mentally rehashing every word his sister had said about the woman.

Animated for the first time since he'd arrived, Maggie had reseated herself at the kitchen table, the sunlight making her glow, and told him the when, where, why and how of Simone Chandler's life history. The salient point being that Simone didn't have a special man in her life, and it was high time she found one. Great. His sister was matchmaking. Brax was sure Simone wouldn't like him knowing all her secrets. Or her failures. Still, he'd listened dutifully. Simone had been a tech writer with her own Silicon Valley business that had taken a nosedive when the bottom fell out of the telecommunications industry. Maybe the ad she'd fallen across, for a trailer "with a real foundation," had been *her* divine intervention when she was down and out. She'd arrived in Goldstone beaten to a bloody pulp by life, but she'd thrived in the high desert air and made Goldstone her home. That was Maggie's version of the story, and she was sticking to it.

Brax didn't ask how anyone could thrive in Goldstone. The burg had fallen to its knees in the flood and taken its last gasping breath in the fire. Now, it was nothing more than a ghost town. Its citizens were taking a helluva long time to figure that out.

For thirty miles, the desert whipped by the windows of his SUV, with nothing but road signs breaking the monotony. That and the vision of blond hair through the rear window of the truck ahead of him. If she was off to meet Carl at some out-of-the-way place, Brax would catch them in the act and put a brotherly end to the affair.

Instead, she slowed at the Bullhead city limit, then pulled into a grocery store parking lot, finding a space near the front while Brax had to cruise the aisles look-

ing for another. Monday morning at The Stockyard Grocery was apparently a popular time. She'd already disappeared through the automatic doors when a car backed out of the spot straight across from hers.

More divine intervention. Brax parked, climbed out, then rested against the back of his SUV to wait. He was a patient man. A cop had to be. Besides, he indulged himself with the image of her platform shoes, tanned legs and short shorts—not that he'd been ogling, merely observing. He preferred voluptuous to emaciated any day of the week, and Simone Chandler was definitely of the voluptuous variety. Even her voice held a sultry, sumptuous note guaranteed to elevate the temperature and raise a few other things, as well. Boredom was nowhere in sight when she returned some thirty minutes later, wheeling a cart full to the brim with paper sacks.

He crossed the narrow aisle. "Let me get that for you." He helped her load the bags into the bed of her truck.

"Did you follow me, Brax?"

"You could say I followed your rear end."

She arched a darkened eyebrow into her bangs.

He stepped back and pointed to the tailgate of her truck and the excess of bumper stickers plastered to the chrome. "Too small to read when I'm adhering to the required distance of one car length per ten miles an hour rate of speed. I had to follow you in here so I could take a good, long gander at your stickers."

She put a hand on her hip. "Should I take it you're done perusing my backside?"

He nodded. "I find that one particularly intriguing." He pointed to a black decal with white letters warn-

ing the unwary, Don't make me bring out the flying monkeys.

"It's The Wicked Witch of the West sending out the monkeys to steal Dorothy away," Simone explained.

"I get the image very clearly." She'd win lovers' quarrels with that one, by getting said lover to laugh himself to death. Or bring him to his knees for an entirely different reason. Damn, he did have it bad when a bumper sticker made him hot. He pointed once more to her truck's rear. "The skulls are a nice touch."

They ringed her license plate, and following her, he'd noticed the eyes lit up when she stepped on the brake.

She bounced on her platforms, felled him with a heart-stopping smile and clapped her hands to her cheeks. "Aren't they absolutely perfect? Whitey found them for me in one of his Harley magazines." Her hands flipped, flapped and waved all over the place as she talked. "You remember Whitey, don't you? He was at the Flood's End last night."

"Beard down to here—" Brax hit the edge of his hand midchest "—and a voice like he's chewing gravel?"

"That's him. I think Mr. Doodle and I are probably the only ones who understand him. Not that anyone can completely understand Whitey." She tapped her temple. "He's a little out there, and my mother would drop dead of a brain implosion if she saw him stick tobacco in his mouth, but he's the biggest sweetie who ever walked the earth." Simone put the last bag in the bed and leaned her hip against the side of the truck. "So, who are you like?"

She dizzied him with her lightning-fast speech, hand movements and subject changes.

Both her eyebrows flashed up this time. "*The Wizard of Oz.* Which character do you identify with?"

"Ahhh." The sound wheezed out of him. "I've never thought about it." He wasn't sure anyone *but* Simone Chandler had.

She saved him from answering by launching into her own preference. "Personally, I'm intrigued by the Wicked Witch of the West. You know, life must have been really tough being a wicked witch." She punctuated with a hand flap and a hair flip. "She's got all that green-tinged skin and that long nose and raspy voice. I think she had bad teeth, too. And her younger sister, the Good Witch, is so much prettier and nicer and everybody loves her and she gets to wear the pretty white dress, while the Wicked Witch has to wear all that ugly black stuff—"

"The Good Witch wasn't her sister."

She gasped, as if he'd blasphemed. "Sure Glinda was her sister."

He shook his head, playing her game, wanting to. Almost compelled to. She had that effect on a man, making him want to do things not in his nature. "The Wicked Witch of the East, who got clobbered by Dorothy's house, is the Wicked Witch's sister."

She gaped. "They're *all* sisters, the north, the south, the east and the west. It's just that two of them are wicked and two of them are good."

He quirked one side of his mouth in what he'd been told was a know-it-all smile. Damn. He *liked* arguing with her. "Nope. You better watch the movie again."

"I'm sure I'm right. The two wicked witches lived in the shadows of their happy, pretty sisters."

Again, the happier, prettier sister thing. He won-

dered briefly about her family, then threw her a curve-
ball. "So who were their parents?"

She stopped, looked at him. Damn, she was cute.
Laughter danced in her eyes as she pretended to pon-
der the question. To no avail. "I don't know."

"Then how do you know they were all sisters?"

She kept up the play, narrowing her eyes at him.
"You're trying to trick me."

He shined his fingernails on his shirt, which said it
all.

She flapped a hand at him. "All right, all right, forget the witches. Who are *you* like?"

Caught. The banter hadn't sidetracked her for long.
"As I said, I've never thought about it."

"Think about it now."

He puffed out a breath. "The Tin Man, I guess."

"Aha." She pointed at him. "The man without a
heart."

"Actually I was thinking tin star. Because I'm a
sheriff."

She snorted. "Lame."

It was. He spread his hands. She might be right. The
man without a heart was not a flattering description. It
reminded him once more of his ex-wife and their
doomed marriage. Maybe if he'd been a better listener.

He brushed the dampening thoughts aside. "It's the
best I could come up with on short notice."

"Maybe *you* need to watch the movie again."

He might need a lot of things, one of them being
more time in Simone's company. Except that she could
be having an affair with Carl. Christ, the thought made
him wince. "I'm pretty sure the Good Witch's name
isn't Glinda, either."

"We could watch it together and find out who's right."

She looked at him, all fresh faced, innocent and hopeful. His heart flipped over—see, he did have one. He wanted to say yes. His duty to Maggie stopped him. Watching *The Wizard of Oz* with Simone was a bad idea all around. If, repeat *if*, she was diddling Carl, she was no friend to his sister. He couldn't bring himself to believe it. Yet he couldn't forget the eagerness with which she'd asked Carl if he'd gotten her e-mail, nor the blush that seemed to cover Carl from head to toe.

He ignored her implied question in favor of saying, "I don't think I've ever had the…pleasure of meeting anyone quite like you. You are…" He paused, scanning her beautiful, lively face. Charming, funny, witty, a little bit kooky. Hell, a lot kooky, but dazzling. Yeah, completely dazzling. "Unique," he finally said aloud.

On second thought, maybe what he'd said wasn't any better than accepting her invitation. Damn.

She laughed. "I'm pretty sure unique wasn't the word you were searching for." She nodded her head knowingly, as if she presumed he'd been thinking something derogatory. "My mother says I'm like a jet engine. Get in my flight path, and I'll suck you in one side and spit your little pieces out the other."

"That's a very nice compliment." He was sure it wasn't a compliment at all. He was also fairly certain he wouldn't like her mother.

She laughed, the sweet sound burrowing into his belly. "Thank you for lying so gallantly," she said.

Damn, he'd wanted to lie for her. He pointed to the truck bed, needing to end the little tête-à-tête before he

got himself into serious trouble. "I hope you haven't got ice cream in there that's in danger of melting."

"No ice cream. Just milk."

They couldn't stand there all damn day, as much as part of him wanted to. He pulled his shades from his shirt pocket and hid behind the dark lenses. No two ways about it, he had to get the freaking question over with and out of the way. For Maggie's sake. "Are you having an affair with my sister's husband?"

Her smile died. His insides twisted with the loss, but he ignored any possible meaning to that.

She gave him a simple, "No."

Just as when he interrogated a seemingly bereaved wife who may or may not have had something to do with her spouse's demise, he didn't apologize for asking. He did, however, wince inwardly. "Then what was in that e-mail you mentioned last night?"

She thought about it for long moments before answering with, "You'll have to ask Carl about that." She bit down on the inside of her cheek. "But I wouldn't have an affair with a friend's husband." She pursed her lips. "Not that I'd have an affair with anyone's husband. But especially not a friend's." She heaved a sigh. "What I mean is—"

Her flustered explanation made him feel like shit. He held up a hand. "I think I get it. Thanks. Gotta run."

After enjoying her enchanting banter, then insulting her nine ways to Sunday, he couldn't get out of there fast enough. Guilty conscience, pure and simple. He turned on his heel, crossed to his truck, and left her standing alone in The Stockyard parking lot.

His problem, however, still remained. He'd asked. She'd denied. But could he believe her?

"STRANGE GUY," Simone muttered as she watched Brax pull out onto the highway and head for Goldstone.

She could have told him the e-mail was a fantasy Carl had wanted her to write for Maggie. Something to rekindle the fire they'd lost. She never should have mentioned the e-mail in front of Brax. A person didn't tell another's secrets, not even in defense of their own character.

She groaned aloud. Okay, so she'd voraciously listened to Maggie reveal all Brax's secrets, right down to the fact that his marriage had gone bust because he'd worked too many long, hard hours, and that he hadn't dated much since the divorce. There was also that little thing about the wife having gotten hitched to him on the rebound from a love affair gone bad. She *really* shouldn't have listened quite so carefully to that part. But listening to secrets wasn't the same as revealing them. Was it?

She tabled that thought for later in favor of musing on the man himself.

You could judge the mettle of a man by who he identified with in *The Wizard of Oz*. It was a rule. "The Tin Man without a heart," she whispered. Hmm. It didn't fit. She was sure concern for Maggie had forced Brax to ask that silly question about Carl. Which definitely indicated the existence of a heart. He also phoned his mother once a week.

It was probably a good thing he hadn't taken her up on watching the movie together. She was starting to like Brax a little too much.

CHAPTER THREE

HALF AN HOUR LATER, Brax was still asking himself the same question. Did he believe Simone when she said she wasn't having an affair with Carl?

The bulk of Brax's job was asking questions, probing the intimate details of people's lives to ferret out the truth, badgering them until they revealed what he wanted to know.

Simone wasn't the usual suspect. She'd committed no crime, staged no robbery, executed no property damage. She hadn't even run a stop sign or driven over the speed limit. He felt like a puppy kicker.

She was a jet engine gone mad, and she'd sucked him in completely. And that was a compliment, in every way.

But did he believe her? Dammit, he wanted to. He wanted to be sucked in. So to speak. Which was the problem. He'd never let lust override intellect or suspicion. But this time, mere lust wasn't the only thing attracting him like the proverbial moth to the flame.

She was different. She was dazzling. Damn, he could imagine her in the middle of a heated argument, shaking her finger at him and muttering between clenched teeth, "Don't make me bring out the flying monkeys." Jesus, wasn't that the most frightening fantasy any self-

respecting man could ever have? She definitely made him hot. Really hot, thinking of how he'd take control of that finger pointed smack-dab at his chest, nibble it a little, lick it, follow the finger bone connected to the hand bone and the hand bone connected to the... Dammit.

He had to be vigilant around Simone Chandler. The woman muddied his brain and made him think with his tallywhacker. She made him put aside morose thoughts and laugh. She made him forget that dark afternoon he'd attended his friend's autopsy. The scent of Formalin and the drone of Hyram's voice dictating dissection details still haunted him. Cottonmouth was by no means immune to violence, but somehow the murder of one of the town's most upstanding citizens had stolen a piece of the town's innocence. In addition to arresting the perpetrator, it had been Brax's duty to protect that innocence. He'd succeeded in the former but failed in the latter. Not to mention that Nick Angel and Bobbie Jones had almost lost their lives, as well.

Damn. Guilt had sneaked up on him again. He'd done a good job hiding his feelings on the subject from everyone in Cottonmouth, but his own culpability ate a hole through his stomach.

Screw it. Self-flagellation could turn into self-pity if you indulged in it too much. He cut off the emotions ruthlessly.

An idea occurred. For appropriate interrogative purposes, maybe he was going about this investigation all wrong. Instead of running away from Simone, closer proximity might be required. Hot pursuit. He was good at that, very good. They never got away when he was behind the wheel.

First, he had other fish to fry. Make that chickens to roast, at The Chicken Coop. The black paint of his SUV soaked up the sun, and heat waves shimmered off the hood as he rolled to a stop in The Chicken Coop's gravel lot. How he'd made it there was beyond him. Thank Christ it was on the highway south of town as Maggie had said, because his mind was *not* on road directions.

Heavily traveled Highway 95 was the main route between Las Vegas and Reno. Though only two lanes wide at this point, it split Goldstone in half. Right on the edge of the highway, The Chicken Coop, with its bright neon sign advertising Girls, Girls, Girls, was perfectly situated to attract truckers and lonesome travelers.

The sunbaked trailer with pale blue siding stood on cinder blocks. A crushed shell path bordered by cacti led to two wooden steps. Five cars flanked his in the lot, all equally dusty with varying degrees of flaked paint and rusty fenders. Thankfully, Carl's relatively newer model truck was not among them.

Behind the double-wide, several smaller trailers formed a semicircle, each with an identical shell path connecting them to the main trailer. Only the cacti were different. The effect was neat but barren.

Sparkling white blinds rattled against a window on the right, then the front door opened. A woman stood there, leaning on the door handle, her blouse gaping enough to reveal the swell of very large breasts.

"Howdy, stranger," she said, like a line out of an old western. He wanted to answer, "Howdy, Miss Kitty," but didn't. Her voice, low enough to be sexy, raised

goose bumps on his arms. Damn, with her upswept cap of gray hair, she resembled someone's mother. *His* mother.

"You must be here for the early-bird special," she purred.

Brax glanced at his watch. A little after noon.

"Well, don't stand there speechless. Come in and check out the menu, Big Boy."

As he climbed the stairs, for a moment he feared she'd remain in the doorway so that he would be forced to brush past her. The idea didn't sit right. She even smelled like his mother, the scent of talcum powder drifting off her like haze off asphalt.

He'd have considered moseying out of the place lickety-split if Maggie hadn't seemed desperately in need of his investigative skills concerning The Chicken Coop.

He supposed the interior was your typical Nevada whorehouse, several settees placed haphazardly about the darkened room, lace doilies in shades of pink and blue covering the lampshades.

The woman patted his back. "I'm Chloe, and these are my little chickens." She waved a hand at four women seated in a circle on the floor at the far end of the trailer. "Day shift," she whispered close to his ear. "Take your pick. What's your pleasure?"

He was no prude, and he'd certainly encountered his share of prostitutes, not as a customer, but on the other end of the law. But Chloe's breast pressed to his arm gave him the heebie-jeebies. He'd complete his business and be out of there pronto.

He raised his nose, sniffing for the sweetly floral aroma Maggie had described. Instead he encountered

only the mixture of heavily abused cheap cologne. The chickens must have dabbed themselves with the same scent.

"Go ahead, Big Boy, don't be nervous. You can get to know them a little first, if you like." Chloe pushed him toward the circle of women on the floor. "Cotton Candy, Chocolate, Peppermint and Caramel." Which did not refer to the color of their skin, but the hue of their frilly look-alike lingerie.

At least she hadn't given them chicken names. Maybe it was a brother's loyalty, but he couldn't imagine Carl choosing a chicken over Maggie.

An open box and a conglomeration of pieces and parts lay strewn about the middle of the girls' circle.

"What ya got there?" he asked.

"It's Chocolate's little nephew's birthday, and we bought him a robot," said Peppermint. Presumably she was Peppermint, based on the red-and-white swirls of her lacy teddy. She might have been pretty if not for the hard glint in her turquoise eyes, which were most likely contact-lens enhanced. And yes, he noticed her breasts. How could one *not* notice, though to his taste, they were overdone. Simone's were less ostentatious, but far more appealing. He wondered if breast enlargement would be considered a tax-deductible expense for a topless dancer or a Nevada prostitute.

"But we can't figure out how to put it together," Chocolate added. She leaned over the box. "*Some* assembly required. Who are these jokers kidding? This is rocket science here."

"Maybe I can help."

The circle parted like the Red Sea to include him.

He hadn't sat cross-legged since he was ten years old and Maggie'd bounced a ball off his privates. She'd always claimed it was an accident.

"Here's the instructions," Candy said, wearing a pink teddy to identify the Cotton Candy of her name. She handed him a ten-page legalese document with a smattering of drawings.

"Well, let's get some light on the subject." He waved at the blinds on a nearby window, and Caramel rose to open them, her backside wiggling beneath caramel-colored lace and ribbons.

Brax studied the diagrams.

"All right, let's get started." He held out a hand, palm up. "Screws." Someone tittered, but slapped the plastic bag full of nuts, bolts and screws into his outstretched hand.

"What's your name?"

"Big Boy."

This time they all laughed. "No, really. We have to tell Timmy who put together the robot."

"Brax."

"That's a funny name. You're not from around here."

"Visiting." His opportunity presented itself that easily. Not that he wouldn't have found another way. He was a cop, after all. Interrogation was his middle name. "I'm Carl Felman's brother-in-law."

"Ah, the brother-in-law. You're a sheriff. Wanna arrest me?"

As in Cottonmouth, word traveled fast and everyone knew everything. Even the chickens. "Wouldn't dream of arresting such lovely ladies." Brax sifted through the pieces on the floor for the one he wanted. "So you know him?"

"Everyone knows Carl. Him and Whitey are fighting over Whitey's outhouses."

Whitey, purveyor of skull license-plate frames like the one on Simone's truck. Brax held out his hand again, like a surgeon asking for his scalpel. "Phillips screwdriver." Thankfully, the kit had come with the proper tools. "They're fighting over outhouses?"

"Yeah. Whitey wants to charge Carl bucks up the ying-yang to excavate his four outhouses."

Brax raised one brow, then pointed to what he believed was the mechanical calf of the robot. Chocolate tossed it to him.

"Bucks up the ying-yang?" he repeated to keep the girls going.

"Whitey wants seventy-five percent of whatever Carl finds."

"Hmm. That's a bit steep. Allen wrench."

"What's that?" Caramel leaned forward to sift through the tools and parts, her filmy negligee falling open.

Brax ignored the sight. A man needed all his concentration when assembling a child's toy. He indicated the hexagonal key near Peppermint's bare knee. With a few twists and turns, he gripped a completed robot leg in his fist.

Peppermint whistled. "Wow, you're good."

He smiled. "Yeah. That's what they all say."

The girls all giggled at once. Brax pointed to the torso. "So, Carl come by often?"

Candy snorted. "Carl? Here? You gotta be kidding. He stinks like an outhouse."

"Worse, he smells like bat shit." Peppermint grimaced.

Caramel threw a nod to her boss. "Chloe wouldn't let him in the door."

"And Maggie would shoot him right between the eyes. Then she'd come gunning for *us*." Chocolate punctuated with an eye roll.

Brax cranked and screwed. Yep, just like in Cottonmouth, everyone knew everyone else's business. It was obvious Carl wasn't getting any at The Chicken Coop.

The front door rattled beneath a pounding fist, and light filled the trailer's other half as Chloe opened up. "Come on in, Big Boy."

Hey! Brax had been Big Boy. Maybe the name wasn't so special. The man that walked in was rail thin and beanpole tall, his grin reminiscent of one of the witch's flying monkeys.

"Oh God, it's The Foot," Peppermint groused under her breath.

"The foot?" Brax asked as Caramel handed him the robot head.

"Jason Lafoote."

Across the room, Chloe waggled her fingers at the chickens. "I'll be right back, girls. Keep our boy there entertained." Then she led The Foot through a stream of beaded curtains.

"Yuk," Candy murmured. "I can't imagine them doing it."

Peppermint slapped her knee. "She doesn't do him. She doesn't have to do anyone. She owns the place."

"What's wrong with him?" Brax asked.

"He's a pain in the ass. He doesn't know blow from suck and in from out."

Nice analogy, that, which Brax took to mean that Lafoote was lacking in the sexual expertise depart-

ment. He attached the head to the torso, then the torso to the legs, and had a brief flashback to that little fantasy about Simone, the flying monkeys, her finger, and him nibbling on it. Damn, he had it bad for the woman.

"And he doesn't tip," Caramel added.

Who? Oh yeah, The Foot. He was losing concentration here.

"Jason's pumping money into us so he can get to Chloe."

Brax figured it wasn't only money Lafoote was pumping at the Chicken Coop. "What's he want from Chloe?"

"He wants to renovate that old broken-down hotel in the middle of town. And he thinks she'll talk to the judge for him."

"About what?" With the robot body, head and legs put together, all he needed were the arms. He held out his hand to Candy who had possession of both.

"The judge won't give him the permits he needs. But Chloe's a good businesswoman, and she sees the boom a gambling resort could be for the town," Peppermint explained.

"He's riling everyone up over the whole thing." Candy glared at the beaded doorway through which Chloe and Lafoote had disappeared. "People are getting pissed. Chloe should stay out of it, because if they get pissed enough, we could find ourselves out on our tail feathers."

Peppermint wriggled her eyebrows. "It could be a big boon for us, too."

"Dream on. He's a cheap sonuvabitch," Caramel grumbled, "and I don't trust him to follow through on a darn thing he says he's going to do."

"I take it you ladies don't like him."

"He's a pussy." Chocolate batted her eyelashes at Brax, licked her lips, then dropped her gaze to his crotch. "We like you much better."

Holy hell. He stuck the right robot arm in the wrong socket. He started over on arm construction and finished in a jiffy. Just in time, too, since the girls had tightened the circle around him, and their liberally applied cologne was starting to choke him. He'd learned everything he needed to know about Carl and the chickens. The information about Lafoote and Chloe didn't appear germane, but he'd store it for future reference, if necessary. Maggie had nothing to worry about; her husband wasn't a customer.

"That's it, I think." He held up the fully assembled robot.

"Wow," they crooned in unison.

Not bad, if he did say so himself. He rose to his feet, his knees creaking after sitting cross-legged on the floor so long.

"You're a genius," Peppermint said.

"You're awfully cute," Candy added.

"So which one of us do you want?" Chocolate asked.

A robot leg almost snapped in his hand. "Well, ladies, now that I've gotten to know you all, the choice is too damn difficult."

"You don't have to choose, Brax." They gazed up at him with identical twinkles in their eyes.

"You can have all of us." Candy smiled and sucked her index finger into her mouth.

"Together." Caramel stroked a finger over her nipple.

He squeezed the robot body so hard the head almost popped off. But he was a seasoned cop and adept at diplomatically extricating himself from unwanted situations. The chickens couldn't hold a candle to Simone, but there was no need to hurt their feelings. "I haven't got that strong a constitution. All that pleasure might be the death of me."

"Oh, come on, Brax. We'll be gentle."

He held up a hand. "No, no, ladies. You're all much too much woman for me. I'm a humble sheriff from California. Catch."

He tossed the robot at Chocolate and got the hell out of Dodge before the chickens tackled him to the floor.

Twenty minutes later, he opened the front door of Maggie's trailer. He found her in the back bedroom tapping on her computer keyboard. "Is Carl usually out late at night?"

She shrugged. "He's mostly home in the evenings. Out in that trailer of his."

Brax ignored her gibe. "Then you must have figured he was diddling someone on the day shift at The Chicken Coop."

"I didn't know they had shifts."

"They do. I learned a lot today." He raised one eyebrow.

She tipped her reading glasses to look over the tops. "What have you been doing, Tyler Braxton? Better not be something our mama would be ashamed of."

A man had his pride, and saying he'd put robot parts together down at the local brothel instead of…that didn't sit right. Even if he was talking to his sister. He hedged. "Among other things, I was interrogating. And I'd be willing to bet my left nu—" He caught himself.

"I'd bet my left eye your husband isn't planning to run away with one of Chloe's Chickens."

"Then what's he doing with our money, and why's he stink like perfume?"

"Did you ever think maybe he's trying to cover up the odor of bat guano?"

She stared at him.

"As for the money, maybe he's planning a surprise trip for the two of you. For your tenth anniversary."

"That was two months ago."

He heaved a sigh. "Maggie, I'm a cop. Invariably I look for the worst in people instead of the best. Suspicion is as natural as breathing. But you don't have to be like me. Give him a break. Talk to him. Calmly. Find out what's going on with him."

She pouted. "It won't do any good."

"Maybe it won't. But it sure as hell isn't going to make things better if he finds out you asked your brother to spy on him." He wasn't good at dispensing advice on relationships, but he knew things would only deteriorate if Maggie and Carl didn't at least try to talk.

Maggie worked her lips from a grimace to a half smile. "Well, maybe. I need to think about it."

"Good. While you're thinking, let me get on the computer." He wanted to check out Simone Chandler's Web site.

GOODNESS, she was consumed by sexual thoughts. Every time Simone tried to describe the hero in her story, he had short blond hair and blue eyes, though her client had asked for tall, dark and handsome. Tall and handsome, yes, but no matter how many times she hit

the delete key, he always came back with blond hair and gazed at her with arresting blue eyes as he crawled down the length of her body to…

It was rather pathetic when you couldn't control your own wayward fingers. For typing, that is.

The phone rang. She pounced on it without checking caller ID. Simone never answered the phone unless she knew who it was. Why, a person could lose an hour of their life if they picked up for the wrong caller.

At the moment, however, anything was better than wayward fingers or wayward *thoughts*. "Hello?"

"You didn't screen."

"Hello, MOTHER." That's how Simone always thought of her mother, in capital letters. "I saw it was you."

"You didn't." Her mother had call blocking, so her number didn't come up. Instead it read, Private.

"It must have been telepathy then." If it *had* been telepathy, she would have been sure *not* to answer. Not that she didn't love her mother dearly. Ariana Chandler was the sweetest, kindest, most thoughtful mother in the world. At least, that's how everyone described her. And she was. Truly. Very thoughtful, caring, helpful, concerned. But these monthly calls were…well, they were like the monthly curse; Simone needed to take a muscle relaxant for five days afterward.

"Did you get the care package your sister and I sent?"

"Yes. Thank you, MOTHER."

"And they fit?" Why did her mother sound so surprised?

"Of course." Actually, Simone had never even tried them on. More than satisfied with her own clothes,

she'd driven to Bullhead and given all her sister's designer castoffs to the Goodwill. She was not a designer kind of girl, and Goldstone was not a designer town. She would have looked ridiculous walking around in Ralph Lauren. If her mother had ever visited Goldstone, she'd know that.

"I knew what an incentive that first box of beautiful dresses would be in helping you with your little weight problem. So I thought you deserved another set. Besides, Jacqueline needed to go through her closet and get rid of last year's fashions."

Simone did not fit into her sister's size zero clothing. She would never fit into size zero clothing. She didn't *want* to fit into them. Her head started aching. She knew her mother meant well, she did, but she really, really didn't think she had a weight problem. Except once a month when her mother called.

"So, how's the job hunt going, dear?"

Simone's stomach lurched. Her mother had never gotten over her daughter's spectacular failure, which had, embarrassingly, made it into the L.A. papers. Even the memory of all those delinquent accounts receivables and unreturned phone calls to insolvent clients gave Simone a migraine. "Don't put all your eggs in one basket," her mother had always said. But Simone had. When the stock market dropped the basket, Simone had gotten crushed beneath the broken shells. Ariana never stopped hoping that Simone would "turn her life around." Despite the amount of time since her business debacle, her mother had not given up.

"It's coming along," Simone fibbed. "I've got a few bites out there but nothing solid yet."

She hadn't searched for a job in three years. She

loved her new life. With all the nifty payment options available on the Internet, she got her clients' funds before she sent them a word. She'd learned that lesson the hard way. Show me the money first. Her alluring fantasy Web site was going gangbusters. "Tell me your wildest dreams," her banner advertised, "and I'll write you a story to send you and your lover into orbit." Sex on the Internet was the hottest thing. Her mother wouldn't get the appeal. Prone to ripping out hair under duress, she'd be bald within three minutes of learning about Simone's venture.

"Well, I've got a whole list of people for you to contact," her mother continued. "And really, please do try to make a good impression. Don't tell them you live in a trailer." Simone visualized her mother's shudder from the sound of her voice. "Have you got a pen and paper?"

"Yes, MOTHER." Simone had DSL, a state-of-the-art computer system into which she could have typed the information as quickly as the spoken word, and an Outlook address book the size of which would rival the one in her mother's PalmPilot. She doodled on a nearby Post-it as her mother read aloud.

"Now, let me tell you what to say in the initial letters. I think for Ambrose, that darling man, you should tackle it this way—" Her mother suddenly sucked in a breath. "You *are* going to wear makeup and fix your hair properly, aren't you?"

"It's a letter. He's not going to see me."

"Well, a positive self-image creates a positive attitude the recipient can sense even through the writing. And you could be such a pretty girl if only you'd—"

The doorbell rang. *Oh thank you God above. Thank*

you, thank you, smooches. "Someone's at the door, I have to run. I'll call you later and you can tell me exactly what to say."

She hung up in the middle of her mother's, "But—"

Brax stood on the outer doorstep, across the expanse of the sunporch. Her heart gave a weird, scary little leap at the sight of him. Then she reminded herself that according to Maggie he was only here for a two-week vacation. And he'd asked her if she was sleeping with his brother-in-law.

"Peace offering." He held the disk case against the screen door so she could read *The Wizard of Oz* on the front. "Drove all the way back into Bullhead to find it."

She stayed on the threshold of her front door and tried to be tough when what she really wanted to do was drag him inside. "I've got it on tape."

He waggled the case. "But this is the anniversary edition. It's got the jitterbug sequence they cut."

"Oh." That sounded delightful. The sneak. He'd already figured out her weaknesses. "Did you know they considered cutting 'Somewhere Over the Rainbow' because they thought it slowed the pacing?"

He opened the screen door and crossed half the porch width. "Some bright guy must have saved their butts at the last minute. So, are we betting on whether they're sisters?"

"What do I win?" Which didn't mean she was letting him in. Brax was dangerous, the type to make her lose control.

"The question is…" His gaze dropped from her eyes to linger on her lips. "What's *my* prize?"

Whoa, the man gave potent eye scan. Nothing at all

like the way Jason Lafoote did it. Maybe Brax could come in, just for the movie, because he'd driven so far to get it. She could always seat him on the other end of the sofa. And make him leave after they watched the movie. She would definitely have to make him leave before she did something embarrassing, like go into meltdown if he touched her.

"Since I'm going to win," she answered, holding the front door wide, "I want…" Well, there were those very nice fantasies she'd been having all day, but she wouldn't clue him in. He'd never know, not in any infinitesimal way. They were *only* fantasies. "I want ice cream. And you'll have to drive out and get it." She backed up.

He followed her into her living room. "Ice cream. Sounds fair. But since *I'm* gonna win—" his voice dropped, and he leaned in close enough to tickle her ear with his breath "—I think I might like to have you lick the ice cream off my cone."

Uh-oh. Now that was a euphemism for tallywhacker she'd never heard before.

And Trouble with a capital *T.*

CHAPTER FOUR

HE SHOULDN'T HAVE READ the teaser on her Web site. A massage scene involving only neck and shoulders, its sensuality still managed to evoke a purely male reaction. It also impaired his manners. That could be the only excuse for what he'd said. Brax had to admit he'd been imagining ice-cream cones, which was not a bad thing in and of itself. But sex complicated matters, especially when he was in Goldstone for only two weeks. He shouldn't have given voice to the image.

She smiled that perfect smile of hers, the one that made him weak in the knees. The dazzle smile. "Shall we get started?"

God, yes.

Beautiful eyes wide, she bit her lip. "With the movie, I mean."

He knew that. "Sure." It was the slickest dialogue he could muster when he felt as tongue-tied as a teenage boy.

He *really* shouldn't have read that teaser. Snippets of it muddled his main goal. Which was...it was...oh yeah, to determine if she could lie without the telling body language that clued a cop into when he was being snookered by a suspect. Yes, that was his goal in coming over tonight.

That and giving Maggie time alone to talk things out with Carl.

He hadn't picked up the movie because he wanted to watch it with Simone in a darkened room, sitting close on that big sofa, drinking in the citrus fragrance of her hair and the sweet scent of her skin. Nope, he'd intended to do a little subtle interrogating.

And that's what he'd do.

"Don't look at me like that," she said suddenly.

"Like what?"

"Like you can't decide whether to cart me off to jail for being an axe murderess or..." Her voice trailed off and she bit her lip again. Her nip plumped the flesh to a lush, red, inviting fullness.

A cop had to be good at schooling his features, keeping his true thoughts off his face and out of his eyes. Brax was usually damn good at it, too, but Simone saw right through him.

Maybe he shouldn't salivate quite so much when looking at her hair tumbling over her shoulders in artful disarray almost as if she'd been in bed when he'd shown up at her door. But then he'd started remembering that slow sensual massage.

He picked up her hand and placed the DVD in it. "Why don't you put the movie in?" That should get his mind off *creamy shoulders* and *a bare nape* begging to be kissed.

She backed up a step, stopped only by the edge of the coffee table. "Popcorn. I should make some popcorn."

He pulled a packet from his back pocket and tossed it on the table. "I brought licorice." Why the hell he'd picked out the candy while waiting in line for the video,

he couldn't say. "Start the movie," he whispered, as if he were talking about something far different. Her scent teased his nose.

The goal, he repeated to himself as she slipped from between him and the table to kneel in front of the TV.

She fumbled opening the DVD, then again trying to get the disk out. Those damn disks could be tricky. Pushing a button, the player flashed on and a tray slid out. She plopped the disk in, closed the tray, then hopped to her feet and skittered across the living room to the couch. Grabbing a remote, she flopped down on a cushion in the corner and pointed.

Nothing happened.

"Darn it," she whispered and poked at the remote a couple of times.

He held out his hand. "Here."

She clutched the gadget to her chest. "I know how to work my own remote."

He glanced at the blank TV. "I don't see anything."

She pursed her lips, narrowed her eyes and pointed again. Still nothing. She pushed a series of buttons in sequence, with the same result. Nothing.

"You're a jinx. It always worked before." She tossed it to him.

He looked at it, pushed one button and the TV came to life.

"How'd you do that?"

He beamed the way Whitey had last night in the Flood's End mirror when she told him he should have been a writer. "Remotes are man's work."

He pushed a series of buttons and magically the opening credits began to roll.

"Sit." She gestured to the opposite end of the couch. "Over there."

He plopped down in the middle, next to her, his knee almost touching hers. "It's more comfortable here."

She looked at him, not the screen, where Dorothy was doing...something. In the fading light of the evening sun, Simone's hazel eyes deepened to a richer shade of green. Her lip biting had transferred a dash of red lipstick to her front tooth. She closed her mouth and licked it off, as if she'd known what fascinated him.

He slid an arm along the back of the sofa until his hand touched the gold of her hair. Soft. Silky. Just as he'd imagined. He took a lock between his thumb and two fingers, stroking it.

"What are you doing?"

Getting lost in the feel of her hair.

Which was not the reason he'd sat so close. No, he'd chosen that exact spot because the sun was setting and the room was darkening, and he'd needed to be close to read the expression in her eyes when he questioned her. At least that's what he'd told himself, so why wasn't he doing some basic interrogation?

She leaned over and snagged the bag of licorice he'd thrown on the table. "Can I open it?"

"Sure."

She ripped the package, pulled out a whip, then offered the bag to him. Brax shook his head.

"I logged on to your Web site." That wasn't what he was supposed to say. He was supposed to ask a question he already knew the answer to, a difficult or embarrassing question about which she might feel the need to lie. To gauge her reaction and analyze how her brain functioned. He was supposed to administer a test.

"Oh." Her gaze flicked to the TV screen. "You're missing the witch."

He heard the music and knew the old witch was riding her bicycle with Toto in the basket. "I've seen this part."

She sucked on the end of the licorice, then bit off a small chunk, chewing as she watched him instead of the movie.

He didn't realize he'd leaned closer until she put the flat of her hand to his chest and pushed. If she'd used her finger, he'd have lost it completely.

"Brax."

"Hmm." He loved the way her lips puckered around his name.

"I might write erotica on the Internet, but I'm not going to lick your ice-cream cone."

His ice-cream cone reacted immediately, as if she'd said the opposite. "Bad choice of words on my part."

"It was?" Was that disappointment in her voice? She bit off two more pieces of licorice and stared at him thoughtfully.

"Yeah." She wasn't an ice-cream-cone-on-the-first-date kind of woman. "I don't know what came over me." A lingering heat from reading about sensual massage had come over him.

And the dazzle of her smile that had flitted through his dreams last night.

She stuck the last bit of red licorice between her lips.

He backed off, leaned heavily against the sofa to run both hands through his hair. Where the hell was his perspective? It wasn't just his life that had turned upside down in Cottonmouth. He, himself, had become topsy-turvy. He was usually rational, analytical and focused.

His reactions to Simone, however, had proved anything but. "I'm exceptionally sorry."

She hummed beside him.

"I'm usually more circumspect."

Then she started to sing along with the movie. Slightly off-key, deeper than Judy Garland's sweet tones, but Simone's voice burrowed beneath his ribs and shot up to grab hold of his heart. Something glistened in her pretty hazel eyes. The notion gripped him that she wasn't singing for Dorothy, but for herself, and she had yet to find her way over any rainbows.

Maggie had told him as much.

He stroked the back of her hand with his knuckles. She sat hugging her knees to her chest, her bare feet flat on the sofa, her toes curled over the edge. She blinked away tears.

He thought she might flick off his touch, but instead she said, "I love that song," then she glanced at him, as if to assess his reaction. "I'm a sucker for sappy movies."

He was a sucker for her. "We should get to know each other better."

She gave him a where-the-hell-did-that-come-from look.

"I mean, we should get to know each other better before we start thinking about ice-cream cones." Not that he couldn't think about them, in the most politically correct fashion, of course. Whatever that was.

She continued to hug her knees. "I bet Maggie already told you everything there is to know about me."

And, he surmised, Maggie had probably told *her* everything there was to know about *him*. "Does that bother you?"

She thought about it, staring at a point on the sofa beyond his head. "No. Everyone knows everything around here. I suppose you want to know about my spectacular failure in the cutthroat tech writing business."

His hand trailed down her leg to her feet where she'd now crossed them at the ankles. "If it's important."

"Important? Of course it's important."

Why? Everyone failed at something or other in their lives. Divorce. Letting your friend get murdered. Countless errors in judgment with eventual disastrous consequences for someone.

He knew Maggie hadn't told her about his Cottonmouth failure. He hadn't given Maggie more than the bare facts without the emotion. He certainly hadn't shared the guilt. He wouldn't burden Simone with it now. But he would listen to whatever she needed to tell him.

"Tell me." *Tell me everything about yourself.*

She rested her chin on her knees and looked at him. "My mother always says I'm like the little squirrel who runs out into the middle of the road in front of a speeding car. I twitch this way and that way, and before I make up my mind which way to run, I get squashed."

Her mother. He really did not like the woman without even having met her. "But you're doing fine now."

He no longer questioned that she'd thrived in Goldstone. He had the feeling that Simone would thrive wherever life dumped her. After all, she'd always have that smile.

She tipped her head to one side. "Yeah. I feel safe

and secure here in Goldstone. This is my home."
Putting her foot down, she tapped against the carpet
and floor of her trailer. "It's got a foundation, you
know. Most trailers sit on cinder blocks, but this one's
got a real foundation."

"It's a very nice trailer."

Simone laughed. Brax couldn't know how many
times she'd heard similar platitudes. "You sound like
my mother. She chokes every time she has to say the
word trailer so she avoids it like the plague."

"I mean it. You seem…" He paused. Probably
searching for the right word again so he wouldn't offend her. "Settled."

It was a good description. Most people never found
that settled place. They were always looking for more,
needing more, never content with what they had. Simone savored the peace Goldstone had brought her.
"I'm doing great. Never better."

"So, what else do you want?"

"It's your turn. I answered, now I get to ask."

He considered her a moment before answering.
"Shoot your question."

She read his face like a map. He thought she'd ask
about the divorce. Most women wanted to know about
a man's failures in love. Not Simone. She'd had too
many failures at love herself.

Like Andrew, her ex-fiancé. Putting it mildly, they
hadn't been compatible in the bedroom. She knew it
was all her fault. But sometimes, well, she got carried
away. Loudly. Once Andrew even covered her mouth
with his hand. It would have been okay, maybe, if he'd
kissed her instead, but he'd used his hand to muffle her
cries. No, her screams. She was a screamer. Oh my

God. Her mother would have been appalled at her lack of control. Excess and exuberance were dirty words in the Chandler household. After that, Andrew simply took care of the problem by not touching her in certain spots.

So no, Simone would not ask about Brax's divorce. "Did Maggie really beat you up when you were kids?"

He laughed, half relief, half openmouthed wonder, she was sure. "Yeah. All the time."

"And you never hit her back?"

"She was a girl."

"But she tortured you mercilessly."

He shook his head. "Never hit her."

"But you did retaliate in some way, didn't you?"

He gave her a crooked smile. "It took years of planning."

"What did you do?"

"Timing was everything."

"But what'd you do?" She waited, feeling breathless and wide-eyed.

"Well…"

"Come on, come on." She twitched her toes under his palm.

The sun had fallen completely behind the hills. The room was dark and intimate. Dorothy was skipping down the Yellow Brick Road. Simone wanted more than Brax's hand on her foot.

The warmth of his skin heated her on the inside. Too much. He chose that moment to withdraw his light touch, as if he, too, felt the sudden intimacy. And needed to break it. She should have been glad. She'd been rushing toward something she feared she couldn't handle.

Instead, she mourned the loss. Jeez, she wanted him to touch her. Badly. Three long years badly.

"In the tenth grade, Maggie had a huge crush on Ricky Meyers. So I invited him over to go swimming because we were the only ones in the neighborhood with a pool, one of those big Doughboy things. I told Maggie he was upstairs in my room and wanted to see her."

She gasped. "You didn't let her walk in on him naked?"

He nodded. "I was only twelve, and I figured she'd get the shock of her life when she saw him changing into his swimsuit."

"You were so bad." But terribly cute.

"Only thing was, Ricky wasn't just changing into his swimsuit."

She cocked her head. "What was he doing?"

"Then, I wasn't sure. She screamed, and he ran out. For weeks afterward, I thought he had sunburn because his face was red whenever I saw him. Beet-red."

"Beet-red."

"Yeah. *Beat* red." This time he stressed the word.

Oh my God. She covered her mouth. *Her* face turned beet-red, she was sure. And it made her think of her afternoon fantasies about Brax all over again. "He wasn't…"

"Yeah. He was," Brax said gravely.

"Sheriff Braxton, that is the worst prank I've ever heard." She wanted to let go with an exuberant laugh her mother would have disapproved of, while the heat in her cheeks reached deep inside, warming those certain spots of hers to conflagration stage.

Brax raised a brow. "Well, I didn't know he was

going to do *that*. I didn't even know what *that* was. At the time." He spread the fingers of one hand, keeping the other in contact with her skin, her arm, her elbow, her calf, the back of her ankle, driving her crazy. "I led a very sheltered life."

"Poor Maggie." She smiled behind her hand.

"I wasn't sure she'd recover. My dad grounded me for a month and told me if she was scarred irreparably by the incident, it would be a weight I'd carry on my shoulders the rest of my life."

"You deserved the worry." The grin on her lips belied the solemn words, but she couldn't help it. Nor could she help her quickened breath and racing heart. "But Maggie must have gotten over it by the time she married Carl."

He laughed then. "All those years of agonizing guilt I suffered, then, when we were drinking champagne after her wedding, she told me she hadn't been screaming at all. She'd been laughing hysterically."

"Laughing?"

"Yeah. Ricky Meyers was a tad on the small side. I never knew it, but she was the one who started calling him Tiny Tim."

"Guess she got you in the end, huh?"

"Yeah. I learned one of life's great lessons very early."

"What's that?"

"Revenge backfires."

She laughed, but when she lifted her eyes to his, the smile died away. His blue eyes were suddenly so hot. Burning, blazing. For her. She hadn't been wanted in such a way in a long, long time. And he did want her. She knew.

He robbed her of her breath. He stole her power of

speech. He warmed her skin and peppered it with goose bumps all at once.

Dropping her gaze, she played absently with her toes. He stroked her forearm. Ooh. He was big-time getting to her.

"I want to kiss you, Simone."

Oh my. The things this man made her feel. He was adorable, like a big huggable grizzly bear with a heart of gold. Did grizzlies have hearts of gold? Well, he did. For the first time in a while, she wanted more than the fantasy on her computer. She wanted to close her eyes and lose herself in his hot touch. As scary as that was.

Very scary. Too scary. She was a baby-step kind of girl. The thought of baring anything, everything, physically or metaphorically, terrified her.

But, oh my, she wanted more. Not all-the-way more, just a tiny bit more. Something nonthreatening, but very sexy, very erotic. Something to tease herself with.

He smelled so good. Purely soap and shaving cream laced with the subtle hint of hot hard male. She'd forgotten what an aroused male smelled like. She'd missed that, too.

Simone raised her gaze to his, the light of the TV flickering across his cheek. Then she tucked her feet beneath her and rolled to her knees, putting her hand on the back of the sofa next to his shoulder, her lips inches from his.

"You know, Brax, I'd like to kiss you. But there's something I'd like even more."

GOD HELP HIM, he was about to complicate things. Against his better judgment. Right now, he'd give her anything. Everything. He couldn't help himself.

"What do you want?" His voice almost cracked like an adolescent.

He wasn't a man who usually asked permission. A woman gave signals. A man learned to read them. He didn't think he was wrong about hers. The quickened rise and fall of her chest, the flush tingeing her flawless skin above the neckline of her T-shirt, and her concentration with her toes. Yet with her, something made him hold back, some indefinable sense that he wanted her sanction. Her unqualified consent to full participation in the sweetest kiss his mind had ever conjured. He anticipated her taste with an intensity so great his hands shook.

He scanned her features, her eyes, her slightly parted lips and drank in the citrus scent of her hair. He wanted the touch of her crimson lipstick and the lingering taste of licorice.

"I want the fantasy," she fairly purred.

"The fantasy?" Which fantasy? His? Hers? He'd die to know what they were.

"Yeah, you know, that whole building tension thing, where you want and you anticipate and you're pretty sure you're going crazy, because it's all you can think about, every moment, sleeping or waking."

Her words were so damn close to the way he was feeling. "And?"

"Don't you remember how it was when you were sixteen? You wanted to touch that girl, whoever she was, so badly, your fingers itched and your whole body felt like it was going to explode."

He'd been seventeen and the girl was Mary Alice Turner.

"You ached for the touch of her breast through her

blouse, wanted the feel of its peak in your palm. You were on the edge, dying, needing."

Simone's voice took him back to that time, that place, the backseat of his dad's Chrysler, sweet, pure, innocent desire consuming him.

"You wanted to get to first or second base, maybe even third so bad you thought you'd die. It was so intense you almost lost it with the thought of touching her most private, intimate spot."

Her voice and his memories seduced him.

"That's eroticism," she whispered. "The wanting and the not being able to have. It made you feel so alive, so aware, so breathless with desire. And when you finally got what you wanted, if you ever got it, you'll never forget that moment." She licked her lips. "Do you remember what that was like, Brax?"

God, yes. He'd wanted Mary Alice with the fervor of teenage hormone overload. He remembered the depths of despair, then the glory of that first kiss and, yes, Mary Alice Turner's nipple against his palm. He never made love to Mary Alice, but he'd wanted to with every fiber of his being. He couldn't remember a time that was more intense or made him feel more alive.

Simone was right. Kissing her right now would be great, having sex with her even better, but if he let the need, anticipation and desire build, he might recapture that feeling of aliveness he hadn't experienced in a long, long time.

Maybe that was another thing that had been filling him with this sense of restlessness. Not only the murder, but also the feeling that life was passing him by without him even noticing. Maybe his memory of Mary Alice had been piqued by the recent goings-on

in Cottonmouth, but he'd wondered a couple of times what had happened to her after she left town. Old hurts, past mistakes, previous errors in judgment. They'd consumed him in recent weeks. His dead friend, his dead marriage, his ex-wife. Maybe he'd never shown her the passion she needed to make her feel alive. He knew he'd never truly felt alive in the marriage.

Brax touched Simone's cheek, then trailed a finger down to her jaw, farther still to the hollow above her collarbone. Again, he trembled with the warmth of her skin. His breath came fast, his gut clenched, and his groin tightened.

He wanted that kiss. He wanted her breast in his palm, his hand in her panties and his body buried deep inside her. But more, he wanted *this,* the wild need clutching his chest, the sense that he couldn't take his next breath without mingling it with hers. The fear that he'd come without a touch, with nothing more than the sound of her voice so damn close to his ear.

She made him feel the blood pounding through his veins, the pulse at his temple, his throat and his fingertips, the rush of heat across his skin. She made him feel fiercely alive.

"I remember," he murmured, his gaze holding hers. "And I want that feeling. With you."

She leaned in, closing the small distance between them, and licked his lower lip with her tongue.

He damn near exploded in his pants.

She did the one thing he couldn't do for himself. She made him forget his guilt. Even if only for a short time.

THE WITCH CACKLED, Dorothy fell asleep in the field of poppies and the Tin Man cried.

Simone realized they'd missed more than half the movie.

Brax watched her with…intensity. His gaze traveled over her face, coming to rest on her lips. Her skin felt flushed, her body more than aroused, her nipples hard and achy. Her stomach fluttered like one of the heroines in her stories.

"We missed the part where we would have found out if they were sisters."

His eyes didn't even flick to the screen. "Yeah, we did."

"Then I guess we're both losers."

He picked up a lock of her hair that rested against her chest, the back of his hand brushing across a nipple for the tiniest moment. A flame sparked inside her.

An answering blaze lit his eyes to a deep blue. "I don't see any losers around here."

"I think you're a nice man."

He grinned. "Hasn't anyone ever told you that calling a man *nice* is the kiss of death?"

"Men don't like to be told they're nice?" She knew that. They wanted to be told they were hot or macho or hunky or virile or big where it counted. But nice? Not.

"There's always a 'but' that comes after nice."

"Not this time. This time it's the highest of compliments. The last nice man I met, I almost married." Oops darn. She shouldn't have said that.

"But you didn't marry him. Nice wasn't so nice after all."

Andrew *had* been nice. "He just had a little phobia about catastrophic failure." As if it rubbed off on those closest to the ruined individual.

"I'm sorry."

She smiled brightly, though her face felt like cracking. "I'm so over it now." Not. Especially not Andrew's disgusted whispers in the dark. That was the worst part. *Simone, the neighbors will hear you.*

Which was why it was much better not to let Brax touch her on any of those certain spots that would make her lose control completely. Now, she wrote about sex without actually experiencing the act. Much safer that way.

"Glad you're over it." Brax wrapped her hair around his finger, let it pull loose, then tucked the lock behind her ear. His touch lingered. He traced the shell of her ear, a barely there caress that sent chills and thrills down her spine.

This was what she'd meant about building the need and heightening the senses with anticipation. He'd understood completely. A kindred spirit, looking for something more than the wham-bam-thank-you-ma'am of a short vacation fling. When he left Goldstone, they'd both have wild memories, even if this moment was all they had. And there would be no embarrassing hand-over-the-mouth episodes or appalled looks in the aftermath.

She trailed the tip of her finger from his Adam's apple to the center of his chest. A light stroke, a subtle caress.

He growled low in his throat. "Say it."

"Say what?" She'd say anything he wanted her to.

"The bumper sticker thing."

She understood. "Don't make me bring out the flying monkeys."

He closed his eyes and murmured, "Say it like you mean it."

She did, gritting her teeth and infusing emotion into the words. "Don't *make* me bring out the flying monkeys."

He captured her finger and drew it to his lips, then kissed the pad. "Christ, that makes me hot."

She laughed. "I'm pretty sure it's *never* made anyone hot before."

Warm and wet. Gentle suction and the caress of his tongue. She was suddenly a mass of jangling nerve endings. Her panties dampened. "I really think you better stop that."

"Does it make you want to go to first base?"

She tilted her head. "What exactly is first base? French-kissing?"

"You've gotta be kidding. It's getting my hand in your bra."

"No way. That's second base."

"Guys don't care about kissing. They want flesh."

"But that wouldn't make sense. Because if putting your hand on my breast—"

"On your nipple."

"—is first base, then that means second base is getting your hand down my pants. But a home run is going all the way. So what's third base?"

He put his forehead to hers and laughed, the vibration streaking all the way down through her chest to her legs and even her toes. "Is this like that old Abbott and Costello routine, who's on first and what's on second?"

"Actually, we were talking about third."

He rolled his head to the side and nipped her ear. "Third is using my tongue on you."

Oh. Ooh. Ahh. She closed her eyes and savored the delicious warmth that spread through her. "I don't think

teenage boys think about *that*. I don't think they even *know* about that."

He chuckled. "Believe me, they know exactly what it is, and they've got some very colorful names to describe it."

She knew what Andrew had called it, and it wasn't polite. He hadn't liked it because Simone got downright embarrassing with her exuberance. "What do they call it?"

This time, Brax laughed outright. "I can't tell you."

"I might have to use the terminology in one of my stories."

"It's a guy code of honor. I can't tell."

"Spoilsport." She pouted. But he'd made her laugh inside and forget about the mutant ache brought on by too much Andrew-thinking. Andrew-thinking was wrong-thinking at a time like this.

Brax tugged on a lock of her hair. "It's an advanced technique best left to experts rather than teenagers. So I guess third is getting you to put your hand in my pants."

She considered his logic. "Maybe."

"I'm right. I was a teenage boy. Kissing is unimportant. Touching is everything."

"So you don't want to kiss me?"

"Kissing is another advanced technique employed by experts designed to make your defenses tumble."

"Hmm. That sounds like seduction. Maybe you're not such a nice guy after all."

"That's what I've been telling you." Then he put his hand on her throat and his fingers on her chin and tipped her chin up. "I want to kiss you. I want to touch you. I want to taste you. I want to be inside you." His

lips brushed hers as he spoke. "But for now, I'll only do it in my dreams. Until I think I'm gonna die. Until I beg you to put me out of my misery."

Ooh, she was in trouble. Very big trouble. He made her tingle. He made her want to scream exuberantly and the consequences be damned.

"I don't know, Brax," she whispered, "I might beg you first."

CHAPTER FIVE

MAGGIE FELMAN STARED at the chalky gray mass on the platter. She'd made Carl his favorite, liver and onions with bacon. Personally, she found it disgusting. Eating organ meat was akin to cannibalism. But she was trying very hard to follow her brother's suggestions. Just as Tyler said, she was giving Carl the benefit of the doubt.

Carl wasn't trying. The bastard.

She'd kill him when he got home, absolutely kill him.

Staring once more at the ruined meal, she wrinkled her nose in distaste. Why had things gone so wrong? And when? Three months ago, four, six, a year? She couldn't pinpoint it, except that she got the sense it was about the time Carl got into the whole outhouse thing. Or maybe bat shit had finally rotted what little brain he had in the first place.

She pursed her lips. That wasn't nice. She took it back. She'd never thought of Carl as a jobless loser, no matter what anyone else said. After all, she'd married him because she'd been attracted to his anti-rat-race philosophy. He made money in…offbeat ways, and they were certainly far from destitute.

Though the medical insurance bothered her. They

weren't getting any younger, but Carl saved money by getting one of those policies that covered only the major stuff. There was also a lifetime limit. That's what terrified her. Her dad's medical expenses had been astronomical. She'd hid all her anxiety from Carl, which caused her to worry even more, and she was pretty sure ulcer treatment wasn't considered "major."

It had gotten to the point where they couldn't even communicate in bed. When they made love, it was perfunctory. They used to make beautiful love together. She just couldn't remember the last time.

Maggie swiped at a tear that had slipped down her cheek. Another followed. Her marriage was falling apart. So was her life. As much as she'd hoped, she knew Tyler's visit wasn't going to fix anything.

The front door opened and closed. Not Tyler. She'd sent him off to Simone's. She'd wanted an extra hour or two to create this wonderful, stupendous, fantastic alone time with Carl. And Carl had ruined it all, as he'd ruined everything else with his silences and his office locking mechanism.

"You're late," she snapped when she heard his footsteps behind her on the kitchen floor. "The liver is ruined."

She opened the door under the sink and slammed the plate against the side of the garbage can until the leathery mess slid off into the trash liner.

"I didn't know you were cooking. You haven't cooked in a long time."

Her self-pity died beneath another onslaught of anger.

She turned on him, narrowing her eyes. She was so angry she could barely breathe. "What? You think

Hamburger Helper isn't cooking? You think it doesn't take time to thaw the hamburger and brown it and add the noodles and stir and stir and heat up a can of corn to go with it?"

Her husband, the filthy rotten bastard, backed up two steps. "Uh, no." He clutched a paper sack to his chest and watched her with a wary gaze.

That pissed her off more. "What have you got in there? Porno magazines? Is that what you do all night in your stupid trailer?" *Is that what you do when you should be spending time with me, making love, real love, with me?*

"No. It's…uh…it's…uh…"

"Cat got your tongue?" She waved the cleaver, so angry she could smack him upside the head with the flat edge.

He eased around her. She turned with each step, making sure he got the full effect of each eye-stabbing look she threw at him.

He pointed. "Trailer. Talk later." One step, then two, closer to the back door.

"Yeah, the trailer. Well, you can sleep out there, for all I care." Her temper rose with every word, as if she couldn't keep them inside any longer. "In fact, you can just drop dead, do you hear me?" Finally she was shouting at him, and it felt so good. "Drop dead, Carl!"

He dashed through the back door at that last soul-freeing bellow. Damn him, damn him. Moments later, she heard the trailer door bang. She could even imagine the lock slamming home. Locking her out.

Then her own words came back to haunt her. The fury whooshed out of her as quickly as it had come. She sagged against the counter, deflated.

Tyler would kill her. She'd handled it wrong. She'd ruined their evening as surely as Carl's tardiness ruined their dinner.

What was wrong with her? What was wrong with *them?*

She folded her arms on the counter and, still clutching the cleaver in her hand, laid her head down.

She didn't have energy left to cry.

BRAX TOOK HIS MOVIE, but left the licorice. Simone sat in her rocker on the porch chewing thoughtfully on another piece as she stared off in the direction his truck had disappeared.

He hadn't kissed her good-night. He'd touched her face, run his thumb over her bottom lip, then held her close for five seconds. It was too long and nowhere near long enough. He hadn't kissed her, but he'd wanted to. He'd been hard against her, and she knew he must have felt her beaded nipples against his chest.

The whole evening had been such exquisite torture. She'd never met a man who understood how incredibly erotic the whole tease thing was. Men weren't built to withstand teasing. They had a name for women who did that, and it wasn't pleasant. The male gender didn't get how good it could be.

But Brax did.

He hadn't told her that teasing was fine if she slept with him in the end. Part of the game, the part that made it even hotter, was not knowing. Even *she* didn't know if they would.

Until this afternoon, the answer would have been a definite no. Now, she wasn't so sure. It was almost worth the possibility of embarrassment and rejection

to see how good it could be. Dangerous, though. She might lose more than her control.

After this evening, she liked the man, not just his hunky body or his cheeky grin. He played her weird games—she admitted they were weird—he laughed at his mistakes, and he was honest-to-goodness sweet to Maggie. What kid brother cared if he scarred his sister for life? That's what kid brothers *hoped* to do.

Not that Simone had firsthand knowledge. No kid brothers, only her sister, Jackie. Jackie hadn't pulled a prank since…well, never. Ariana Chandler didn't tolerate pranks from little beauty pageant queens, particularly not her daughters.

Sometimes Simone wished Jackie *had* played a joke, even if it was on her only sister. Jackie didn't pull nasty tricks, she didn't lie, and she always followed the lifesaving creed, "If you can't say something nice, don't say anything at all." Most of the time, Jackie *didn't* say anything, especially around their mother.

She had the sudden urge to call her little sister. It wasn't terribly late, if Jackie was home and not attending some elaborate gala. She dialed Jackie's private line.

"Hello?" Her sister always answered the phone tentatively, as if she were sure of neither her caller nor herself.

"Thanks for the clothes," Simone said, remembering her mother's admonition.

"I'm sorry."

"For what?"

"I tried to say it wasn't such a good idea."

"It was a wonderful idea. I loved them." Some lucky lady shopping at the Goodwill was in for a treat.

"I know how you really feel, so thanks for saying that."

Simone's thoughts regarding the care package were not Jackie's fault. It would have been blasphemy to mention that perhaps her sister deserved better than to have to wear size zero clothing, as well. Simone decided to move the conversation forward. "You'll never guess what I did tonight?"

Someone else might have suggested something outrageous, like a Lady Godiva-like ride through the streets of Goldstone. Jackie just said, "You know I'll never guess."

Jackie didn't like guessing games. One could say the wrong thing, and that made a girl vulnerable. Jackie was ultracareful. She had to be, living with their mother.

"I watched *The Wizard of Oz* with a man. And he was the one who brought over the movie." Okay, she'd suggested it earlier in the day, but he didn't have to take her up on it. They hadn't watched much of it, either. They hadn't even played the jitterbug sequence. Simone didn't care.

"Someone in Goldstone appreciates *The Wizard of Oz?*" Jackie didn't say it the way her mother did, with that high falsetto I-find-that-hard-to-believe tone. Jackie's voice was never steeped with judgment, but always…neutral.

"He doesn't live here. He's visiting his sister."

"I'd like to see Goldstone. At least once." Wistful thinking murmured in an equally wistful voice.

"You could come for a visit."

"Mother's not going to visit Goldstone."

"I meant *you* could come. Alone."

"Oh." Jackie was only two years younger, but she'd never lived outside of an Ariana Chandler household, and Simone was beginning to think she never would. True, Jackie had her own suite of rooms with her own entrance. If she didn't want to see Ariana for days or even weeks, she didn't *have* to.

Ariana, however, didn't raise her daughters that way. They dined together every night. MOTHER carefully selected Jackie's clothes, Jackie's hairstyles, Jackie's friends and Jackie's opinions. It was Ariana's way of taking care of Jackie.

Simone had dealt with her mother's overbearing good intentions by running away to college right out of high school.

Which was why she'd also run into a few problems along the way, her mother had stated flatly. The only thing Ariana had approved of was Andrew. She'd adored him, his Stanford degree, his Porsche, his proper East Coast well-to-do parents and the way he kissed Ariana's hand when she'd deigned to visit twice yearly.

God, she was depressing herself. That wasn't why she'd called her sister. She'd called because Jackie was her best friend, and, like a starry-eyed teenager, she'd wanted to tell her sister all about Brax.

"It doesn't matter about you visiting, Jackie. I know you're really busy and don't have the time." She offered Jackie that excuse. "I only called to tell you all about *him.*"

"Yes," Jackie answered breathlessly, with the tiniest bit of emotion and excitement in her voice, "tell me all about him."

For the next few minutes, they oohed and aahed to-

gether like the innocent, happy, carefree teenage girls they'd fantasized about being.

She was still smiling when she hung up. Someday she would get Jackie to visit. They could have such fun. Mr. Doodle would adore Jackie. Simone hugged the phone to her chest and stared out into the night beyond her porch. Though the moon was at its smallest crescent, stars sparkled. Jackie should see how beautiful the desert was at night, without city lights obscuring the sky or the stars.

Something moved beyond the end of the lane. Hers was the last trailer, and the road at that point led up to the town's park, a dirt lot with strategically placed plastic trash can lids to simulate a baseball diamond.

The shadow was too big for a coyote, and it didn't move with the loping amble of the wily animals.

Her skin prickled. For a moment, she felt as if the thing crouched and watched. Her. She had the sudden terrible feeling it, whatever it was, had been watching her the whole time she talked on the phone with her sister.

For a moment, the crescent moon slid behind a cloud. When it slipped out again, the shadow at the end of the lane was gone.

Simone rubbed her arms. It was her imagination playing tricks on her. Silly. Still, she locked up tight, both the porch screen and her front door.

BRAX HADN'T ASKED Simone a single pointed interrogative question. He didn't care. In fact, he'd revealed more about himself than he'd learned about her. He didn't care about that, either. Simone wasn't sleeping with Carl. She wouldn't do that to Maggie. That secret

e-mail was not about an affair. Something else, not that. He'd stake his tarnished reputation on it. Maybe Carl was hitting up Simone for love life advice. He might even have asked her to write a story with which to surprise and delight Maggie, a peace offering to fix whatever was wrong in their marriage. Yeah. That explanation set well with him.

Brax was whistling when he entered the front door which opened straight into the main part of the trailer. Ahead was the kitchen and kitty-corner, the den, where Maggie sat, staring sightlessly at the TV.

She sat cross-legged on the couch, arms over her chest, her chin drooping. There was not a smile within a mile of her.

Damn. The little talk with Carl had probably degenerated into a big argument.

He dispensed with the formalities and sat on the heavy lacquered wood coffee table in front of her. "What's wrong?"

She stared at his chest as if she could see right through it to the TV. Her eyes were red rimmed, her cheeks blotchy, and telltale tears left tracks down to the edges of her mouth. "He's out in his office."

"What did you say to him?"

She looked at him sharply. "I didn't say anything inflammatory."

Whoa, girl. He held up his hand. "I didn't mean that you did. But what happened?"

"I made dinner. He came home. He went out to the trailer. And he's been there ever since." Her lower lip trembled. "He didn't even eat dinner, and I made his favorite. Fried liver smothered with onions and bacon. I had to throw the whole thing away."

Egads. The trash sounded like a good place for that meal, but Brax didn't comment. "What happened in between the time he came home and when he went out to the trailer?"

Her gaze dropped once more to the middle of his shirt, her lips flattened, then she twisted her mouth back and forth. "Nothing."

"Mag-gie."

"All right already," she snapped and proceeded to fill him in.

When she'd finished, her mouth twisted, her nostrils twitched and her eyes filled with tears.

"It's okay, honey," Brax murmured soothingly. "Do you want me to talk to him?"

"No."

"Tell me what I can do to help." Because he felt too damn helpless watching her cry.

"You can't do anything. I know that. I really blew it, Tyler. I shouldn't have gotten mad."

"He shouldn't have come home late." Though, in Carl's defense, he hadn't known Maggie was gonna go all out with the liver and onions. Brax withheld a shudder.

She sighed. "Yeah, you're right."

"Let me talk to him, maybe smooth things over."

Her brow creased with a militant frown, and he knew he'd said the wrong thing. He couldn't figure out what was the right thing.

"I want you to skip the talking part and beat the crap out of him like big brothers are supposed to do."

"I'm your little brother."

"You're bigger than me. And you're bigger than Carl. So go beat him up and tell him it's for me."

He smiled.

The corners of her mouth turned up. Not a full smile, but better than the morose expression that had spoiled her face when he walked in.

He tapped her nose, then rose and stepped away. "How badly do you want me to hurt him?"

"Make him real bloody."

All right, he'd give Carl one more crack. He'd probably get no further than he had last night, but he couldn't stand watching Maggie rip herself up this way.

His obsessive thoughts regarding Simone would have to wait until later.

"By the way," she said as he backed out of the room to do her bidding. "I have to go to the Manor for our monthly tea party tomorrow."

The Manor? "A tea party?" He got a bad feeling that she was going to make him tag along.

"Our Manor of the Ladies is the local old folks home, and we all go once a month. I told the ladies you'd want to meet them, and they're really excited."

He cocked his head and eyed her warily. "How many ladies?"

"Well, there's Agnes and Rowena and Myrtle and Nonnie. But don't call Myrtle Myrtle. Call her Divine. She hates Myrtle. In fact, I think she hates her mother for giving her that name."

Agnes, Rowena, Nonnie, and Divine-not-Myrtle. He wondered which would be more difficult, beating the crap out of Carl or facing four little old ladies across a tea table.

"Umm, are you sure you need me on this one, Maggie?"

"Don't whine. And yes I need you. They'll be very disappointed if you don't attend with me."

"I never whine."

She dipped her head and looked at him through her eyelashes. "Simone will be there."

Ahh. The crux of the matter. His sister's matchmaking at work again, in that singsong voice she used when attempting to manipulate.

He didn't care that she'd slyly maneuvered him. She'd used the magic word, or rather the magic name. Simone.

"Sure. I'll go."

Then he left to metaphorically beat the crap out of Carl before his sister started crying again and got him to agree to *really* do it.

BRAX KNOCKED on the trailer door. Carl opened it a scant three inches, revealing nothing more than one eye.

"Yeah?"

"Gotta talk to you, Carl. Let me in."

"About what? I'm really busy." Carl offered only another three inches, his face and body filling the opening so that Brax could see nothing of the interior of the trailer.

Marital issues required subtlety. Revealing that Maggie was inside crying wasn't the smart course. "You looking at porn on the Internet? Let me see."

Carl's nostrils twitched. "No, I'm not looking at porn. Did Maggie send you out here?"

Busted. "I take it you're not going to let me in." What was the man hiding in there? "Fine. Let's go out for a drink." He'd loosen Carl up with a beer. It had worked last night.

Yeah, and he'd gotten himself into a hair-raising discussion on communication with the opposite sex. He wasn't looking forward to more, but he did have familial duties and obligations.

"I'm not in a drinking mood, Brax."

Damn. Things were bad when a man didn't want to drown his sorrows in a frosty mug of beer.

What would entice Carl? Brax tried to remember the last few months of his own marriage. What had *he* done to drown out his wife's bouts of crying followed by endless silences? "How about a game of pool?"

They'd probably have to drive into Bullhead, but a man had to do what a man had to do. While he was there, he could drop off *The Wizard of Oz*. Maybe pick up another movie to watch with Simone. What else would she like? Was she a *Singing in the Rain* kind of woman? Yeah. Definitely.

Shit. Carl stood in the barely open doorway saying nothing.

"Okay, not pool." He drew another blank, a testament to the fact that he didn't really know his brother-in-law well. He made the commitment to himself to get to know Carl better, starting right now.

Carl finally made the next move. "Darts."

"Yeah. Darts." Brax hadn't thrown a dart since he was in college, and even then, he hadn't practiced enough to get really good. Skill level, however, didn't matter in this instance.

"All right." Carl glanced back over his shoulder. "Let me…clean up in here."

"I'll wait out by the truck."

Brax figured Carl had acquiesced merely to get him out of the door of the trailer. What was he doing in

there? Brax's immediate reaction was to flash his badge and intimidate his way inside. Carl being his brother-in-law, however, required more stealth.

Like plying him with beer and darts, then driving him back home to talk with his wife.

CHAPTER SIX

THE EVENING WAS comfortably warm half an hour later when they climbed out of Brax's SUV in Bullhead. Monday night was a helluva lot more crowded at The Dartboard than at the Flood's End on a Sunday. Whether it was the day of the week, the entertainment or the fact that The Dartboard offered scantily clad waitresses, Brax couldn't be sure. By the looks of it, the majority of Bullhead's male population—and probably most of Goldstone's, too—was in attendance. They had to take a ticket and wait for one of the ten boards set along the far wall opposite the bar.

Brax muscled his way through the three-deep crowd at the bar and ordered a couple of beers while Carl claimed a miraculous recently vacated table at the edge of the dart range. They could have waited for one of the bar girls, but there was a good chance they might both expire of old age by then. Brax figured he needed to loosen Carl's tongue with some brew as quickly as possible.

Expect for the occasional "turn left here," Carl had been mum on the drive. That, however, had been part of Brax's plan. He'd let Carl stew in silence, then he'd interrogate—excuse me—persuade him to talk over a beer and a friendly dart game. With the decibel level

on the deafening side, Brax didn't have high hopes for much serious conversation, though. At least not without the alcohol. And a little more of that divine intervention.

The patrons were on the rough side, mostly wearing jeans and worn T-shirts in a multitude of colors. Long, scraggly beards were a fashion statement. The smoke-infested air they breathed would choke a chicken. Bad analogy. The chickens were too high-class for a joint like The Dartboard.

Returning to the table, he slid one foaming beer to Carl and squeezed into the chair opposite. The place erupted in hoots and hollers as some skilled and talented player did…something. Brax couldn't see over the throng, but by the sound of it, the accomplishment had been stupendous. Brax was jostled from the left and stabbed in his right ear by a pointed elbow.

The Dartboard was a bad idea for any man-to-man gritty and to-the-point discussion. Dammit, he should have started on Carl in the truck, but he'd been anticipating a crowd more on par with the Flood's End. He was also damn sure that Carl had intended it this way. A smile creased Carl's mouth as he stretched his five-foot-ten frame for a gander at the dart action.

"How long you think we'll have to wait for a board, Carl?"

He shouted but Carl cupped his ear and mouthed, "What?"

Brax was sure the man was snickering at his own cunning. "When will we get a game?" he enunciated distinctly so Carl could lip-read.

"Probably by Friday night," Carl shouted back.

Snookered. He hadn't credited Carl with being so

cagey. His brother-in-law was damn talented at it, too. Friends eased between the tables, slapping him on the back, joking, laughing. Brax didn't strain to overhear.

Divine revelation wasn't going to come from a bit of backslapping with the good old boys.

Maybe he could clear the bar by arresting them all for overcrowding. A sign over the door indicated the maximum occupancy at fifty, but this herd exceeded that by a multiple of at least three.

His throat scratched, and his head ached from cigarette and cigar fumes. He found it hard to even fantasize about Simone and her lovely smile. Someone had stepped on his right foot and broken his toes, or at least it felt like it. The cool sizzle of beer down his throat helped.

"Carl, you got three choices," he yelled.

Carl lifted an eyebrow.

"You can tell me how you're going to do right by my sister."

The one eyebrow dropped, and Carl raised the other.

"Or we can go outside, and I'll beat the crap out of you for making her cry."

Carl held up three fingers indicating he wanted to hear Brax's third option.

"We can muscle in on a game of darts."

A wry smile curved Carl's lips, then he pointed through the sea of spectators to the dart floor.

Brax almost sighed. In truth, he preferred the third choice himself. Talking about so-called issues or fighting about them were equal pains-in-the-butt. He ignored the small voice whispering, "wimp, wimp." Why did women think it was so easy to bare your soul? Or to listen to someone else baring theirs?

Brax rose, taking his beer in hand, then they shoved through the throng, guarding their mugs with their arms.

"All right, who's the most likely candidate to be intimidated into letting us in?"

Carl strained forward, looking left, then right, and back again. A smile split his face. It was damn near the evil mien of a maniacal serial killer. Not that Brax had ever dealt with one. Not a real one, at any rate. Nick Angel didn't count. That crap about him being a serial killer had all been gossip.

His brother-in-law was a goofy-grin kind of guy, making you wonder if there was much up there in Carl's brain. But the smile that spread across his face now, well, it was pure shit-eating malevolence.

Brax leaned out to glance down the line of shooters, but he couldn't pick out Carl's mark.

Still smiling, Carl dipped back into the crowd and made a beeline for what looked like the last board. Brax followed. Carl called out before they'd even reached their destination. "Hey, Lafoote, how about letting us join your game?"

A hush fell, like the moment the minister steps up to the pulpit or a cop walks into a friend's dope party. Where moments before Brax's ears had pounded with the din, they now rang with the sudden silence.

Lafoote. Alias The Foot. The man the chickens had called a variety of demeaning names. What had the girls said about him, besides the fact that Lafoote wasn't man enough to handle one of them, let alone all four? Oh yeah, Lafoote was planning to renovate the old hotel—though from what Brax had seen, he'd be better off razing it to the ground and starting over—and he was plotting the venture with Chloe.

The two men faced off. The bar's atmosphere darkened, the air heavy and charged, like the hours before a hurricane hit land.

"Let's play a game, Lafoote." Carl seemed to stand a little taller and a lot straighter. To him, this was no game.

Lafoote's opponent, a dark, wiry guy who would have looked dangerous even without the dart clutched in his fist like a weapon, retreated three steps. A two-foot half circle opened up around Lafoote and Carl, like kids on a playground when the class bully finds a victim.

Falling back into a gunfighter position like something out at the OK Corral, Lafoote widened his stance and put his hand on his hips as if preparing to do a quick draw. "Well now, Carl, since we're almost done here, that doesn't seem like the politic thing to do at the moment." He pointed to his companion. "My friend here is beating the pants off me, and I'm sure he's enjoying the fact that I'm no challenge. You, on the other hand, Carl, I'm sure you excel at the finer points of the game, considering the number of hours you practice each day. And that on top of managing to excavate at least four outhouses a week and discovering untold buried treasures. Why, Carl, that is what I call total dedication to a worthwhile pursuit."

Carl's confident smile vanished.

Lafoote was smooth all right. With Muhammad Ali's "float like a butterfly, sting like a bee" finesse, he'd called Carl a dart-playing, outhouse-excavating loser. Lafoote's lanky opponent was still trying to figure out if he'd been insulted, too.

Completely shut down by Lafoote, Carl could only

sputter. His face turned red, and it wasn't with the same stain of embarrassment that had tortured his features last night at the Flood's End. This was spontaneous combustion. This was Monday night in the boxing ring. This had the potential for collateral damage that rivaled Goldstone's flood and the fire combined.

Brax had been a cop for coming up on sixteen years. The best strategy an officer could apply was to head 'em off at the pass. He put a hand on Carl's shoulder. Don't grab, don't pull. Gently bring 'em back to their senses. But Carl shrugged his hand off and squared off against The Foot.

"Listen, you little weasel, you'd better take your dog-and-pony show out of Goldstone before something bad happens to you," Carl growled and clamped his mouth. His teeth ground as if he were breaking down gravel into sand. His fist clenched, unclenched, clenched again, so hard his knuckles turned white, and the beer mug in his other hand trembled. His breath headed toward a full-blown pant while his eyes bore the haze of a bull gone mad.

If he'd had a gun, Carl more than likely would have shot the weasel.

"Are you threatening me, Felman?" The weasel, however, didn't seem to know how close he was to dying. Or at least to sustaining a broken nose and a few loose teeth.

Brax shoved his own beer into the hand of a convenient onlooker and insinuated himself between the two combatants. Three inches taller than Carl, Brax blocked his view of Lafoote.

"We're going to the Flood's End, Carl."

Carl's breath puffed like a steam engine. "Butt out, Brax. This is between me and Lafoote."

"Sheriff Braxton, he's threatening me." The glee in the weasel's voice was about to earn him an elbow in his belly if he didn't shut the hell up, but Brax concentrated on Carl.

Wider and taller, Brax gave Carl the cop look, the one that said I'm hauling your ass to jail, or telling your wife on you. "Back off, Carl."

If Lafoote made a move or a sound, if anyone did, Carl would go off like a powder keg. What caused the animosity between the two men, Brax didn't know, and right now, didn't care.

He met Carl's gaze. The blaze of anger in Carl's eyes was downright frightening. Brax's concern for his sister rose a notch.

Brax met Carl stare for stare, muscles bunched. "Let's go outside, Carl." He debated mentioning Maggie's name, then decided against it.

Moments passed. Brax could almost feel the trapped breaths of the onlookers. Finally, Carl's gaze dropped. The flare of his nostrils receded. Brax clapped him on the arm, then wrapped his hand around Carl's biceps and turned him, steering them through a quickly parting crowd. "It's too fricking loud in here, and there's too many people for my taste, Carl. I'm getting claustrophobic."

Carl moved like a zombie. They reached the end of the bar, and the door was in sight. Almost clear. Brax half expected The Foot to throw some irritating parting shot at Carl and start the whole damn thing over.

He reached the door, slammed it open and practically shoved Carl through.

He'd learned three things. First, something overly odd was going on between the resort developer and the

outhouse excavator. Second, Carl was much closer to the edge than even Maggie seemed to think. And third, Carl was not spending his time at The Chicken Coop, but at The Dartboard. Which should please Maggie.

"Let's get the hell out of here." Brax climbed in. Almost meekly, Carl followed suit on the passenger side.

Once they were on the highway headed back to Goldstone, Brax released the tension in his neck and shoulders. "What the hell was that all about?"

"The man's a fucking asshole." Carl's voice was a low-pitched growl.

Brax didn't know Carl well. He could count on one hand the number of times he'd met the guy face-to-face. So his experience was limited. Still, he'd never heard Carl use that particular word. Not even last night, when it was a guys-only outing.

"Why's he piss you off so much?"

"It's that fucking hotel."

O-kay. The road wasn't heavily traveled and the closest headlights were far in the distance. Carl was on the edge about the whole business. Why? People didn't want the hotel, but Carl's reaction was way beyond simply not wanting the renovation.

He put on his best-buddy routine to ferret out the answer. "I agree he's a dick of the first order all right, but ya had me a bit unnerved in there. I mean, I'd hate to have to tell Mom you had homicidal tendencies." He decided a little levity would ease the tension while at the same time impress upon Carl that his uncharacteristic behavior was bordering on bizarre.

Carl snorted with what Brax hoped was a chuckle. "She'd drag Maggie off to *Divorce Court* if she heard me use the *F*-word."

His mother loved that judge on *Divorce Court.* "Up to this point, she's been quite fond of you, Carl." He threw that in, though it wasn't the truth. "But you're pushing it, pal."

Carl glanced at him. "Let's keep it between us, okay? Your mother scares the crap out of me. Last time she got mad at me, she gave me the 'look.' I was afraid for my life."

Ah, *that* look. The infamous look from Brax's childhood emphatically stating, "if you do that one more time, I will be forced to scream. And then I'll tell your father." There'd always been hell to pay when his mother got that look.

Enid Braxton treated nothing lightly, especially not a "potty mouth." Brax could still taste the soap at odd moments. "I don't know, Carl, it was a dual *F*-word. That's pretty serious."

"What do I gotta do to get you to keep it a secret?"

"Tell me what's going on here, and I won't rat you out to Mom."

Carl was silent.

"That crap going down wasn't like you." At least Maggie had never complained of a temper.

Still no answer. With a quick glance, Brax found him staring out the windshield, a crooked smile on his lips, the headlights of the oncoming car glinting in what Brax was terrified might be moisture. It was the saddest damn thing he'd ever seen. What was he supposed to do if Carl actually cried?

"She still loves you, man." He had to say something.

Carl didn't remark on it. Instead, he returned to Brax's original question. "Lafoote knows how to push

a man's buttons. Can't say I've figured out how he does it, but he knows what to say to set a man off."

"What's he got against you?"

Carl sighed, quirked his lips and shook his head, as if the actions explained it all. "It's the hotel. Nobody wants it, and he won't take no for an answer."

There was more to it than that, but Carl wasn't gonna spill without some manipulation. "So you were gonna rip his throat out over some hotel project?"

"He's an asshole."

"You said that already, Carl."

"Is asshole okay with your mother?"

"Ass is fine if you drop the hole. It's in the Bible." Brax allowed a moment of silence without pressing for an answer.

Finally, Carl shifted in his seat. "He thinks I put Della up to stalling him on the permits and licenses he needs."

"Della?"

"Della Montrose. She's the county judge and the city mayor."

"And did you put her up to it?"

"She was as against it as I was."

"You know, Carl, I don't really get the whole problem. A resort would create jobs and bring income to the city and county." Hell, maybe they could even afford to pave some of the roads.

Carl turned and looked at Brax fully. "Would you want a bunch of gamblers, drunks and whores moving into Cottonmouth?"

"Whore is a strong word." It seemed too crude for the chickens. "And you've already got The Chicken Coop."

"It's the quantity and quality, Brax. We're a small town. We want it to stay that way. That's why most of us are here."

Hard as it was to believe, people came to Goldstone by choice.

"They'll want to start building houses and apartments and condos," Carl went on, "because their employees will need somewhere to live. Then there'll be laundromats and gas stations on every corner. And before you know it, they'll want to put in a shopping mall." He shuddered as if that signaled the decline of modern civilization.

"On the bright side, at least you wouldn't have to drive thirty miles to get your groceries and you wouldn't run out of gas between here and Bullhead."

"Only tourists run out of gas." Goldstone did actually have a gas station, but from what Brax had seen, they'd tacked another twenty cents a gallon onto the price.

"Goldstone's eventually gotta come into the new millennium."

"Maybe," Carl muttered. "All right, sure. But it's not gonna be done by some outsider who looks like a weasel and acts like an ass." Carl turned away to stare out the window. "One of these days, someone around here's gonna surprise everyone."

And that someone would be Carl himself? What, was he planning on finding a treasure trove of lost diamond rings beneath one of Whitey's four outhouses?

Damn. That was harsh. Carl wasn't a bad guy. He'd given his wife quite a nice roof over her head, even if it was a trailer, and up until a few months ago, Maggie had actually seemed happy most of the time.

Could the two events be more than coincidence? When had the Lafoote hotel business started? Did that coincide with Carl's behavioral changes Maggie described?

Were the two connected, and how? He was thinking like a cop and treating Carl's outburst like a crime.

Hell, he was far better at solving felonies than mediating marital squabbles. At least usually. The now-familiar stab of guilt reminded him why he'd left Cottonmouth.

Brax turned back to the original cause for alarm. "So Lafoote thinks you sabotaged him and he's pissed."

Carl snorted. "Yeah. I don't know why I let it get to me back there."

Brax knew. Lafoote had implied that Carl was a loser in front of an overcrowded room full of men Carl probably played with regularly. Any man would be pissed. The near rage in his eyes, though, had been unsettling.

That hadn't been because of the hotel. Something deeper was brewing. Brax was willing to bet Carl himself didn't consciously know the reason. He'd fought with Maggie, then he'd gone ballistic when Lafoote had intimated he was a loser. The implication was clear. Carl thought of himself as a loser, Maggie exacerbated the situation and Lafoote tapped into it either as a lucky hit or a man adept at exploiting another man's weakness.

Sometimes a man would do just about anything to prove he wasn't a failure.

That was the frightening part.

"Carl, things are getting out of hand. You and Maggie need to sit down and talk over your problems."

"I've tried."

"No, you haven't. You leave early, you're gone all day, and when you're home, you closet yourself in your trailer." Christ. He sounded like a woman nattering at her husband.

"I've got important things to do."

"Nothing's more important than your marriage and your wife." He should have listened to his own advice before his own marriage had gone belly-up. "I'm not trying to butt in."

"Yes, you are."

"All right, I'm butting in because I care about Maggie's happiness."

"Brax, it's not—"

Brax cocked his head and skewered Carl with a sideways look. "I'll tell Mom you said the *F*-word."

Carl turned. Brax heard a snort. Then a real chuckle. Finally, Carl's voice rose to a falsetto note. "Oh, please, please, Brax, don't do that."

"Then ask my sister out on a date tomorrow night. Talk everything through."

Carl threw up his hands. "All right, fine. You win."

"And don't take her to a burger joint."

"What kind of loser do you think I am?" Carl laughed, then stopped as if he heard his own words. In a subdued tone, he added, "I'll take her some place real nice. For steak. We haven't had a good steak in years." Carl turned in his seat once more. "Hate to leave you all alone, buddy."

Brax smiled. "Don't worry. Just do your duty by my sister."

Besides, Brax didn't intend to spend the evening alone.

CHAPTER SEVEN

As SHE ENTERED the Manor's small dining room on Tuesday afternoon, Simone smoothed her navy polka-dot skirt. She always dressed up for the monthly tea party. The ladies appreciated it.

Our Manor of the Ladies was clear on the other side of town from The Chicken Coop. Though no fancy resort for rich oldsters, it was at least a real building, with sand-blasted formerly white siding, neat walkways and a magnificent view of the desert wonderland. Currently, the most magnificent view was in the dining room itself.

A familiar hunky-blond sheriff-type sat next to Agnes. Not that Simone had a thing for sheriffs.

She had a thing for Brax.

Looking at the back of Brax's head, Simone's heart beat a little faster and a nice shot of warmth started in her chest, then spread to her extremities. Silly to get so worked up over the back of a man's head. Or his broad shoulders. Not to mention his muscled arms.

The chair next to Brax was empty. They, all the ladies plus Maggie, Chloe and Della, had made sure of that, Simone knew. She checked her watch. Two-thirty. She wasn't late, they were all early. Two round tables that usually seated four had been pushed together at the

back of the room by the open windows. A flowered paper tablecloth was set with teaspoons, a variety of paper napkins, plates of fragrant baked goods, two tea-pots and mismatched china cups the ladies foraged from various Bullhead thrift stores and garage sales. The colorful array was rather enchanting.

Rowena, the darling, half rose out of her chair to wave at Simone. "Yoo-hoo, we're over here." Not that Simone could have missed the group with only five ta-bles in the otherwise empty dining room. All the ladies of the Manor were invited, but only the usual suspects were in attendance, Rowena, Nonnie, Agnes and Di-vine. The four originals.

Rowena had a quaint British accent that had never worn off despite the fact that she'd lived in the U.S. since the war. World War Two, that is. With a charm-ing cap of blue-gray hair and a frilly pink blouse giv-ing her a bosom she didn't normally have, Rowena looked quite the queen for a day.

Rowena yoo-hooed a second time, to be sure Si-mone heard.

Della waggled her fingers in greeting, then went back to whispering in Maggie's ear.

Brax turned, ran his gaze over her white blouse to her filmy skirt, then smiled. Her heart did a little jig when he pulled out the chair next to his and patted it. She could almost feel the pat on her rear end.

Her feet couldn't move fast enough, and goodness, her hands trembled the tiniest bit as she sat, then scooted the chair forward. His knee brushed her thigh. His hand slid from the back of the chair to her shoul-der as he gentlemanly assisted her.

His little caresses were more than enough to whet

her appetite. Had she recommended light touching last night when she talked about building anticipation? Or had the man simply discovered the technique on his own?

She was darn near panting by the time he'd unfolded her paper napkin and placed it across her lap, the back of his hand barely skimming over her stomach.

"Sweetie, you look so pretty," Agnes crooned. Her bright red lipstick had seeped into the lines above her upper lip. She'd be mortified to know, but Simone couldn't tell her now.

"Doesn't she look lovely, Brax?" Nonnie added. Though the oldest of the four ladies, she bore the most youthful appearance, her brow smooth, as if she'd practiced all her life not to frown.

"Pretty? Lovely?" Divine piped up. "Men don't use those words, you idiots. Right, Brax?"

Her face heating, Simone glanced at him. His lips flirted with another smile at their obvious matchmaking.

"What do men say, Brax?" Rowena fluttered her eyelashes coyly.

Chloe flapped her hand at the four elderly ladies. "You're embarrassing the poor boy. Aren't they, Brax?"

"No, ma'am. None of you could possibly cause embarrassment. And being in the company of such *lovely* ladies is an honor," he added, stressing the adjective.

Goodness, the man was flirting with *all* of them, giving each in turn a wide smile with lots of shiny white teeth. In unison, they tittered and simpered like prim schoolgirls.

It was the sweetest thing Simone had ever seen a

man do. The ladies of the Manor soaked up his compliments as if starving for male attention. Which they probably were, since all were over the age of seventy. Only ladies lived at the Manor, and *these* ladies adored male attention.

"Ain't he a doll? Do you know what he did at the Coop the other day?" Chloe beamed.

Simone's heart skipped a beat and her tummy did a somersault. Brax had been at The Chicken Coop?

Brax coughed, looked pointedly at Chloe, then reached for his water glass.

Chloe didn't seem to notice, or if she did, she ignored his polite warning. "The girls bought this ridiculous robot with a million parts for Chocolate's nephew, and Brax spent all his time with us putting it together. He didn't even get a chance to—" Chloe jumped, then glared at Rowena on her right and Agnes on her left, as if they'd both kicked her under the table.

"It was my pleasure to help out, Chloe," Brax countered. "A nicer group of ladies I've never met." He smiled that irresistible smile, sweeping the Manor ladies with a look. "Present company excepted, of course."

Then his hand dropped to the outside of Simone's thigh, stroking her with his knuckles. She gave him to the count of five, relishing the tingle of his touch, then reached beneath the table and put his hand back where it belonged.

He'd assembled a robot for the chickens. Why he'd gone there in the first place wasn't her business.

Still, she was terribly glad he hadn't partaken.

It was time, however, to redirect the conversation. Brax might not be embarrassed. Simone was another

story. "Maggie, you look…wonderful." She hesitated at the last moment because Maggie didn't look wonderful at all. She looked…haggard.

The blusher on her cheeks appeared almost garish against her pale skin. Bags sagged under her eyes, and a deep frown puckered her forehead as well as her mouth. Unhappy didn't accurately describe her. Wretched was more like it.

Maggie gave her a wan smile.

"She looks like crap," Divine barked, then added, "Tell us what's wrong, honeybunch."

"She had another fight with that bastard Carl," Della announced, "and she doesn't want to talk about it."

So that's what all the whispering had been about.

"He's a rotten, no-good bastard." Maggie might not want to talk about it, but Della certainly did, patting Maggie's hand and adding, "You'd be so much better off without him."

Simone felt honor bound to intercede on Carl's behalf. For Maggie's sake, as well. After all, Carl had ordered that fantasy. He'd paid for it, too, wouldn't take no for an answer even though Simone didn't want his money. Making payment showed commitment, a desire to fix things. "He's trying, Della."

But why hadn't he given Maggie the fantasy, acted it out with her? Simone was sure he hadn't, not yet. Maggie wouldn't appear so beaten down if he had.

"Trying, schmying," Della said. "He's a man. They don't even know how to begin." She added a glare for Brax. Della had started picking on Carl recently, but then Della picked on men period.

Not that Della wasn't a very attractive woman. Somewhere in her midfifties, her hair was still a golden

cloud atop her head and her makeup application was flawless, accenting her high cheekbones. She kept a trim figure, and her attire was always impeccable, usually skirts that reached the knees or slacks with matching blazers, though she did wear jeans for casual occasions. Neatly pressed jeans, and minus the faded wash look.

She was a well-ironed woman, with few wrinkles marring her face and none marring her clothing.

Brax cleared his throat. "Perhaps we should save this discussion for a more private moment." A good sheriff, he headed off trouble before the tea party degenerated.

With Della, it didn't work. "Don't you care that your sister's miserable?"

Della was fiercely loyal to her friends, and though she'd always known Maggie and Carl as a couple, she naturally took Maggie's side due to hours spent over coffee and low-fat pastries.

Now she'd turned her fierce loyalty against Maggie's brother.

"Out of respect, I don't air my sister's problems in public."

"Said like a man who thinks a woman should be seen and not heard. We're supposed to suffer in silence. Well, this isn't public. We're all friends here. We all care about Maggie and we want to help her." The sun caught the sparkle of moisture in her eye.

Della cared and Della wanted to solve everyone's problems. She hurt as much as her friends did when something bothered them. Yet sometimes she didn't know when to stop.

Next to her, Maggie shrank in her seat as if she wanted the earth to swallow her up.

"I said later," Brax repeated. Simone had to admire that he stood his ground against Della's ferocity.

Della's eyes narrowed and her nostrils twitched as if she'd encountered a particularly nasty odor. Simone had seen that particular look more than once.

Brax didn't deserve it. He wasn't a criminal Della was sentencing.

Simone simply had to jump to his defense. "Della, I think—"

Chloe didn't let her finish. "Shut up, Della. The boy's right. This isn't the time or place."

"But you know she'd be better off without him—"

"Brax said later, and I said shut up." Chloe sat taller in her chair and glared across the table, almost daring Della to open her mouth again. "I think you ought to apologize to Brax."

Della's eyes flashed. Chloe was going a tad too far.

Brax shot the table at large a winning smile. "No apology necessary." Then he deftly redirected the topic away from his sister. "Can I have one of those delicacies?"

"Scones. I made them myself. They let us use the kitchen here, you know," Rowena popped in, relief in the rapid pace of her quaint British accent. "I've always loved baking, but with my chosen profession, I never had much time. Since I came here, why I bake to my heart's content, don't I, girls?"

"You should taste her trifle," Nonnie added. "Delicious."

"Trifle isn't baked, you silly woman," Divine burst in. "It's custard and whipped cream."

"Don't forget the sherry on the ladyfingers," Agnes trilled. "Rowena always puts extra sherry. It's simply orgasmic."

Brax almost knocked his water tumbler over. He cocked his head and stared at Agnes as if he wasn't sure he'd heard correctly. Then he grinned, which Simone determined meant he had decided he'd imagined the word. After all, Agnes, with her pile of gray hair knotted and confined in a silvery hair net with tiny sparkles of glitter certainly didn't look as though she'd say orgasmic. Simone covered her mouth to hide her smile, though it would have been terribly embarrassing if Brax had understood.

He came out with, "I'd love to try it sometime."

"And then there's her nut torte," Nonnie added, as if afraid a moment's lull in conversation might give Della another opportunity to start in on Carl. "It's made with crushed nuts, no flour or anything. It's amazing. And there's—"

"Pass him a scone, Nonnie, before he expires of hunger," Rowena admonished.

"Ladies first."

"Oh no, you're the first man we've entertained since Chloe opened the place," Agnes revealed. "Gentleman callers first."

"Oh yes, yes. And jam and butter." The plate of scones rattled against the jam pot as Nonnie passed them to Brax with slightly palsied fingers.

"I can't wait." Brax took the offering, but his glance shot speculatively to Chloe.

Our Manor of the Ladies had been Chloe's brainchild, and she'd funded a goodly portion of it, then chided town dignitaries to raise the additional monies. It had taken almost a year, but finally, the Manor had opened to its first residents, the four women now seated at the table.

"Here's your tea," Agnes said, passing the cup. Lukewarm liquid sloshed into the saucer. "And you must have milk and sugar, the way the British drink it. Rowena taught us that."

"Thank you, ma'am." Brax poured milk, stirred sugar and spread jam and butter as the ladies tweeted around him like birds.

Maggie surreptitiously swiped at something beneath her eye. Simone ached for her. Della, while caring deeply, wouldn't understand that her behavior had only made matters worse.

What to do, what to do? She'd find Carl and tell him to let the fantasy work its magic. He should act tonight. Which meant Simone would have occupy Brax so that Maggie and Carl could be alone.

She'd be forced to invite Brax for another movie. What would he like? *The Adventures of Robin Hood* with Errol Flynn. Even better, *Captain Blood*. Yes. Perfect.

"Oh my, would you look at the size of his hands." Eyes wide, hand over her mouth, Agnes was agog.

Brax stopped with a bit of scone halfway to his mouth. Then he extended his arm to look at the aforementioned hand.

He quirked an eyebrow. "Is there something wrong with my hands?"

"Oh no," Nonnie chirped.

"They're so large," Agnes went on with awe in her voice.

His gaze flashed left to right, from one lady to the other, his question shouted in his glance.

"You know what they say about a man's hands, don't you?"

Oh my God. Catastrophe was coming. Simone opened her mouth to divert it just as Brax said, "No, what do they say?"

Agnes let the words burst forth. "Why, that the size of a man's hands is directly proportional to the size of his penis."

If he'd been drinking his tea or eating his scone, Simone was sure he'd have spit mouthfuls across the table. As it was, his pupils dilated and the scone dropped to his plate, landing with a splat, jam side down.

"Is it true?" Nonnie asked with wide-eyed innocence.

Simone's cheeks flamed. Why, the old jokesters.

"You two stop that right now. My mother always says the tea table isn't the place for discussing..." Simone searched for an appropriate euphemism and fell back on, "Tallywhackers." Brax was going to think that's all they talked about in Goldstone.

Agnes hid behind pouring tea for everyone else and passing out the cups as someone—maybe Divine—snickered. Nonnie blinked behind her jeweled, cat's-eye glasses and said, "It isn't?"

Rowena sampled her scone and pronounced it, "Magnificent, if I do say so myself. And, my dear, in our profession, penises are always the first thing we wonder about."

"Former profession," Chloe corrected.

Rowena sniffed. "If men realized the virtue of an older, experienced woman, it wouldn't be former, darling."

"Here, here." The ladies clinked cups, china tinkling in the dining room.

Brax had yet to pick up his teacup or his upside-down scone. Now that was a squirrel-in-the-center-of-the-road look if Simone ever saw one.

Divine tapped Maggie's arm. "You didn't tell him, honey?"

Maggie, silent and morose up to this point, twisted her paper napkin until it fell apart in her fingers. "I didn't think I needed to."

"Tell me what?" Brax croaked. His voice probably hadn't cracked like that since he was thirteen years old. He had to *know* what was coming. In fact, Simone could have sworn he ducked slightly as if to ward off the blow.

"Our Manor of the Ladies is a home for former ladies of the night," Divine explained.

"Chloe built it for us," Rowena added.

"Sadly, many of us aren't terribly good at saving our money for old age," Agnes admitted.

"We never thought we'd reach old age," Divine scoffed. "What with AIDS and all that."

"Speak for yourself." Rowena tipped her head with a queenlike gesture in Divine's direction. "I always insisted on protection even before it was fashionable."

Brax made an odd sound, either horrified laughter or he was choking on the scone he'd just popped in his mouth.

"But Chloe came to our rescue." Nonnie acknowledged credit where credit was definitely due.

"Isn't she the most wonderful person?" Agnes said on a grateful sigh. The others nodded their heads like bobbing apples.

Simone couldn't agree more, but Chloe, flustered by the glowing compliments and admiration, busied herself with buttering a second scone.

That's why Chloe was the only one in town who wanted Jason's resort. Most thought it was because she wanted increased traffic through The Chicken Coop. Which was true, but Simone suspected she wanted the extra cash flow to support the Manor. Fifteen ladies now lived in the small rest home, but she constantly received new petitioners. Chloe had a hard time saying no.

Brax finally swallowed the scone. He raised his dainty teacup, looking ridiculously fragile in his big hand, and saluted each one. "Here's to the most gracious quartet of ex-ladies of the night I've ever had the pleasure of meeting." Then he inclined his head toward The Chicken Coop's madam. "And to Chloe for her generosity."

They all drank to his toast.

What a sweet guy. He could have run screaming from the room.

Agnes pointed to the hand still holding aloft his teacup and said, "So, don't keep us in suspense. Eight inches? Or more?"

AFTER NUMEROUS OFFERS of aid, they'd left the Manor Ladies to tea party cleanup duty. His earlier shock had receded. A home for ex-prostitutes, only in Goldstone. Having made it through teatime, Brax wiped the proverbial sweat off his brow as he stepped out onto the Manor's front porch, Simone a pace in front of him. She was close enough for him to draw in her fresh fruity scent. "All I can say is, thank God I didn't screw up and call Myrtle by the name of Divine."

Simone snorted in disgust. "Her *real* name is Myrtle, and you were *supposed* to call her Divine."

He did remember, but he'd wanted to see Simone's smile. The feminine snort was the next best thing. "Thank God I managed not to call her anything at all."

Simone glanced at him over her shoulder, her hair blowing into her eyes and sticking for a moment to her freshened lipstick before she pulled it free.

He had a sudden vision of lipstick prints all over his body.

"You were terribly sweet, you know."

His turn to snort. "Remember what I said last night about nice? Goes the same for sweet. Men aren't supposed to be sweet," he finished, the last word rife with his disgust.

She patted his forearm in comfort. Damn, what the slightest touch from her did to him. He shouldn't have played with her in the dining room, shouldn't have touched her thigh, her silky hair, or laid her napkin across her lap where he wanted to lay his head. Sheer torture, his actions had built the tension and anticipation she'd seduced him with last night. Her very proximity shot his testosterone level into the ozone.

"Aren't you going to drive Maggie home?" Simone asked.

Thankfully, she found the perfect question to bring him back to earth, solid ground and his sense of responsibility.

At the far end of the lot, Maggie fumbled with her car keys at the side of her clean, white four-door sedan. Last year's model. Carl certainly didn't skimp on the vehicles they drove. Brax wondered at their debt-to-equity ratio.

"She wanted to be alone." He didn't consider himself ineffectual in most cases. He had, however, been practicing quite a bit of ineffectual behavior lately.

"My mother says a gentleman should always see a distressed lady home."

In this case, Brax had to agree with Simone's mother wholeheartedly. He'd offered to drive Maggie home, but short of snatching the keys out of her hand, there hadn't been much he could do about it. Maggie needed some alone time. The discourse with Della Montrose at the tea party had deteriorated almost to blows. He was sure witnessing that hadn't helped Maggie.

Which made him extremely glad Della had been the first to leave, before the second pot of tea had been emptied or the last scone demolished.

"Perhaps you'll let me make up for my lack of chivalry by walking you home." It was only a mile. Everything was only a mile away in Goldstone.

"I wasn't criticizing—"

"Any more than was deserved," he finished for her.

She nodded as if in agreement. "And how do you know I didn't drive myself over?"

He glanced around the near-empty lot, now that Maggie had pulled onto the highway. "I didn't find my favorite bumper sticker." That and the fact that she wore flat sandals more conducive to walking than the platforms he'd admired. She'd painted her toenails a pale pink.

Her mouth lifted in a slight smile, not as dazzling as the usual, but enough to raise his pulse rate. "Of course, while we're walking," she said, "you intend to ask all about how you can help Maggie."

"The thought had crossed my mind." That was his strategy behind accompanying her home. A secondary plus to that plan was its guarantee to keep his mind where it belonged instead of on Simone's pretty pink

toes, shapely ankles and what she wore beneath that polka-dot skirt fluttering in the breeze. "I think you're a better choice than your friend, Della."

Simone sighed and started across the parking lot to a path Brax now saw headed back into Goldstone proper.

"I don't know what got into Della. She's usually more..." Searching, Simone tipped her head from side to side, her hair brushing her nape and shoulders, then she shrugged. "Diplomatic. Being a politician, she doesn't usually go off like that."

Brax had his doubts. There was a pinch to Della Montrose's lips and a hardness in her cold blue eyes that said she went off on a regular basis. "Why doesn't she like Carl?"

Simone flapped both hands, then dropped them to her sides. "It's not that she doesn't like him. She loves Maggie. Della came to Goldstone about the time Carl brought Maggie home as his wife, and both being new, well, I think they naturally became the best of friends. She's very protective of her friends."

An admirable trait, though somehow it did not make him appreciate Della. "How long has she been mayor?"

"Seems like forever, since she had the office when I got here. But I guess it's been about six years. And she's been the county judge for almost the whole time she's been in Goldstone."

The path they followed widened to a gravel street. The old schoolhouse stood a block to the east, the stone façade crumbling, and a twelve-foot chain-link fence surrounding it. A dog barked off to the right, answered by another perhaps a block farther down, and cars whooshed by on the highway a few hundred feet away.

Other than that, they could have been alone for all the activity *not* happening in Goldstone on a Tuesday afternoon.

Brax would dearly love to be alone with Simone, if not for the fact that he liked her too much in addition to wanting her. With liking came responsibility, commitment, relationship questions, and a woman's desire for a man to share his emotions.

He nipped that line of thinking in the bud. "So Della's protective. Seems to me a better way of handling the rift between Carl and Maggie would be to talk it through with her. Isn't that what women do best? Talk?"

Simone stopped in the middle of the road, put her hands on her hips—he really did wish she would stop touching her own body parts, it was driving him nuts—and cocked her head. "I get the sneaky suspicion there was something derogatory in that remark."

He held up his hands in mock surrender, then took her arm and steered her down the street. "No, no. I meant that women seem to need to talk things out with someone else."

"Like we can't make our own decisions or need someone else to tell us what to do?"

"Hell, no. That is *not* what I meant." He was glad he had his hand on her or she might have gone careening down the road. The militant female blaze in her eyes burrowed beneath his skin the same way as the thought of her finger poking his chest. She had spark. He wanted to ignite it. But not this way. "I admire the way women talk over a problem, come to a conclusion and act."

"Hah."

"What's that supposed to mean?"

"Men hate talking."

He gave a shrug, letting his hand fall away. "Yeah. But we admire that women are able to do it." At least when it was amongst themselves.

"And?"

"And, I'd like you to talk to Maggie. Because I'm inadequate at it."

She dropped her gaze to her toes. Obviously his plea wasn't what she wanted or expected. She wiggled the toes on her right foot, then her left, a mesmerizing performance.

"You know...I..." She bit her lip.

"What?" The only good thing was that he'd turned the tables on her by admitting his flaw.

She tipped her head up to look at him through her lashes. "How about if I talk to Della and get her to let up about Carl?"

"Maggie needs more than that." Something he should tell himself instead of palming his responsibilities off on Simone.

"They've known each other longer. I think Maggie will open up to Della more than me."

He smiled wryly. "Della seems more concerned with getting Maggie to leave Carl."

"She was just edgy today, that's all."

"I noticed."

"She's been edgy since Jason Lafoote came to town."

"Because of the resort?"

Simone turned then and headed down the slight incline toward her own street. Brax followed, catching up just as she mumbled, "Everyone hates that resort."

"Except Chloe."

"Chloe has her reasons, I'm sure."

"To fund the Manor?"

Simone tucked her hair behind her ear and nodded. "I'm pretty sure that's the reason. More business. But not to line her own pockets. She's very selfless, you know."

Hard to believe that a whorehouse madam could be selfless, but Brax had to agree Our Manor of the Ladies could be nothing but an altruistic endeavor. He couldn't find the hitch in it anywhere. "The ladies certainly love her."

"We all do."

"I didn't know Maggie knew her so well."

She rolled her eyes, then gave him the dazzle-smile he'd been waiting for with bated breath. "Everybody knows everybody in Goldstone. Really well."

An exact repeat of Maggie's words yesterday, and precisely as it was in Cottonmouth. Only difference was, Cottonmouth didn't have a madam or a whorehouse, and the only chicken coops were the genuine articles.

One thing he still found puzzling. If Maggie knew Chloe so well, why had she sent him down to question the woman instead of asking Chloe herself?

Not wanting to air dirty laundry came to mind. Even in a town the size of Goldstone, people wanted to keep their secrets.

Brax wondered how many secrets Simone was keeping.

CHAPTER EIGHT

"I'LL TALK TO DELLA. She's the best one to help Maggie. I promise." Simone felt like a traitor. Or maybe something else. A heel. Not quite right, either, too harsh. The person caught in the middle. Writing snippets for the Doodles to play with was fine. Giving Carl a fantasy when she knew he and Maggie were having problems was downright stupid.

Not that she'd thought of it that way until she figured out Carl hadn't even used the story. At least not that she knew of.

"I'd rather you did it."

Brax had walked her all the way home, hoping to change her mind, she was sure. Now he waited for her answer on her front walk, within touching distance, while she stood on the step trying to figure out how to get away with a fib.

She couldn't risk talking to Maggie. What if she revealed something she shouldn't? "I'd probably say the wrong thing." She had a very big mouth sometimes, especially when she didn't know how to bring up the subject. "My mother always says I speak before I think."

"Your mother's wrong." A hard edge filtered through his voice. "You're perfect the way you are. And you'll say the perfect thing."

A nice sentiment, but Simone knew her mother was right.

"Della. She'll do it. I'll buy her a drink at the Flood's End and talk to her. I swear."

"Why don't you want to talk to Maggie?"

Darn. She'd forgotten he was a cop. They always asked why. Not that she'd had any real experience with cops, but that's how they acted on TV. Now, if only she had a really good reason. Other than the fact that she was a bigmouthed coward. She looked over his head at the row of rusted barrels lining the side of her neighbor's house. Thinking, thinking… She gave him a modified version of the truth. "I'm afraid of making things worse. A woman has to *want* to talk. You can't butt in and tell them they *need* to talk. It gets their back up, then they won't listen at all."

He put his hand on the door frame, but didn't interrupt. A good sign he was buying it.

"But she's talked to Della. So Della's the logical one to do it. And I'll make sure Della doesn't go off half-cocked again."

"Following your logic, Della won't like you butting in and telling her what to do, so she'll ignore everything you say, and handle Maggie all wrong."

"No, no, it's okay to butt in if you're asking a woman to help *another* woman. It's only bad when you're talking about a woman's own problems."

He opened his mouth, clapped it shut, looked around, then finally said, "I'll never understand women."

"That's okay. We understand men and that makes everything work out."

He laughed, his eyes crinkling at the corners. She

should have told him that her mother always claimed she could talk a person in circles until his or her head exploded, but Simone didn't want Brax to know he'd been had.

He tugged her hand. "Come down here."

"Why?"

"Because I want your lips within two inches of mine when you feed me a line of crap like that."

BRAX DIDN'T BELIEVE HER. He might not understand women on a personal level, but he for damn sure knew when someone wasn't telling the truth. It was all in the body language. Most people couldn't tell a lie while they looked you in the eye. Simone was no different. At least not in that respect.

Yet it was an absurd thing to lie about. Why not tell him the truth about why she didn't want to talk to Maggie about this thing going on with Carl?

His calves strained as he climbed the steep hill to Maggie and Carl's home. Their trailer sat on a plateau overlooking Goldstone, and the high desert elevation worked his lungs.

The thought of that e-mail tore a hole in his belly. He'd been done with that suspicion last night, convincing himself the e-mail meant nothing, that Simone wasn't having an affair with Carl, she was true-blue, and all the rest of that rot.

So why didn't she want to talk to Maggie? Guilt?

No one was home when he got to the top of the hill, though Maggie had left the back door unlocked for him. She'd been gone most of the morning, now she'd disappeared again. Carl's truck was absent, too.

Brax got a bad feeling. He wished he'd told Carl

burgers were okay. Anything. As long as he and Maggie went somewhere together and talked.

Three hours later, as Brax sat in the darkened living room, the lock clicked on the front door.

MAGGIE UNLOCKED the door and dropped her purse and keys on the foyer table. Not that her *trailer* had a real foyer like a real house should have. Another burst of anger shot through her chest. No foyer, no real house and no man in her bed wanting to slip his hands beneath her nightie in the dark.

He'd even forced her to send her brother down to The Chicken Coop to check up on him. She couldn't ask Chloe herself. That would have been worse than the scene at the tea party.

Bastard. If Carl were standing right in front of her, she'd have kicked his butt. All the way back to Vegas and that stupid wedding in that stupid chapel with those stupid flamingos that Carl had insisted on.

A shadow shifted in the living room. She marched three paces forward before she realized it wasn't him.

It was her brother. Tyler sat in the dark family room just as her father had done when she'd been late coming home from a date. Dad never said a word, but he was good at saying "I'm so disappointed in you I can't even speak," with just a look. She couldn't see Tyler's expression, but she didn't think it would be any more sympathetic.

Dammit, she had a right to her anger, her tummy-clenching, spine-wrenching, teeth-gritting anger. Carl was cheating. She knew it in her bones.

"Where ya been, Maggie?" Tyler said, soft as steel.

"Where do you think I've been? Out looking for that

no-good, dirty rotten bastard husband of mine." Life wasn't fair. She'd been a good wife...Carl had been less than a dog.

She marched into the kitchen. The Elvis clock ticked on the wall, his pendulum legs swinging. The only other sound in the trailer was Tyler's footsteps across the linoleum as he followed.

"I would have come with you if you'd asked."

She didn't turn on the kitchen overhead, but moved to the light of the foyer overhead lamp. "I didn't want you with me."

She opened a cupboard, slamming the door against its neighbor, and grabbed a wineglass. The last remaining wineglass from the dime-store set she'd bought when they were first married. She didn't even own a crystal wineglass. Carl would have broken it just as he had the others in this set. Clumsy oaf. She'd only broken one of them, and she hadn't been tipsy, either, but doing the dishes the morning after.

"Maggie, come into the family room and sit and talk." Tyler touched her arm.

She flung him off. "I don't want to talk. I want a glass of wine." Wine out of a box, because that's how she saved money. While that bastard was salting it away for his floozy. Who was she? What was she like? Where'd he meet her? Maggie hated her without knowing the answers.

"Tell me where you looked for him."

She'd driven around Bullhead for hours, out into the nice neat suburbs where the houses were real houses, with manicured cactus gardens and decorative rock formations and fountains and paved driveways. "Bull-head."

"I take it you didn't find his truck."

"No."

"He might be playing darts. He goes to The Dartboard a lot."

She whirled on him. "The only darting he was doing was sticking his thing in some other woman's bull's-eye."

He took a step back. Bastard. Men always took a step back.

She didn't let him, stomping to within a foot to poke her finger in the center of his chest. He flinched.

"He's fucking some bitch in heat and you know it and when I catch him I'm gonna Bobbitize him and I'm gonna stuff his tiny little dick down the garbage disposal and grind it up so they won't be able to sew it back on."

His eyes widened, and he opened his mouth. Open, close, open, close, like a fish, but nothing came out.

She whirled again, headed for the refrigerator and her precious box of cheap, stupid wine. "I hate this house. I hate *him*. He's gonna be sorry. He's gonna be really sorry."

"Maggie, I don't think he's cheating on you."

Her cold, numb fingers wouldn't close around the refrigerator handle. Little spots flashed before her eyes. She couldn't seem to catch her breath. "You don't think? What do you know? You don't live here, you don't know anything. He gets drunk and goes out so Elwood will arrest him and throw him in jail so he doesn't have to come home to me. You're so stupid. You're all so stupid. I know what's going on. I know what he's doing. I'm gonna kill him when I catch him and throw his parts down his goddamn outhouse holes."

The glass in her hand suddenly smashed against the counter. Tiny shards pricked her face, her throat and her arms. She closed her eyes in time to take the sting against her eyelids.

Her glass, her last precious stupid cheap glass, gone, just like that. Like her marriage. Like her life.

"Maggie, honey, sweetie."

She felt Tyler pry the stem out of her fist, then wipe the shards from her cheeks and shoulders.

"Don't move," he whispered, "it's all over the floor. I'll clean it up."

She couldn't have moved if she tried. Sudden light beat at her eyelids. The paper towel holder rattled. Water ran in the sink. Air currents shifted as he moved, wiped the counter, around her feet. A cupboard opened, the trash can lid flipped up, then slapped shut.

"There, there. It's okay." Soothing voice, soothing words, as if he was talking to a child.

Her lip trembled. She opened her eyes. Tyler's face blurred, then came back into focus. His eyes, almost slits, searched her face. Two deep grooves bit into his cheeks from his nose to his mouth, and his eyebrows almost touched in the middle, his frown was so deep.

"I'm sorry," she whispered. She'd upset him. No, she'd damn near scared the bejesus out of him. "That was so stupid."

"Don't worry."

Tears welled up until she couldn't see him clearly anymore. Legs suddenly weak like the aftereffects of an adrenaline rush, she wanted to crumple to the floor and lie there. For a long, long time. Drained. Empty.

"Do *you* think I'd be better off without him?"

Tyler put his hand on her shoulder and rubbed. "No.

You were happy before. You'll be happy again. This is just a bad patch, I swear."

Then, almost hesitantly, he pulled her into his arms. Rocking her, he stroked her hair, the way their mom used to do when she was a kid. God, she missed that. Someone to stroke her hair as she fell asleep. She used to make Carl do that sometimes.

A fresh wave of tears rushed to the surface. Her throat clogged and her nose stuffed up. Tyler rocked, stroking and murmuring while she cried and cried and cried until she didn't think she could have any tears left.

"Why didn't he come home tonight?" she muttered against his T-shirt.

He answered, though she was surprised he even understood her mumble. "I don't know. But when he does come home, we're all gonna sit down and talk. You, me, and him." He pulled back, then tipped her chin up. "Look at me."

She did. He was a blur.

"He's not having an affair, Maggie. I don't know what's going on with him, sweetheart, but it's not that."

"Are you sure?" She wanted to believe him, she really, really did because she hated, *hated* feeling this way. Helpless and lost and broken-down.

He nodded gravely. "Yeah, I'm positive. Together, we'll find out what it is, honest. When he gets home."

RETURNING FROM her evening walk, Simone opened her sunporch screen door. She was almost to the front door when she cocked her head and turned. Darn it. She'd locked that door. She stared at it a moment. Actually she remembered locking it when she went to bed last night. She didn't have a clear memory of locking

it when she left for her walk. She racked her brain, but she couldn't come up with the image of turning the lock.

Sighing, she opened the front door instead. At least she'd remembered to secure that one.

What was up with this weird need to lock her doors? She was jumping at coyote shadows in the night. This was Goldstone. Nobody locked up. Besides, she didn't have anything worth stealing. Oh, her computer. There *was* that. At least she backed everything up and kept the disks in a drawer. Hmm, what about the fantasies she'd created for her clients? Could they be used for blackmail? Nah, she was sure there were far juicier secrets lurking in Goldstone than anything she'd ever written about.

On to more important things. Earlier, with her feet eating up the gravel streets, Simone had come up with a plan.

The smartest thing she could do was talk to Carl himself and get him to fork over the answer to her question. And force a commitment as to when he was going to put that darn fantasy to the test. Yes. Perfect plan.

Except that Carl wasn't online. She'd e-mailed him five times. Then she'd called his office number—she couldn't call the house itself. He hadn't answered. She'd left her number and a terse message, but there was no blinking light on her machine. Simone tapped in her password and checked her e-mails. Carl hadn't replied to those messages, either. He was ignoring her, darn it.

She understood Maggie's feelings when Carl disappeared for hours on end.

Only one option remained. She'd have to go over there and pound on his door. Well, not pound, because Maggie might hear. Or Brax. Simone had to keep this private. At least until she'd talked to Carl. After that, well, it might be best to come clean and tell Maggie all. First, she'd warn Carl of her intentions.

She felt better now that she'd established a good solid plan.

Simone opened her closet door and perused the row of clothing. She needed black to blend in with the dark. Wouldn't do for Maggie to spot her crossing the driveway. In the end, she chose a black T-shirt and black leggings.

The phone rang. Carl! She jumped on the receiver. "Darling!"

She was getting terribly lax with checking caller ID. For the second time in two days, she'd let her mother take her by surprise. Why, she hadn't even practiced her deep breathing before picking up.

"Hello, MOTHER." Come to think of it, why was Ariana calling in such quick succession? Unusual. Simone's antennae went up.

"Jackie tells me you've got a new man in your life. Why didn't you tell me yesterday when I called?"

That was her mother, no beating around the bush. She'd probably plucked the information out of Jackie with a tweezerlike torture device. "He's not exactly my new man."

"What? He's your new dog?"

"I mean he's not my man. He's just a man. And he's not in my life. He's visiting."

"He's visiting your life? Spoken like a transient. I

knew that godforsaken town was going to be bad for you."

She should have made Jackie swear she wouldn't tell. Then again, her mother probably recorded all Jackie's phone conversations just to nip anything unsavory right in the bud.

Simone tried again. "He's visiting his sister. Remember Maggie? I've mentioned her to you before."

"Holy Mary Mother of God," Ariana shrieked, though she was as WASP as the Archbishop of Canterbury. "She's the latrine cleaner's wife. And you've fallen for that woman's brother?" Simone heard a violent rustle, and her mother panted over the phone lines.

"Carl doesn't clean latrines. And I haven't fallen for Brax. I only met him a couple of days ago."

"Brax? What on earth kind of heathen name is that?"

"It's a nickname. A shortened version of his last name." Why was she trying to explain? The more she said, the worse her mother would get. Ariana was magnificent at twisting words, her own as well as others. Simone knew she meant well, but her mother didn't know when to let well enough alone.

"Does he clean latrines, as well?"

"*Nobody* cleans latrines." Irritation slipped through her voice.

"Don't use that tone with me, young lady."

Simone pinched the bridge of her nose. "Sorry, MOTHER."

"If this kind of insolence is any indication of what that man is teaching my poor little girl…" Ariana let her words trail off, expecting Simone's apology.

Simone was well used to the maneuver, and she'd long since given up engaging in battles she'd never

win. The best countermaneuver was to give her mother exactly what she wanted. Then get the heck off the phone. "You're right. He is a bad influence. I didn't realize until this moment, but you're so right. MOTHER, you are so wonderfully astute."

There was a short pause as if Ariana suspected sarcasm. If she did, she chose to ignore it. "I am, aren't I? I love you and I worry about you. It's a mother's instinct to protect her young."

Some mammals *ate* their young. Ooh, that was an awful thing to think. "It's lucky Brax is only visiting. But I won't give him a by-your-leave from now on." Brax wouldn't give *her* a by-your-leave if he caught her sneaking up to Carl's trailer, not after she'd refused to talk to Maggie. He would not understand.

"You're such a smart girl. And you always listen to your mother." A long-suffering sigh traveled across the line. "But your sister. I don't know what I'm going to do with her."

"Jackie?" Jackie had been *born* soaking up their mother's every word, and suddenly Simone knew why her mother had let her off the hook so easily with Brax. "What's wrong with Jackie?"

Another sigh. "Oh, I don't know. She's acting strangely. She hangs up the phone when I walk in her room."

Her mother had barging-in-without-knocking down to a science, all in the name of taking care of her daughters. "I'm sure Jackie just wants to give you her undivided attention."

Ariana didn't get the sarcasm. Or, more likely, she was too wrapped up in the drama of the situation. "No, no, it's a quick, furtive sort of thing."

"Oh my."

"And I've caught her in little lies about where she's been and who she's said she was with and what time she got in. Simone, I think your sister has," gasp, "a man friend."

"Noo!"

"Yes!"

"That's terrible." Good for Jackie. She deserved a little happiness. A lot of happiness.

"I don't know what to do about it. She's so naive. I know she'll get herself hurt in the end."

"She's a big girl, MOTHER." Sometimes a daughter had to make her own mistakes or she never learned. So great was her desire to protect, Ariana didn't understand that.

Her mother snorted, a very un-Ariana-like sound. She was probably so distracted she hadn't even heard herself do it. "He must be after her money."

At least it would give Jackie the chance to get out of their mother's smothering house. Simone loved her mother, but all that caring stifled a person. "But maybe he's not. We should give her the benefit of the doubt, don't you think?"

"Simone. Your sister has no sense of judgment when it comes to men. Remember that horrible Wesley person?"

Jackie had been eighteen and the "horrible Wesley person" a horrible twenty-five. Ariana had made sure Jackie's heart got broken before Wesley had a chance to do it himself. Simone had always wondered if he'd really taken that payoff money or if Ariana had him shanghaied to Europe. Ariana was capable of a lot of not-so-nice things in the name of love.

Simone was suddenly tired of her mother's voice and her mother's worries. No one, least of all Simone herself, would ever convince Ariana to let Jackie have a life of her own. "There's the timer on that yummy pan of brownies I'm making. I better get them out of the oven."

Another gasp. "Simone, you can't eat a whole pan of—"

"Oops, I can smell them burning. Gotta run."

Now that was a dirty trick to play on her mother, but all was fair in daughterhood, especially when your mother was Ariana Chandler.

Besides, she had Carl and Maggie to worry about and time was wasting.

CARL DIDN'T COME HOME. In the end, Brax had to go searching for him.

His own hands had done their fair share of trembling in the kitchen and his breath had wheezed from his chest as he'd watched his sister literally fall apart before his eyes. Then they'd sat in the living room for two hours, the longest two hours of his life, while she alternately talked and cried.

He hadn't been able to say a damn useful thing. But he'd listened.

Finally, he'd pulled her to her feet. "You get some rest, honey. You're exhausted."

"Only if you go out and find Carl for me."

He didn't see that he'd have any more luck than she had. He was used to hunting criminals, not his sister's husband. "I don't like leaving you alone."

"I'm used to it." She gripped his hand hard. "I need you to do this for me."

How could he say no, even if his instinct was to stay and protect her, if only from her own dismal mood? "I'll do whatever you need."

"Go see Elwood."

He quirked an eyebrow.

"Sheriff Teesdale." She dipped her head and her voice dropped. "Maybe Carl's in the holding cell sleeping it off."

"Does he do that often?"

"Only when he's trying to get away from me. And if he isn't there, maybe Elwood's seen him."

Maybe Elwood knew at whose house he'd parked his truck so Maggie couldn't find it. Damn.

She looked so forlorn, she might have read the thought. He stroked the straggly hair back from her face. "I'll check there first. Take a nice bath. You always did love a long, hot bath."

She grimaced. "Yeah, with you yelling at me through the door and telling me to get out so you could take a leak."

"The trials and tribulations of being a one-bathroom household."

"You always were a brat." Maggie sniffled, but a hint of a smile curved her lips.

"Yeah." More like a model brother, putting up with her the way he had. "At least you're old enough to have wine with your bath." Women liked wine in the tub, though he could never understand the fascination with lying for hours while the water went cold. "I'll pour you a glass."

She sniffled. Her brow puckered and her mouth trembled. "I broke the last wineglass."

Shit. "I'll buy you a whole new set, I promise."

"I have others. But that was my first set after we got married. And Woolworth's is out of business."

Ah God. He was an ass, forgetting, or rather, not having understood the correlation between a bath, a glass of wine and the shards he'd mopped up and thrown in the trash. "You got any chocolate?"

She stopped crying long enough to question him with a look.

"Chocolate and wine in the tub." Maybe that would take her mind off things. His ex had kept a special tin of chocolates on the bathroom counter. Upon pain of death, he was never allowed to touch them, and as far as he knew, she only ate them when she took a bath. Three had been her limit.

Fifteen minutes later, Maggie was in the tub, the sweet scent of bubbles wafting under the closed door and filling the trailer. Brax pulled his keys from his jeans pocket and let himself out the front door. Crickets chirped and somewhere an owl hooted. Below, the lights of Goldstone trailers gleamed across the highway, but Maggie's plateau lay in the complete darkness of a moonless night. Distant music wafted on a gentle breeze.

First stop, the county jail and Sheriff Elwood Teesdale.

Something rustled the weeds at the edge of the driveway. A dark shape scuttled to the top of the incline toward Carl's office trailer.

"Carl?" If it was, where had he parked his truck? His usual spot lay empty.

The shadow, too small for the bulky Carl, stopped, crouched, then sucked in an audible breath and held it.

Brax crossed the drive and caught the unmistakable

feminine scent. The sweet tang of citrus. A fragrance that had driven him crazy most of last night when he'd tried to fall asleep. Now she wore a tight T-shirt and black leggings that outlined every curve of her body.

Simone.

CHAPTER NINE

"WHAT THE HELL are you doing sneaking around in the dark?"

Oops. "Well...umm..." Darn it, she should have had an excuse prepared. With Brax looming over her, she couldn't think straight. So she told him the truth. "I was looking for Carl."

"Why?"

"I decided that Carl was the one who needed a talking-to."

He was probably glaring at her, but beneath the cover of darkness, she couldn't tell for sure. He widened his stance as if he were hunkering down for battle. "I've already talked to him. You think you can do better?"

She shuddered in her white tennies. Maybe that's how he'd seen her when she'd thought she was sneaky and stealthy. White against black. "I thought he might listen, you know, coming from a woman and everything."

He glanced at the trailer. "Carl's not here."

His answer said he didn't believe her reason for being here, nor did he think it worth countering her argument. "Oh."

"In fact, I don't know where he is. And Maggie hasn't seen him since this morning. So why did *you* think he might be here?"

She backed down the driveway a step. Then two. "An unlucky guess. Since he's not here…I should be going." Three steps.

He moved in a flash to her other side. Now she was two steps above him instead of below. "Tell me why you really came."

She pivoted on one foot. "I just did."

"I asked you before if you were having an affair with Carl. You said no." His tone indicated he needed to ask the question again.

This was what she'd been afraid of. Brax finding her. She'd told herself the worrisome thing was Maggie seeing her. Not. At least not as much. "I did say no. And the answer is still no."

"What was in the e-mail you sent him?"

"Nothing important."

"Was it cybersex?"

She almost laughed, but knew *that* would be a big fat mistake. "Don't be silly."

He crumbled the distance between them as if it were paper in his fist, and suddenly, he was right in her face, all six-foot-something, fire-breathing, two-hundred-twenty-odd finely honed pounds of him. "My sister is in there crying herself *silly* because she thinks her husband is having an affair with some *floozy,* and I want to know if that *floozy* is you."

His finger stabbed within an inch of her eyeball. Or so it seemed. She should have been pissed, most normal women would be when accused of adultery for the second—or was it third?—time. But darn, she was a sucker for a guy who didn't even try to hide his worry over his sister's problems.

"No. No, it's not me," she whispered, as if the smaller her voice, the calmer he might get.

"Then tell me what was in that goddamn e-mail."

His shout boomed against her eardrums, and she struggled not to put her hands over her ears. Would Maggie hear and come running? Please, God, no. Tense white lips and stark lines etched Brax's face as if it were made of marble.

"I don't think he's having an affair at all." Though she wasn't so sure of that anymore. Could it be Carl had her write that story for someone other than Maggie?

His jaw worked and his hand fell to his side, bunching into a fist. "Tell me."

"I can't."

"You won't."

"It's Carl's business."

"Carl is fucking my sister over. I don't give a goddamn about his privacy or his business." Brax turned, stalked three paces, turned again.

He scraped a hand down his face. His fingers trembled. His whole body quaked.

This was how Maggie had felt, he knew. Helpless. Angry and impotent. It made a man want to lash out. It made a woman want to Bobbitize.

"I'm sorry. That was uncalled for." At least the level of anger with which he'd shouted at Simone.

He wasn't normally a bully. Still, he couldn't come right out and say he believed her. Something was off. Obviously, she wasn't the floozy with Carl at this very moment. Equally obvious was that she didn't know where Carl was. But Simone was hiding something, and innocent people had nothing to hide.

What was in that e-mail? He knew. Dammit, he

knew there was sex. That's what she did, write sex. But was it something she'd written for *both* Carl and Maggie?

This damn trip had been a bad idea all around. He'd have been better off facing his failures back in Cottonmouth. Though the same sense of helplessness had consumed him, he'd had purpose, a killer to subdue, justice to mete out and a gun to back him up.

With Maggie, he hadn't a clue how to help. He closed his eyes, tipped his head back to let warm night air skim his face.

Simone's touch on his cheek brought him back.

She smoothed her thumb across his lips. "As much as we want to fix things for other people, most of the time they have to do it on their own."

"Seems like a cop-out."

"It's better than beating your head against a wall you can't break through."

Light sparkled in her eyes. With no moon, he couldn't figure out where it came from. Maybe from within her, like a creature of the light, not one of the dark in which he usually dwelled. In her view of life, there would be no murderers, no drug addicts, no wife beaters, no child abusers.

"Make me feel good," he whispered, his lips inches from hers.

"But you're still mad about my e-mail to Carl."

"Let's pretend that e-mail doesn't exist. Let's pretend Carl and Maggie are inside making love and everything's perfect and right with the world." He wanted only the scent of Simone filling his head, the taste of her in his mouth, the feel of her skin beneath his fingers. "Kiss me and screw the rest of it for now."

Her gaze searched his as her fingers stroked his cheek. Then she touched her lips to his, lightly brushing, before she retreated. He exhaled with a sigh.

"More," he murmured.

She gave him her lips once more, then her tongue. Warm, wet, delicious. The taste of cherry lip gloss burst in his mouth, filling him up. She rose to her tiptoes, wrapped her arms around his neck, her breasts pressed against him. His hands on her hips, he gathered her closer still, diving into the moment and forgetting everything but this, everything but her.

She moaned, the sound vibrating through him. He wanted skin. Slipping beneath the hem of her shirt, he savored her soft flesh. He kneaded muscle, stroked high to the edge of her shoulder blades, then angled his head for a deeper, finer taste of her mouth. He took her with his tongue, relishing her as he would her deepest, most intimate parts.

When he couldn't breathe for want of her, he backed off, nibbled her lips, then trailed kisses along her jaw to her throat. He sucked, nipped, licked, and lifting her off her feet, crushed her against him a moment before letting her slide down his body until her feet were once more firmly planted on the ground.

Her peaked nipples rubbed his ribs. His cock pushed insistently at her belly. He wanted to bury himself inside her, and he wanted to hold her just this way with the promise of nothing more. Anticipation trapped his breath in his throat and tension tightened every muscle. His pulse drummed at his temple, and his heart pounded against his breastbone. The night breeze across his hair felt like the caress of her fingers, and the chirp of the crickets were like sweet nothings murmured in his ear.

He felt alive and drowning in sensation, drowning in the feel of her body and the roar of his blood through his veins.

"Christ, I needed that." He slipped his hands down to skim the waistband of her leggings.

She rubbed her nose along his collarbone, her hair tickling his chin.

Damn, she felt good. "You were right."

"About what?" she muttered into his chest, her breath hot against his nipple despite his shirt.

"That definitely qualified as first base. I must have been insane when I said kissing wasn't important."

"I told you anticipation was everything."

He ran his hands up her sides, rested them at her ribs, his thumbs brushing the undersides of her breasts.

If they could stay, like this, forever.

He'd promised Maggie he would find Carl. Forever with Simone in his arms wasn't an option. He'd had a taste, like a drug addict's fix, and it would have to sustain him. She'd calmed him. She'd thrown his doubts to the wind. Now he had his duty to perform.

"If you see Carl, tell him I'm looking for him."

She pulled away at his words, though he hadn't meant them as either criticism or censure. She tugged the bottom of her shirt back into place, then drew both hands through her hair and flipped the ends into order.

She looked at her toes as she spoke. "I'd tell you if I could, Brax. But I can't betray Carl."

He knew. The e-mail. They were back to it. This time his blood didn't threaten to boil over. In an odd way, he commended her stoic support, support Carl most likely didn't deserve. She'd written a sex fantasy.

Of that much he was sure, all doubts erased. She'd probably intended for Carl to read it with Maggie. But Carl hadn't.

That was the disturbing part. Carl had kept it to himself. Younger woman. Midlife crisis. A man like Carl might let himself believe that something existed between him and Simone.

After all, a woman didn't share her most secret intimate fantasies with a man unless...

He was losing that feeling again, that calm, almost mellow memory of her in his arms.

He backed away because he wanted to stay and reignite the glow. Pretty damn badly. "You still gonna talk to Della?"

"I promised I would. We're meeting at the Flood's End."

"And you never break a promise."

She stared at him, as if she were trying to figure out if that was sarcasm in his voice.

He should have told her it wasn't. A man who'd spent his career cleaning up after other people's lies and broken promises, he actually admired her commitment.

Even if it was misguided and added to his sister's misery.

SIMONE WAS TEN MINUTES LATE for her drink date with Della at the Flood's End.

It was that kiss, that lovely, toe-tapping, bone-melting, butterfly-inducing kiss. It muddled her brain. With her fingers idiotically caressing her lips in a tactile reminder, she'd stood at the top of Maggie and Carl's driveway long after Brax's taillights disappeared into

the dark. She'd closed her eyes and relived every glorious moment of it. This was bad, very bad. She headed toward excessive and exuberant emotions.

He'd done an about-face after his outburst and apologized. She might have been able to stay mad at him if he hadn't done that. Then he'd kissed her. She didn't know what to think. Except that he was probably as mixed-up as she was.

But gosh, she'd felt bad for him. Agony had ridden the stark lines of his face. He'd set out to solve Maggie and Carl's problems, but he'd set himself up for failure. Simone knew, since she was intimately familiar with failure.

Maggie and Carl needed more than a shared fantasy, if Maggie's pale drawn face at the tea party meant anything. Not to mention Brax's obvious concern. More than concern. He'd worked himself into a tizzy, spouting bad language, his fists bunched. Signs of a worried brother.

She couldn't find Carl, Maggie had cried herself silly, and despite that devastating kiss, Simone was sure Brax blamed her for the trouble. Della was her last hope when all else had failed.

Seated at the bar next to Whitey, Della was drinking one of Mr. Doodle's strawberry daiquiris. Doodle was a daiquiri master, perhaps because that had become Mrs. Doodle's favorite libation since they'd visited Hawaii last year.

"You're late." Clad in a Western-style shirt and a pair of jeans that looked as if they were straight off the store shelf, Della appeared freshly pressed and smelled freshly perfumed. Simone felt underdressed in her black outfit.

Della pushed a second fruity concoction across the table. Topped with whipped cream, a souvenir umbrella and a hot pink swizzle stick, the offering resembled a creation straight from a posh Hawaiian hotel.

"I'm sorry about being late." Her mother said one should never breeze through an apology lest the receiver finds it insincere. "I mean, I'm really sorry. I don't even have a decent excuse." Kissing Brax wasn't an excuse, it was a revelation, one she didn't want to share with anyone.

"You're forgiven." Della licked away her whipped cream mustache.

Thank goodness. Simone waved at the line of friendly faces along the bar, with a special wink for Whitey. She loved everyone in Goldstone, but Whitey, for some reason, held a special spot in her heart. He claimed he'd name a character after her in his next book. Whitey was always writing a new book. The man had a prolific mind.

"Mr. Doodle, you've outdone yourself yet again." Simone sipped the delicious drink and smacked her lips appreciatively.

Brax's kiss had tasted better, true, but there was no point in giving the comparison to Doodle.

A smile split the seams of the elderly man's dear face. "Next I'll try my hand at a Lava Flow. The wife was especially delightful after that Lava Flow she had in Hawaii."

She tried not to think about the Doodles' delight. "I can't wait." She turned to Della. "Let's get a table."

Mr. Doodle made excellent drinks as well as perfecting the art of eavesdropping. He'd probably manage to

overhear every word they said even if they did move, but Simone wanted to present at least some challenge.

Tuesday was as good a drinking night as Friday, and the Flood's End had only two empty bar stools, including the one Della had vacated. Simone followed her friend to a table by the wall.

The TV over the bar blasted some all-sports channel, and a slot machine belled-and-whistled in the back room while coins clanked into its metal tray. Horten had hit another jackpot of one degree or another. In her three years in Goldstone, Simone had yet to see anything but the back of Horten's head. He was a slot machine addict, and he always seemed to break even. Simone had heard on the grapevine that just as he was about to lose his last quarter, miraculously he'd win a jackpot that would keep him playing—and losing again—the rest of the night.

She'd long suspected Doodle had rigged the machine to keep Horten away from the real casinos where he'd assuredly lose every quarter he had, plus the shirt off his back, the trailer off his lot and the rusted cars from his front yard.

Simone let Della settle in, took two more heavenly sips of daiquiri, then went to work. "All right, give me the scoop, poop. What's going on with Maggie and Carl?"

Della perused her drink, twizzled her swizzle, then took a leisurely sip, holding the stick aside with her forefinger. "Haven't you ever heard of the subtle approach?"

"My mother says I don't have a subtle bone in my body. I'd hate to prove her wrong." Actually, Ariana *was* wrong. Simone had learned subtlety at a young

age. In the Chandler household, subtlety was the *only* way Simone got what she wanted.

"Your mother is the one without a subtle bone."

"You don't even know my mother."

"You draw such good word pictures, I don't have to."

She steered Della back to the most important topic of the evening. "I'm worried about them. Tell me everything."

"I'm not sure how much I should say. If Maggie hasn't told you herself." Della spread her hands for emphasis.

"All right, so you want me to drag it out of you."

Della raised a perfectly arched eyebrow. "Another strawberry daiquiri might help."

Simone fluttered her hand. "Oh, Mr. Doodle, could we have another round?"

He whisked a pitcher from beneath the counter, filled two glasses, shot them both with whipped cream and shoved in the umbrellas and swizzle sticks.

"My tab, this time," Simone said as he set down the new and gathered the almost empties. She always paid her miniscule bar tab at the beginning of the month, when she usually found that Mr. Doodle had undercharged her.

Alone again, she simply stared at Della.

She didn't know the mayor as well as Maggie did. They were friends, true, but she'd never felt the urge to bare her soul to Della. She liked her, respected her, admired the wonderful job she did, but Della had always seemed a tad removed.

That's why Della's vehement flare-up over tea had

seemed so odd. There was more to it than Maggie and Carl having a fight. Or two. "Now, spill, Della."

"I want you to know that I've really been trying to convince Maggie that everything's going to be all right."

"Could have fooled me at the tea party."

"That was a culmination." With her thumbnail, Della picked at a knot on the table. "After seeing Maggie in that terrible state, I couldn't take it anymore."

Maggie had been a fright, that was true, but Brax was right. Her friends should be talking her down off the ledge, not climbing up there with her. "I understand how you feel. But we'll help Maggie more if we remain calm. She needs a shoulder to cry on."

"I'm really trying not to cast judgment. But Simone, even I don't hold out much hope."

"It can't be that bad." Carl had asked for a sex fantasy to rekindle Maggie's fire. That meant something. Simone tried to squash the fear that it wasn't Maggie's fire Carl wanted to light.

Della shook her head, pursed her lips and stared down as the dollop of whipped cream on her daiquiri sank below the surface. "I think Maggie's right. Carl's planning on leaving her."

Della's words hit her like a blast of icy arctic air. "No. That's not possible."

Della stirred, then stirred some more until the scoop of whipped cream melted into the mix. "She told me he's been taking money out of their bank account. When a man starts sneaking money out of the joint checking, it means he's leaving."

"Maybe he needed the money to start his outhouse business."

Della snickered. "Right. I think he invented outhouse excavating and bat caving to cover his disappearances."

"What about the ring he found? The diamond ring?"

"He probably got it out of a gum ball machine at the Stockyard." Della dropped her chin and peered at Simone through her lashes. "He could have gotten the ring anywhere."

But...but... Simone glanced at the bar to make sure Whitey was engrossed in the TV, then lowered her voice. "What about Carl and Whitey's four outhouses?"

"For show, I think. Carl wants everyone to believe he's pissed at Whitey for not letting him at the outhouses. But I bet he's as happy as a bat in bat guano that Whitey's holding out."

Carl just couldn't be such a big fat liar.

What about the fantasy? Why would he have asked Simone to write it for Maggie if he wasn't trying to patch things up? But he'd never said it was for Maggie. Never.

Oh my God. She had to face the truth here.

The erotic tale Carl had her write was for another woman. Simone had helped him carry on an illicit affair behind Maggie's back. She was a party to his deception. She was a backstabber. Even if she hadn't known his real intention.

She'd saved all his e-mails detailing exactly what he'd wanted. When she got home tonight, she'd review every single one.

"Who's he running away with?"

Della shrugged. "I don't know. I wish I did. Lord knows I've tried to help Maggie, but I can't get her

hopes up that this isn't bad, really bad. It's better she understands now so that when it happens, it isn't such a terrible surprise."

"Couldn't you be wrong, Della?" Simone didn't know much about Della's life before Goldstone. In fact, she didn't know anything. Had Della had a bad marriage in which her husband cheated on her? Was she looking for the worst in all men?

"I know men, sweetie, and I know I'm not wrong. Haven't you noticed that he's been losing weight?"

Now that Della mentioned it, Carl might have dropped a few pounds. You noticed the slightest weight loss on a woman, but a man, well, that was harder to distinguish. Now that she thought about it, though, Carl's clothes did seem to hang more loosely on him. "What does that mean?"

"*Cosmo* magazine says that when a married man starts losing weight, it's because he's got his eye on someone new."

"*Cosmo* says that?"

"Yes, *Cosmo*," Della said with a reverent lifting of her chin.

"Couldn't it mean that he got health conscious?"

Della snorted, then looked at the lipstick mark she'd left on her glass. Reaching into the purse she'd plopped on the edge of the table, she pulled out a compact and freshened her lips.

Makeup perfect once more, she said, "You really need to read *Cosmo* more. You haven't got the slightest idea how a man's mind works."

And *Cosmo* did? Wasn't it written by women?

Still, she did have the stomach-dropping sensation that Della and *Cosmo* might be right.

BRAX DIDN'T FIND Carl at the county jail, nor did he find Sheriff Elwood Teesdale. After 9:00 p.m., the only person working the county jail was the 911 dispatcher who informed Brax that the sheriff was hot on the trail of a dangerous thief who'd robbed the minimart at gunpoint earlier that evening.

Carl hadn't shown up at the jail. In fact, Teesdale hadn't thrown him in the clink for public drunkenness in over a week.

Brax had then taken a quick jaunt up to The Dartboard in Bullhead. No Carl. After driving every street and back road around Goldstone, Brax still hadn't found Carl's truck. Nor had he seen or heard evidence of the sheriff's manhunt, no flashing lights and no sirens. Waiting at a stop sign on the highway, he massaged his temples.

He had the sinking feeling Maggie was right. Carl was bunking down in some floozy's bedroom.

But Brax couldn't go home to Maggie's trailer without Carl in tow. He'd promised.

He had only one hope left. Flood's End. He'd gone by earlier. Carl's truck wasn't there, so he'd driven on. Bartender Doodle, however, might provide other leads he could follow up.

The neon sign atop the Flood's End called to him. Amidst trailers like hulks in the darkness and the occasional telephone pole outlined against the sky, that glaring neon sign was a beacon to a thirsty traveler. Which hit home the other reason the Flood's End beckoned. Simone had said she was meeting Della.

Simone was the drink and he was the one thirsting for her. As a panacea for his troubles, she was infinitely superior to downing a glass of whiskey.

His eye on the guiding neon light, Brax pulled into the lot outside the Flood's End. Cheers pounded out through the open door, and as he stepped onto the porch, he could make out the fuzzy outline of a sports announcer on the TV above the bar and Simone at a table against the right wall.

The cheering ended abruptly as Brax passed through the door. Eight pairs of eyes surveyed him until one set blinked. Whitey. He recognized a few of the other faces from his sojourns around town, but could associate no names. Whitey mumbled something, perhaps a greeting.

Doodle slapped his hand on the bar. "The brother-in-law. Sorry, son, I forgot your name, but come on in. We're watching the world cricket match. Take a seat."

Only two remained. Brax chose the stool closest to the exit, the one separated from the rest by the bartender's escape hatch.

"What'll you have, boy?"

Brax pointed to the drinks on Simone's table. "I'll have one of those."

Doodle cackled, leaned closer and said under cover of another hooting for the cricket team, "Well, now. Which one? Simone's as sweet as apple pie and baseball. But Della, she's more like the apple the snake offered Eve."

Whoa. That was a pretty damning statement. "Why don't you like her?"

Doodle vigorously shook his head, his tight white curls springing in all directions. "Love her. Heart of gold. But she's a born politician, and big state governor or small town mayor, they all make promises they can't keep. Only really good thing she's done is get all

us residents our own burial plot in the Goldstone Cemetery. For free. All we have to do is pay to get the hole dug."

That was certainly a rousing recommendation.

Doodle tapped his arm. "Don't let on I ever said that."

Which part? "Our secret. Even torture won't get it out of me." Of course, everyone at the bar probably heard all the old man said. "Now back to the original topic, I wasn't referring to the ladies, but to the drinks on their table. Care to make up another batch of the stuff?"

Doodle reared back. "You can't have a froufrou drink like that. Those are only for ladies."

Brax knocked the side of his head. "What was I thinking? Beautiful ladies scramble my brain. A beer is what I meant to say. Whatever you've got on tap."

Doodle poured and slid the glass down the bar into Brax's waiting hand. Then he followed it with a damp cloth sopping up the trail of liquid from the bottom of the frosty mug.

Used to the regulars, Doodle obviously preferred talking up the newcomer, since he didn't leave after depositing the beer. "Brax. I remember the name now."

"Right." Brax took the opportunity to ask about Carl. "You seen my brother-in-law this evening?"

Doodle shook his head and mimed a frown. "Ain't seen him since you two were here on Sunday."

Brax had hoped, but he hadn't actually believed finding Carl would be that easy.

"He have another fight with Maggie?"

Brax neither confirmed nor denied. "I'm out looking for a drinking buddy," which seemed as good an explanation as any.

"Well, after you finish your beer, check on over at the jail. Carl sometimes sleeps off his fights over there. Leastwise, Teesdale might have seen him somewhere."

"I was trying to locate the sheriff. He likely to stop by?"

The sound of a siren took up its banshee wail, growing louder as if the pursuit car headed straight for the Flood's End.

Blue-red stripes flashed across the walls and patrons, then the siren cut, the engine died, and the lights were doused.

"Looks like ya found the sheriff."

CHAPTER TEN

DOODLE FISHED a bottle of Heineken from somewhere deep beneath the bar, opened it, then tilted a frost-laden mug and poured with a minimum of foam. He slapped both the mug and the bottle onto the bar.

"Doodle, you're a god come down from Olympus to save the parched throat of a lowly sheriff," Teesdale said as he reached for the "nectar of the Gods."

"Sheriff, a good man deserves the best a poor bartender can offer." Doodle leaned on the counter.

Sheriff Elwood Teesdale downed half the glass, sighed with his eyes closed, then poured the remainder of the bottle. He waved a hand. "Gentleman, as you were. Just put on the siren so you'd know to clear out all the illegal nose candy before I descended."

A hush had fallen when the sheriff pulled his wailing cruiser into the lot. Now a few laughed and all went back to watching the cricket match.

"Simone. Mayor. Don't mind me." Teesdale tipped his Smokey the Bear hat to the ladies, then tossed it on a nearby table. A day's wear in Goldstone's heat had mashed his hair in a ring around his head. He kicked a chair out with his foot and sat with his back to the wall nearest the door.

"Tough night, Sheriff?"

"The worst of my life, Doodle. Needed a nip to calm the old nerves." He held up his hand, showing off a case of the shakes as bad as any thirty-year alkie would have.

Sheriff Teesdale was your average Joe. Average height, average weight, average number of lines ctched into his face for a man somewhere close to his mid-forties. Brown hair a medium shade cut to a medium length, it was neither a buzz cut nor touched his collar. He bore no distinguishing characteristics, and his voice held no distinctive inflection. His looks were those of a man no one noticed in a crowd or the kind over which neighbors exclaimed, "He always seemed so ordinary," when the police uncovered his wife's body buried in his backyard.

Brax had never bought the ordinary explanation, but he had to admit, Teesdale was the personification of the term.

Doodle cupped his hand over his mouth and said to Brax, "Sheriff likes to unload after a bad one. Ask him, cop to cop. It'll do him a world of good."

Brax understood the need to unload, though he'd never been one to do it. As ranking officer in his department, he didn't unload with his subordinates. Bad for morale as well as for maintaining discipline. Nor had burdening his wife with his job stress been an option. That cut his choices down to none.

Until recently, he'd never had the need.

Doodle flapped a hand in his direction. "This is Carl's brother-in-law."

"Heard all about you, Sheriff Braxton." Teesdale stretched out his legs and crossed them at the ankles. "Sorry. I'm sure you came here to get away from shoptalk."

"Not a problem, Sheriff. But I did stop by to see you earlier. Wondering if you've seen Carl lately."

Teesdale scratched his head. "Can't say that I have."

"Maggie thought maybe he'd been by to visit you."

"Nope." Teesdale flicked a piece of lint from the brim of his hat. "Hasn't visited for at least a week or more."

That was it. Brax himself would have to spend the night in jail so he didn't have to face his sister.

"So do tell, Sheriff. What was all the fuss about?" Doodle was obviously bored with the topic of Carl.

The sheriff shook his head soberly. "It was a desperate situation, Doodle. More than half a dozen times, I thought I was a goner."

The man was a born storyteller, relating the tale with the-fish-was-really-this-big exaggeration.

Doodle pointed the remote and lowered the TV's volume. The boys grumbled and groused. "You can see, ya don't have to hear, too. Sheriff, sorry for their bad manners. Go on."

"Well, Doodle, I'll tell you. Jody was damn lucky to escape with her life. That woman's fast on her feet, thank God, or we'd have been cataloging blood spatter on the walls from now until Christmas."

"Jody's the clerk over at the minimart," Doodle muttered out of the corner of his mouth, "and that woman couldn't move fast if her ass was on fire."

"He made her lie down on the floor, and she had the good sense to let him take as much as he wanted," Teesdale went on. "Nothing good comes of facing down a man with a gun over a few material things. Especially when they belong to your boss."

Simone sipped at her drink, watching Teesdale, and

Della twisted in her seat. The bar boys had even tuned out cricket. Brax figured knocking over the local mini-mart was the most infamous crime Goldstone's sheriff ever saw, and the man was playing up to his audience for all he was worth.

"Then she called you?" Doodle prompted.

"At the time, I was surveying the landscape out my office window." Which meant he hadn't had a damn thing to do. "The perp exited with his bootie. Couldn't see his face in the gloom."

"He had a jump on you, then, didn't he, Sheriff?"

"That he did, Doodle. But I tracked him."

"From his shoe prints?"

"No. Something much more damning." The sheriff paused for effect. "Twinkies wrappers. Every twenty yards or so. See, I stopped long enough with Jody to find out exactly what the desperado was after. Stole the entire display of Twinkies. Ten boxes. Followed the trail right to the brigand's front door."

"Amazing detective work, Sheriff."

Teesdale nodded in acceptance of the accolades. "Took years of training, and a lot of psychological know-how. See, I deduced it had to be someone who loved Twinkies. I further surmised that Mud Killian, who buys a box of Twinkies at least every other day, was the most likely suspect."

"Mud's Mama Killian's youngest. He's twenty-one, but a might tetched in the head." Doodle did another aside explanation for Brax.

"So when Mud opened his front door, I was prepared to register every bit of evidence. The first thing I noted was the Twinkies cream on his upper lip. Gave me probable cause to search the premises. And there

they were, in the middle of the kitchen counter. Nine boxes of Twinkies. He'd eaten one box, which I verified by counting the number of Twinkies wrappers I'd collected while hot on his trail. I impounded the rest."

"Damn, Sheriff. Good work."

"Thank you, Doodle. But are you truly aware of the implications here?"

"No, sir. Maybe you should tell us."

Teesdale uncrossed his ankles and leaned forward with his hands on his knees. "Remember the Twinkies defense?"

"The Twinkies defense?"

"That fellow over in San Francisco who shot the mayor because he OD'd on Twinkies? Don't tell me you don't remember. The case was a landmark."

"Sheriff, can't say that I—"

Teesdale whipped out a hand. "Don't say another word, Doodle. I'm shocked and dismayed. But since you don't remember, I'll explain. Mud Killian could have OD'd on those Twinkies and wiped out the entire town. He had the arsenal to do it."

Doodle slapped his hands to his cheeks. "Sheriff, you're a saint. Thank the Lord for providing you to us."

"Don't mention it. It was my duty, and I couldn't have done otherwise."

"What's gonna happen to Mud?"

"The heinousness of this crime deserves the stiffest of punishments. I did what I had to do. I confiscated his cache of squirt guns, then I informed his mama."

Doodle's breath wheezed out. "Holy Christ, Sheriff."

Teesdale did the sign of the cross over his chest. "I know, I know. Mama Killian's retribution is too terrible to imagine. I figure I'll take a ride over there to-

morrow and make sure she hasn't staked him out over an anthill for longer than twelve hours." He drained the last of his beer, then smacked his lips. "Delicious brew, Doodle."

"Have another, Sheriff. On the house. Can't do enough for the man who saved the entire town."

Teesdale rose to his feet and plopped his hat on his head. "Thanks for the generous offer. But for now, folks, I gotta turn in. The wife'll be worrying herself sick over me, and I have a busy day tomorrow, what with all those dastardly criminals to incarcerate and Mama Killian to subdue." He put a hand over his heart. "Better make sure I remember my nitroglycerine, just in case. The old ticker may give out in the face of Mama's wrath."

Teesdale tipped his hat. "Night, Doodle. Night, Simone, Mayor." He turned, encompassing the assembly at the bar. "Gentlemen." Then he gave a nod to Brax. "Nice to meet ya, Sheriff. Drop by for a little shoptalk anytime."

"If you see Carl, send him home ASAP."

"Will do. Like Little Bo Peep's sheep."

Teesdale saluted, then left.

If the sheriff hadn't seemed quite so tickled with himself, Brax would have felt for him. The humiliation of capturing criminals like Mud Killian was a cop's nightmare, a job reserved for screwups who couldn't make it in a big city department. Hell, Teesdale wouldn't make it in Brax's county department.

Still, tracking a Twinkies thief was a sight better than working a good friend's murder case.

"Simone. Mayor." Brax stepped up to their table and all those butterflies she'd gotten when he walked in came back for another rally in her tummy.

"We'd ask you to join us, but it's past my bedtime." Della tipped her arm to look at her watch. "Will you look at that? It's after eleven." She jumped up, grabbed her purse, hugging it to her chest as if she thought Brax might suddenly stare at her breasts.

He was much too much a gentleman for that. Most of the time.

"I've got to be up early for a breakfast talk at the Rotary in Bullhead," Della explained. "Those Rotarians, you know, as much fun as a barrel of monkeys. Gotta go. Bye, Simone."

Della rounded Brax, turned, scrunched her eyes and zipped her lip in a warning that said, "Do not tell this gorgeous, hunky man a thing."

The long line of gawkers at the bar fell like dominoes. Della had a killer wiggle in tight jeans, especially when she wore those lace-up suede boots with three-inch heels.

Simone cocked her head at Brax. "Do men know that the reason women wiggle when they walk is because of the high heels?"

"Something your mother says?"

"No. It's an observation I just made." It also guaranteed to sway his thoughts if he suddenly got the idea to ask how her talk with Della had gone. "It never occurred to me before. But that's why we do it."

He cast an eye after Della as she disappeared through the door. "I think some women do it because they can."

Simone wasn't exactly sure what that meant, especially regarding Della, but then he held out his hand to her. She forgot about caring what he meant. "Can I walk you home?"

She wanted to take his hand so badly the butterflies in her tummy jumped all the way up to her throat. She looked at his hand, then back up at him. "You can walk me partway. Just to the corner."

"Partway? Why not all the way?"

Did he notice his own little double entendre? His eyes sparkled, and she figured he did.

"Because." First, he might try to kiss her—and she'd let him—and second, she needed to look at Carl's string of e-mails on her computer. Alone. She stood, avoiding his hand, and tried to pull the hem of her T-shirt down over her butt, but it was too short.

"It doesn't cover your tush," he whispered in her ear, setting off a nice chain of tingles, "but I promise not to look."

"You're a very bad man," she whispered back. With her head held high, she paraded through the empty tables. "Night, Mr. Doodle. Night, boys."

More than a few brows rose in speculation as all noted Brax close on her heels. "Brax is going to walk me home. Partway."

"Uh-huh, Simone." Doodle covered his mouth.

Snickers and chortles followed them out the door.

She turned on Brax in the parking lot, out of sight of the open door. "You shouldn't have offered to walk me home."

"What kind of gentleman would let a lady walk home alone? Today you said I needed to be more chivalrous."

Trust him to remember and throw it back at her. "You let Della walk home alone."

"I said lady."

She gasped and opened her eyes as wide as they'd go.

Brax held up his hands. "I meant, she's the mayor, not a lady."

She jammed her hands at her waist and leaned forward.

"What I mean is—" He stopped, eyed her. "You did that so I wouldn't ask you what Della said."

Darn. He caught on. She turned. "Walk me to the corner."

"Don't walk so fast. We'll get there before you have a chance to tell me."

"Tennies. They always make me walk too fast." She hummed. "I don't think I should tell you. You're not going to like it." She made sure she stayed a pace ahead of him so that she couldn't see his eyes.

"Can't be worse than Teesdale saying he hasn't seen Carl."

"Oh." She hadn't even given a thought to his disappointment on Maggie's behalf. A chill crept across her shoulders. Wouldn't it have been nice if Carl was sleeping it off in the jail? "Why didn't you ask him to search for Carl?"

"If the sheriff is worth anything at all, he figured out he should do that when I asked him if he'd seen Carl."

That didn't sound as if he thought much of Sheriff Teesdale. Maybe the Twinkies story didn't have all the drama of chasing a real murderer through dingy back alleys as Brax was probably used to, but the sheriff was still something special.

She didn't realize she'd stopped until Brax ran into her back. "You don't like the sheriff?"

"Seems like a stand-up kind of guy."

"But?"

"I didn't add a but."

"There was definitely a but there."

He laughed, softly, then harder. Finally, he bent over, putting his hands on his knees as he completely lost it.

"What?"

He raised his head. The light of a street lamp sparkled in his eyes. "I have never in my life met anyone like you. I don't think you even know how hilarious you are."

She pouted her lower lip. "Hilarious doesn't seem like much of a compliment." Sexy, seductive, beautiful, smart, those were compliments. Hilarious was something you called Groucho Marx.

He walked his hands up his thighs until he was straight and towering over her, then he put his hand on her cheek. "You have no idea how much of a compliment it is."

"That makes me feel better." Yeah, right.

He stroked her cheek with his thumb, and all the laughter drained from his gaze. "It doesn't matter what Della said or if she talks Maggie into feeling better. I think it's too late."

The chill she'd felt earlier skittered from her nape to the bottom of her spine. "You think he's going to leave her."

He smiled gently, but his eyelids drooped with sudden fatigue. "I arrived too late to do anything about it."

"It takes two to fix something, Brax. And you were never one of the two that could do the fixing." So why had she thought her little fantasy would help? A question without a good answer.

"You said that before. Still feels like sh—crap."

"It's all right. You can say shit. I'm a big girl, and I can take it. It'll work out, Brax. I'm sure it will."

She squeezed her eyes tightly shut and prayed, *please, God, let Maggie be the one Carl's talking about in his e-mails.*

"What are you doing?"

Her eyes popped open. "Praying."

"Hope it does some good."

It had to. Brax stared at her. She stared at him. And finally she had to ask, "Wanna kiss me good-night?"

Taking her elbows in his hands, he pulled her close until her nipples touched his chest and his lips brushed the tip of her nose, then her lips themselves. "Yes. I wanna kiss you. But I'm not going to."

Ooh. That was too bad. "Why not?"

"Because I'd rather dream about it tonight. Because in my dreams, I don't have to stop with kissing. I get to unbutton your shirt—"

"I'm not wearing a shirt with buttons."

"Shh. I'm seducing you with my words here."

"Sorry."

"As I was saying, I unbutton your shirt, use my tongue to push aside the lacy bra and take your nipple in my mouth."

She wanted to press her nipples hard against his chest. "What about the part where you bury yourself to the hilt? The hero always does that in romance novels."

He rubbed his lips on hers. "Burying to the hilt comes at the end. Before that, I'm going to make you come nine ways to Sunday with my fingers, my lips and my tongue."

"Oh." Oh my goodness. She was turning to mush. Excessive, exuberant, dangerous mush. She moved so her lips grazed his jaw. "All in your dreams?"

"For now."

BRAX PUT BOTH HANDS on the doorjamb of the Flood's End. "Wanted to let you boys know that Simone is home safe and sound. Figured you'd be worried about that."

They looked at him as if he had a screw loose, not caring one whit if he did or didn't climb into Simone's bed. The geezers loved her. She could do no wrong.

He backed up one step on the porch. "I'm getting into my truck now. Going back to Maggie's."

They still didn't care. But he wouldn't tarnish Simone's reputation. Not for anything.

In those moments when he'd held her by the elbows and fantasized about tasting her with his tongue anywhere and everywhere, he'd decided—for the third or fourth time—that whatever was in that e-mail between Carl and her, he, Brax, didn't give a damn. It wasn't something that would hurt Carl's marriage to Maggie.

Simone was sweet, she was funny, and she wasn't a liar. But Brax was going home in a week or so, and his relationship track record sucked the big one. As much as he wanted to taste her again and again, it was better to leave Simone in his fantasies. Dream girls were satisfied with very little.

Five minutes later, his SUV chugged up the steep drive. The trailer was dark, Maggie's car was exactly where it should be, and Carl's parking spot was still empty.

How was he going to tell Maggie he'd failed?

Worse, how was he going to tell her he believed Carl was about to leave her and break her heart?

SIMONE STARED at the computer screen until her eyes started to cross. It was impossible to tell if the heroine

was Maggie. She'd exchanged three e-mails with Carl, asking for further clarification on certain details.

He'd replied with specific answers.

But was the woman in the fantasy supposed to be Maggie? She was blondish, like Maggie, but Carl's description was of a seemingly younger woman with much fuller breasts. For that matter, the hero of the story was younger, taller and thinner.

Maybe Carl had imagined them both young, perfect and agile.

Simone couldn't make a determination.

Darn it, why hadn't he given her names to use? Instead, she'd written the whole thing with pronouns. Which was easy when the story involved only the hero and heroine.

With a sudden burst of frustration, she pounded the side of her monitor, then, for each of his stupid, damning e-mails, she hit the delete key so hard she almost broke a nail. "Darn you, Carl."

She dashed off a new e-mail.

"If you're planning what I think you're planning, you are dead meat. And I do mean dead meat. Rotten, maggot-infested, buzzard bait."

She felt only marginally better.

She just hoped Carl came back to read the e-mail. At least that might mean he and Maggie still had a chance.

"ARE ANY OF HIS CLOTHES missing?" Brax asked as gently as possible.

They sat at the kitchen table, no food between them, just mugs of coffee that Brax had prepared. The morning hours had ticked by like molasses running uphill.

No crunch of tires on the gravel drive, not even a phone call. Carl hadn't come home last night, and he hadn't returned today. Maggie refused breakfast. She'd skipped lunch, too. Though he forced himself to eat, Brax sure as hell didn't feel like it while watching his sister's life go into meltdown.

"No." Maggie's voice was emotionless, except for that hard sharp edge that would have flayed flesh from bone. Stone-cold anger glittered in her eyes.

"Did you check?"

She gave him a one-eyed glare without turning her head. "I don't have to check. I do all the laundry and all the folding, but I refuse to put his crap away. There are four piles sitting two feet high on the dresser. Just like yesterday and the day before that. So no, he hasn't taken any clothes." Her lip lifted in a snarl. "He's probably planning to buy all new stuff with my money when he gets wherever the hell he's going."

"Now, Maggie, you don't know..." Brax stopped himself before she got the chance to cut him off. Last night's bath had not relaxed her. It had turned her hard and cold and determined to kick Carl out if he did come slinking back.

Brax started again. "He didn't leave a note."

"My point exactly. He didn't even leave a goddamn note. He walked out on me without even so much as a one-line explanation."

"Even the police require twenty-four hours before accepting a missing person's report. Maybe we should hold off judgment."

She lifted her arm, looked pointedly at her watch, then put her hand flat on the table. "He crawled out of my bed at five o'clock yesterday morning. That makes

it almost thirty-six hours. He's gone. And you know what, Tyler, I don't care. I really don't care. Della's right, I'm better off without him. He can fall off the edge of the earth and die for all I care."

"Now, Maggie."

"Don't you dare 'now Maggie' me! You're wearing the most pathetic hangdog face because you *know* he's gone as well as I do."

He didn't want to believe, but he couldn't deny. He hadn't known Carl had it in him, but the man had proven to be quite a liar. Carl sat solemnly on the passenger side of Brax's vehicle and promised he'd take his wife out to dinner. He'd poured out his anger at Lafoote and the resort. He'd confided. Yet all the while, he'd been planning to leave. Maybe that was how he'd show them all he wasn't a loser. By taking off and making a better life somewhere else. He'd probably return ten years from now with a beautiful young wife, two kids and enough money to buy all of Goldstone.

A knock on the front door carried through to the kitchen. Brax jerked his head up.

Maggie snorted. "If it were him, he wouldn't bother knocking. It's probably UPS."

Her knees creaked as she rose. It was yet another sign of her stress.

There came the murmur of voices, then nothing, not even the closing door.

His heart started to pound and his blood rushed like a raging river in his ears. Rising, Brax knocked his mug over. A stream of coffee dripped off the edge of the table onto the floor. He left it behind as he followed the voices to the front door.

Sheriff Teesdale stood on the doorstep, his hat in his

hand, the same ring of crushed hair around the top of his head. He worked the brim back and forth, then pulled it through his fingers, turning his hat in an endless nervous circle.

Maggie didn't move. Some time before Brax stepped into the hall, she'd jammed a fist to her mouth and wrapped an arm around her waist.

Teesdale looked at him as if he were a lifeline. "I'm sorry. Real sorry."

The words weren't necessary. The sheriff's eyes said it all.

Brax had delivered bad news too many times. He'd felt for the victims of the tragedies, the car crashes, the hunting accidents, the drownings, a million ways to die. Christ. It tore up his gut observing the myriad ways in which people reacted.

Yet he'd never even contemplated being on the receiving end, nor his sense of utter helplessness as he watched Maggie. Just watched. Unable to move. Unable to touch. Incapable of comforting. The sensation was akin to total paralysis, right down to his vocal cords.

Carl hadn't run away. He was dead.

CHAPTER ELEVEN

"WHERE'D YOU FIND HIM?" The words burned his throat, the thought tormented his brain.

The sheriff glanced at Maggie, then answered Brax. "The gorge." He pointed off to his right. "The chickens found him. They were out there dirt biking."

"On a Wednesday?" Brax didn't know why he bothered to ask.

"Chloe gives 'em Tuesdays and Wednesdays off," Teesdale explained. "He musta fallen from one of the trails up above. Lots of bat caves and stuff in that area."

"He was really out splunking," Maggie whispered.

"Honey, why don't you let me talk to the sheriff for a minute?" Brax tried to steer her from the front door, but her feet remained secured like a rock.

"How long was he there?" she asked.

Brax's heart broke.

The sheriff twisted his hat into a misshapen mass. "Yesterday. Morning. I think." He looked at Brax, helpless, silently asking for guidance.

Brax had none to give, but he briefly shook his head. The less said in front of Maggie, the better. He had questions, but the answers could wait. Maggie's feelings were more important now. "Give me your card. I'll call you."

Teesdale stuck his hand in his khakis' front pocket, then the back. Finally he found the small stack in his shirt pocket and peeled one off.

Brax reached around Maggie and shut the door as the sheriff walked away.

"I'm tired," she said, staring at the floor. "I think I'll take a nap."

"Yeah, yeah, good idea, sweetheart."

He hadn't a clue what was a good or a bad idea, hadn't a clue what to do for her. He'd handled grief so many times, he'd have called himself an expert, but he'd never figured on handling Maggie's. When his father died, he'd grieved, they'd all grieved together— Mom, Maggie and him, comforted one another. But this was in a class of its own.

Sudden, unexpected death always was.

HE CAN FALL OFF THE EDGE of the earth and die for all I care.

Maggie curled into a ball beneath the covers, making herself as tiny, as unnoticeable as possible.

Tyler had left her alone in her room. He couldn't stand to be near her. How could she blame him, even if he was her brother? What kind of wife told her husband to drop dead? She covered her ears, but the words wouldn't go away. How many times had she said it when she got so angry her thoughts spewed out like Linda Blair spitting pea soup in the *Exorcist?* Oh God, oh God. She didn't even have the excuse that she was possessed. She didn't have any excuse. She was a terrible, horrible wife. Like a woman on one of those detective shows who fed her husband antifreeze.

Drop dead, Carl!

Her last words to him. When he'd crawled out of bed the morning after, she'd pretended to be asleep, hadn't even opened her eyes. Hadn't taken one last look or said one last thing. Something nice. Something sweet.

Something to remedy *Drop dead, Carl!*

And he had dropped dead. Just like she told him to.

Her belly cramped. She curled around the pain, nursed it. She'd had nothing more than coffee since the tea party. The caffeine ate a hole in the lining of her stomach. Good, good. Penance. Payback. What kind of wife? Oh God, what kind of wife?

I'm gonna kill him.

Throw his parts down his goddamn outhouse holes.

I'm gonna Bobbitize him.

I'm gonna stuff his tiny little dick down the garbage disposal and grind it up so they won't be able to sew it back on.

She pulled the pillow over her head, but she couldn't shut out the words. Her own words, her own horrible, terrible, unforgivable words. Oh God.

Now I lay me down to sleep, I pray the Lord my soul to keep. I'm so sorry. I'm so sorry. Please forgive me.

The pillow snuffed out her breath for a moment, but then she found she could drag in air through the cotton fibers. She pressed the pillow tight over her mouth, but still she could breathe. Mashing both fists against the cotton covering her mouth and nose, she finally got what she wanted. She couldn't breathe. If felt so good in a panicky, unreal sort of way.

You're a bad, bad woman, Maggie Felman. May God forgive you.

She deserved to die.

Her legs started to move as if they didn't even be-

long to her. Her feet rub-rub-rubbed against each other, then they twitched back and forth on the sheet, faster, faster, as if trying to run away. Her head tipped down, her mouth opened, and a tiny inhale of hot air filled her lungs. Then her hands tossed the pillow aside, and she gasped and gasped.

God, she hadn't even been able to hold herself down for five seconds. She couldn't even stick it out until her lungs hurt and she saw spots before her eyes. Isn't that what happened?

Had Carl been in pain? She didn't want to think about it, but she couldn't squeeze her brain shut any more than she could hold a pillow over her face until she suffocated. Hear no evil and see no evil were easy. All you had to do was shut your eyes and cover your ears. Thinking no evil was harder. And speak no evil? She should have learned to shut her mouth a long time ago.

But Carl knew she was a drama queen. A forty-two-year-old drama queen. He knew she screamed and shouted and said all sorts of things she didn't mean. Why, once, when her dad was dying of cancer and she'd gotten mad at him about…something, she'd told him to drop dead. Her cheeks had caught on fire and that surrealistic I-can't-believe-I-just-said-that feeling almost made her heart seize up. She couldn't picture the look on his face or in his eyes anymore. She'd blocked it out.

"I didn't mean it, Daddy. I didn't mean it." She couldn't remember why she'd gotten mad. Everyone knew you weren't supposed to get mad at people who were dying. What could have made her so angry that she'd forgotten his disease for that split second?

The episode should have cured her. Normal people would have taken their medicine, and never done the like again. But she'd never been normal, and she hadn't been cured. Diarrhea mouth, Carl called her. But Carl knew that, and he knew she didn't mean all that stuff.

He loved her anyway. He wasn't leaving her. He was out looking for caves when it happened. It. The unthinkable.

Was there such a thing as karma? Like maybe because she'd said it so many times—because she'd said it to her father who was dying—the cosmos or God or whoever was out there decided she needed to learn a lesson, so they tipped Carl into the gorge.

She grabbed the pillow she'd tossed aside and clasped it to her chest. Fingernails biting into her palms, she hugged that pillow as tight as tight could be.

Why did she do these things? Why did she say them? Why did she get so angry?

"I'm so sorry. I didn't mean it. I'm so sorry. I didn't mean it." She chanted under her breath, over and over, as if that could make the impossible possible. Like maybe if she said it enough, the cosmos and karma and God would bring Carl back. And she'd never ever say drop dead to him again. She'd never say it to anyone, not another living soul. Not even a dead one.

Her thoughts stopped whirling around and around. She looked at the ceiling.

"I promise I'll never say it again."

The house was very quiet, as if it were listening, waiting. She held her breath. In the afternoon, the wind sometimes picked up. The old antenna on the roof—

the one Carl kept saying he would take down since they got satellite—usually creaked. Back and forth, back and forth. Today it was eerily silent.

"I promise, I promise." She crossed her heart.

There were always noises in the desert, yet today, there was nothing. As silent as a tomb.

She sat up, leaning back on her hands. Her wrists hurt, the angle awkward.

"Please, God."

The clock had stopped ticking. Carl found it at an old junk shop, and he liked it better because it lacked a snooze button. She remembered him winding it yesterday morning as he sat on the edge of the bed. Her eyes closed, she could almost hear the whir of the springs as he cranked. It should have been good for a week. But the clock had stopped.

She scrambled to the edge of the bed, reached down, grabbed her slippers and yanked them on.

The clock had stopped ticking. It was a sign.

"Tyler," she called, yanking open the bedroom door.

It was a sign. God had listened.

The man they found in the gorge wasn't Carl.

SIMONE WATERED her cacti. They said you weren't supposed to water cacti, but sometimes guilt overwhelmed her and she gave them a little drink. Especially on hot, dusty afternoons like this.

She'd tried writing, but her erotic fantasies seemed to have dried up. She'd been reminded of the story she'd sent Carl. She'd surfed the Net for a while, but found nothing more entertaining than the enticing detail that Britney Spears had worn blue panties under white slacks and the thong showed

right through. That was the headliner on her service provider's home page, which was above "coed's kidnapping caught on tape" and "son decapitates mother with sword." Jeez.

She didn't hold out much hope that kidnapping and murder would headline above the color of a rock star's panties any time soon.

Simone had learned about blue underwear and white pants when she was nine and Johnny Bremerton told everyone to check out her butt. Her mother had not been pleased. Suffice it to say, Simone never wore blue underwear again.

The color combo would undoubtedly become a new fashion fad just as it was cool for girls to show their bra straps. And it would still headline over murder and mayhem.

Her watering done, Simone cranked off the faucet and curled the hose beneath it. Behind her, something creaked. Creak, creak. The hair on her arms rose. Bent over as she was, her bottom felt exposed in the short jean skirt. She whirled, crouching like an action figure in a fight-to-the-death battle, and shrieked.

Jason Lafoote sat in her rocking lawn chair. Creak, creak. Forearms stretched along the armrest, he rocked, watching her with hooded eyes.

"How do you always manage to sneak up on me like that?" Her breath rate dropped back to normal. Almost.

"I didn't sneak. You just didn't hear me over the conversation you were having with yourself."

Yuk. "You can leave now. I'd rather talk to myself."

"I came by to offer my condolences." Jason rose from the chair, though its rock continued for a few moments more.

She eyed him warily. He had something up his sleeve if the lip curl and that smug look in his sneaky eyes meant anything. "Condolences for what?"

"Why, the loss of Carl Felman, of course."

God. Carl had run away. Maggie must have found a note. Or something. How did Jason know so quickly? And why did he see fit to bring her the news personally? "I'm sure it's all a mistake. He'll be back."

"Not unless he's Lazarus rising from the dead." The man couldn't help sounding tricky and smarmy.

"What's that supposed to mean?"

"Don't tell me you haven't heard?"

Prickles of unease raced up and down her arms. In the hot afternoon sun, a sweat broke out on her upper lip. "Heard what?" Her voice cracked in the middle.

He rushed to her side, putting a hand on her arm as if he thought she might faint.

She jerked away. "Don't touch me."

"Oh Simone, I'm so sorry, I thought you knew. I thought everyone knew."

She didn't want to know. It wasn't true. "Know what?" she whispered.

"They found Carl's body out in a gorge somewhere. He fell. He's dead."

"No." She bent over, clutched her stomach, felt the hot dog she'd eaten for lunch rise up into her throat.

He stroked her back. She hated it, but she didn't have the strength to throw him off. No, no, no. Not Carl. Goldstone was safe. Nobody got hurt in Goldstone. "There's a mistake."

"I heard it from the sheriff."

"There's got to be a mistake," she said again, a whisper to herself, a plea to some higher power.

"I'm sorry, Simone. I didn't think. I shouldn't have told you like that."

She hated him for doing it. "I have to see Maggie."

"I'll drive you over."

She stood and backed away from him, almost tripping off the edge of the patio. "Go away."

"But Simone, I've thought it through. I'm going to dedicate a wing of the hotel to Carl. The Felman wing. And—"

She slashed her arms in the air, shouted at him. "Shut up about the hotel. Nobody cares about the hotel. There isn't going to be any hotel."

"But Simone, please, I want to help you."

"Go away." She drew in a deep breath. "Go. Away."

Then she shoved past him into the house, slamming the sliding door and locking it as she raced to answer the ringing phone.

At first, Simone couldn't find the cordless. Then she dived between the couch cushions from where the sound emanated, grabbing the phone with both hands and holding it to her ear.

"Hello?"

"Simone."

"Oh God, Brax. It's not true, is it? Tell me it's not true."

After a long sigh, "Come over. Maggie needs me to do some things for her, but I'm not leaving her here alone."

Oh God, it was true. If it wasn't, he would have asked her what she meant. "But how? What happened? I don't understand."

"I'll tell you when you get here. And Simone, bring Della with you. The more friends Maggie has with her now, the better."

He hung up. She clutched the phone to her ear another minute, an eternity. She wanted to cry, she had from the moment that awful man had thrown out his Lazarus allusion. She'd had five minutes to get used to the idea.

She never would. Carl couldn't be dead. The image was so frighteningly...forever. Like marriage was supposed to be. *Till death do us part*.

God, she had to get to Maggie right away.

BRAX HAD CALLED Teesdale, forcing Maggie to listen on the extension as the sheriff said he'd done the ID of Carl's body himself, and no, there was no doubt in his mind that the chickens had found Carl and none other.

Maggie wouldn't believe. Guilt drove her insistence. She'd said some shitty things about Carl, today and last night. She'd also said some shitty things *to* Carl. She hadn't cried as she'd told Brax, in fact, she'd sat backbone straight, as if the confession were penance.

Now she wanted to prove it wasn't Carl they'd found.

Brax couldn't allow her to ID Carl. He'd promised to go himself, to do it for her. She'd agreed. But he'd needed someone to make sure Maggie stayed put. The heart-stopping thought that she'd follow him forced his phone call to Simone. He wanted Della for added pressure. Simone might prove to be a softie, but Della would stand steadfast.

"Do not let her leave the house," was his last command before he headed out to Goldstone's county buildings. The stricken look on Simone's face was too much to bear.

Teesdale met him in the front office, a four-by-four,

white-walled square with an opening behind which the dispatcher took 911 emergencies, service calls, and otherwise acted as the sheriff's administrative aide.

"This isn't necessary."

Brax put up his hand. "It is."

"It's a bitch when the next of kin doesn't want to accept what's happened. Usually guilt or hoping for a miracle."

"It's neither." It was both, but he didn't like Teesdale's notion that he could talk to Brax as if he were just another cop. Goddammit, at this point, he was next of kin. "Let's review the case." First. He didn't relish getting down to the details after he'd seen Carl.

Teesdale turned, led the way to his office, took a seat behind a desk cluttered with a mess of files and disorganized piles of paper, and indicated the spare chair for Brax. The letters had long since worn off his grimed keyboard, and greasy fingerprints on the monitor obscured anything that might have been visible from Brax's vantage point on the other side of the desk.

"You know most of it," Teesdale began. "Hard to say until the medical examiner takes a look, but I'd venture he'd been there along the lines of twenty-four hours."

Despite having no training as a doctor, there were signs a cop picked up from experience. Brax didn't ask for clarification. He'd see for himself soon enough. "Your most likely scenario?"

"Lost his balance and fell. Even from the bottom where we found him, you could see skid marks down the side. It's not a straight fall, but it's steep and rocky as hell."

"Speculation on cause of death?"

"Don't like to speculate."

Brax understood, as much as it sounded like a cover-your-ass comment. "Fair enough. You want to tell me about the truck?"

Teesdale shrugged noncommittally. "I was getting to that."

"Luckily everyone in town knows about your finding Carl's truck or I might not have heard that detail." He doubted Teesdale would have bothered to tell him about it otherwise. A guy with a vaguely familiar face had given Brax the tidbit when he'd paused at the stop sign on the other side of the highway.

"You'd have asked."

Teesdale was right about that. But Brax didn't like the impression that the man wasn't forthcoming. "Where exactly did you find it?"

"Bottom of the trailhead just south of town. Lots of hiking trails up into those hills. You'd be amazed how pretty it is in the spring. First time we ever lost a hiker, though."

Brax realized he hadn't driven out far enough last night. He'd been looking for Carl's truck parked in a floozy's driveway, as Maggie had suggested.

"Think he was dead before he hit the bottom?" Could he have saved him if he hadn't assumed Carl was plundering a neighbor's wife instead of sniffing wildflowers.

Christ, he could not, absolutely would not go back to tell Maggie that Carl had taken hours to die, all alone, at the bottom of some godforsaken gorge.

"Can't speculate," Teesdale said again.

No more of an answer than Brax expected, but a piss-poor one anyway. He put his hand on his knees and shoved to his feet. "Let's do it. Where's your morgue?"

Teesdale quirked his mouth. "We don't have a morgue here. Hell, Goldstone doesn't have a hospital, not even a clinic, let alone a morgue. We have to take him up to Bullhead."

"You should have told me. I would have met you there."

Teesdale spread his hands. "He's not there yet."

"If he's not in the morgue in Bullhead, then where the hell is he?"

The sheriff shrugged. "The basement."

Brax pointed down without saying a word.

"Yeah. 'Bout the coldest place we have around here."

"You've gotta be kidding."

"Hey, we aren't some big city department with all the frills, bells and whistles like some sheriffs are used to."

"I haven't got a morgue in my facility, but I still wouldn't store bodies in my basement." Christ, it was almost laughable, would have been for sure if it wasn't Carl lying down there.

"They're coming tonight."

"So why did you move him out of the gorge?" For that matter, what the hell had they transported him in? Surely not the back of a department cruiser. Worse, what evidence had they destroyed in the process?

Whoa. This was no murder investigation.

"Critters," Teesdale said as he led Brax through the jail proper. Six cells, all empty except for the pungent aroma of a heavy disinfectant which failed to expunge the underlying scent of urine. Brax hated to admit it, but though his department and budget were most likely multiple times the size of Teesdale's, he couldn't rid

his own facility of the smell despite the king's ransom in county funds he'd authorized for disinfectants and cleaning crews.

And he was dwelling on the prevalent fragrance to avoid dwelling on the critter comment.

Brax could only pray that Maggie was right and Carl wasn't in Teesdale's basement. How the hell was he supposed to bring up the subject of critters with her?

The sheriff started down a rickety set of curving metal stairs that shook under his feet. Brax followed, the winding effect and the subtle shake enough to make a drunk queasy. The only light that followed them down came from the eight-foot-high windows from the floor above.

"You sure you want to do this?"

"She's my sister."

"Yeah." Teesdale pulled on a string hanging above his head.

The body lay on a metal workbench against the back wall. A blue sheet draped the man-size shape, hanging down the side of the bench.

"Okay, stand out of the light. I'm only gonna uncover one side."

"I can't tell from a look at one side, Teesdale."

"I'm telling you, the other side isn't going to help you identify him."

Brax had seen his share of horrific sights. Carl could be no worse. "Pull it back all the way. My sister is counting on a decent identification."

Sometimes those horrific things happened to people he knew. He remembered the last time, his friend, the sound of that autopsy buzz saw, or whatever Hyram had called it. He should remember, he'd heard the name more than once, but he didn't.

He could not explain to Maggie why they'd have to subject Carl's body to that indignity. Then again, Nevada laws and regulations might be different. Maybe he could get Teesdale to forgo the autopsy in this case since it was clearly an accident.

"Holy shit."

Teesdale had pulled back the sheet while he'd been thinking.

"Critters," the sheriff said again.

"Christ." They'd made fast work of the left side of Carl's face yet the right remained completely intact. Like a Thanksgiving turkey where you'd carved the left breast and saved the right one for tomorrow night's dinner.

Only critters weren't so neat about it. Nor had they picked him clean.

Brax drew in a breath, more to ease the ache in his chest than for the air itself. Though there was evidence of skin sloughing, the body hadn't reached putrefaction stage, and the smell was still manageable, perhaps because Carl had been out in the open instead of a hot, humid place. Desert air was dry.

If you didn't look at the left side of his face, you could almost think he was...

Not in a million years did Carl look as if he was sleeping. The dead just didn't look as if they were sleeping, no matter how many times you saw that on TV or read it in a book. Or heard it in a mortuary. They looked *dead*. Even without the ravaged half face. Slack jaw and drooping facial muscles robbed the body of every last ounce of humanity. They also smelled dead, even before decomposition set in. A body lost control of all muscles. A body had to be cleaned up.

"I gotta go."

"Need a bucket, Braxton?" It wasn't said unkindly, but with the knowledge that when tragedy happened to someone close, when the victim was family, it didn't matter how many goddamn times you'd seen death. Distance changed perception.

He still didn't need a bucket.

"I'll call you about the arrangements. We need to talk about whether an autopsy's actually necessary."

"Oh, it's necessary," Teesdale said, bristling.

Brax realized he hadn't phrased it correctly. Maybe he should have begged Teesdale not to put Maggie through it, though forgoing autopsy warred with his cop sensibilities. A cop always wanted to rule out foul play. Things set better with an M.E.'s rubber stamp.

Teesdale held up his hand before Brax could re-word. "And it's my call." He pointed to his badge. "See that? Little lettering? County Coroner?"

As a brother, Brax knew he should fight for his sister, spare her the pain of knowing her husband's body would be dissected like a frog in biology class. As a cop, he knew he should look more closely, ease Carl's head to the side, peruse the wounds on both the skull and other areas of the body. He'd let himself be caught between the proverbial rock and a hard place.

Brotherly duty or cop common sense?

For the moment, neither choice mattered.

Right now, one person consumed him. Maggie. Duty to his sister dictated he tell her that an open casket service would be a bad idea. He could almost handle that task. It was the other fact tearing his chest open.

The last words Maggie had said to her husband would forever be, "Drop dead."

CHAPTER TWELVE

DELLA'S HAND WRINGING was beginning to wear on Simone's nerves, mostly because she felt like wringing her hands herself. She'd picked up Simone, and they'd driven over together, both silent, both in shock. Della had started the hand gesture the moment Brax left.

Carl was dead. Dead. *Dear God, please don't let it be true.* But the hard, implacable lines of Brax's face when he walked out the door haunted her still. Simone knew he didn't think Sheriff Teesdale had made a mistake.

"I shouldn't have been so hard on you yesterday." Della's voice hitched.

Maggie flapped her hand as if she didn't have a concern in the world. "Oh, Della, don't even worry about it. I know Carl and I will work everything out when he gets back."

Della glanced at Simone, a frown puckering her brow. Was denial normal? Was Maggie cracking up? She was actually chipper in a jittery, agitated sort of way, her fingers tap-tap-tapping, first the arm of her chair, then her knee, her cheek, and back to the chair.

What would they all do if—when—Brax came back with solid confirmation? The very idea made Simone shake inside and out.

Maggie's brittle smile scared her spitless, and worse, Simone didn't know what on earth to do or say. She had never dealt with death or grief. Her father was dead, but her parents had divorced when she was very young. She hadn't seen him again, and his death had come over the TV on the six o'clock news as if he were no more to her than a face in *People* magazine. In fact, that's all he was. She didn't have grandparents or aunts or uncles or cousins that she'd ever known. Her mother might actually have been hatched.

Simone's pseudo-fairy-tale life didn't give her any clues on how to help Maggie. She'd known Carl for three years, and all she wanted to do herself was rock on the sofa and repeat over and over, "I can't believe he's gone." How much worse it must be for his wife of ten years. Simone couldn't even imagine.

Carl. He was sweet and funny, and God, she would miss him deeply. How could he be gone forever?

Her heart flipped over and twisted in, out, and around on itself when she thought of that nasty e-mail she'd sent last night. She wished more than anything she could take it back. Hit the recall icon.

Wherever he was, Carl would have already seen it. He could see everything now. Would he forgive her for getting so angry with him last night?

She jumped up before she actually started wringing her hands along with Della. "Do you want me to make you some tea, Maggie?"

Brax had been gone for an hour. She'd made Maggie three cups of tea. Each time, she seemed to add a little more sugar and a little more milk, as if somehow the sweetener and cream would soften the blow when it came.

"No thanks. Brax will be back soon, and I don't want to be rushing off to the bathroom every five seconds. I might miss the moment he walks in with Carl."

Oh God.

Simone hurried into the kitchen to make the tea anyway. She could still hear them in the family room, Maggie's voice high and excited, Della subdued, the roughness of tears edging her tone.

When she returned with the tea, thicker and creamier than before, the late-afternoon sun had moved beyond the windows, hitting the bedroom end of the trailer. A hush fell along with the relative darkness in the living room. Maggie's eyes had become smoky hollows in her face.

The front door burst open. Maggie jumped up, raced halfway across the room, then reached out a hand, her fist closing, clenching, as Chloe barreled into the trailer.

"Oh my God, sweetie, I would have been here sooner." She offered no explanation for why she hadn't been. "I brought you some Xanax. Drugs are a girl's best friend at a time like this."

While Della shed the tears Maggie couldn't and Simone offered the comfort of tea, Chloe delivered tranquilizers. Simone almost begged for one herself.

Maggie flapped her hand. "Oh, Chloe, I don't need any Xanax. Brax went to prove it wasn't Carl they found. The sheriff made a mistake."

Chloe clamped her lips, swept first Della then Simone with a potent, questioning glare. They both, in that order, dropped their gaze. "Sweetie, I talked to the chickens—"

Maggie turned, stomped to the sofa and threw herself down. "They made a mistake, too."

"If it wasn't him, Maggie, then where do you think he is?" In the kindliest, grandmotherly tone, Chloe asked what Simone had been terrified of asking. Concern etched lines into Chloe's plump face, but her foot slapped a no-nonsense beat on the linoleum.

They waited through an excruciating two-minute silence. Simone had never understood how truly long two minutes could be. Maggie's Elvis clock beat in the kitchen, each tick and tock like a minor explosion. Chloe breathed like a dragon waiting to shoot fire. Della sniffed. Maggie hummed.

Simone prayed for Brax to come home.

PANDEMONIUM STRUCK the moment the front door opened.

Maggie flew across the room and into his arms. Brax closed his eyes and clutched her to his chest. Swallowing past the ache in his throat, he held her tightly a moment longer.

Then he gripped her arms and gently set her back. Her wild eyes searched his face, reflecting desperation. Panic. Raw guilt. He'd do anything to give her the answer she needed. Fucking anything. His choices had died in Teesdale's jail.

"Maggie, honey, it was him."

"No." She struggled in his grasp, then lifted her chin, and stared him down. "That's a lie."

Her eyes. They tore him apart.

He opened his mouth, but the words took forever to come out. "I'd never lie to you about this." She needed to hear the truth.

"It's not him. I'll prove it to you. I'll show you." Head down, she battled against him, butting his chest.

"I'm going to see whoever it is, and I'll show you you're wrong."

Jesus. He wanted to bleed off her pain like a lanced wound, but the only thing he could do was make sure she never carried the memory of Carl's ruined face in her mind. Or her heart. "You can't do that, honey, believe me, you can't."

With a mighty shove, Maggie pushed him back against the door, his hip glancing the small hall table. It shook, then tumbled. The thick glass bowl on top bounced off the linoleum, flipped, then landed on a weak point and shattered.

"See what you've done," Maggie screeched. "Carl always puts his car keys there. Always. And he's gonna be so mad. He's gonna be—" She covered her mouth.

His chest ached as if the tiny shards had sliced straight through the flesh and bone to his heart. It thrashed and bled behind his ribs.

Brax flattened his hands, bracing himself as Maggie's pain washed over him like a hard unforgiving rain. Then he did what he had to do. "You're not going to see him, Maggie." He spoke with a strong, sure voice, but the breath he dragged in shook his soul and burned his windpipe. "I'll take care of everything."

Jesus, God, look how he'd taken care of everything. His sister had shattered in front of him as surely as the bowl had shattered on the floor.

He closed his hand over Maggie's shoulder. "Sit down, honey." He turned her to the family room. Her feet moved like an automaton, as if her outburst had drained the fight from her.

He started to guide her into the worn lounger.

"That's Carl's chair." Maggie's voice hitched and

her body jerked, her calf ramming the coffee table. He caught her before she fell.

"Sit here." He gently pushed her down into the corner of the couch. Someone hovered nearby. Simone. Her scent drifted over him, but he couldn't let it soothe. He couldn't let his own pain ease a fraction while Maggie's agony ripped her in two.

Brax pushed aside the tea mug and a plastic bottle of pills, then sat on the wood coffee table.

"It's not him," Maggie whispered.

He cupped her cheek. His eyeballs stung as if the sweat had run off his brow. He blinked, cleared his vision, then found his voice. "Yes, it is. I swear, honey. You have to face it."

She shook her head, swiping at her eyes. "He didn't leave me?"

"No, honey, he didn't." His heart broke in two and each breath was like a knife wound. He didn't know what the hell to do for her. Useless, helpless, he told her the things he hoped she needed. "He loved you."

Maggie started to rock. "I don't understand, I don't understand," she chanted under her breath.

"He—" His voice broke. "He fell. He was hiking, and he fell. It was an accident."

Maggie's bottom lip trembled. "God'll never forgive me. Never."

Brax held her face with both hands and fruitlessly tried to dry each of her tears with his thumbs. Nothing would stop them. "Yes, He will. He already does. I promise, I swear."

Maggie leaned forward and buried her head in the crook of his neck. She shook against him with the force of her sobs.

"I told him to drop dead and he did," she said finally. Loud and clear, her confession. "He dropped dead like I told him to."

Her words vibrated inside him, in a deep hollowed-out place. A place that knew guilt, that lived with it, writhed in it. If he could make it so she didn't live that way for the rest of her life. If he could fix it, if he could take away her pain.

"Where he is right now, Carl knows you didn't mean it, honey." He continued to murmur, meaning lost in the low pitch. It didn't matter what he said. It was the soothing sound of a voice she needed, anybody's voice. Carl's voice. But he could never give her that.

Stroking Maggie's back with one hand, he bent his chin to her shoulder, rubbing his eyes with his thumb and forefinger as if that would somehow ease the pain for both of them.

His fingers came away moist.

"I brought some Xanax," someone whispered, the sound dropping like a dead weight in the room.

Chloe held the small bottle out to him.

"Get me some water." Behind Maggie's back, without loosening his hold on her, he deftly unscrewed the protector cap and shook a pill into his hand. He didn't even give himself a chance to question the wisdom of accepting drugs from a whorehouse madam. As a lifesaver, he'd have grabbed at anything.

Chloe handed the glass she'd fetched to Simone and Simone handed to it Brax, their fingertips brushing.

He took the water with a slight tremble in his hand. He couldn't look at her.

Brax tipped Maggie's chin with the hand holding the little blue pill. "Take this."

She looked at the tiny tablet. "I don't want it."

God help me, please take it. Please. He'd break clean in two if he couldn't end it for her somehow. Even for a few short hours. "It'll help you sleep."

Fresh tear tracks trailed down her cheeks.

"Put out your tongue."

She did, like a child. He dropped the pill, then tilted the glass of water against her lips. Maggie drank with her eyes closed, then swallowed.

"Are you sure it's Carl?" she murmured one more time.

Resting the glass on one knee and the bottle on the other, Brax leaned his forehead against hers. His head ached, his heart bled, and his insides leaked out on the floor as if he'd been gut-shot.

He hammered her last hope into the ground. "Yeah, honey, I'm sure."

How LONG WOULD the drug take to work?

Simone knew if she witnessed the tableau for one more second, she'd die.

Watching them was agony—Maggie, a pitiful shadow of the woman she'd been two days ago, and Brax, a good man brought to his knees by his sister's grief. Despair turned his eyes a light blue and his lips a faded white. Stark grooves of pain slashed his features.

She could do nothing for him. Nothing for Maggie. Nothing to ease their anguish. Nothing could ever take away what Maggie had said to Carl.

Maggie would live with those words for the rest of her life.

Simone's eyes filled with hot tears. Chloe's arm

slipped around her shoulder, hugging her close. As a mother would.

Simone wished someone, anyone, could have done the same for Maggie. And for Brax.

HIS EYEBALLS throbbed from the inside out. A headache pounded at his temples. His sister's life had gone to shit, and he'd failed miserably at doing anything to help her. The only sure thing was that he would not allow Maggie to see Carl. Christ. He'd never let her face that. In the gloomy hallway outside his sister's bedroom where she rested, Brax shoved his hands through his hair and let his breath out in a sigh.

When he opened his eyes, Simone stood in the hall. He wanted nothing more than to wrap his arms around her, bury his face in her hair and hold her.

Until Maggie woke up.

Simone padded down the hall, stopping when her fresh citrus tang was enough to ease the ache behind his eyes. Earlier her scent had offered comfort he couldn't take. He filled himself with her, breathing deeply of her gentle fragrance.

"Is she sleeping?" she asked.

"Yeah." He ached to touch her, even her hair, but he kept his hands at his side. "Never thought I'd think it, but drugs are a damn good thing."

She put a hand to his cheek. "How are you doing?"

He felt worse than Carl had looked, like critters had eaten away half his heart and half his soul. "I'm fine."

"Liar," she mocked gently.

"I wish I was. A liar, I mean. Then I could have told her it wasn't him down in…" He stopped. Simone

didn't need to know Carl was stuck like garbage down in the jailhouse basement.

"You did the right thing. She has to face it eventually."

He had the churning sense that Maggie wasn't close to facing anything. Her voice thick and slurred, she'd begged him to stroke her hair while she fell asleep. Even though he was younger, he'd felt more like her father. Watching her, he'd hurt so bad inside he'd almost lost it and cried while he'd rubbed her matted, messy hair.

His heart seized with the memory of Maggie's last whispered words before she succumbed to a drug-induced sleep.

Maybe he didn't accidentally fall into the gorge.

She'd looked at him with the same frenzied hope she'd had when she sent him down to the sheriff's to make sure it wasn't Carl's body. Then she'd verbally kicked him senseless.

Maybe somebody pushed him, Tyler. Maybe somebody killed him. You have to find out who did it. Carl can't rest until you do.

Maggie couldn't rest until she'd assuaged her own guilt by proving that someone else had done worse to her husband than she had. Words, some so fucking momentous, others so fucking useless.

The only saving grace God had given Brax was letting Maggie fall asleep before he had to answer her plea.

Maggie could sleep, but she'd never rest. He knew he'd do whatever she asked. He had to. And when the evidence showed Carl had lost his footing and fallen without any help from another's hand, Brax would

have to tell her that, too. There wasn't enough Xanax in creation to ease the pain she'd face then.

Simone soothed with a soft, wordless murmur. He wanted to sink into her comforting touch, lose himself in her warmth.

"I think you were right, Brax," Simone murmured in the gentlest of voices.

"About what?" Even her voice stroked his aches.

"You are like the Tin Man. All along, he had a heart as big as a mountain. He just didn't know it."

Brax knew he had a heart. It lay in pieces at her feet.

Putting his hand over Simone's, he held her palm to his cheek. He couldn't tell her in words what her touch meant. He couldn't express how badly he wanted to take the comfort she offered. He could only let her know through his gaze and the heat of his hand over hers.

Then he let go, ending the moment before he begged for so much more. "I have to check out Carl's office."

"Check out his office? Why?" She covered her mouth, muffling her small exclamation. "Life insurance and stuff? Do you think he had any?"

He hoped to God Carl had some sort of insurance to help see Maggie through. A free plot in the Gold-stone Cemetery wasn't going to do it. "We'll see."

Looking for an insurance policy now wasn't his intention. Maggie would ask him what he'd done to find Carl's supposed killer the moment she woke, and the sooner he could lay her latest fear, qualm, need, desire, or whatever the hell it was to rest, the better for her. In the long run, she'd have to accept that Carl's death was a terrible accident.

His cop skills were the most he had to offer. His consoling abilities sure left a lot to be desired.

What a woman needed at a time like this was her
mother. Theirs was more than a couple of hundred
miles away.

Shit. He should have phoned Mom hours ago.

"Have to make a call," he muttered, easing past her
in the hallway. Simone trailed him into the family room
where he made the smartest move of the day, maybe
of his life.

He called his mother.

SIMONE WATCHED Brax talk to his mother. He raked his
hand through his hair so many times, it had become a
mass of tangles snagging his fingers with each new
pass.

He squeezed his eyes shut as he spoke. His feet
shifted, his body moved constantly, a hand on his hip,
then his neck, kneading, finally back to his hair again.
As if movement were the only thing keeping him sane.

Della had fled to the kitchen, ostensibly to get
them all a glass of wine. Simone needed something
mind-numbing.

This was a crisis. An emotional one. Della hid from
it in the kitchen. Simone wasn't doing any better. But
Chloe, she'd turned out to be a godsend for more than
Our Manor of the Ladies.

Chloe patted the couch beside her. Simone wanted to
touch Brax, anything to ease his tense shoulders and the
harsh slash across his brow. That moment of closeness in
the hallway, when he'd let her cup his cheek, had passed.

By the time he'd concluded the call, Simone had
taken Chloe's offer, accepting the woman's comforting arm around her shoulders.

Brax turned. Anguish and anger lit his eyes. She had

the feeling he could smash his fist into the wall and not even feel the physical pain. Then he cleared his throat, pointed in the general direction of Carl's office trailer, and said, "I'll look for those papers."

Simone half rose to follow him. Chloe pulled her back down.

"Let him go, honey."

"I have to do something. He's hurting so bad, Chloe."

"He needs to fight his demons by doing. It's a man's way. So let him alone to do what he has to."

Simone pulled back, examining Chloe's soft, powdered face. "How'd you get to be so smart about men?"

Chloe smiled. "It's my job, sweetie pie. What you have to do for him is be strong and take care of his sister because he can't do it right now."

The kindly madam pricked Simone's conscience with that directive. "I don't know how to deal with Maggie's grief."

"Nobody does, sweetie. What do you think you ought to do?"

"Wait here until Maggie wakes up or her mother arrives."

"That's the secret. Be there for them when they need you."

Simone managed a small smile. "Chloe, you amaze me." Simone would stay as long as Brax and Maggie needed her.

Chloe patted Simone's shoulder to indicate all was settled, then raised her voice to call, "Della, where's that wine?"

MAGGIE HAD SAID Carl always left his keys in the bowl when he came in. The broken bowl. One of the ladies

had cleared the mess away while Brax had tucked Maggie into bed.

The keys weren't in the bowl. Shit, he'd really lost his ability to think clearly. He should have asked Teesdale for Carl's personal effects. His keys would have been among them. He'd be damned if he'd go charging back to ask. What would it matter now to Carl if he broke the trailer door down? After first testing to make sure it was locked, Brax retrieved a crowbar out of his SUV.

Damn, it was liberating not to have to worry about obtaining a search warrant.

The weather-strip was degraded, the door loose. Brax popped it open with a minimum of effort or damage. After two days closed up in the summer sun, the air inside the trailer gushed out hot and fetid. Drawn shades suffused the place with an eerie gloom despite the early-evening light outside.

He put a hand on the doorjamb, a foot on the metal step, and paused. He'd search the place because he had to give Maggie some sort of peace, and because doing something pushed out the memory of her tear-streaked face. Finally, he hauled himself inside. Conducting a visual inspection of the small trailer, he felt along the left wall for the light switch and flipped it on.

Damn. Carl was exceptionally neat. Or rather he *had* been.

Obviously a false assumption, Brax had presumed the neatness in the house was due to Maggie. The desk, a battered Salvation Army variety, was clear of scattered papers and files, with only a closed spiral notebook off to one side. Not even a speck of dust lurked at the base of the computer. A small bottle of air squirt

for cleaning keyboards sat by the monitor and next to that, a spray can of glass cleaner. A bottle of aspirin, a pencil holder, magnetic paper clip dispenser and a Post-it pad neatly lined the edge of the calendar blotter. The blank calendar squares stared up at him, providing no clues as to Carl's schedule.

Beside the too-neat desk sat an equally empty trash can lined with white plastic.

If a kitchen or dining nook had ever existed in the trailer, Carl had long since torn them out. Pale blue indoor-outdoor tiles carpeted the floor. A door at one end led presumably to the bathroom. A large, slanted drafting table abutted one wall with four wooden four-drawer filing cabinets, scarred but polished to a glossy shine, lined up next to it.

The drafting table drew Brax's gaze. Three topographical maps covered its surface, each held down with sliding clamps. Carl had written no notes in the margins, but had marked several spots with a red X. Outhouse excavation? Brax discerned that the marked spots were not within Goldstone township, but located in the vast hills and valleys. Caves? He surmised that each X registered a potential site for one of Carl's spelunking sojourns.

The maps neither proved nor disproved murder. They simply confirmed what everyone said; Carl had taken up spelunking. Brax turned from that dead end to the filing cabinets.

The first cabinet contained past tax returns for the last seven years, as required by law, all neatly labeled with subfolders for various types of transactional backup.

Brax would return for further examination if neces-

sary. More importantly, he wanted Carl's bank statements, the siphoning off of money being the first thing Maggie had complained about. Before she'd ranted about the floozy.

His heart jumped into his throat, then beat a path to his gut. Damn it, he couldn't afford to think of Maggie in ranting terms. He was a cop; she was a citizen with a concern regarding her husband's death. Anything else screwed up his objectivity.

Hell, at this point, he needed to look up the definition of objectivity in the freaking dictionary.

He moved on to the next cabinet. Bingo. Hanging folders and files sorted by institution and account and filed by year. Damn, Carl had accounts with almost every major stock and investment establishment. What the hell?

Brax pulled out the first folder. He gave a long, low whistle upon opening it. A 401K account, the balance of which was more than Brax's net worth. He drew out the latest statement for each of the accounts and laid them on the drafting table, flipping through each to peruse the contents. When he was done, a quick calculation rounded to the nearest ten thousand staggered him.

Carl had almost a million dollars spread out in bonds, stocks, real estate partnerships, gold coins. The diversification ran the gamut. He even owned railroad cars, for God's sake.

Where had Carl gotten the money for all this? Maggie had said they were doing fine, but this was far more than fine. This was unseemly, given the fact that they lived in a trailer in a broken-down town full of losers. Why was Carl, a rich man, hiding out in the desert?

Hiding out? Running from an embezzlement scheme? Brax was developing a melodramatic streak in his old age.

Maggie wanted answers. The first answer was going to have to come from her. Where had the money come from and why hadn't she told him the full extent? She was his sister, and this investigation was personal, and he resented the hell out of being kept in the dark.

The minor irritation washed away the residual ache and galvanized his actions. He flipped through the checking account statement. Carl had withdrawn cash at regular intervals. How could he spend three hundred bucks at a whack? Brax pressed the computer's on button. Carl, unbelievably, had jotted down the user ID and password on the inside cover of each account folder.

Did he think that feeble lock on his trailer door would keep out anyone bent on ransacking his financials?

The computer booted up, then requested a password. Brax snorted. He was no hacker. Thank goodness all he had to do was open the spiral notebook neatly placed to one side of the desk. Sure enough, there it was, along with his e-mail codes.

Carl, where the hell was your head when you wrote this down?

Brax typed in *onehotmama*, trying not to think about what it meant. He accessed the Internet, requested the site, and punched in Carl's ID and password for his checking account, then scrolled through the transactions, starting with the most recent. A few checks had cleared, an ATM withdrawal, a branch withdrawal—

Holy shit.

Carl drew out three thousand dollars the morning he died.

CHAPTER THIRTEEN

DAMMIT. CARL HAD withdrawn three thousand in cash. *Three thousand.* Then he'd gone for a hike? In Brax's gut, the man's actions didn't make sense.

Carl and Maggie had been having marital problems. Maggie had reamed him. Carl displayed an overzealous reaction to a dart game and a proposed resort. Then he'd cashed out three thousand dollars and fallen off the side of a mountain.

Coincidence? Not in Brax's experience. Though he believed her reasons for crying murder were due more to her own sense of guilt, Maggie might be right.

Could the money have been on him when he died? Did Teesdale take it? Brax thought the sheriff incompetent, but not a thief. More importantly, Carl's unidentified assailant would have gotten to the money first. Before the chickens and way before Teesdale.

Dammit, dammit. Brax should have known something more was up than ten years of marriage becoming routine. Carl had bled the bank account for weeks in small but consistent amounts. Maggie had told Brax that, and the statements confirmed it.

Money and murder went hand in hand.

Brax, for his part, had wanted only to smooth things over, bring the issue to a swift resolution, and get back

to his vacation. He'd fobbed his responsibilities off on a bestselling relationship book. He'd *planned* to give his sister short shrift.

Now Carl was lying in Teesdale's basement. Jesus. He should have done something. Anything. Instead, he'd fucked up his duties.

Same as he had in Cottonmouth. He'd ignored signs screaming at him.

His initial thought was to wake up Maggie. Now. She had to know more than she'd told him. Her husband had a net worth of almost a million, and, by her own admission, she checked his balances online. Did she know about all the accounts? Why was she hiding shit from him when she'd flat-out asked for his help?

One last unbearable thought pounded at him.

Had Maggie discovered the withdrawal, then followed Carl up that trail, and fought with him about it?

He was a cop, and the golden rule was look to those closest to the victim first.

He would not follow the rule with his own family, and he didn't give a goddamn what anyone said about that. He'd make damn sure Teesdale didn't follow it, either. Brax's gut told him Maggie's reactions were born of guilt over her last words to Carl. If she'd had anything to do with his death, then for the last two days, she'd given the performance of an Academy Award winning actress. No. No one could have faked her reactions along the way. Not the ballistic anger, nor the disabling pain. Maggie had denied to herself that Carl was dead, then she'd cooked up the murder scenario. To appease her own guilt. That was all. Nothing more.

So where the hell was the money?

The cash or a paper trail leading to it had to be

somewhere in Carl's office. When Brax found it, he'd tackle Maggie. In the morning, when she'd made it through this first hellish night and the temporary oblivion provided by Xanax.

He closed his eyes, took a deep breath, draining his anger as he exhaled. Emotion, whether it was anger, self-pity or guilt, interfered with a job to be done. It always fucked up an investigation, and he damn well couldn't afford the luxury of self-recrimination. He needed a clear head.

Brax flipped through the notebook. Carl had written down, presumably, every credit card he possessed and his insurance policies, with contact name and number, from home owners to car, including a life policy. The pen used appeared to be the same, black, with the same degree of legibility, as if Carl had cited all the pertinent information in one fell swoop.

Why? Nobody was this methodical. Even Brax, who considered himself relatively organized, would have to scour his wallet to obtain each and every credit card number. Thank God the billfold had never been stolen. Had Carl truly been about to leave Maggie and written out the data in order to help her pick up the pieces once he was gone?

Brax found the remaining pages of the notebook empty. He opened each desk drawer on the right side to uncover only the usual assortment of office supplies. Almost the usual. A calligraphy set lay in the bottom left drawer. Calligraphy didn't seem Carl's style. Nor did the fact that he owned an extensive quantity of colored pens.

He started on the left-hand drawers, only to find more of the same innocuous reserve of office supplies,

and a well-read science-fiction book by a guy named Waldo Whitehead. Brax recognized the author and the name of the book, *Death Game,* from the bestsellers lists. Damn, the title was strangely prophetic. Carl hadn't struck him as a reader, and a desk drawer was an odd place for it. He flipped through, hoping for a secret cache of notes that would explain everything. Yeah. He could hope, but he was a cop, and he knew things were never that easy. The book contained nothing of interest. He left it on the desktop.

Shoving the rolling chair back from the desk, Brax returned once more to the filing cabinets. If Carl had been idiotic enough to write down all his passwords and methodical enough to detail all his credit facts, he might also have written down, in detail, what he'd used the money for. Hopefully including the three thousand he'd withdrawn yesterday morning.

The answer had to be somewhere in this goddamn trailer.

He yanked open the first drawer on the third filing cabinet. It contained documentation on major purchases, the cars, a new stove, the Jacuzzi on the sunporch. He'd kept every warranty booklet and instruction manual for everything he owned, right down to the four-slice toaster he'd bought over three years ago. In alphabetical order by type of purchase, the booklets filled the entire cabinet, though Carl hadn't crammed the drawers, leaving plenty of space in between for new additions.

He had not, however, documented any new purchases beyond those expenditures he'd made for his spelunking equipment. As Maggie had testified, he'd used his credit card for those items, and the last major purchase had been made over four months ago.

No three thousand anywhere and no accounting for where the money had gone. Nor anything indicating what he'd done with smaller amounts he'd taken out over the last few months. Shit.

The fourth cabinet turned out to be empty, as if Carl had planned for future expansion. At least, Brax presumed it to be empty until he got to the bottom drawer.

A paper grocery sack had been shoved in but not squashed down. Two spools of ribbon, one red, one silver, their unsecured ends curling, lay on top.

Paper sack. Something about a paper bag…and… and…ah, he had it. Carl came in with a grocery bag the night of the Big Fight. Maggie had accused him of buying porno magazines to entertain himself. Carl had not revealed what was in that bag.

Brax batted aside the spools of ribbon and lifted out the bag, taking it over to the drafting table. Too light to hold even one magazine, he unfolded the evenly turned down opening.

Heavy-weight, antiqued scrolls, each tied in a bow with a red or silver ribbon, filled the bag to capacity. He pulled out one, marked with the calligraphed number six. The bag, in total, gave up twenty rolls, each with a number painstakingly written in a different color on the right end.

Hence the calligraphy set and the unusual number of pens. Every detail an investigation uncovered always had a reason. A detective just had to find out what it was.

Brax scattered the scrolls, prowling through them until he located number one. He stared at it far longer than necessary, his belly screaming with that bad feeling common to cops and people snooping where they didn't belong.

The ribbon knotted when he tried to undo the bow. In the end, he slipped it off, the bright red cascading to the floor. Unfurling the paper, he pressed it flat to the table. The ridiculous curlicue font, made more difficult to read by the fact that it was in bold, confounded him for a moment. He flipped on the desk lamp attached to the top of the drafting table, and the words suddenly jumped out at him.

He followed three paces behind her, leaving room between so that he could watch the play of sinuous calf muscle as she walked. Her short skirt barely covered her butt cheeks, her bare legs smooth and tan, and her boots topped with bulky hiking socks.

Jesus. This could not be what he thought it was. He kept reading.

The contrast of feminine to utilitarian raised his temperature. Sex was about alluring contrasts and minute sensuous details. A soft breeze blew across his back, then caught the hem of her skirt, lifting it. He'd hoped for a tantalizing glimpse of silk. Instead, he was rewarded with firm, delightful flesh.

Brax folded his arms, laying his head down. Damn, damn. The fantasy. Simone had written it. He'd know that voice anywhere. He'd dreamed the words of her Web site teaser over and over. Her writing was unmistakable. He forced himself to read on.

She scooped at the skirt, laughing and turning to him. "Oops. Guess I forgot my underwear." God, he wanted her. Here, now, under the hot sun, against the warm earth.

Brax read until there was nothing left to read. To his everlasting shame, his jeans bulged with a painful erection. Though the room was empty, he felt like a voyeur. He'd eavesdropped on Carl's fantasy.

On Simone's fantasy.

Jesus, he could only pray it wasn't their fantasy. Simone and Carl. God, no. He could pray, but he was beyond hope.

The woman in that fantasy was not Maggie. Yes, Maggie had blond hair, but there, the similarities ended. Simone had described herself. She'd beefed Carl up to stud status, letting him do his fantasy lover bit six times in different spots along a mountain trail. He'd managed to come six times, too.

Six sex scenes in the space of twenty pages, all so vivid that Brax had a hard time not imagining himself doing those things.

Godammit. She'd written a sex fantasy for Carl. Brax had known it, in his heart and gut, he'd known. He'd wanted to believe she wrote it for Maggie and Carl, starring Maggie and Carl, the way Doodle had said Simone wrote snippets for his wife.

Goddamn Simone.

That woman was not Maggie. No forty-two-year-old woman could possibly contort her body into those positions. He wasn't sure a twenty-year-old could, either. That was definitely not Maggie.

Shit, shit, shit. The money, the withdrawals, now

this. Why had Carl printed each page out on fancy paper, then rolled them into a scroll and tied them with a fricking ribbon? Godammit.

At first, he retied the ribbons. Five pages in, he no longer gave a damn. The untied scrolls had rerolled themselves and cascaded to the floor as he tossed them aside. They crackled beneath his quick stride to the computer.

His flesh hot, his body aching, he booted up Carl's e-mail program, flipping back to find the password page in the spiral notebook. Sure enough, the e-mail sign-ons were there, too. Brax typed them in, then perused the e-mails in each of Carl's folders. Nothing from Simone, nothing from her Web site. Carl hadn't saved the original message. And Brax wanted to see it. He needed to see where the hell that fantasy came from. He had to have it before he accused her.

But Carl had left no trail. He'd documented every goddamn detail of his life, but he hadn't kept Simone's e-mail. Brax clenched his fist with the need to pound the desk in frustration. Afterwards, he could never say why he decided to download Carl's unread e-mails.

He waited an eternity for fifty-two e-mails. When they hit the in-box, most could immediately be marked as spam. Only one held any meaning for Brax.

An e-mail from Simone's Web address. His fingers trembled as he guided the mouse and clicked.

"If you're planning what I think you're planning, you are dead meat. And I do mean dead meat. Rotten, maggot-infested, buzzard bait."

Her words hit him like a left jab to his jaw.

Jesus H. Christ. Simone had threatened Carl. Now Carl was dead. Buzzard bait, just as she'd said.

SIMONE HEARD a car engine turn over, but by the time she'd rushed to the window, the drive was empty. Brax's SUV was gone.

"Where's he going?"

Della came to stand at her side. They both stared out into the dusk.

"I don't know." An obvious answer, unless Della thought she'd suddenly become a mind reader. Where he'd gone was less important than why he'd rushed off without coming back inside. Brax had found something in Carl's trailer, but what? And why had it sent him driving off without a word?

A shiver ran across Simone's shoulders, and she rubbed her arms to dampen the trail of goose bumps.

BRAX CHARGED INTO Teesdale's office to find the man perusing the pages of a magazine. He'd changed from his rumpled uniform to casual and left his hat on the credenza behind him. He read for another thirty seconds before closing the periodical and setting it on his desk. Gently.

"Have a seat, Braxton."

Brax didn't take a seat nor did he start his questions in the order of priority. He'd leave Carl's personal effects, including the cash, for last. A whammy at the end.

Wrong. The most important question was for Simone. He'd whammy her *after* Teesdale.

"You're not insisting on an autopsy just to piss me off, are you." It was not a question.

Teesdale put his feet on his desk, crossing his ankles. The tread of his boots had almost worn through. "It's routine."

"Bullshit."

Arching a brow, he said, "What makes *you* think we need an autopsy? Not two hours ago, you seemed mighty against it. For your sister's sake, I think you said."

"Carl's the only witness to the event, and I want to know what his body testifies to." In the basement, he'd been thinking with his heart instead of his head. He couldn't bury it in the sand anymore. The money shouted foul play. Foul play shouted Maggie's name. Then of course, there was Simone and the fantasy. And that e-mail. He'd get involved because he had to.

It never occurred to him to simply cover up what he already knew.

"Bullshit," Teesdale mimicked. Then he flexed his jurisdictional muscles, though he kept his tone mild. "You think you know something. Better tell me or I'll have to throw you in a cell for obstructing justice."

Fighting words, but the sheriff's lackadaisical manner and attitude suggested he didn't care one way or the other what Brax knew or what the autopsy might reveal.

"Let's work together on this." Not wanting Teesdale mucking with things at this point, he'd keep Carl's finances to himself until he could pigeonhole the sheriff's abilities. "Tell me when the autopsy's scheduled for."

"When the M.E. gets back from his conference." The sheriff leaned forward, flipped a couple of pages on his day calendar. "Saturday, probably."

Three fricking days. "Doesn't he have an assistant that can do it?"

Teesdale snorted, then outright laughed. "Yeah, right."

"You don't seem too fucking concerned about it."

The man shrugged. "You work with what you've got."

"Where the hell is Carl now? Still down in the basement?"

"The boys from Bullhead picked him up an hour ago. Don't worry, he'll be patiently awaiting our M.E."

Worry? He was goddamn crazy with the scenarios racking his brain. Scenarios involving his sister. Or Simone.

Dammit, he should have examined Carl's body closely.

"Three days isn't good enough, and you know it, Teesdale."

"Sit down, Braxton," he said, with more force than previously. The sheriff put his feet on the floor and rolled his chair closer to the desk.

Brax sat, not in deference to Teesdale's command, but due to the weight of his own failures sitting heavy on his shoulders. He'd fucked up royally. He hadn't checked Carl's body. He hadn't asked any questions about the crime scene. He hadn't even considered that there *was* a crime scene. With the four chickens riding their dirt bikes through the gorge, and probably a horde of lookie-loos, any evidence would now be obliterated.

In short, he hadn't adhered to the training of a long career in law enforcement. He would not, however, allow further self-recrimination to get in the way now.

"I'm going to interview the chickens and go over the site where they found him, including the spot from which he presumably fell." He'd have to ask the girls about the money, too. Even chickens might be tempted.

There was Lafoote's involvement to be considered, as well, the hotel being the big money game in town.

"I've got it handled."

He didn't give a damn if he was stepping on the sheriff's toes. "This is more serious than following a trail of Twinkies wrappers to Mud Killian's doorstep."

"You don't say?" Teesdale drawled.

Brax wasn't in the mood for a pissing contest. He wanted to do right by his sister. The money Carl withdrew shouted out that Maggie was right. Carl hadn't tripped and fallen over the edge of the cliff. "Let me give you the benefit of my recent experience." His stomach cramped, his words a reminder of why, besides Maggie's plea, he'd wanted this hellish trip in the first place. "The faster we move on this, the more likely we are to bring it to a satisfactory conclusion. Every tick of the clock is our enemy."

For the first time, Teesdale reacted with something more than a drawl or a negligent wave of his hand. His jaw tightened and nostrils flexed. "I have a helluva lot more experience in my left toe than you've had in a lifetime."

"I'm sure Goldstone has been a gold mine for you."

Teesdale curled his lip. "L.A. Ten years. RHD."

Shit. LAPD, Robbery-Homicide Division. Ten years. Had he been washed out? Probably. LAPD to tiny, forgotten County Sheriff wasn't just a step down, it was a fall into the abyss.

Teesdale leaned forward, narrowed his eyes, his teeth gleaming through a mirthless smile that looked like something on a death's head. "I can see you're dying to know what I did to get the boot out here."

"Yeah, sure, why don't you tell me?" The story ob-

viously stood between him and what he needed Teesdale to do on Carl's death investigation. He'd hear the
man out, then get on with business.

"You got any gangbangers in Cottonmouth, Sheriff
Braxton?" Teesdale used the title as a slur.

Brax had faced worse than gangs. A suspect list
consisting of people he'd known for years. People he
considered friends, yet suspects in the murder of a respected man they'd all known.

"I can see you think you've got your share of shit.
And maybe you do. But you ain't seen nothing till you
see what they're capable of."

"I'm sure Goldstone is…" He'd been about to say
"more your speed," but thought better of the sarcasm.
Obviously Teesdale had seen things the ordinary citizen couldn't comprehend. "Preferable," he said instead.

"Preferable, yeah." Teesdale punctuated with a short
bark of laughter. "There are a lot of things preferable
to digging an eight-year-old girl out of the city dump
where her killers tossed her body like trash after rap-
ing her until they'd damn near ripped her in two, and
then slammed a lead pipe into her head so many times
it looked like a squashed pumpkin."

Brax had been wrong. There were worse things.

The sheriff's voice dropped, and his gaze focused
on something far beyond Brax's shoulder, memories
long in the past but never forgotten. "We got them.
Four. Fifteen, fourteen, eleven and ten. Minors." He
swallowed, his Adam's apple sliding with difficulty
past a lump in his throat. "I testified, but I didn't wait
for the verdict, never even read about it. Got out of
there the next day."

Brax didn't blame him for that.

Teesdale closed his eyes, a shudder twitching his shoulders. "My little girl was eight at the time." Then he stared Brax down with a dark-eyed, crazy-man look that only a father could wear. "You can bet your goddamn ass I'd rather be trailing Twinkies wrappers to Mud Killian's door than dreaming about my little girl topped with nothing but a squashed pumpkin head."

Teesdale hadn't been drummed out. He hadn't run away. He'd done the only thing a man afraid for his sanity could do, the very thing a father *would* do.

Brax was used to meeting glare for glare, did it all the time and always came out on top in the exchange. This was different. This was beyond his ken. Teesdale was right. Despite being a cop, Brax's world didn't contain children who preyed with such viciousness upon other children. Monsters made out of little boy parts. Jesus H. Christ.

"Carl withdrew three thousand dollars out of his checking account yesterday morning before he went hiking."

"Throwing me a bone, Braxton, because my little story tugged at your heartstrings?"

"Nope." Though it had. "Just asking for help from the good Sheriff of Emerald County." He'd intended to slam the sheriff with the cash thing, but Teesdale's brief story changed that plan. Given the choice between gangbangers or Mud, Brax would have taken to trailing Twinkies wrappers himself. The man would know his craft after his years of experience, and Brax's best hope for keeping Maggie safe was to work with him rather than against him. "How old is your daughter now?"

Sheriff Elwood Teesdale smiled and dropped five years' worth of lines from his face. "Almost sixteen. She's the prettiest little thing I've ever seen. Already planning which college she wants to go to. I'm thinking Stanford. She's as smart as a whip. Wants to be a doctor."

"I'm sure she'll be whatever she sets out to be."

"Yeah." He sat back in his chair and folded his hands across his belly, once more the contented small town sheriff whose biggest case involved Twinkies and a perp called Mud. "Now, about that cash. Maggie have any idea what he used it for?" Teesdale asked.

"She's sedated. I'll ask her as soon as it's possible. But I'm not holding out that she'll have any useful answers." He *knew* she wouldn't. "Don't suppose you found an easy three thousand on the body or in the truck?" The question had to be asked even if he knew the answer would be in the negative. The whereabouts of the cash lay in the identity of Carl's killer.

"I'd have given it a mention if I did," Teesdale said dryly.

"Yeah, I'm sure you would have." He met the sheriff's gaze head-on, and those few seconds belied the near accusation in his question. Teesdale would have demanded where the hell it came from. Not salted it away.

"I plan on dropping by the bank tomorrow to see if anyone remembers seeing Carl," Brax said.

The sheriff didn't pull the old "stay out of my case" thing. "Good idea."

Brax couldn't say he'd been having a whole helluva lot of good ideas lately. "Now tell me why you want the autopsy."

Clasping his hands over his belly and drumming his fingers, Teesdale didn't answer directly. "I take it you think the money is talking murder instead of a simple fall."

"I take it you'd agree with me on that." Brax stared him down and waited.

Teesdale rolled his lips, wriggled his mouth, let out a long sigh, then gave Brax what he'd both been afraid of and needed to know. "Carl had an odd depression on the side of his head."

Brax didn't have to ask if it was on the side the critters had been at. He'd have noticed anything on Carl's good side.

"I'm no medical examiner, but I've seen crushed skulls before and this wasn't caused by any rock he hit on the way down. Too uniform, in my opinion. Like he'd been struck *with* something rather than landing *on* something."

"The sooner we get that autopsy then, the better. We'll need time of death." Maggie had been out during the morning and part of the afternoon, returning in time to dress, then drag Brax off to the tea party.

She didn't have an alibi if Carl had died before two o'clock.

"I've got a call in that might help speed things up."

Brax almost laughed. The sheriff *had* been giving him a hard time. He didn't bother to ask what that call might do. This was Teesdale's jurisdiction, and with LAPD RHD under his belt, the man had a right to it. Hell, he'd know all the back doors in his own county.

Brax broached another topic on his mind. "What do you think of Jason Lafoote?"

"As our man?" At Brax's nod, Teesdale snorted. "No motive."

It was a long shot, but the only one Brax had. "Carl told me he got the judge to hold up those permits." In as many words. "Could be Lafoote held it against him."

Teesdale stroked his chin. "Doesn't make sense. What would be the point? Della would still stand in the way. If it was Della at the bottom of the gorge, now that'd make some sense."

"With Carl out of the way, Lafoote could have been hoping Della would change her mind."

"Too much risk that she wouldn't. If the permitting, or lack thereof, was the motive, doesn't make sense he'd hit Carl first."

Nothing made sense at the moment. A sense of the situation only came after hours and sometimes days of investigation of the small, seemingly meaningless details.

"Why don't you see what a background check on Lafoote comes up with?" Brax phrased it as a question rather than an order. It was still Teesdale's case.

"It couldn't hurt," the sheriff agreed.

Brax came to his next question. He hated to do it to Maggie, but it had to be asked. "Any gossip around town about Carl and another woman?"

Teesdale chuckled, though Brax couldn't find the humor in it. "Not a whiff of that kind of thing. I guarantee you, if Carl was stepping out, we'd all know about it."

"The judge doesn't seem to think it's out of the realm of possibility."

"Della." Teesdale rolled his eyes. "Men aren't high on her list. She even thought I was having an affair two years ago when my wife went to L.A. to visit her mother. Told me I oughta stop my cheating ways and beg forgiveness."

"You got any other bright ideas?"

"If I did, I wouldn't be sitting here on my ass."

Shit. He'd been hoping Teesdale's Goldstone knowledge would provide some leads. "I'll still give Lafoote a try. Tomorrow." Tonight, he had other priorities. Maggie and Simone. "First thing tomorrow, I want to go up to the trail above the site." Doing it now, in the dark, might destroy any evidence.

"I was planning on heading out about seven. Think you can be up that early?"

The sheriff should have already made the trek up there, but it was too damn late to make recriminations. "I'll be there. At the trailhead where you found his truck." Early was good, he'd make it back in time to be at the bank close to opening.

Brax rose, then stuck out his hand, neither apology nor guilt, simply acceptance.

Teesdale stood, took the offering, shaking hard and fast.

"Find anything interesting in the truck or his personal effects?" If the depression in Carl's head didn't come from the fall, then everything he'd had on his person constituted potential evidence.

Teesdale tipped his head and pushed his hat farther back on his head. "Funny thing about that truck. Carl's fingerprints were missing off the door handle and the steering wheel. At least on the spots where they should have been."

So, Teesdale had dusted. Good.

"And funny thing about his keys."

Brax waited out the good ole boy routine. Being a cop, he appreciated that stringing things out garnered more reaction.

"Can't find those keys. Weren't in his pocket." Teesdale looked down, then wriggled his hand into the front pocket of his jeans. "Funny thing about pockets on a pair of jeans. Things don't slip out easily." He glanced up. "Carl was wearing jeans. And I checked 'em. Not tight, but tight enough, if you catch my drift." The set of car keys he pulled out caught on the upper edge of his pocket, held, then pulled free.

"Was he wearing a jacket? Maybe he took it off up on the trail."

"Yeah," the sheriff snorted. "A likely scenario. He got overheated, pulled off his jacket, slipped on a rock while he was struggling to get his arm out of the sleeve and fell all the way down. Of course, the jacket managed to disengage before he actually tumbled."

"Won't know until we get there. Seven. I'll be there."

He left the office. The sheriff's chair squeaked behind him.

Brax had one thing to be grateful for. The sheriff had never mentioned talking to Maggie regarding her whereabouts at all times during the day Carl had taken a dive off that trail.

In the parking lot, Brax stuck his hand in his pocket for his keys. The night had grown cooler, but not cool enough to warrant a jacket. His car keys had gone into his front pocket. Reaching down for them, he didn't figure they'd have fallen out even if someone had turned him upside down and dumped him on his head.

So what had happened to Carl's keys?

Brax stopped at The Chicken Coop before heading back to Maggie's place. As Teesdale had claimed, the chickens added nothing new to the mix. Brax hadn't

expected anything more, but not questioning them would have been dereliction of duty.

Only when he was back in his car and headed along the highway to Maggie's did Brax allow himself to think about Simone.

Simone, spinner of fantasies. Simone, who'd sent Brax's now-dead, apparently murdered brother-in-law a threatening e-mail. Not just threatening. Pissed as hell.

Which was how Brax felt as he thought once more about that salacious fantasy.

He'd have a few choice words for the author before the night was over. He'd get some answers even if he had to interrogate her with a light in her face like some zealous, forties-style cop.

CHAPTER FOURTEEN

SIMONE WISHED she was a nail biter or a hand wringer, but her mother had drummed both bad habits out of her at an early age. Either gesture would have helped ease some of the tension she now felt. Brax had come home. He drove up, but hadn't entered the trailer, not for an interminable ten minutes.

When he did finally come in, a paper bag crushed beneath one arm, Brax had pointed at her, told her to get her stuff, and said he'd drive her home. Then, as if belatedly remembering manners, he'd asked Chloe to stay with Maggie for a little while longer.

No one argued, not even Simone. Chloe shooed her out with a flap of both hands.

Now the paper bag sat on the armrest between them. She trapped the questions racing through her mind in her aching, parched throat. Half her brain wanted to know all the answers. Now. The other half, left or right, she couldn't be sure, wanted to crawl into the backseat, lie down and sob until neither a tear nor a single thought remained.

The silence in the 4Runner shouted out her guilt.

She'd betrayed Maggie by writing that fantasy. Instead of bringing Carl and Maggie together in bliss as

she'd intended, Simone had most likely driven a wedge of lies between them.

Her tummy flip-flopped up and down with every movement of the wheel. It sank, then climbed back up to her throat. It wasn't a clichéd description, but an actual roller coaster in her stomach. That same sudden seesawing fear that hit upon first realizing you'd done a terrible thing or made a horrible mistake. It could be a life-on-the-line thing like changing lanes only to suddenly hear the shimmy of air brakes and see that semi's grill up close and personal in your rearview mirror and not being able to figure out where it came from. Or it could be something as simple as suddenly remembering the Visa bill was due yesterday.

That's how she knew she'd done a very bad thing to Maggie and Carl. Now Brax knew, too, signs of his knowledge riding his tensed lips and his narrowed eyes. He bore the implacable cop look of a patrolman who'd stopped her for speeding. He didn't even need the mirrored sunglasses to pull it off. That look and the paper sack between them chanting "open, open, open" said it all. It wasn't a funny commercial running through her head.

He wheeled into the gravel drive and came to a stop behind her truck, boxing her in should she try to escape.

He reached across her, yanked her door handle, his arm brushing her belly. She shrank at the contact and his stiff command, "Inside."

Not "get out of the car," or "could we please go inside and talk," just that hard-edged order.

In other circumstances, she would have given him the finger and a dirty word. Instead, she had only one

thought. *I wrote a fantasy, Carl's dead, and I sent him an e-mail saying he'd be buzzard bait.*

Okay, that was three thoughts. If she could have limited it to one, she might have been able to forgive herself.

Brax stood at the passenger side door, holding it open, waiting. So intent on her own thoughts, she hadn't moved, hadn't heard him shut his own door or seen him walk around to her side.

She climbed out, staring at his chest then his boots as she clutched her purse to her chest.

He graciously extended his arm for her to proceed, but slammed the car door. She'd left her door unlocked, stupid girl. Jason Lafoote's obnoxious aftershave still wafted out as she opened the screen, as if he'd been waiting once again on the sunporch. Of course, that could have been from the other night. The man's essence lingered like a bad smell.

The sun having gone down behind the hills, her trailer lay in near darkness. She flipped the light switch to banish both the intimacy and the fear.

Of course, her fear remained. Her beloved Goldstone had been struck by tragedy. Tragedy always came in threes.

She hadn't cleaned up. The sofa cushions were askew from her mad search for the portable phone. Last night's wineglass sat on the coffee table, lipstick stains smudging the rim and the evaporated remains of white zinlike sludge at the bottom. Cracker crumbs dotted the wood surface.

Brax bypassed her, dropping his paper bag onto the table. It landed with the soft plop of lightweight contents.

He pointed to the couch. "Sit."

She wasn't a dog, but she sat obediently, legs together primly, feet curled up against the sofa bottom, and hands clasped on her thighs.

Brax did not ease her discomfort by sitting beside her. He remained standing, the overhead light behind his head keeping his eyes in shadow.

"The fantasy you wrote for Carl. Tell me about it."

She twisted her hands in her lap. The fantasy. The bane of her existence, the harbinger of bad things to come. "Didn't we already go over that the other night?" Sort of?

"Quite frankly, I don't remember what the fuck we went over the other night. All I remember is kissing you. Then finding out Carl is dead the next day."

Bam, bam, bam. He shot her down, picked her back up, then blew her away, all with three devastating sentences.

She didn't know what to say. The ridiculous urge to hum a toneless tune came over her, but she held it at bay. Maybe if he hadn't given her such an open-ended question. "Could you ask me something that requires a yes or no answer, because I really don't know where to start." Her eyes started to cloud up.

"How about this?" He bent, grabbed the grocery bag, ripped the top open, and dumped the contents on her coffee table.

Rolled pieces of paper scattered all over the table and onto the carpet, some squashed, some in perfect scrolls, others tied with pretty silver and red ribbons.

She touched one, picked it up gingerly, as if it were a snake that might sink its fangs into her if she moved too quickly.

"You did write that, didn't you?" He indicated the pile with a stab.

Unrolling a scroll, her own words jumped out at her.

He slid his fingers into her creamy center, taking her gasp of pleasure into his mouth, tasting his own essence on her tongue.

Oh my God, it was the end of the blow job scene. And the start of another one. She looked at Brax and almost asked if he'd read it. Oh my God, he'd probably read the whole story. *The whole darn story.* She blushed, heat spreading through her entire body. She remembered writing the scene. She remembered how she'd grown moist writing. It hadn't involved Maggie and Carl. There'd been only herself with her dream lover, and her body had ached for his touch. Her heart had ached for a figment of her imagination.

"That was a yes or no question."

"Ye-es." Her voice cracked.

"Did he give you instructions on what to write? Doodle says his wife gives you instructions."

She swallowed, but couldn't get her voice above a whisper. "Yes. And yes."

"How explicit were his instructions?"

"That's not yes or no." God, her voice sounded all wobbly, and hot tears burned at the backs of her eyes. She knew her reactions didn't make sense. But she couldn't think, she could only feel. Somehow, that fantasy she wrote for Carl set off a horrible chain reaction that led to him falling into the gorge. An untenable thought, but she couldn't help it.

Brax shoved the coffee table out of the way and hun-

kered down beside her. She realized she had been staring at the paper, the ink suddenly running down the page from three wet splats.

He took her forearm in a gentle but firm grip. "What did he tell you to write?"

She was going to start blubbering. Any minute. And then she wouldn't even be able to think, let alone talk. She rushed in before the onslaught. "He wanted something out in the open on a long walk. He described what he wanted the characters to look like and what they should be wearing and where he wanted them to stop, then he told me to make up the rest myself." She bit her lip and sniffed. "The...you know...the sex part."

Brax jerked to his feet, and with his back to her, ran both hands through his hair. Then he turned back to her, his eyes stark, pained. "What was he going to do with it?"

Her lip trembled. She sucked it in and bit down hard, hoping the pain would fight away the tears. Then everything inside her rushed out at once. "He was supposed to read it to Maggie. At least that's what I thought he was going to do. Della said Maggie was upset about stuff, and I could tell she was. Then Carl asked me to write a story and I thought it was for them, so that they could make everything better." She hiccuped and sniffled and started blubbering as she'd been afraid she would. "I wanted to make it all better, but neither of them would tell me anything. And it didn't sound like Maggie even knew about it. So I got scared he didn't have me write it for Maggie, but for someone else. That he'd been having an affair, and I'd actually written a story he read to some...some...bitch. Now he's dead, and I sent him the most awful e-mail. I feel so terrible."

Her nose ran, her eyes hurt, and beside her Brax smelled so good, like…well, it wasn't like anything she could describe, a little sweet, a little sharp, a clean male scent that made her want to bury her face against his shoulder.

"You sent him a nasty e-mail because you thought he'd tricked you into writing something for his lover. That's all you did. It wasn't a crime."

She sniffed and nodded and stared down at that paper with all her erotic fantasies and dreams running down the soggy page.

She'd failed. Again. Worse than putting all her eggs in one basket and losing her business, her career and her fiancé. Worse than being a screamer. She wanted to make things better for everyone, for Maggie, for Carl. She'd failed miserably at that.

And now Carl had died.

"If I hadn't written that fantasy, none of this would have happened."

He stroked a finger down her wet cheek and murmured in her ear. "You keep telling me I'm not to blame. Well, same goes for you. What happened to Carl wasn't your fault."

THE TENSION ACROSS Brax's shoulders eased. Simone was telling the truth.

She looked at him, mascara smudges beneath her eyes, her nose reddened, and tear tracks down her pink cheeks. "It's not?"

Money had played a role in Carl's demise. Brax felt the truth in that as if it were written in Carl's own blood. "Writing a fantasy for him doesn't make you responsible for his death."

Christ, he was an ass. He'd browbeaten her confession out of her only to find that she'd been playing The Good Witch of the North and waving her magic wand to fix everyone's problems.

If it were that easy, Maggie and Carl would have done it themselves. Simone had said it herself, but she hadn't believed her own words.

He smoothed one cheek dry even as another teardrop fell. "If he didn't use it the way you intended, that was his fault, not yours." He tapped the paper on her lap. "The fantasy is beautiful."

"Oh my God, you read it."

"Yeah, I read it."

"All of it?"

"Every single word."

She dropped her head, burying her face in her hands. "This is awful. This is so awful."

"I'm an idiot. I saw your last e-mail, and I wanted someone to blame for Maggie's pain." He touched her hair. "I was wrong."

She sniffled, then raised her head slightly to look at him, her hands still covering her mouth. "Did Carl kill himself?"

He had no idea how much to tell her, but he couldn't let her go on thinking that. "No." He pushed her hair away from her face. "Carl left behind a lot of unanswered questions, but that isn't one of them. Not in my mind."

"What about Sheriff Teesdale's mind?"

"Nobody thinks that. Whatever happened to Carl, he didn't do it to himself."

She shuddered and closed her eyes. "Did somebody kill him?"

"I…" Maggie would say it tomorrow, even if he didn't say it tonight. "It is my considered opinion that someone did."

Tears spilled over her lower lids once more. "Oh my God, oh my God. No one in Goldstone would hurt him. Nobody."

He steeled himself to handle her emotion. Simone would never do things half-measure. When she smiled, she did so from the inside out, and when she cried, she sobbed. Brax did the only logical thing he could. He sat beside her and gathered her into his arms. Pulling her onto his lap, he rode out the pain with her, whispering all the while, "Don't cry. It's okay. There's no need to cry. Don't cry."

But she didn't stop. Helplessly, he ran his hands up and down her back, through her hair, along her arms, but he couldn't stop the flow. She'd run from the big, bad city to the safety of Goldstone, and suddenly found that secure place she'd built for herself had fallen apart. Carl's death had rocked her trailer off its foundation.

His T-shirt moistened beneath the onslaught. Her body shook, and she pulled her legs onto the sofa, curling into him, into herself. Powerless to do more for her, he murmured soft nothings against her hair, pressing his lips to the silky strands.

When her sobs faded to snuffles against his chest, he raised her chin with his finger and kissed the tip of her nose.

"I'm a mess," she whispered, wiping beneath one eye.

"Yeah. Your nose looks as red as Rudolph's."

She laughed, then hiccuped. "I'm sorry for going off like that."

Her gentle laugh loosened the knot in his abdomen. "Don't be sorry." He pulled a tissue from the box on the side table. "Here. Blow."

That done, she held out her hand. He plucked another, which she used to wipe the mascara smudges from beneath her eyes.

"Trust a woman to have the tissue handy," he said, hoping to make her smile a little.

She did. Softly. Too sadly. "Sappy love stories always make me cry."

She'd admitted that, and he'd witnessed. She'd almost cried when Dorothy sang "Somewhere Over the Rainbow."

Balling the tissues, she put them on the table, then smoothed the flat of her hand down his chest. "I got your shirt all wet, and it's covered with lipstick."

"It'll dry, and lipstick won't show on the black."

"You're awfully understanding."

Right. The most he'd been able to do was let her cry in his arms.

"Thanks for letting me get that out."

She was thanking him for doing nothing? "It was my pleasure." He'd almost broken down himself. First Maggie, now Simone. He felt beaten to a pulp.

Her tangy shampoo tickled his nose, her bare skin against his arm heated him, and the gentle swell of her breasts suddenly seemed to mesmerize him. When she cried, he'd offered the comfort of touch. Now, with her lying across him, her breath caressing his neck, his body started doing some thinking of its own.

Shit. Maybe the right place, but certainly not the right time. He patted her arm in a hopefully comforting gesture, then tried to ease her off his lap.

She burrowed deeper, her face to his throat, her

arms wrapped around his neck. He didn't have the heart to push her away, and instead pulled her closer still. God, she smelled good. In a world that had suddenly gone rancid, she was fresh and clean and everything his mind and body craved.

A few more moments, that's all he'd take. One more deep breath to fill himself with her scent. He nuzzled her hair, then grazed her forehead with his lips. She tasted salty. In all that sobbing, she'd gotten her tears all over herself.

Damn, she was beautiful. She took him to a place where death, murder, pain, guilt and anger didn't exist. There was only her woman scent and her baby-soft skin.

Brax cupped her throat, tracing the line of her jaw with his fingers, then down to test her racing pulse.

SIMONE LIFTED HER HEAD.

She couldn't have said whether she raised her face or he tipped her chin, but their lips met. Mouths closed. Gentle. Sweet.

She felt as if she'd been alone and untouched forever. His taste was a balm to her soul. Just a kiss, just one.

She threaded her fingers through his hair, massaging his scalp. Then licked his lower lip. Only this. She wouldn't ask for more. He groaned, tightened his hold on her and opened his mouth to her tongue. He bent her over his arm, kissing her with his lips, his teeth and his tongue, his hands at her back, his chest to her breasts and his erection riding her hip.

Okay, so that was a little bit more than she'd planned, but God, she could almost believe he kissed

her with everything he had. Reverently. In a way she'd never been kissed except in her fantasies.

Her breasts rose and fell against his chest. Leaving her lips, he pulled back, his hot gaze touching her flushed skin. He trailed a finger down the slope of breast to the scooped neckline of her T-shirt.

Please, please, please, more.

But there he stopped. Waiting for her permission. Gentleman Brax. Darn it. She almost wished he'd do it, touch her, so she didn't have to make a decision.

What if she never got another chance? She'd die a shriveled prune. Living on fantasy didn't cut it. Not now. Maybe tomorrow, she could return to her Goldstone way of life. Right now, she needed Brax.

"Second base," she whispered. Then she guided his hand to her breast, cupping his palm over her tight nipple.

It wasn't enough. It was too much.

"Jesus," he breathed against her hair.

Lying back against the arm of the sofa, she offered herself like a meal. "I know I'm selfish, but I don't care right now. Please touch me." She was almost beyond thinking.

He smoothed a hand across the flesh above her T-shirt. "What happened to heightening the anticipation until we're crazy?"

What had happened to her sense of decorum? Poof, gone.

She bit her lip, wriggling in his lap. "This *is* crazy. We shouldn't. *I* shouldn't make you. I know Carl's gone, and Maggie's hurting terribly. I know it's wrong to want this." Wrong, yes, but she steered his hand once more to her breast, rubbing his finger back and forth against the tight, aching bud.

His blue eyes darkened, blazed with heat. "Don't think about the rest. Not right now." His body surged beneath her. "Just think about how goddamn much I want you."

His words. They were almost out of control. The way she felt.

Then he pulled aside the lace and cotton of her bra and bent his head to take her in his mouth. Crying out, she held him to her. He sucked her like candy, searching for the sweet center. Cradling her shoulders against his arm, he plumped her breast, stroking the underside with his thumb. Rough texture, but oh so sweet. He soothed her skin with his fingers, then took her nipple with his mouth and tongue.

She almost shouted with the pleasure, only at the last moment clamping down with her teeth on her lip. Raking both hands through his hair, she used the tips of her fingers, her nails. A soft moan fell from her lips.

He found the strip of exposed flesh above her waistband and dipped his finger into her belly button. It tickled. She jumped, her belly quivering with the anticipation. Fire exploded inside, consumed her.

He threw his head back and held her down, rocking his cock against her. "I want third base."

"I don't remember what it is." But she wanted it, whatever it was.

He stilled, his gaze roaming her stomach. "My hand in your panties."

"Yes, please." Her voice came as a tremulous whisper.

Shimmying, she pulled up her skirt for him, baring her need and her desire as blatantly as she revealed the white thong riding her hips and intimately cupping her sex.

"Want me, Brax. Want me badly. Until you feel like you're gonna scream if you don't have me."

With a fingertip, he traced her through the cotton panty, pushing deeper until he found the nub of her clitoris. A hum vibrated in her throat, and she tipped her head back, exposing her neck to his lips. He nipped, then licked, still playing her through her panties. Then he palmed her, shoving his hand between her thighs. Tightening her legs, trapping him, she soundlessly begged for more.

"Christ, you're hot down there."

She opened her eyes to his deep blue gaze. He was so beautiful. "Uh-huh."

Dragging his fingers over her once more, he teased the skin along the elastic line across her belly.

She lost every last one of her inhibitions as well as her fear. "It doesn't count as third base," she murmured, "unless you're inside my panties."

"What's it called when it's outside the panty?"

"It's called the shortstop tease, and it isn't a nice thing to do to a lady." She wasn't a lady, not the way he made her feel, not the way she wanted to cry out. But she didn't care. She wanted to feel good, for a little while.

He stroked back and forth, back and forth, until she thought she'd die if he didn't delve beneath the darn elastic. She wanted all of him.

He wasn't going to reject her. At least not yet, not until…later. She'd deal with it then.

He grinned down at her. "Are you sure it's not nice?"

Her skin tingled, and her body heated, moistened, readied. She became one of those heroines in her stories. She licked her lips, wriggling in hopes his fin-

gers might slip beneath the panty line. "I guess it's nice. But it could be a whole lot nicer."

"Isn't the anticipation better? The wanting, the needing, like your whole body's going to explode. The feeling that you'll die if I don't put my fingers inside your sweet, hot, wet—"

She snapped her hand over his mouth. "I think you're throwing my own words back at me." Slightly altered, of course. But oh my God, it was how she felt.

Pulling her hand away, he grinned like a feral animal, all white teeth and predatory eyes. "Yeah. Ain't it great?"

It was. She ached for his touch from the inside out. On its own, her body moved in rhythm to his stroke, building toward climax with nothing more than his heady male scent, the tactile memory of his mouth on her breast, and the rough texture of his big, beautiful hand against her stomach.

Don't think, just do.

She grabbed the back of his neck and pulled his head down until his mouth touched hers. "It's perfect." She nipped his lip. "Make it more perfect. Please. Pretty please." She shouldn't beg. Begging wasn't done. It suggested a girl was about to lose control.

Simone couldn't help herself.

She probed his mouth with her tongue, greedy for his taste, and pressed her breasts hard to his chest. Her heart raced and she gave voice to the breathless pant of approaching orgasm.

He tugged on her hip, working the panties down, while she wriggled, helping him and driving herself crazy with all the squirming.

Tingles like fireworks sparklers accompanied the

touch of his fingers all the way back up her calf and thigh. He slid a finger over her clitoris, then deep inside her, and she went off like a Fourth of July display. Thighs clamped, inner muscles contracting, spasming, she cried into his mouth with unladylike abandon. He took it all, took her kiss, made it his own, drank in her screams, devoured her like the predator he was. With short, sharp movements of his hand, he forced her to ride the edge until she trembled with orgasmic exhaustion.

Then he held her, caressing her lips, nuzzling her cheek with his nose, and soothing her tensed limbs with gentle strokes. She was warm and tingly and snug and…

What had she done?

Had she screamed? Sort of. Against his lips. Which was better than having him put his hand over her mouth. But still. She'd been in a fugue state. The sobbing, the crying, then his touch, his kiss. She'd lost her mind.

This was the problem with letting hormones and emotions take over. She didn't care how she behaved while she was under the influence, not until it was all over. Then splat, she came down off the high.

She tugged at the bottom of her skirt to at least cover her pantyless state. "Well, that was incredibly embarrassing."

Brax kissed her eyelids. "That was heaven."

"You barely touched me, and I totally lost control." She'd screamed. She closed her eyes, too embarrassed to look at him.

He rubbed his nose to hers. "This is very unmanly to admit, and I probably shouldn't, but I've never made a woman orgasm like that in my life."

"That's why it's embarrassing."

He held her chin. "Look at me."

"I can't."

He shook her lightly. She opened her eyes to his laser-bright blues.

"That was too fucking incredible for words," he whispered, his hot, husky voice caressing her.

She blinked. "Oh."

"I want to make you do it again, but this time I want to be inside you."

No one had ever taken everything she had to give and asked for more. No words had ever made her feel so special. He couldn't possibly mean it. Her heart beat faster and her eyes clouded up. "But it was so unladylike."

He gave a short bark of disbelieving laughter. "Do not tell me your mother dictated orgasm etiquette to you."

Not exactly. "Why would you bring up my mother at a time like this?"

"I swear I heard her voice coming out of your mouth."

She gasped. He hadn't figured out who her mother was, had he? "You've never even heard her voice." She worried her lip. "Have you?"

"I know a quote when I hear one."

"Oh." She squirmed. It wasn't a quote exactly, more like an overall rule of permissible behavior. "Nothing, including sex, should ever be done to excess."

He laughed outright this time, throwing his head back. She wanted to lick his throat as it moved.

"There is definitely one thing that should be enjoyed to excess and that's an orgasm." He tipped her

chin, holding her gaze. "The world would be a better place if everyone came like you did."

Oh my God. He didn't care she was a screamer. He wasn't like her ex-fiancé. He resembled one of the heroes in her fantasies, actually enjoying that she was exuberant and excessive. She could hardly believe it. "What does that mean, Brax?"

"It means, make love, not war."

"I think that's a sixties slogan."

"Smoking too much of the happy weed or not, they did know a good axiom when they heard one."

"You might have a point." Wriggling until she could lean an elbow on the sofa arm, she put space between them. She wanted him to throw his arms around her and hug till she popped. She wanted to give him everything she'd been holding back for three years. All her exuberance. "I know another good axiom."

He slid down, resting his head against the couch to watch her through hooded eyes. "And what's that?"

She trailed a finger from his throat to his belt, then laid her hand on his buckle. "One good turn deserves another."

His gaze turned hot, a fire sparking beneath those seemingly lazy lids. "What did you have in mind?"

She drew a hand down the bulge in his pants, then cupped his erection. She felt bold and free, like one of her characters. "What base are we on if I touch you here?"

He covered her hand, pressing harder. His gaze captured hers in an endless moment.

Then he whispered, "We're halfway home."

quite holding her nape. "I know I'd want someone to give the comfort I have. I know I will..."

He pulled his fingers away, leaving a warmth, her breast like a warm pudding. She quivered under the touch before his fingers, slightly colder, gripped. He murmured something. Suddenly, huffy. I blinked.

Brax didn't like love, my lady.

I stood in the silence again.

CHAPTER FIFTEEN

BRAX WANTED HER MOUTH ON HIM. He wanted to fill her with himself. More, he needed to experience that moment again, when she flew apart with his touch, cried out his name, and for one infinitesimal flash of time, drove the ache from his vital organs.

She'd admitted feeling selfish because she'd wanted to forget for a while. She couldn't imagine how much more he had to forget.

Halfway home. He wanted to *be* home. All the way home, deep inside her.

"I think if you so much as touch my bare flesh, I'm a goner."

A shadow flitted through her eyes.

"I want to come in you, with you. It's not a bad thing."

She dropped her head, stroked him through his jeans with her cheek. He knew how she'd felt when he played with her panties.

He pulled her up by her arms, guiding her to straddle him. Her skirt at her waist made it easier, and the enticing aroma of hot, wet woman threatened to fog his brain and cloud his judgment.

She tugged down her skirt modestly, hiding the very part of her he wanted most.

"I didn't bring a condom," he said, running his hands up and down her arms. "Are you okay with that?"

She shrugged, her hair falling forward. "Yeah. The pill. You know."

Being on the pill, probably another unladylike habit. Her mother jumped even higher on his shit list.

"You don't have to be ashamed."

She stared at the center of his chest. "The only men I've been with since I came to Goldstone were in my dreams. It's sort of pathetic to have stayed on the pill."

He pushed her hair back behind both ears. "Hopeful. Not pathetic. And my good fortune. Do you know how much I want you?"

She shook her head.

"I want you more than I wanted Mary Alice Turner in the backseat of my dad's old car when I was sixteen."

He hadn't given her a name when she'd first introduced him to the theory of anticipation, but he knew she understood exactly what he meant. When she closed her eyes and leaned into him, her nipples brushing his chest, he also knew he'd given her what she needed.

"More than Mary Alice when you were sixteen?" Barely a whisper on her exhale.

"Yeah. Way more."

Sliding her skirt up and tilting his hips, he pressed her down and rocked against her center until his cock screamed, until she moaned softly. "We're gonna have an accident here if you don't undo my belt buckle pronto."

"Yes, Sheriff."

Nimble fingers made fast work of both belt and zip-

per. She rose up on her knees, giving him a gorgeous view of naked womanhood, while he pushed down on the jeans until his erection slid free.

"Oh, it's beautiful. May I touch it, Sheriff?"

He laughed, then groaned as she took him in hand. Closing his eyes, he savored her cool grip. "Jesus."

Her hair cascaded over his face as she slid her hand down, then up. "Does that feel good?"

"Better than ice cream on a hot day."

"Is that a not so subtle plea for me to lick your cone?"

He curled his fist around hers. "Hell, no. I'd never survive that."

"Never say never."

Hot and playful, she made him want to laugh and come all at the same time. Just as he wanted her to smile over her tears.

He pried her fingers loose. "You've got about two seconds before I—"

He almost lost it as she slid down on his cock hard and fast, taking him all the way inside her sweet, lush body, then settled in for the long haul. Or what he hoped was a long haul.

"Is this what you wanted, Sheriff?"

She stole his breath. He couldn't answer, could only hold on to her as his hips surged, driving higher and deeper inside her.

Her fingers dug into his arms as she tipped her head back. "Oh my God, that feels so good."

She couldn't know how damn good. Or maybe she did. Looking down at him once more, she grabbed the bottom of her T-shirt and pulled it over her head, shaking her gorgeous hair loose. Her nipples peaked tanta-

lizingly through the lace bra. He grabbed her by the waist, pulling her close to take the sweet tip in his mouth. She arched, strained, cupping the back of his head as he sucked her through the lace.

"You taste good," he whispered. He kissed the swell of breast above her bra, then licked her throat and finally leaned back to look in her eyes. "And you feel good around me." He wanted her heat. Trailing his fingers along the crease of her thigh, he put his thumb to her clitoris and stroked.

She moaned. "Brax, oh, Brax." She moved with him, slightly, forward, then back, riding his touch as well as his cock. The fingers of his left hand bit into her hip.

"Are you ready?" he whispered with his single last ounce of control. So much for the long haul.

"Oh please, I am so ready."

He couldn't hold out a second longer, thrusting up hard, wrapping his arm across her waist and holding her tight to meet him. She rose and fell, biting her lip, panting, her gaze never leaving his.

"Let go, baby," he murmured. "Let it go. God, I want to hear how good it feels."

His muscles bunched, his thighs shrieked, his thumb played her, then he rammed home one last time, and lost himself in her. A moment later, her body spasmed around him, and she screamed out her pleasure with abandon.

DARN. SHE'D SCREAMED AGAIN. Loudly. Mr. Doodle probably heard her over at Flood's End.

Brax still held on to her, squashing her breasts to his chest, pumping warm breaths against her neck. He

cupped her butt, stroking, as her heart rate slowed, the flush on her skin dimmed, and the throb of him inside her subsided.

"Kiss me," he whispered against her hair.

"What?"

"Kiss me so I know you didn't use me merely for sex."

Putting both hands on his shoulders, she pushed back. He watched her with a somber face and dancing eyes.

"I didn't use you, Sheriff."

"You called me Brax a few minutes ago. Now I'm back to being Sheriff. Kiss me so my ego doesn't get wounded."

She wanted to laugh almost more than she wanted to kiss him. His petulant lower lip won out. She laughed.

Both hands dropped to her butt, and he pulled her snug.

"I like being inside you." He brushed his lips over hers. "I love the way I can make you scream."

"Hold me, Brax." *Please God, let him mean it.* Brax wouldn't lie about a thing like that. Not when he knew it was important. And he did know.

He squeezed her tight in his arms. She wanted to stay that way forever. Safe, warm. Excessive and exuberant.

Then he eased her away, kissed her nose, her cheeks, finally her forehead. "More than anything, I wish I could stay with you." He searched her face a moment. "But I have to go in case Maggie wakes up."

Icy water suddenly rushed through her veins, chilling her skin, raising goose bumps, and turning to crystal around her heart. "I forgot."

"I wanted to forget."

Suddenly tears were as close to the surface as they'd been when she'd thrown herself sobbing into his arms. "I'm sorry. I'm so sorry. I don't know how I could have done that when Carl's—"

He held her face and her gaze in a powerful grip. "Don't take away from what we did. It's the only good and beautiful thing I have. And I needed it."

"But—"

He shook her lightly. "Carl's dead, and I have to ask Maggie some real shitty questions even though I know she'll fall apart. So let me keep what we did without turning it to shit, too."

She pressed her lips together, sniffed. She'd been terribly selfish in begging, almost forcing him to make love to her. Then she'd followed it up with her it's-all-about-me guiltfest, never even considering how Brax felt. "You're right. This was ours. I won't take it away."

"Good. Now kiss me."

She leaned in for a kiss sweeter than she'd ever tasted. Just a meeting of lips and a tear's salty taste at the corner of her mouth.

Then she rose, pulling free of his arms and his body, the loss of contact tugging at her insides.

"I'll be back in a minute." She grabbed her T-shirt off the sofa beside him and ran.

Cleaning up in the bathroom seemed so demoralizing. It should have been like one of her fantasies, where there was no mess, no fuss, no bodily functions, and your hair and makeup remained perfect.

Instead, the stark fluorescent lights beamed down on ratty party hair, washed-out skin bare of blush, and

highlighted the mascara streaks and the smear of lipstick on her chin.

Oh God. She shouldn't have thrown herself at him.

She should have at least made him turn out the lights.

She rubbed the lipstick off her chin, wiped away the mascara smudges and smoothed her hair. If only she could have removed her bad thoughts as easily. Brax had told her not to be ashamed, not to destroy the beautiful thing they'd done.

Beautiful. He'd used that word, hadn't he? She'd screamed out loud, and he told her he loved it.

"It was beautiful," she whispered, then returned to him.

He'd fastened his jeans and belt and tucked in his shirt. The only reminder of their interlude was the slight ache between her legs.

He held out his hand. "Come here."

Even in her platforms, she fit securely beneath the arm he draped around her shoulders.

"Kiss me goodbye."

She'd have liked it better if he'd said good-night instead of goodbye, but she raised her lips to his. Once more, he filled her with sweetness and she could have sworn her morose thoughts flitted away into the night.

Until a car door slammed out on the road and voices wafted on the summer breeze.

He leaned his forehead to hers. "Expecting someone?"

"No." It was probably Sheriff Teesdale for Brax. With more bad news.

Her screen door whined and the porch creaked beneath footsteps, then the front door resounded with a loud knock.

"Better answer it," he said, brushing his lips across hers.

She did. Her heart dropped to her stomach, and her stomach plummeted to her toes.

Her mother stood on her doorstep.

MAGGIE CREPT to her bedroom door and listened.

"I need to get out of here, Chloe."

Della. In the hallway by her room. Whispering. The thin, wooden inner doors did nothing to muffle their voices.

"Wait until Maggie's brother gets back. We can't leave her alone."

Tyler was gone. That was good. The dark room spun, dust bunnies from under the bed stuffed her head, her lips felt like thick slugs and her wobbly legs threatened to collapse. But she was awake, and she knew what she had to do. Tyler would have stopped her.

"You stay. I can't wait," Della said.

"Buck up, Della."

"How can I face her after the horrible things I said yesterday?"

"We've all done things we wish we hadn't." Chloe paused. "But we do what has to be done in the aftermath."

"When she's in her right mind, she's not going to forgive me."

Maggie held her breath in case they might hear her in the silence.

"Della Montrose, if you leave before Brax gets back, I'll…" Chloe stopped.

"You'll what, Chloe?"

"Don't make me say it, Della."

Maggie never heard the actual threat. They left the hallway outside her door, though she was sure Della didn't drive off. Their arguing was a good thing. They'd never notice her leave.

She couldn't remember what Della had said yesterday. She couldn't even remember yesterday.

Except that yesterday, Carl hadn't been dead. She couldn't remember what that felt like. She could only feel the hollow ache in her chest, the pain in her temples and the screech of her own words like nails on a chalkboard. *Drop dead.*

For the first time ever in their marriage, he'd done exactly what she told him to do.

See, that was the thing. Carl never would have done what she told him to. If she'd shrieked "don't drop dead," then he might have fallen into the gorge to spite her. That's how she knew someone else had made him fall.

But how was she supposed to explain that to Tyler? Even she knew how asinine it sounded. He'd say it was grief, disbelief and Xanax talking. In fact, he might have said something like that before she fell asleep, uneasy despite the Xanax. She couldn't recall. She only remembered wishing her mother was here.

She had to go see the chickens. The chickens had found him. Maybe he'd been alive when they did. Maybe he'd said, "Mighty Mouse pushed me."

Maybe he'd said he forgave her for being a whacked-out, PMSing, premenopausal bitch.

Maggie had to know.

"DARLING." Her mother glided through the doorway, forcing Simone back two steps. "After that phone call last night, I knew you needed me desperately."

What phone call? Simone could only stare, wide-eyed and slack jawed, with total and complete amnesia about last night.

Her mother patted Simone's chin. "Close your mouth, sweetie. God only knows what airborne germs there are in this place."

Then her mother's china-perfect eyes landed on Brax.

"Oh my. Who *is* this marvelous person?" She held out her hand like a queen expecting him to go down on one knee for the worshiping hand kiss.

Most men usually did.

"This is…this is…" Simone was sure she'd hyperventilate if she said his name. Or faint.

"Brax," he supplied for himself. He didn't take the proffered hand nor extend his own. Simone couldn't bear to look at his face.

He was seeing her mother. For the first time. In the flesh. Men killed for a glimpse of her mother up close and personal.

While Simone stood aside in a pantyless state. Oh God, where were her panties? *Please, not on the sofa.*

"It's such an exquisite pleasure to meet you, Mr. Brax," Ariana simpered. Why was she pretending Simone hadn't told her about Brax on the phone last night? "I couldn't have imagined anyone of your ilk would live in such a…place," she finally added, her lips plopping around the word. Her eyes roamed the trailer, from the ancient orange shag carpet and ratty sofa to the dirty wineglass and cracker crumbs on the coffee table.

Oh my God. The coffee table. Covered with the be-ribboned scrolls. It was the ones devoid of ribbons, over half the pages, that freaked Simone out. The ones her mother could read if she got close enough.

Simone made a mad jump for the table, almost tripping over a bump in the shag. She grabbed the bag and crammed in papers, careful not to bend too much and expose her bare behind. "I should have cleaned up a bit." *I should never have been born.*

"I'll help." Brax leaned down, scooping up one of the scrolls that had rolled off between the table and the couch.

And there were the darn panties.

His mouth quirked.

She almost dived on them, grabbing the scrap of material and three more scrolls, then shoving the lot into the bag.

"One more," he murmured, and darn it, he was laughing at her.

She glared at him, then took the roll, stuffed it and squished the bag to her midsection.

"Well, that's all cleaned up." Her blood roared through her ears like a freight train. Red faced, she gave her mother a sheepish smile. "Sorry."

She might have hidden the panties, but her mother wasn't done with her yet. "Darling. How could you even think of entertaining such a handsome man without makeup?"

Simone slapped a hand to her cheek. Horror of horrors, her mother had caught her with no makeup. A social gaffe worse than not wearing panties. Worse than blue panties under white slacks.

Setting elegant hands at the waist of her delicate sky-blue silk pantsuit, Ariana gave Simone a head-to-toe examination. "Why, darling, you're looking—" she glanced at Brax, then adjusted her word choice "—robust. The food here must agree with you. But you know what animal fat can do to a buxom figure."

"It gives a woman curves that appeal far more to the male eye than a bony stick figure."

At the sound of Brax's deep voice, Ariana Chandler stopped her hands in midflutter, arms raised, her bracelets jangling until they slipped down her forearms to rest at her elbows.

Some meteorological phenomenon sucked all the air from the trailer and replaced it with a storm cloud that built right over her mother's perfectly coiffed blond head. A storm built in eyes so blue they could only have sprung from a contact lens case.

Thunder in the desert could shake a trailer from its cinder blocks, but one of her mother's rages was a woman-made storm of unparalleled force.

Though not meaning to, Brax had insulted her mother's...bony stick figure.

"Ariana, I am not dragging in every damn bag you brought. Get out here and pick out what you want."

"Kingston." Simone blurted his name as if he were their savior. Which he was. Kingston Hightower, her mother's manager, was the only person on earth, man or woman, who could bring one of her mother's tantrums back to dead calm. In two seconds flat.

She grabbed his arm, dragged him over the threshold, knocking aside the suitcase dangling from his hand, and threw her arms around him. With her lips at his ear, she whispered desperately. "Do something. She's going to explode."

Brax would never recover. A man of steel who dealt with dirty, rotten, low-down criminals every day of his life, he'd never faced Ariana Chandler. He didn't know what she could do.

"For you, Simone," Kingston whispered back, "any-

thing." Then he set her on her feet, and threw an arm around her mother's shoulders, trapping Ariana's fragile figure beneath his beefy arm. Six foot four with a physique like Mr. Universe from 1975, Kingston immobilized her mother's approaching cataclysmic outburst with an immovable arm.

"Ariana, sweetie-honey-baby, could you please help Jackie figure out which bag you want for the night. We'll bring in the others tomorrow."

"Kingston, I need everything," Ariana whined. She only ever whined for Kingston, though she'd never allowed her girls the luxury. Not for Kingston or anyone else.

Someday, he'd marry Ariana. When her star had faded, and she realized she couldn't do without him.

"Introductions, please, Simone." Kingston, having been with her mother for the last twenty years, was the father Simone had never had.

"This is Brax." She said it out without stumbling this time, but didn't bother to explain the relationship. They didn't have a relationship, unless you mentioned Carl's death, Maggie's breakdown, or the last half hour on her living-room couch.

"Brax, this is my mother."

He shot her a self-satisfied look saying he'd known all along. She shot him down with the rest of it. "My mother. Ariana *Chandler.*"

He raised a brow that said, *yeah, I got that.*

She almost thought for a moment he didn't know.

Sticking out his hand, Brax said, "Didn't catch your name."

"Kingston Hightower, at your service."

A firm handshake dispensed with, silence fell for

several seconds while Brax stood there. Saying nothing. Doing nothing.

He really didn't know. Simone's heart jumped to her throat with hope and glory, then dashed itself as quickly on the rocky shores of reality. He'd know soon enough. Then he'd be on his hands and knees begging forgiveness for the stick-figure comment.

Two bags thumped to the floor and her sister leaned against the doorjamb to catch her breath. Flawless skin that had never braved harsh rays without sunscreen, ethereal blond beauty like a water nymph and the fragile figure of a Greek goddess, men wept at Jackie's feet in adoration.

Next to her, Simone looked like Brunhilde out of the "Ride of the Valkyries."

The end was near. Simone stepped inevitably toward it. "And this is my sister. Jacqueline Chandler."

She saw the moment Brax made the connection. He cocked his head, glancing from Jackie to Ariana. Three times. His eyes widened imperceptibly, then his gaze finally rested on Simone.

She shrugged. "You've probably seen them at the movies."

Kingston laughed heartily. "That's an understatement, sweetheart." Said like a good PR man. "He's seen them on the Academy Awards every year."

"Sorry." Brax shook his head. "Don't watch the Academy Awards." Then he graciously added, "But I've seen a couple of movies and enjoyed the performances."

He didn't expound. He didn't effuse. *He didn't grovel.*

Simone's heart started to pound. With the extracur-

ricular workout in the last hour, the organ was close to expiring.

Kingston broke the silence and Simone's knot of tension with practical matters. "Show me where to put your mom's bags."

"In my room, I guess. I'll have to change the sheets."

Her mother gasped. "Kingston, we can't impose on Simone. I didn't know her trailer would be so small. We need a hotel." She waggled her fingers at Simone, her bangles jangling. "Darling, is there a Ritz in that town down the highway?"

Kingston snorted. "A Ritz? We're not in Hollywood anymore, Dorothy. Simone's trailer will do fine."

Ariana afforded them all a very pretty pout.

"You came all the way here to see Simone. So let's spend some quality family time."

Quality family time? With her mother? Simone would rather pick a million cactus needles out of her foot with tweezers.

"Besides, Jackie's tuckered out." Kingston pointed to Jackie, then the two bags at her sister's feet. "Simone, sweetie, could ya show us where to go?"

Brax snorted at Kingston's unintentional pun, though sobered quickly when Ariana flashed him a look. "I'll help," he offered.

"Got it," Kingston said, grabbing both bags in one hand and putting his arm around Jackie's shoulders to guide her.

Simone led them away. Leaving Brax alone with her mother.

Her gorgeous, not-a-day-over-thirty-nine, adored-by-millions, movie-queen mother. Next to her, Simone was a chunky frump.

It was like asking a connoisseur if he preferred chopped liver to pâté de foie gras.

"So, TELL ME, how long have you known my sweet little Simone?" She fluttered her eyelashes.

It looked as if she had a nervous tick in her eye.

Ariana Chandler. Didn't that beat all. Simone had her polished, classic beauty, but Ariana's was a poor imitation of Simone's brilliant dazzle smile. Too practiced. Brax figured she wiped it off at night the same way she'd remove her makeup.

She batted her extraordinary lashes once more, and leveled him with the sultry, come-hither look of Marilyn Monroe.

Not working. At least not on him. "Let me think. How long have I known her? Three days, six hours and—" he glanced at his watch "—thirty-six minutes." He smiled. "And I've cherished every moment. You've got a wonderful daughter." Though he couldn't figure out where Simone had inherited her dazzle.

Instead of answering—probably working on a good comeback—Ariana flicked a white handkerchief across the sofa cushion, peered at it, then sat. Draping her arm across the couch back, she folded one knee beneath her and extended her leg, revealing toned thigh and calf encased in silk, and trim ankle strapped into dainty sandals. A practiced position designed to display shapely attributes. Ariana Chandler's assets came off as a tad better than ordinary when compared to her daughter Simone.

Pretty damn dexterous for a woman her age, she'd kept herself in reasonable shape. Her face wasn't bad, either. Simone was close to the thirty mark, which put

her mother near fifty, if she'd had Simone when she was a kid herself. Then again, she probably charged off a very good plastic surgeon on her taxes as a deductible salary expense.

Ariana patted the sofa. "Why don't you sit beside me and tell me all about those three days, six hours and thirty-six minutes? I'm dying to know. Simone's so inhibited when it comes to…" She simpered and fluttered, then added, "man talk."

He wanted to laugh. In disbelief. The invitation resembled a come-on more than any request for a friendly chat. This woman was a piece of work. In the space of five minutes, she'd called her daughter fat, demoralized her for not wearing makeup on her fresh beautiful skin, trashed the trailer with a mere look, and now she wanted to know about her daughter's sex life.

All right, he was biased. He already had a strong dislike for Simone's mother before he met her, and before he knew she was the Ariana Chandler.

Being a movie star was not a point in her favor.

If familial duty didn't call him back to Maggie's side, he would have plopped himself right down beside her on that couch, and told her the many ways in which she could not possibly hold a candle to her daughter.

He didn't have time for a boxing match with Mommie Dearest. Even more importantly, he wouldn't leave Simone alone with the aftermath of a verbal knockout.

"Sorry. Gotta run."

"I suppose you're anxious to leave this." With a flourish, she indicated the trailer's early seventies decor. "You'll be glad to know I'm here to help Simone get out of this awful place."

"She's quite happy here and doesn't need your help."

"Oh, come, Mr. Brax, nobody could *want* to live in a…trailer." She wrinkled her nose. Extremely unattractive. Amazing she hadn't checked the expression in a mirror and expunged it from her repertoire.

"You underestimate the joys of trailer life." He now had a great appreciation for Simone's sofa.

"Why, it could blow away in a heavy windstorm. I've been so worried about her."

Right. She worried about her own image if it should get out to the press that her daughter lived in a trailer out in the middle of nowhere. *Friday Night Fights* or not, he couldn't allow the woman to disparage the life Simone had chosen for herself. "Her home's got a solid foundation. Believe me, nothing is ever going to blow it or her away."

A small sound, maybe a gasp, caught his attention. In single file at the bedroom hallway, Simone, the waiflike Jacqueline, and the manager, a protective hand on the sister's shoulder as she leaned lightly against him.

Simone stared at Brax, teeth worrying her bottom lip.

He ignored the mother in favor of her daughter. Closing the short distance, Brax kneaded Simone's nape, pulling her forward to murmur against her hair. "I wouldn't leave you alone for a moment with the dragon lady if I didn't have to."

There, in front of her mother, her sister and whoever the hell the big older guy really was, Brax leaned down for an openmouthed taste of her, savoring her sweetness for several seconds longer than a goodnight kiss necessitated.

HER HOME'S GOT a solid foundation.

Her trailer? Her life? Simone felt sure Brax meant both. He actually understood. He knew what Goldstone meant to her, the underlying significance. He appreciated where she'd been, and why she'd never leave. He grasped the meaning of home.

In that moment, Simone fell hopelessly in love with Tyler Braxton.

CHAPTER SIXTEEN

CHLOE AND DELLA jumped him the moment he opened the trailer door. Going automatically for the weapon he wasn't carrying, Brax nevertheless crouched into a defensive posture.

"She's gone."

"What do we do?"

"I haven't a clue where."

"It's been half an hour of hell."

"You should have left your cell phone number."

He tried to make sense of who was saying what and what it all meant. "Maggie's been gone to God knows where for half an hour but you didn't have my cell number, yet you didn't call Simone or get in your car and drive less than a mile to her house?"

"It wasn't our fault." Della put a hand over her mouth.

Chloe pointed. "Della panicked. I couldn't leave."

"I did not panic."

"You threatened to stick your head in the Jacuzzi motor and turn it on if I left. I'd call that panicking."

"You're exaggerating, Chloe."

"Ladies. Excuse the expression, but please shut up. Now."

In his experience, ladies didn't usually do what you told them to, but in this case, these two did.

"Only one of you answer. Did she sneak past you?"

Chloe did the honors. "She pried the window screen off in the bedroom."

"You noticed half an hour ago. But when was the last time you checked if she was there?"

"We didn't check," Della said, staring at the floor. "You said she was asleep, and we didn't want to risk waking her."

Dammit, he'd been gone almost an hour and a half. Shit. Shit. Shit. Giving in to his desire for Simone had been the worst mistake in a long line of stupid mistakes he'd made lately. Not the act itself, that was beautiful, but the timing sucked.

He'd told Simone not to sully what they'd done.

Maggie's disappearance did it for them.

"Did you call the sheriff?"

The two looked at each other, then the floor, and both answered simultaneously. "No."

"Shit." His vocabulary suddenly seemed limited.

He pulled his cell from its holder on his hip just as an electronic excerpt from Tchaikovsky's "1812 Overture," minus the canons, shrieked from somewhere deep in the family room.

With the agility of a high-dive champion, Chloe lunged for her bag on the coffee table before Brax had a chance to hit 911.

Chloe looked to Brax. "The chickens have Maggie."

What the hell was Maggie doing at The Chicken Coop? He knew in the next split second. She was doing her own investigation, starting at the source, the witnesses who found his body. Damn those detective shows.

"They don't know how long they can hold her off,"

Chloe relayed. "It's a terrible mess. She's gonna kill Whitey any second now. Holy hell, I hear her screaming like a crazy person."

"Tell them we'll be there in two minutes." Brax pointed at Della. "You stay in case she somehow gets away before we arrive and comes back here."

Della groaned mournfully. "But I'm the last person she'll want to see. I can't handle it."

Chloe shook her by the shoulders. "Della. You're the mayor and the judge of this town. Start acting like it."

Shit, shit, shit. Someone had to gain control. Because Brax had certainly lost it.

"THAT MAN WAS incredibly rude." Ariana paced the short length of Simone's living room, her brilliant blue sandals blending with the orange shag like high school pom-poms.

"Ah, Ariana, honey, you're miffed because Brax didn't fall worshipping at your feet. I think the boy's smitten with our Simone." Kingston put his arm around Simone's shoulder and hugged her off her feet.

"What does he do for a living in this godforsaken place? Sell used hubcaps?"

"He's visiting." Of course, she'd already told her mother that, along with the fact that Brax was Maggie's brother, but Ariana never could resist a good dig. "He's a sheriff in Cottonmouth."

Her mother made a face. "Cottonmouth? That's a disgusting name for a town." She sniffed condescendingly. "Trust a gambling and prostitution state like Nevada to allow such a thing."

"Cottonmouth's in Northern California."

"Hmmph. *Northern* California. Well, that says it

all." Anything north of Hollywood counted as the back-woods to her mother, even if it was part of the great state.

"Don't mind her, honey, she's jealous," Kingston said loud enough for her mother to hear. Kingston never seemed to care what her mother thought. Maybe that's why her mother took his blasphemies without throwing him out on his ear. Actually, Simone never had understood why her mother tolerated it. Another of life's great unsolved mysteries.

"Jealous, Kingston? Oh please. Of what? She lives in a trailer, for God's sake. And did you see this town? Why it doesn't even have a decent spa."

Goldstone didn't have a spa at all, and her mother would shrivel in the dry desert air. But her daughter thrived. Maybe Jackie needed some good desert air, too. She seemed so pale.

"Simone is standing right here, Ariana. You don't have to talk like she's in the next room. I think her trailer is…" Even Kingston had to search for a kind word, "special."

And it had a foundation. Brax said so. Simone's heart beat a little faster, and she couldn't help a tiny smile.

"Any trailer is an abomination," her mother said, as if a trailer was the next-worst thing to an outhouse. "How could you do this to me, Simone? How *could* you? If the press ever gets wind of this…" She threw herself on the sofa, covering her eyes with her arm.

Simone opened her mouth, but Kingston fought her battle for her. "She didn't do it *to* you, Ariana. This is *her* home, and it doesn't have a thing to do with you. I'd venture that she didn't even consider you when she bought it."

Anathema to her mother, the idea that the world didn't revolve around her. "You're coming home, Simone. I won't hear another word about it. You can have your old suite at the house. But don't even think about redecorating in orange."

"She's not coming home, Ariana."

"Kingston, will you please stop talking *for* her. The girl's old enough to talk for herself."

Talk for herself? Ariana didn't think she was old enough to even think for herself.

They looked at her. Expecting something. It was so much easier to tell her mother what she wanted to hear when all Simone had to do was hang up the phone afterward. She took the coward's way out. "You can sleep in the master bedroom, MOTHER." Of course, her whole trailer would fit in her mother's bedroom suite, and there wasn't a speck of marble or brass to be found anywhere. "Jackie and I can take the guest room." Which had a queen bed, where they could giggle and tell stories all night long as they had when they were children. "The couch isn't very long, Kingston, but it's better than the floor."

Kingston laughed. "Maybe your mother should take the couch. She looks so at home there, doesn't she?"

Ariana rose, smoothing imagined wrinkles from her silk pantsuit. "Thank goodness, I brought spare sheets. I like my own with the proper thread count. Jackie, sweetheart, would you mind taking care of it? And don't forget to get the atomizer out of my overnight case to spray the bed."

"Yes, MOTHER." Yes, Jackie minded, or yes, she'd do it? Simone thought she detected capital letters in her sister's voice. Jackie had hung back in the hallway, out

of sight, out of mind, out of the storm, during the entire exchange.

Simone almost laughed. The thought of Academy Award-winning Jacqueline Chandler changing sheets bordered on the absurd. Just as it was easier to tell Ariana what she wanted to hear, it was always easier to do what she said. If she was close enough to throw eye daggers at you. Suddenly it was getting hard to say her mother meant well.

"I'll help, Jackie."

Jackie turned back along the hall, Simone followed, hoping her mother's voice would do a fade-out.

"Kingston, I need a drink. See what she's got."

"Yes, Ariana. Whatever your little heart desires." Kingston Hightower took her mother's orders as though they were a source of great amusement. He always had. Simone had often wondered what her mother would have to say or do to breach his equanimity.

"And if there are any mice lurking in the cupboards, you are driving me to a decent hotel, even if we have to go all the way back to Vegas."

"Of course, Ariana. You know your every wish is my command." Laughter lurked in his voice.

"And when is she going to write darling Ambrose? If she'd just do herself up and wear a little makeup. I don't know how to help her anymore when she won't even…" Fade out.

THE DRIVE TOOK FIVE MINUTES. The longest five minutes of Brax's life.

Two flood lamps spotlighted pandemonium in The Chicken Coop's lot as he wheeled in. His tires spewed

gravel in all directions, the ping-ping of it hitting damn near every parked car and spraying the two combatants and four referees.

Dressed in varied length shorts and crop tops and without their distinguishing lingerie, Brax couldn't tell which chicken was which, but two held Maggie back by her arms.

Brax yanked his car door open and caught her words. Hell, she was shouting so loudly all of Goldstone must have heard her.

"I know you killed him, Waldo Whitehead. You thought he was going to dig up those damn outhouses of yours in the middle of the night and stiff you out of a cut of whatever he found."

Then she threw herself at Whitey, hands outstretched, fingers curled into claws.

With a mighty effort, the chickens held her back just before she'd have scratched his eyes out. The bearded man jumped, stumbled, then fell on his ass.

"Maggie, stop it." Brax didn't know her. She was a crazy wild thing, her hair flying in all directions, spittle at the corners of her mouth. Psycho time. It would have been cliché if it hadn't been his sister.

For a moment, one small part of his mind stepped back to assess the situation with an unbiased cop's eye. At the end of a self-proclaimed knock-down, drag-out fight with her husband, Maggie Felman had threatened to cut off his family jewel. She had disappeared for most of the next morning during which, at some point, her husband had fallen to his death. The autopsy report might very well come back determining time of death to be within the window of her opportunity. She now threw accusations of murder around like a crazy

woman. Or a crazy-*acting* woman desperate to throw suspicion onto someone else.

Shit. Damn. Brax was closer to losing his lunch than when he'd been tasked with cleaning up after a ten-car pileup on the highway involving a semi's lost brakes.

Please God, don't let my sister be an out-of-control Mack truck.

Whitey garbled something, the only recognizable part being his utter terror.

Brax seized the distraction like a lifeline.

A chicken, Peppermint by the scent of her, grabbed Brax's arm, and whispered in his ear. "It's a game they played, that's what he said, that he would have let Carl have the outhouses in the end."

Brax closed in on Maggie and the two chickens with death grips on her upper arms. Their muscles flexed and rippled with effort. He didn't know how much longer they could hold her, but he couldn't gauge the transfer of power at this point. If he tried to take Maggie too soon, she could bolt. Either for Whitey's throat or into the night where Brax would never find her. The desert was too damn dark and too damn easy to hide in.

"Maggie, honey, let's calm down. Let's talk." He held up both hands in a peace gesture.

"He killed him, he killed him."

With more unrecognizable rhetoric from Whitey, Peppermint murmured once again, like a UN interpreter deciphering a foreign language for Brax. "He'd never kill Carl over an outhouse. The first edition of *Death Game* Carl found at Goodwill, maybe, but not the outhouses."

"Why the hell is he saying he had a reason? He'll

set her off again. Shit." Then louder, so his sister could hear, he brought out the big guns. "Maggie, Mom'll be here soon. You don't want her seeing you like this. You know what she'll do."

Suffer heart failure, that's what she'd do. Maybe he shouldn't have called her. Seeing this Maggie would break her heart.

"Come on, sweetie, let's go home so Mom doesn't worry."

Maggie stared at him, her face a garish collage of harsh lines and hollows in the flood lights.

"Mom's going to be mad, isn't she?"

She morphed from ferocious feline to whimpering child so quickly moisture sprang to his eyes. His skin prickled as if someone walked over his grave. "She's not going to be mad. She's going to be sad. Let's go home and get you cleaned up."

"You don't think Whitey killed him? I can't leave if he did."

Brax eyed the man's white beard and scrawny chest. "Nah, Whitey didn't kill him. It was somebody else, somebody we don't know."

Behind him, someone gasped. Had to be Chloe.

"Maybe it *was* the book. I forgot all about it." Maggie suddenly wore the most beatific look of hope.

Brax hated to crush it. "Nobody kills anybody over a book."

"It's a first edition." The chicken with nothing to do but watch uttered that. Cotton Candy? She'd need a good lecture about the art of talking a jumper off a window ledge.

Maggie started pointing and jabbering. "See, see. It could be."

"Listen to me, Maggie. The book isn't important."

Another interpretive whisper in Brax's ear. "Carl could have sold it on eBay for a thousand dollars."

Which explained why Carl had *Death Game* in his desk drawer. It had to be the same book Maggie referred to.

The sound of crunching rocks once more issued forth from Whitey's mouth.

The chicken clucking in his ear was starting to fray Brax's nerves, but he needed the info. "He says he's still got author copies left, and he doesn't need the thousand dollars because he got six figures on his last advance."

Brax whipped his head around to stare at her. "What the hell are you talking about?"

"Whitey. Waldo Whitehead."

Bestselling science fiction writer Waldo Whitehead was the old geezer sitting on his butt in the gravel? Jesus. That was the name Maggie used when Brax first climbed out of his car.

What the hell did it matter now except to bring Maggie back to the real world? "Honey, listen to him. He's got more money than Carl ever dreamed of and he's got a whole box of copies of *Death Game* in his house. He didn't need the one Carl had."

Whitey, aka, Waldo Whitehead shook his head vigorously in agreement.

"So let the nice chickens go, and we'll go home, okay?"

"But what about Carl?" she moaned. "Somebody pushed him off the trail. I can't let them get away with it."

Everybody stared, four pairs of chicken eyes, a

mother hen, a rooster who'd lost his cockscomb while sitting on his ass in the gravel. And Maggie. Brax's broken-down sister.

To lie or not to lie, that is the question.

"Sheriff Teesdale and I are going up the trail tomorrow morning. We'll look for evidence. I swear to you, Maggie, I will not sweep this under the rug. I'll do right by you and Carl. I promise."

After interminable moments, she let the chickens lead her to him. His damn hands shook as he put his arm around her shoulders and tucked her close. The passenger side door stood open, and he helped her climb inside, strapped her in carefully, then shut the door. Chloe hoisted herself into the backseat.

"Somebody murdered him?" Caramel?

Brax gave them all a nod. "Most likely."

"We'll boil the asshole in oil." Maybe Cotton Candy.

"We'll draw and quarter the bastard."

"We'll cut his balls off." He was sure that was Chocolate.

He'd never known chickens could be such a bloodthirsty lot. Brax held up his hands in supplication. "Enough or I'll have to haul you all in for vigilantism."

Beyond them, Waldo Whitehead still sat in the gravel as if he'd lost the use of his legs. Brax strode to him. Waldo "Whitey" Whitehead, supplier of skull license plate frames and author of *New York Times* bestselling science fiction novels. Brax stuck out his hand and hauled the man to his feet.

"How much were you going to charge Carl for the outhouses?"

"It was the percentage we were haggling over. I wanted fifty-five and he wanted fifty-five."

Amazingly, Brax understood every word, as if there were a phantom chicken at his ear interpreting. Or Whitey merely affected the garble for incomprehensible reasons. "Why didn't you settle for fifty-fifty?"

Whitey dusted off the seat of his worn trousers. "What's the fun in that?"

The scrawny man might have gotten the jump on the much beefier Carl if he'd charged him from the rear. But what would have been the fun in that? Outhouse haggling would be over in the snap of a finger.

"What about the first edition?"

"I only wanted to sign it. Can't stand one of them being out there unsigned, though I know there's a million anyway."

"How badly did you want that signature on it?"

Whitey stroked his beard, then opened his musty brown eyes wide. "How badly do you think, son?"

Brax had read in some magazine, probably while waiting in the dentist's office, that Waldo Whitehead's last two-book contract had topped the million mark. Murder was about money, desire, love, greed, fear, pain, envy, or a host of other strong emotions. Except on the part of the occasional serial killer, it wasn't about fun.

Waldo hadn't needed money. More than likely, he'd needed to wage the war with Carl for his own amusement. Innate logic dictated that Waldo wouldn't do away with his entertainment source. "Badly enough to hold out on those outhouses, I'd wager."

The old man smiled, the barest of crinkles at his eyes and a forehead smooth enough to make Brax wonder at his age. "Gonna miss that boy something fierce. Think I'll name my next hero after him. Carlsonicus Felmanicus. What d'ya think?"

"Nice ring. I think Carl would like that."

Like Teesdale, Whitehead had chosen a different path, where Twinkies wrappers and outhouses symbolized a better life. Life out of the fast lane. Minus the pressure.

Brax envied them.

He might be making another monumental mistake, but in his judgment, Whitey didn't fit the killer profile.

Brax slapped his hand on the hood as he rounded the front of his SUV, then turned back. "If any of you think of something important, the slightest detail, call Sheriff Teesdale."

The word would be all over town before the sun came up. By tomorrow morning, everyone in Goldstone would know Carl hadn't merely fallen to his death. He'd been murdered.

MAGGIE SPENT the five-minute drive with her head against the window. She snuffled, sniffled, wiped at her nose and her eyes, then started all over again.

Brax didn't know how to help her.

Chloe did more for her than he could by leaning forward from her backseat position and slowing rubbing Maggie's arm. Up and down, up and down. It mesmerized his peripheral vision.

A convertible sat in his spot at the top of the drive. Brax pulled in next to it and cut the engine. He unbuckled Maggie's seat belt as Chloe climbed out and opened the door where Maggie rested her head.

"Come on, sweetie," Chloe crooned like the mother hen she so obviously was.

Brax took Maggie's other arm, and together they led her to the front door. It opened before they reached it.

Light spilled out, silhouetting a tall, gangly figure.

Jason Lafoote, hotelier. The object of Carl's animosity the night before he died. What the hell was he doing here?

Maggie turned her head to murmur in Brax's ear. No chicken whisper, the sound chilled his bones. "That man did it. He pushed Carl. I know it. I feel it. It's all because of him."

She was calm. She was sure. Her voice was damn scary. The level of menace in her tone churned in his belly.

Lafoote stepped forward with the most abject look of sorrow and sympathy that had ever graced a Hollywood screen. Ariana Chandler couldn't have done better.

"Maggie, my poor, dear woman." He clasped her hand in both of his. "I had to rush over and offer my condolences. This is the most terrible of terrible things."

Maggie let him touch her without recoiling, but Brax felt the instinctive flexing in her arm.

His own instinct told him to lickety-split pull her away from the sallow, scarecrowlike man.

The observer in him held back. And watched. He didn't like himself, was in fact starting to hate the part of him that could so callously analyze his sister's reactions.

He'd never know what she'd been about to do because Chloe pulled her away and shot Lafoote a look. "This isn't the time, Jason. Go away."

"But—"

"I said go."

When Madame Chloe meant business, few men dis-

obeyed, Brax was sure, and Lafoote wasn't one of the brave few who might. He scuttled to his car.

"Take Maggie inside," Brax told Chloe, then went after the weasel. He had questions he wanted answers to.

"Hold on, partner." He stopped Lafoote before he could throw himself into the front seat and escape.

Lafoote matched him in height, but Brax was almost twice as wide. The man protected himself in the vee of the car, holding the door in front of him like a shield. "I'm very sorry to have disturbed you."

"I apologize for my sister. She's not thinking clearly." The best tactic was nonconfrontational—until Brax was ready for the slam.

Lafoote bobbed his head. "Carl's death is terrible, just terrible. I don't hold her anger against her."

"Yeah. And with Sheriff Teesdale calling it murder, Maggie's beside herself."

"The sheriff thinks Carl was murdered?"

Brax could have wished for better lighting, but as it was, Lafoote showed appropriate surprise. He could almost see the man's mind digesting that. "Yep. Pretty damn sure foul play was involved. Course, I had to tell the sheriff about that disagreement I witnessed the other night."

Lafoote cocked his head. "What disagreement?"

Again, the reaction seemed fitting. Either the man was one helluvan actor, or he didn't remember. "At The Dartboard. Thought you and Carl might knock each other's block off."

It registered. Lafoote blinked. "Well, that was just a friendly game. I'm surprised you'd call it a disagreement."

"Carl seemed to think you were pissed as hell at him for not backing you on getting that resort open. Pissed. As. Hell." He wanted Lafoote off-kilter. "Had to tell the sheriff it seemed like more than a mere disagreement."

"Well, well—" Lafoote sputtered.

Brax waved him off. "Didn't seem too friendly to me, but I'm sure Sheriff Teesdale will ask you all about it tomorrow." He scratched his neck. "What's got him really curious is why you and Carl were at the bank together yesterday. Right before Carl got himself killed." It was a long shot, but there was nothing that said a cop couldn't make up a few stories to rattle a suspect's cage.

Lafoote took a long time answering. Another telltale sign. Sometimes, a suspect had to really think about his answer. Innocent, confused people usually blurted out, "huh?"

"I really don't have any idea what you're talking about."

An inconclusive answer. "You weren't with Carl yesterday?"

Lafoote blinked over extraordinarily black eyes. "No."

"Where were you then?"

Another pause. Too long. Maybe he couldn't remember a day ago. Then, "I was in my office mostly. I had a lot of calls to make."

"Hmm," Brax muttered, then stared the other man down for several seconds. "I'm sure the sheriff will talk to you about that tomorrow, too. So you might want to get hold of some phone records to prove it."

Lafoote jangled his keys. "Of course, I'd be more than happy to talk to the sheriff. And answer any ques-

tions he has which might help find the dastardly culprit. If Carl really was murdered. I'll let you get back to Maggie."

That was a funny thing. Most people would have asked why the sheriff was interested in what they'd been doing when Carl died. Lafoote just wanted out. Interesting.

Watching Lafoote's car disappear at the bottom of the hill, Brax's instinct was to follow, see what he got up to. But Brax had deserted Maggie one too many times tonight, with disastrous results. Tomorrow, Mom would be here and Maggie could be in no better hands.

Besides, he'd set the stage for Teesdale to do a little probing tomorrow. If Lafoote had anything to do with Carl's death, he'd be a stark raving lunatic by the morning wondering what the sheriff had on him.

He found Della, Chloe and his sister in the living room.

Della tipped Maggie's chin. "Drink your tea, sweetie." The woman had found her backbone once more.

"What did Lafoote really want?" Brax needed to know.

Della patted Maggie's back as she spoke over her head. "What he said. Condolences. Even Jason Lafoote will at least wait until tomorrow to try to turn this to his advantage."

Brax had a gut feeling Lafoote wanted something far more. Maybe to hide his own complicity by visiting his victim's widow?

"Someone murdered Carl, Della." Maggie hiccuped.

"Nonsense, honey. Carl fell."

"Elwood doesn't think so."

Della jerked her head to look at Chloe. "Why not?"

Chloe pointedly flashed her gaze to Maggie's tear-stained, ravaged face. "Let's talk about it later."

The Elvis clock hit the midnight mark, bursting into a shortened, tinny rendition of "Viva Las Vegas." Brax was suddenly so damn tired. He'd never been so glad to have two women hovering around his sister as he was when the worst day of Maggie's life finally gave up the ghost.

CHAPTER SEVENTEEN

"YOU OKAY?"

As soon as she'd heard Brax's voice, Simone took the portable phone into the bathroom, locked herself in and sat on her fluffy chenille toilet seat cover.

"I'm fine. How's Maggie?"

"Not so good. Mom should be here tomorrow. She'll know the right thing to say."

Simone ached inside for the weary sound of his voice. If she could have wrapped his pain up in her arms and made it all better, she would have. Honest to God. She didn't know any more than he did how to fix things for Maggie.

"Don't let your mother give you any crap," he said.

Give her crap? Her mother? "Never."

"You're beautiful just the way you are."

She appreciated the sentiment, but it was like saying, "I accept you with all your faults." She didn't want him to think she had any faults. Even though she did.

"You're beautiful and desirable and the way you smile turns me inside out." His voice was a sweet purr in her ear. "And you're gorgeous without a speck of makeup."

She put a hand to her bare cheek, then her lips. "Not even lipstick?"

"Perfect without it, like I said. But lipstick does have its uses for appropriate activities."

"Like what?" Lipstick on the dipstick? Or the ice-cream cone? Or…

"I'll have to show you. Some things require demonstration."

Oh my. She had her own vision right there across the phone line.

"I need to give you a heads-up." His voice changed, from softly seductive to no-nonsense sheriff.

She felt a twinge in her chest. Bad news cometh.

"It's going to be all over town tomorrow that I think Carl was murdered."

She'd forgotten. Well, not forgotten, but she'd put that slip of time they'd talked about Carl in a corner of her mind where she didn't have to look at it. Or think about it.

"Tomorrow Teesdale and I are going up to the spot where Carl allegedly fell. So I won't be around to take any of the fallout off your shoulders."

"Fallout from what?"

"Your mother."

Oh, he was sweet. Thinking about her at a time like this when his sister's husband had been murdered. Tears oozed at the corners of her eyes. "I'll be fine. Brax, I—"

"Yeah?"

She'd been about to blurt the unblurtable. That she loved him. Silly. It wasn't the time. And he'd think it was some posttraumatic stress thing anyway. "I'm really sorry about Maggie and Carl. But thanks for everything tonight."

He chuckled. "You don't have to thank me for giv-

ing you two great orgasms. The pleasure was all mine. Not to mention the one you gave me."

"That's not what I meant." Even with distance between them, her cheeks flamed, because she had meant that, among other things. "I was talking about, well, you know, how you sort of defended me. When my mother arrived."

"There's nothing to defend. Remember that, okay." His voice grated with a hard edge. "You're perfect."

Just the way I am? She managed not to beg to hear it again. "I'll remember."

"Good night, Simone."

He was gone before she even had time to say goodbye. She blew him a kiss anyway.

Then someone pounded on the thin bathroom door. "Simone. How can you have only one bathroom in this place? It's uncivilized. I have to remove my makeup and perform my nightly regimen."

"I'll be out in a minute, MOTHER." Simone didn't have a nightly regimen. Besides, as her mother had pointed out, her makeup was already gone.

She quickly took care of necessities, washed her hands, then brushed her teeth. Over two minutes. Her mother stood outside the door, tapping the toe of her feather-trimmed mule. She'd already changed into an elaborate golden robe that cascaded down her figure and swirled at her ankles. She should have been a forties starlet.

"All yours." Simone smiled brightly.

"Is there any mold in the shower?"

"I squirted it down before you came. Should all be dead as a doornail by now."

"That is not funny, Simone," her mother said, closing the door.

"I thought it was." Kingston laughed heartily from the living room as he shook out a sheet with which to cover her ratty couch. "Jackie, since you did such a good job making your mother's bed, why don't you help me?"

"I'll do it, Kingston," Simone offered. Jackie was a guest, after all, not a servant. And her sister had already had to put the extra thread count sheets on the master bed.

Kingston refused her offer. "Your sister will help. You go get your pretty little self into bed." He dropped his voice. "Before your mother gets out of the bathroom. You know she'll be in there at least an hour."

Jackie, now changed into paisley silk pajamas, sidled by her.

Simone watched with indecision as Jackie grabbed one end of the sheet, smoothed it, and began tucking it beneath the cushions.

Kingston flapped a hand. "Go, go, go."

She wasn't needed, she wasn't wanted, and her mother had taken over her room, spraying it with the cloying scent of roses. It would take days to air out. She closed the guest room door, slipped off her T-shirt and skirt, and pulled on her *Beauty and the Beast* nightshirt.

Crawling beneath the covers, she heard fragile Jackie's voice. Was she crying on Kingston's shoulder? Probably. Simone had done her share of that over the years. Kingston had very big shoulders, and he was a good listener.

Simone should have lain awake, consumed with thoughts of poor Carl and Maggie, her sister's faint cry-

ing and the remembered feel of Brax inside her, but she was almost asleep when she heard the snick of the door and then felt Jackie climb in beside her.

"Are you all right?" Simone whispered.

She heard Jackie's indrawn breath, held, then let out with a long sigh. "I'm fine."

"Is it true?"

Jackie rustled the bedclothes, then settled. "Is what true?"

"That you're seeing a man? *She* thinks you are." Neither of them needed to specify who she was.

She could see her sister's nod in the weak moonlight falling through the window.

Simone was dying with curiosity. "Who is he?"

Jackie stared at the ceiling for a long time. "I don't want to jinx anything." She turned. "Do you mind?"

He was probably some megastar. A little kernel of hurt lodged next to her heart, but she understood Jackie's fear. Look at what happened to the hapless Wesley.

"Don't tell her about him," Simone said. Their mother would find a way to get rid of him.

"He wants it out in the open," Jackie whispered.

"Keep it for yourself." Relationships didn't last long in the public spotlight. Even without an Ariana intervention. "A little while longer."

"He's not like Wesley." Jackie read her mind. Or made her own comparisons. "MOTHER won't scare him away. I know it."

Simone hadn't imagined the capital letters that time. "She won't want to let you go."

Her sister turned, pulling her knees to her chest, the covers fluffing up around the childlike position. "That's why we're here, you know."

"To get you away from him?"

"No. To get *you* away from your sheriff."

Impossible. Unless her mother was a fly on the wall earlier tonight, she couldn't have known how necessary to the mere act of breathing Brax had become.

And he was leaving. Soon. The thought depressed her. She pushed it aside to think about Ariana. "I don't get it. I hardly told her a thing when I talked to her last night."

"She was listening in when you called me the other night."

She should have known Jackie wouldn't rat her out. And that her mother wasn't above lying about how she got the information.

"We'd have been here yesterday at the crack of dawn, but it took her a day and a half to pack and make all her phone calls."

"Why would she care, Jackie?"

Jackie snorted. If Ariana heard the sound, she'd shriek. Chandler women did not snort. "You're such a silly goose. You don't even hear the way you talk about him."

"How do I talk about Brax?" Simone whispered. Her stomach fluttered with the way she felt about him.

"Like he's the sun, the moon and the stars. Your voice sparkles. I even heard it on the phone." Jackie paused, tucking her hands beneath her cheek. "And when he kissed you tonight, it was like we weren't even in the room. That scared her. Badly. You should have seen her face. I'm sure there was a wrinkle. You'd never have known she got a BOTOX injection before we left."

Ariana's face had seemed a little fixed.

"She doesn't want to let you go."

Simone puffed air through her lips. "You're the one she won't let go. I'm miles away already."

"Are you?"

"Well, sure. I live in Goldstone, a state away, and worse, I live in a trailer."

"If you're so far beyond her control, why don't you tell her you're not looking for a job? Or that you aren't coming back, ever? Or that you write sexy little stories on the Internet?"

Oh my God. Simone almost squeaked. If her mother ever found out, if the press ever found out. Well, it would rival the Paris Hilton scandal. "How do you know about that?"

Jackie smiled. Simone only ever witnessed that look when her sister was up on the movie screen. A special glitter. As if Jackie came to life only behind the camera, when she wasn't standing in their mother's shadow.

"I do know how to use a computer. Maybe I'm one of your clients," Jackie whispered through a smile.

Simone gasped. "You are not."

But Jackie didn't answer. Instead, she said, "You think you do what you want, Simone, but you're not free."

"I have lots of freedom." Tons. "I don't wear size zero clothing."

Her sister's smile faded, and the twinkle in her eyes dimmed.

"I'm sorry. I didn't mean that the way it sounded." Simone had, and guilt made her clamp down hard on her back teeth.

"It's okay. That's why I have to tell her about him. Soon. I need to be free, too."

"Are you in love?" Suddenly, they were in high school again and whispering secrets to each other in the dark.

"He's special. When I'm with him, I feel giddy, like I can't stop smiling. And when he touches me, Simone, it's like I can't catch my breath. Like I'll die if he stops."

She knew exactly what her sister meant.

"I don't want to crawl out of his bed and sneak home. I'm twenty-eight years old, and I don't want to sneak around." Jackie pushed a lock of her silky, blond, perfect hair out of her eyes.

Simone squeezed her hand. "I guess you better tell her."

"I'm scared. Isn't that silly?"

"No." When facing her mother, Simone reverted to the eight-year-old child caught sneaking a chocolate kiss up to her room. It was a closely guarded secret that most people would never ever admit aloud, except in a psychiatrist's office, but there was always an authority figure in your life, the one person who made you quiver like you were eight years old. Or a jellyfish.

That icon happened to be her mother. Jackie was no different when it came to the Ariana effect.

"We could wake her up right now and tell her together." Like when they were kids, she and Jackie holding hands in solidarity.

Jackie gasped, choked, then laughed. "Don't rush me."

"Tomorrow?"

"When the time is right."

"Will there ever be a right time?"

A tear pooled in the corner of her sister's eye.

"She can't hurt you unless you let her." Which is

why Simone lived miles out of Ariana's sphere. It didn't seem as brave as she'd thought, more like running away. "Let's make a deal. I'll plan to tell her that I'm not taking that job with darling Ambrose, and you plan to tell her that you're in love."

"Okay." Jackie sniffed.

"And, Jackie? I really am happy for you. Don't let her take it away, no matter what."

"She might not have to. I don't think he's going to wait much longer for me to break the news to her."

Would her lover leave her if she didn't? If he put that kind of price on Jackie's love, he wasn't much of a man.

But then Simone wasn't much of a woman if she couldn't tell her mother to take that job and shove it.

Or if she couldn't tell Brax how she felt about him.

BRAX POURED HOT WATER over the tea bag in the mug. At the rate they'd all been forcing tea down her throat, Maggie would float away. It was better than wine out of the refrigerator box. He wanted her as clearheaded as possible for the forthcoming discussion regarding Carl's finances. The adrenaline burst at The Chicken Coop seemed to have wiped away any residual Xanax cobwebs.

He'd gotten rid of Chloe and Della with the promise that he would call if Maggie needed them, though it had taken fifteen minutes and extra Xanax tucked safely in the kitchen cabinet.

Maggie had then taken an extended-stay trip to the bathroom to freshen up while he'd grabbed two minutes to call Simone. He'd have given his Cottonmouth house to stay with Simone through the night, nestled against her sweetly scented body, his nose nuzzling her

hair as he whispered beautiful sentiments like wards against her mother's scorn. But he couldn't be with her.

Maggie needed him. With all the needs weighing him down, Simone's, his own, Maggie's need took precedence.

The upcoming interview was necessary if he were to provide answers. The key to Carl's death was the cash. Brax had to know if she had any idea what he might have done with three thousand.

He carried the mug of tea to the family room, shoved the coffee table back with his foot, then sat in front of Maggie. Handing her the mug, he made sure her fingers curled securely around the handle before letting go.

"I'm sorry, Tyler. That was wrong. Carl would have been humiliated."

"I wasn't embarrassed, Maggie."

Elvis marked the half hour with a one-Viva chirp.

She wrapped the mug in both hands. He was glad he'd added enough milk so that she wouldn't burn herself.

"I didn't kill him."

"Maggie—"

"I know that's what you've been thinking. The police always look at the spouse first. And I haven't been exactly calm and unemotional."

"Calm and unemotional can be a bad sign."

"I know you've had your doubts."

"Maggie, I haven't…" He had. His gut twisted with doubts from every angle. He'd misjudged how bad the marital situation was, and he'd misjudged the people in the town. He couldn't figure out which bad judgment had led them to this sorry state, Maggie's, Carl's, someone else's. Or his own for minimizing how bad things had gotten between Maggie and Carl.

Brax stopped denying. He wouldn't convince her, because she'd latched onto the truth. All he could do was ask what needed to be asked. "Tell me about the money."

"The money he was taking out?"

"The million dollars in all of his accounts."

"Oh that." She wriggled her lips. "Carl was very good at investing."

That put it mildly. And explained nothing. "You said you guys were doing okay financially."

"And I was right, wasn't I?"

"A million dollars is a helluva lot better than okay." And investing wasn't "this and that," which had been her original explanation. Irritation flashed momentarily. Brax squelched it.

"Why's the money so important?"

"Maggie, when I first got here you were pissed he was salting some of it away. I saw those withdrawals. What he took was a drop in the bucket." Even the last large chunk.

"It wasn't how much he took that mattered."

He held up his hands. "I know, I know, it was the fact that he took it at all. But where did he get all of it in the first place?" And why the hell would he live in Goldstone?

Why the hell not? It was good enough for Teesdale, Whitey and Simone, who just wanted a home. Good enough for Doodle, who coveted free burial plots.

"He used to be a stockbroker. He knew all about that stuff."

Carl? In a Wall Street three-piece suit? He couldn't quite grasp the image.

"He lost everything on Black Monday," Maggie continued.

"Black Monday?"

"Nineteen-eighty-seven. The stock market crash. People jumped out of windows."

Brax tipped his hand. "Thought that was in '29."

"Obviously, you didn't have any money in the stock market or you'd remember October 19th."

He'd probably been taking college midterms at the time. The stock market, no. "So he lost everything. Guess he recouped."

"Carl learned from his mistakes."

Brax wondered if he'd ever learn from his own mistakes.

"He got back in and stayed in until right before the last election. That man knew right when to get out, I'll tell you."

"So why did he think he was a loser?" After that conversation on the way back from The Dartboard, Brax had no doubts on Carl's self-esteem issues.

Maggie shrugged. "I think he believed everything he did since then was luck. That he could lose it all again just as easily. I don't know for sure."

Only Carl knew.

He moved on to the next question. Carl's withdrawals had been a source of irritation to Maggie, not a catastrophic event. Which left Brax with the money Carl had withdrawn the day he'd died.

He took her hand, though he knew it would do nothing to lessen the impact of what he had to ask. "Why would he take out three thousand dollars yesterday morning?"

Maggie stared at him. He couldn't tell a thing about her emotions. Surprise, shock? Then her eyes misted, and he knew it was pain. More pain heaped

on all she'd already suffered. "Because he was leaving me?"

"Between all of the accounts, he had fifty thousand in cash. If he was going to leave you, he would have taken everything." At least Brax would have taken it if he were planning to run off. Take the cash stake to start over with, leave the wife with the investments. Everybody's happy.

Brax didn't buy the running-off scenario.

"Think, Maggie. Why would he need three thousand in cash?"

"I don't know."

"You said he was acting weird. Do you think someone was blackmailing him?"

"Over what?"

He didn't have a clue himself. "Maybe he was going to try to buy out Jason."

Maggie shrugged. "Buy out the hotel? With three thousand dollars?" It sounded ridiculous, but Jason Lafoote's hotel angle was the only money deal going on in town.

"How did he feel about Lafoote and the hotel?" He already knew about the animosity, but he avoided leading phraseology. Maggie had already stated flatly that Lafoote was Carl's killer.

"Like everyone feels. He makes promises he won't keep. He'll turn Goldstone into a strip mall. Carl hated that idea."

"There was more to it than that, Maggie. Carl was angry, more than the idea of a resort and a strip mall warranted."

She shook her head. "I don't know, Tyler. I really don't. Carl said he didn't want that resort, and he talked

a bunch about how to stop it with Della." She closed her eyes and sighed. "I really didn't pay all that much attention."

He felt her own sense of damnation in that statement.

"Did you ever see them together?"

Maggie cocked her head. "No. I guess not." Then she dipped her chin as it started to tremble. "Carl wasn't around much."

"So why did you say Lafoote killed him?"

She sniffed loudly and when she spoke, tears distorted her voice. "I don't want it to be someone I know."

Nobody ever did.

He stroked her hand and put a stop to the painful interview before he did permanent damage. "I think we both need rest." He needed it if he was going to be any use tomorrow. "But you have to promise me you won't sneak out again while I'm sleeping."

She sniffled. He lightly shook her shoulder. "I'm going to take care of things for you, but I have to know you're here and safe, okay?"

"I'm sorry for worrying you, Tyler. You sleep. I promise I won't go out."

"Mom will be here tomorrow. You'll feel better."

She gave him a look, her eyes swimming in tears, her lip quivering, and he knew what she was thinking. At this moment, she didn't believe she'd ever feel better.

He was afraid she might be right.

Which made his mission all the more important. For Maggie, he had to find out what happened to Carl.

BRAX WAS DREAMING about firm legs, thong panties and ice-cream cones. Simone was melting his banana-flavored double scoop with her lips.

He'd die with anticipation before she got down to his crispy sugar cone. His blood rushed through his veins and pounded against his eardrums.

He reached one hand out to cup her beautiful cheek. Warm and wet. And red. She gave him the dazzle smile through a mouth half-eaten off by critters.

He jerked, half sat, and dragged air into his aching lungs. The dark room had given way to a lighter gloom. The pounding wasn't in his dreams, but on the trailer's front door.

Simone's ruined face, like Carl's in the jailhouse basement, haunted him still.

Jumping from the bed, he yanked on his jeans and shirt. A squint at the clock revealed the time to be half past five on the beginning of another hellacious day. A good day never began with a nightmare and less than four hours sleep.

Teesdale with news was the only logical early-morning caller he could think of.

Instead, he found his mother on the doorstep.

"Do not tell me you drove through the night, Mom." He'd have to beat her if she had, after he hugged the living daylights out of her.

"Don't be a Silly Putty." Enid Braxton flapped her hand at him. "Of course, I didn't. Rockie was good enough to drive. He's such a dear boy."

"Rockie?" He glanced over the top of her head, which didn't quite reach the center of his chest.

"He's parking the car on the other side and getting the bags."

His mother had a gentleman friend. Would wonders never cease? On her seventieth birthday, last year, she'd decided that her steel-gray hair lightly tinged with blue

looked like a Brillo pad—or was it S.O.S? He could never remember which was pink and which was blue. She'd rinsed out the tint, bleached out the gray, then added a hint of red. Something had gone terribly wrong, but Brax loved her too much to tell her the blue scouring pad beat the pink floor mop hands down.

"Now where's my hug?" she demanded, her arms wide.

"Right here." He scooped her up, hugged her tight, thanked the good Lord for her safe deliverance, then set her back on her feet.

"Now how's my Maggie?"

"Not good." Just before turning in, she'd hit the tears again like a drunk hit the bottle after a dry spell. If you looked up the word *inadequate* in the dictionary, his picture would be the pictorial example. He'd finally gotten Maggie to bed. "She's still sleeping if all that pounding didn't wake her."

"Tyler, you're not too big to put over my knee for impertinence."

"Yes, ma'am." He kissed her flower-scented hair for good measure.

"Yoo-hoo, Rockie, we're over here."

How had the elderly gentleman managed to drive if he couldn't even figure out where the front door was?

Except that this was no elderly gentleman. Hell, he couldn't be much older than Brax, with a Palm Desert tan and a weight-room build. Two suitcases dangled from his hands.

"Don't you say one word, Tyler. He's my gigolo."

Gigolo? He couldn't get the word past his paralyzed throat muscles, let alone push the thought through his mushy brain.

"He thinks I'm a rich widow with pots and pots of money. So don't you dare tell him any different. Or you'll have to drive me all the way back home because he'll dump me like Mr. Potato Head."

"Isn't that 'like a hot potato'?"

"What-evver." Said with a perfect Valley Girl twang.

Brax was sure someone had dropped him into the middle of a *Twilight Zone* episode. Or worse, *The Outer Limits*. There was always a nifty little moral at the end of *The Outer Limits*.

He couldn't for the life of him figure out what this moral was going to be.

He would *not* ask his mother if she and Rockie… made whoopie. His dad would roll over in his grave.

Brax pointed somewhere in the vicinity of the bedroom hallway. "Maggie." Half choking out his sister's name. "Help Maggie, and Rockie can come in, no questions asked."

Unless Rockie actually touched Brax's mom. Then, he'd have to deck the guy. No questions asked.

His mother blew him a kiss as he stepped back to let her in.

He almost let her get away until another horrifying thought trembled on the edge of his brain. "But he is *not* sleeping in the same room with you."

"You're so old-fashioned, Tyler. You sound just like an old man."

Women, even his mother, had aged him.

CHAPTER EIGHTEEN

BREAKFAST USUALLY consisted of coffee, hot, strong and sweet.

Which made her think dreamily of Brax.

"Simone, you'll make your double chin worse leaning on your hand that way." Her mother tapped the firm flesh beneath her own chin.

Simone's hand went reflexively to her throat. Double chin?

"Honey, pass me another muffin, would you?" Kingston waggled his fingers toward the plate just out of reach in the middle of the table.

She'd pulled out all the stops this morning by toasting English muffins and breaking into one of Mrs. Killian's jars of homemade marmalade. Kingston took two from the plate Jackie offered him.

Her mother had delicately eaten half of a half.

"Darling, it's terribly stuffy. I could barely breathe in my room last night. I barely slept a wink on that bed. There's an awful dip in the middle that I kept falling into like the Black Hole of Calcutta. And I do believe I detected eau-de-dirty-socks. Open a window or a door, would you?"

What her mother probably smelled was the swamp cooler and nothing like dirty socks. But Simone duti-

fully rose to open the front door for fresh air. She could certainly use a little herself. Maybe it would help her double chin syndrome.

She patted the underside of her chin as she opened her front door. Della almost knocked right on her face.

Simone squeaked, her heart breaking into the two-step. "You scared the heebies out of my jeebies."

Worse, she wondered what on earth could have made Della rise before her customary ten o'clock? Judge Della Montrose never let the clerks schedule court before noon.

"Is it Maggie?" she whispered, her voice trembling.

"When I left last night, she was fine. Well, as fine as fine can be under the circumstances." Della's voice was equally low, befitting those circumstances.

Everybody was fine. She was fine, Brax was fine, Jackie was fine. Now Maggie was fine, too. Fine was an overused, meaningless word that didn't mean diddly.

"I have to talk to you about something else." Della glanced over her shoulder at the long, black car nestled against the short picket fence. Goldstone dust now covered the body panels, hood and roof, clinging like barnacles Kingston would have to scrub off. "Whose car is that?"

"My mother's. She came for a visit."

"Simone, don't keep your guest standing on the doorstep. It's extremely impolite," Ariana called.

Holding the door wide, Simone added, "I made fresh coffee." Her mother had gulped the last of the previous pot as if it were water despite the fact she claimed caffeine was bad for her nerves and bad for the skin.

Della was perfectly decked out, in flattering navy-

blue slacks and blazer and her blond hair fastened se-
dately atop her head. Perfect, with the small exception
of a skewed eyebrow that reached much higher than the
other, giving her a lopsided appearance. Simone felt
like tipping her head to bring Della's face back in line.

She'd almost shut the door when she remembered
MOTHER had dictated that it be open. Turning, she ran
smack into Della's solid back.

Simone sidled around her, noting the glassy eyes
and dropped jaw of stargazing.

Della, not usually a stutterer, stuttered. "Y-you're,"
came out, then she completely lost her power of
speech.

"Simone usually has better manners. I'm Ariana
Chandler." As usual, her mother held out her hand like
a queen expecting a curtsy or a kiss. Brax had sorely
disappointed her last night when he hadn't acted
appropriately to the gesture.

Della, agog, took Ariana's finger in two of hers. A
mortal touching a goddess.

"That's my sister, Jackie."

"Si-mone. Your sister's name is Jacqueline."

Maybe her name was Jacqueline, but *she* was Jackie
and always would be, no matter how many awards she
garnered.

Kingston half rose. "I'm Kingston Hightower, hanging on to the coattails of these lovely ladies and basking in their reflected glory."

"You've never hung on anybody's coattails." Jackie
spoke. More than one word and without being spoken
to first. Amazing.

Simone did the expected honors. "Della's our mayor
and judge"

"Oh goodness, the mayor *and* the judge. How utterly impressive. We can see Goldstone is good for the women's movement."

Della beamed at the compliment. But Simone knew that facetious tone. She put a stop to anything else that might come. "I promised Della coffee. Cream and sugar?" In her haste, she suddenly forgot how Della took hers.

Kingston pushed back his chair and, with an elegant hand flourish, offered it to Della. "You ladies sit. I'll bring the coffee. It is my greatest pleasure to serve."

He glanced at Jackie. Jackie glanced at him.

Very weird. Subliminal messages. Did Jackie suspect that Kingston had finally tired of being Ariana's glorified gofer? Always affable, a big man with a big laugh and even bigger shoulders, Kingston had taken a stand against Ariana twice. Once after Wesley, when he'd forbidden Ariana to ever interfere in her daughter's love life again. After that, she'd interfered surreptitiously, with cutting comments but no overt action—at least that anyone knew of. The second time had been over Simone herself, when her mother had a tantrum over news of Simone's catastrophic failure. Kingston told her to shut up—yes, those very words, *shut up*—then he'd offered both his shoulders for Simone to hang on to.

Kingston brought the coffee, cream and sugar. Della spooned and stirred, creamy liquid sloshing onto the saucer of her dainty cup as she stared at the visions seated across the table. Ariana and Jacqueline Chandler. In the flesh.

Simone saw it written all over her face. Della was starstruck.

"You said you needed to tell me something?" Simone prompted, finally capturing Della's attention by kicking her foot.

Della stared blankly for fifteen seconds, as if she couldn't remember what she'd come for, let alone her own name. "Oh, yes." She toyed with her cup. "Look what I've done, clumsy me." She noticed the overflow in her saucer for the first time.

Simone tapped her hand. "Don't worry about it. You said Maggie was fine…" She let the question hang in the air.

"Yes. She is. I think. But I've been doing a lot of thinking, Simone. I really couldn't sleep last night."

"Who is Maggie, dear?" Ariana could not allow herself to be left of center stage for long.

"Maggie's our friend."

"Her husband was murdered yesterday." Della raised her eyebrows, the cockeyed one almost disappearing beneath her bangs.

"The day before actually, but they didn't find him until yesterday." Simone felt a little tremor thinking about Carl alone in the gorge all night long. Had he suffered?

"Oh my."

"Who killed him?" Trust a man, Kingston, to go right to the heart of the matter.

"Brax doesn't know."

"That rude man who was here last night?" Her mother couldn't resist a little dig.

"Brax is a sheriff."

"I thought he was sheriff of some tiny burg in California."

"He's a county sheriff, but since he's Maggie's brother, he's helping Sheriff Teesdale."

"Elwood Teesdale is *our* sheriff," Della explained. She turned to Simone. "What else did Brax say? About why Elwood thinks Carl was murdered. I still don't understand. I tried to find Elwood this morning, but they said he was…tracking."

"They went up the trail where Carl fell."

"But why do they think he was murdered? No one would tell me anything last night." Della turned her cup in her saucer.

There hadn't been a murder in Goldstone since Della took the city reins. There hadn't been a murder since…well, maybe not since Wyatt Earp shot some gunslinger right in the Flood's End before it was called the Flood's End. Mr. Doodle renewed the bloodstains once a year with red lacquer. When Brax and Sheriff Teesdale brought in the villain, Della would preside over the trial. Her first murder trail, at least in Goldstone.

"Maybe it's better you don't know anything," Simone said. "Isn't there something about bias?"

"That's for the jury," Della scoffed, "not the judge."

"This is all so confusing. I feel a migraine coming on." Ariana put a hand to her forehead. "The thought of you living in a town where a murder's occurred. It doesn't *bear* thinking about. We have to get you home." Grabbing Kingston's hand, Ariana hung on, giving an effective performance. "You must convince her, Kingston. She can't stay in this awful, crime-ridden place."

"Brax will take care of everything." Brax the hero, Brax the savior. Every pair of eyes settled on her as if she'd said the two glowing phrases aloud. She hadn't. Had she?

"I'm going back to bed. Wake me up when this night-

mare is over. Or you find a Ritz nearby." Ariana exited with a hand to her brow, Kingston guiding her by the elbow.

"Your poor mother."

Yes, her poor mother. She'd take to her bed before she'd willingly gave up center stage to a murder investigation. Her mother always got the last word, even when she wasn't in the room.

Jackie picked up the empty plate. "I'll toast more muffins."

"Jacqueline Chandler toasts her own muffins?" Della's husky awed whisper fell into a hush with Jackie at the far end of the kitchen ripping apart muffins.

"Yeah." Her sister might actually be capable of wiping her own butt, too. Why did people insist on thinking Jackie incompetent? Or maybe Della meant that movie stars were supposed to have scads of servants to see to their every desire.

Simone suddenly wanted to drop the subject of movie stars and Academy Awards. "So, you wanted to know what Brax told me? Well, he didn't tell me anything except that he and the sheriff were going up there." She pointed to the western hills. "I don't know why they think it was murder, they just do. I believe him."

Della sat there for a long moment, the fingers of her left hand covering her mouth, her gaze fixed on the blue-flecked tiles around the base of the pellet stove. Then her eyes misted over. "I've made a decision. I've thought about this all night."

"What?"

"Jason Lafoote wants to name a wing of the hotel after Carl. I'm going to grant his permits with the proviso that he does it."

Simone gasped. "You can't do that, Della."

"It's the only thing this town has to give Carl. I won't stand in the way of his memory being kept alive."

"That's ridiculous. Carl hated the hotel. It's a resort. For gambling. No one's even going to know the name of some wing."

"Jason's going to commission a statue and put it right in the front lobby."

Simone spread her hands, pleading. "This is a ruse he's cooked up. He said something about it yesterday. He's playing on your sympathies."

"I'm doing it for Maggie."

"Maggie's not going to care about a statue."

Della grabbed her hand, squeezed. "Simone, you didn't see her late last night. You wouldn't recognize her. She needs something badly. I have to do this for her."

"Brax and the sheriff finding Carl's killer is what she needs."

"What if they never do? What if it was some transient who followed Carl up there thinking he had a few bucks in his pocket?"

That's what they were all hoping for, wasn't it? That it was someone none of them knew.

Simone wrote a fantasy, sent a nasty e-mail and now guilt gnawed at her belly. Della told Maggie she was better off without Carl. She'd even called him worthless and useless or other names Simone couldn't quite remember. Maybe the statue was more about Della asking Carl's forgiveness than anything to do with Maggie.

Her fingers started to hurt in Della's hard grip.

"Say you'll back me on this, Simone. Chloe will, I know, then everyone else will fall in line."

She chewed on the inside of her lip. "I'm still not sure it'll be good for Maggie."

"It will. She'll see how we all honored Carl. It won't bring him back, but it will show her that we all loved him."

It would also go a long way to helping Della forget the things she'd said at the afternoon tea party. Guilt was a terrible thing. It burrowed deep and changed the course of lives. It gave Jason a foothold in their town.

A lump in her throat, Simone nodded. "All right. For Maggie."

Della closed her eyes and fervently whispered, "Thank you."

"So you want me to squeeze Lafoote." Teesdale was ahead on the trail.

"Yeah. I got him primed with all that crap."

"All right. I'll give it a shot."

With Maggie finally in his Mom's tender care, Brax was free to follow Carl's trail. He'd arrived at Teesdale's door a little after six, and, as he'd presumed, the sheriff was already on the phone and making plans. He'd been more than happy to make an earlier trek into the hills.

At the edge of the path, Teesdale suddenly leaned over, bracing his hands on both knees. "Will ya lookee here."

Metal glinted in the sun. Keys.

"Hmm," Teesdale mused. "Same make as Carl's." A rubber protector with the truck's emblem covered one key. "How do you suppose they got here?"

Identically braced on his knees, Brax suggested, "Fell out of his pocket?"

Teesdale turned his head. "You tried, didn't ya? Last night. Saw you down there in the parking lot. Don't come out so easy, do they?"

"Maybe he looped them through his belt and they came loose." Brax played devil's advocate.

"We found the truck there." The sheriff pointed to the dirt lot a hundred yards back down the path. "And we found them here. Awful quick for them to work themselves loose."

"Nothing says it couldn't have happened that way."

"Nope. Nothing says that some lazy ass wipe who didn't want to walk too far didn't throw 'em down here after wiping his prints off Carl's truck."

Brax nodded. "Nothing says it didn't happen like that."

Teesdale whipped a paper bag from his back pocket, snapped it open, put his hand inside and plucked up the keys with the bottom of the sack, then turned it inside out. "We'll take them with us." Then he dropped a swatch of the paper bag and grounded it to the spot with a rock.

It took them less than half an hour of power hiking to reach the small plateau above Carl's resting place, a mere dust speck in the gorge below, where the chickens had come close to running him over. Yellow tape, fluttering in the morning air, marked the precise location.

Teesdale stood at the edge of the drop and pushed back the brim of his hat. Sweat trickled from beneath the band.

They'd pulled up twenty yards short of X marks the spot, saving the pathway for further analysis as they

worked their way up to the plateau. It would have been a likely rest stop for Carl to take a slug from his bottle in the miniscule shade of a tall, rounded rock sticking out of the side of the hill. Brax took a slug of his own water. The morning hadn't reached the high temps yet, but the hills had already begun to bake, shimmering waves of heat rising off the rocks.

If it had been his scene, Brax would have brought an ID tech, or at the very least, a processing kit. The extent of Goldstone Sheriff's Department's evidence kit was a box of rubber gloves the dispatcher's wife had swiped from the hospital in Bullhead, paper lunch sacks from the minimart and a disposable camera.

"That's where he went down." Teesdale pointed.

One long scuff mark marred the hillside. Carl's journey was not a straight fall, but a steep, protracted roll, interrupted by small rock formations and scrubby brush. Nothing large enough to grab onto or stop Carl's descent in progress.

Brax squatted, resting his elbow on his knee, to study the dusty trail. "You say it's pretty well used?"

Teesdale came down to his level. "Couple a hikers a week maybe. I'd be damn surprised to find it devoid of footprints."

Brax could make out layers of faded shoe prints. A light breeze blew over them, shifting the puffy dirt granules as if they were snowflakes. If there had once been a tread to match to a shoe, it was probably long gone even before they'd found Carl's body. A fine layer of dust coated everything in Goldstone, from the cars to a trailer's white siding, and it took barely more than a breath to move the fine stuff around.

Shoe prints weren't going to solve the case. The

most they'd provide was icing on the cake once a shoe to match to was found.

Simultaneously, they rose and stepped to either side of the path, Teesdale taking the cliff side and Brax the opposite.

If they were lucky, they'd find a bloody rock that had been used to crush Carl's skull before he was pushed over the side.

They weren't lucky. They found nothing. Teesdale took a couple of pictures of partial prints. If a scuffle had ensued, evidence of it in the sand was long gone.

Having made slowly decreasing circles around the area, they finally stood above the very spot Carl had fallen. Brax squatted for a closer examination of the sector. You saw a helluva lot more at ground level than if you stood, looking down.

Most important was what he didn't see. "There are no shoe prints here." As if someone had cleared the area.

At the edge of the path, Teesdale hunkered. "Interesting."

Brax turned on the balls of his feet. "In fact, there aren't any from here—" he pointed approximately five feet above the fall site "—to there." Approximately five feet back down the path. From the base of an oddly shaped rock to the edge of the drop.

"Well, hell. Ain't that cause for speculation?"

As evidence, it sucked, but a killer was never caught by one spectacular find. It was always the small things which, when added together, could be brought to put pressure on a suspect until he or she cracked under the mounting weight.

Retreating, watching to make sure he stepped into

the footprints he'd already made, Brax backed up. And kept going even as his feet felt the slight rise. He had no idea what he'd see, if anything at all. But he'd been trained to survey a scene from every angle and from every possible level—ground, waist, eye and above, if you could. Each gave a different perspective.

Ten feet back up the hillside, he dropped to a hunker once more, one foot flat, the other taking his weight on the ball.

The plateau, the path, the rock. One side still in shade, the other in the heating sun, the rock rose at an angle from the hillside. For a moment, he almost smiled. Wide at the base and cylindrical, with a slightly rounded bulge at its peak, it jutted like a hardened penis.

He didn't think Teesdale would appreciate the analogy. And it certainly wasn't appropriate to the mission.

But he couldn't take his eyes off that rock.

It reminded him of something. Yeah, yeah, a cock. But something else. Something at the edge of his mind.

Jesus H. Christ. It was the rock in Simone's fantasy. The first stop where the woman had pushed her partner back against that rock and taken him in her mouth.

Shit.

"Think we're done here," he said, rising to his feet.

Teesdale glanced up. "We are?"

"Yep." Brax considered pushing on up the trail, but he couldn't remember all the landmarks in the fantasy. The landmarks themselves had left the least impression during his read-through. His mind had focused on other, more vivid details. "I've got to get to the bank when it opens."

First, he had a more immediate connection to investigate. Like why Carl had requested a fantasy that took place on the very trail from which he'd fallen to his death.

CHAPTER NINETEEN

HER MOTHER HAD EMERGED from the bedroom fifteen minutes later draped in yet another pantsuit, this one emerald with a flowing train behind it. She'd artfully arranged herself on the sofa, the orange material a perfect backdrop to the emerald silk. Della had refused to leave, sitting on the opposite end of the couch basking in Ariana's reflected glory.

Simone had refilled the coffeepot three times, visited the bathroom twice and turned on the swamp cooler. It didn't help.

"Simone, you really shouldn't wear yellow. It makes your skin sallow."

She almost jumped up to exchange the yellow tee for pale peach. But Jackie gave her a look. *Don't you dare.*

"Simone, you have lipstick on your teeth. I can see we're going to have to take you for another makeup application lesson at Guittard's when we get home."

She ran her tongue across her front teeth until it hurt.

"She's such a pretty girl, isn't she, Della? Of course, if she'd had Jacqueline's looks and my talent, she could have been a star. But Simone's got her own special charms." Ariana beamed as if she'd said something wonderful.

What charms? According to her mother, she was fat, she needed a facial badly to reduce blotchiness, and her hair had turned to straw in the dry desert air.

She wasn't sure how much more of her mother's exalted presence she could take without going stark raving mad. Or melting into a puddle of gooey tears.

She almost welcomed the telltale crunch on her gravel drive and the sharp slam of a car door.

She knew without seeing that it was him. Brax. Her hero. Come to her rescue. Standing at the door, she took in his brisk stride up her front walk, her chest swelled with emotion. Oh my, oh my, he was so…

Pissed.

He grabbed her by the arm even as she opened the screen door.

"We have to talk." He stopped, suddenly noticing the four pairs of eyes focused on him. "About that bag I brought over last night."

"The bag?"

"Yeah. The paper bag." He widened his eyes with meaning.

"Oh. The bag." Her hand fluttered, then she managed to point to the back of the house. "I put it away. In the guest room."

"Let's get it." His teeth clamped sharply.

Carl's fantasy. What could he possibly want with the fantasy now? They'd been through all that last night. He'd gotten over his initial anger. Hadn't he?

Obviously not, if the pinch of his fingers on her upper arm meant anything. He didn't hurt her, but neither was he letting her go anywhere without him.

She let him lead her down the hall past her office to the guest room, the silence in the living room beating at

her nerve endings. Brax pulled her in and closed the door.

Thank goodness she'd made the bed.

"Where is it?"

"In the closet."

He followed at her heels, then breathed down her neck as she pulled the bag from its hiding place. He took it from her numb fingers, then dumped the contents.

Her panties landed smack-dab in the middle of the bed.

They both stared for two long, slow heartbeats, long enough for Simone's face to reach conflagration stage.

"I hid them in there last night. I guess I forgot."

He spoke after the longest time. "I didn't forget. Not a thing. Sorry I barged in like that."

"My mother already thinks you're unforgivably rude."

He laughed, a short bark. "No extra harm done then." Taking her hand in his, he pulled it to his lips for the briefest brush of his lips. "We have to go through the story again. I saw the rock, right where Carl must have fallen. It's real. And I'm wondering how many other landmarks in there are real."

Real? "What rock?"

He pulled her close, chest to chest. "*The* rock. Where you wrote that she—"

"Oh my God, *that* rock." The blow job rock. She would never, ever write another fantasy in her life. Well, not for anyone she knew. She did have to make a living, after all.

"I want to go back up there. I want to see what's at the end of that trail."

"It's a big cave." Carl had her end it there, before the couple went inside. "Do you think it's real, too?"

"Highly likely. I want to know why he was so specific. You said he gave you the physical details to use."

"Yes. What does it mean, Brax?"

"Hell if I know. That's why I'm going up there. Someone killed him on the trail he told you to write about. It could be simple coincidence, but that story is like a map, and I want to follow it to its conclusion."

"I shouldn't have deleted all his e-mails. We could have used those. It would have been easier."

He unrolled several scrolls and arranged them by number, stopping to glance down at the script. "It would have been easier on *me*." He looked at her, his gaze deep blue. "Reading this the first time damn near killed me."

What exactly did that mean? She wasn't stupid. She knew all about lust and anticipation and that the way to a man's heart wasn't through his stomach. But still... "Do you think I look insipid in yellow?"

"What?" A line furrowed between his eyebrows.

"Nothing. I..." *I am totally stupid and moronic asking a question like that at a time like this.* Her cheeks heated with the silly schoolgirl insecurities that question revealed.

"It makes you look..." He struggled for the right thing to say. "You take my breath away whatever you're wearing."

That was still about sex. She wanted, needed more, but was afraid to ask for anything. She pointed to the neatly scripted scrolls. "Do you want to follow it like a treasure map?"

Simone flattened page one even as it struggled to snap itself into a tight roll again.

A map. That's exactly what her fantasy was. Brax pointed. "See that view you've described?"

The rise of the hills off to the left, the muted sound of highway traffic and the courthouse clock tower.

"I saw it when I was coming back down. This is the same trail." Brax looked at her. "Did he tell you to write it that way?"

"I told you last night. He gave me all the details to use. Except the…"

Except the sex parts. That Simone got to make up for herself. Yes, Brax knew. How could he forget? Those were the parts he'd damn near memorized despite himself.

Page three. He found himself smoothing it out almost reverently. His favorite page. Damn. The effect was worse with her citrus scent swirling around him and the warmth of her arm pressed to his as they knelt together at the side of the bed. He leaned over to read.

> The huge cylindrical stone jutted out from the mountainside like a phallic symbol of the gods, casting its shadow over the gorge below. Long, wide, with a rounded cap at its peak, it resembled an erect cock, beckoning them to worship at its base. She pushed him back against the rock, her hand flat against his chest, sliding down through the buttons she'd opened. Her fingers trailed his abdomen to the snap of his jeans.

He knew what was coming. His body knew it, too. The Simone effect. His jeans were suddenly a tad too tight and heat rose to his face.

"Uh, that's the rock." Yeah, the rock. Think about that. Not what her characters were doing on the rock.

Taking him in her mouth, she circled the tip with her tongue.

Shit. Think about the meaning of the rock itself. "Picture the jut of it out over the path."

"Yes. He called it a phallic symbol."

Damn. It was that all right. With Simone next to him and her words on the page tempting him, the symbol was overpowering, and her words like the call of a seductive siren.

"And the vista view from that rock." The view, yeah, that's what he'd noticed right off. "It's the same."

"The same as what?"

He hesitated too long.

"That's where Carl fell," she said for him. He nodded and she closed her eyes. "Are you sure it had to be…"

In Cottonmouth, murder had never become routine. But it hadn't been a shock since his first year in the department when he'd found Dick Monahan's body at the bottom of Lucas Tinsin's bonfire. Property line dispute.

"It was the same spot," he said.

Carl's keys had not slipped out of his pocket and the wind hadn't miraculously swept clean the very quadrant of path from which he'd made his tumble.

The hazel of Simone's eyes deepened to stark green magnified by the shimmer of tears. "They're all my friends, Brax."

And you never wanted to find that the smile and good humor of someone you knew could harbor the

soul of a killer. You'd bait a trap, thinking you had total control over the outcome. You'd avoid facing it until suddenly other lives hung in the balance.

Even then, a man didn't always learn his lesson. His lesson had started with murder in Cottonmouth. He was learning it all over again in Goldstone. Anyone was capable of anything if the circumstances were right and the anger burned hot enough.

Anger such as Maggie's.

"Don't." She stared at him with wide, frightened eyes.

His mouth dried up. "What?"

"I know what you're thinking."

She couldn't know the depths to which his mind could sink. Especially the depraved notions he had about his own sister.

"Maggie didn't do this," she said. Emphatically. With a hint of terror.

He struggled to breathe. How could she read his mind so easily? He took her shoulders in his hands, holding her still. "I don't blame her if she did. Bad things were going on in her marriage. I ignored them."

"You can't blame yourself for Carl being dead."

He turned the statement around on her. "Didn't you blame yourself because of a fantasy and an e-mail?"

"You showed me I was wrong. I still feel bad, but then I think of what you told me."

Christ. There was such an overwhelming wealth of trust in her statement. Trust he wasn't worthy of. "It's not the first time I've minimized a situation."

"Hindsight's twenty-twenty. It only works in hindsight."

Another time, he might have laughed. How could he

explain that a cop couldn't afford hindsight? "I didn't come to Goldstone for a vacation." One could actually say he'd been running away. Like Simone. Like everyone else in Goldstone.

"Why are you here then?"

He steeled himself, then gave her a confession he'd given to no one else. "I let a friend get murdered."

"Did you kill him?"

He rubbed her arms almost absently. "You know that's not what I meant. He was killed. It was preventable if I'd been paying attention the way a cop is supposed to."

She put a hand to his cheek. "I think you did everything in your power. I *know* you did."

If only things were that simple. In Simone's world, maybe they were. "The truth is that I didn't."

"If you didn't kill him, and you didn't know he was going to be killed, then it isn't your fault."

"Simone—"

She stopped him with a soft kiss. "You can't save everyone from the bad things that will happen to them, Brax. I wish I hadn't written that fantasy. But I'm not sure Carl would be alive even if I hadn't. And I'm not sure your friend would be alive if you'd done anything different. You can't be sure, either."

Just as Teesdale couldn't save an eight-year-old girl. But he could save his own child. And he'd done it by coming to Goldstone and giving her a safer life.

"You can only do your best, and I know without a doubt that's exactly what you did. But you can't do your job if you blame yourself for things you can't control."

He knew that. It was damn near the same thing he'd been telling himself.

"I know you *know* that," she said, though he hadn't said anything. "But you don't believe it."

"Are you some sort of mind reader?"

She put her face to his chest and shook her head. "No. But I think you tend to think like me. So I'm telling you the same stuff I always tell myself."

They were alike? Sweet, innocent Simone? And him? "It was my job, Simone, and I failed." Christ, how did she get him to admit these things aloud? "Your guilt over that fantasy and what I did are two completely different things."

She looked at him, then whispered, "Are they?"

He opened his mouth to shoot off a quick retort. She gently covered his lips with her palm. "Think before you say it. Is the guilt, not the circumstance, really that different?"

Asked that way, he suddenly wasn't so sure.

She must have seen that uncertainty in his eyes. Or read his mind again. "Don't answer now," she said. "Just think. Very carefully."

He tipped her chin up and lightly kissed her nose. "I'll think." He would. Later. When he knew what had happened to Carl. For now, the revelation eased something deep inside him. Her simple acceptance of his biggest mistake was more than he'd believed possible.

Simone smiled, flipping his heart with her dazzle. "Let's talk about Maggie and the ridiculous notion that she pushed Carl."

"I don't—"

She ignored him. "You know, if Maggie was angry, she'd have shot Carl right then and there, not followed him up a mountain trail looking for a perfect place to push him off."

Jesus, the way her mind worked. Icy logic confirming exactly what he wanted to hear.

"And she wouldn't have risked that Carl might not be dead when he hit the bottom."

Brax stared at her.

"If you're really, really angry, you just want them dead and you don't care about making it look like it was an accident."

He blinked.

"That's why the death penalty doesn't work. Because people don't think first, they just act. At least most of the time."

"You scare me, Miss Chandler." She made him hot, actually, the way she smelled, the way her mind worked. Her defense of Maggie. Her belief in him. She could turn any man's thinking around, and so help him God, he needed that. Now.

"Someday, I'll write a murder mystery," she told him.

Putting a hand to her face, he smoothed his thumb across her cheek. "I think you write a mean fantasy. I wouldn't give up your strong suit."

"There can be sex in mysteries."

"Hot sex?"

"Oh yeah. All that threat of danger and lives at risk. Very fast, very hot and very sexy. Against-the-wall kind of sex where they don't even have time to get their clothes off."

He put a finger to her lips to shush her. "You better stop right there or we'll never finish this mission."

She pulled his finger away. "You wouldn't dare. My mother's out there."

"I don't care." He waited, his gaze roaming her face.

"But you'd be embarrassed when we walked out afterward. Humiliated even. She'd look at you like you were…" She stopped, her eyes wide and bright with glimmering emotion.

"Look at you like you were what?"

She didn't even seem to notice that he'd used the same pronoun, turning the statement back on her.

"Like you were life's greatest disappointment," she whispered.

Her scent screwed with his common sense. He let it. He pulled her hand down to the hard bulge in his jeans. "Does this feel like I'm looking at life's biggest disappointment?"

She stared at him through wide, disbelieving eyes. More than anything, he needed her to believe. In herself. In her power over him. Last night, her skin had glowed with mortification after she'd lost herself in his touch, in his arms. This morning he wanted to reward her with that same loss of control, but this time he'd teach her its glory, see her revel in it. At this moment, bad as the timing was, it was a gift he had to give her. She'd given him something equally precious, her acceptance and her trust. He wanted to drown out the sound of her mother's disapproving voice. She needed him. He needed her.

He pressed her hand, rubbed himself with her palm. "This feels like anticipation, like I don't give a flying rat's ass who's out there or who hears or how they look at us afterward. This feels like I'll go crazy if you don't do exactly what that story says."

She worried the inside of her cheek.

"Please. Put me out of my misery," he murmured, a hair's breadth away from taking her lips with his. "I'm begging you."

She looked at him as if no man in her life had ever begged for her touch. "Stand up."

He did as she commanded, rising, giving her, on her knees, all the power over him.

She undid his belt, slowly pulling the leather free of the buckle, her palms resting on him as she gazed up. Taking even longer to unzip him, she stretched out the thin wire of his tension.

She tugged at his waistband. He helped her push the jeans over his hips until she'd exposed him completely. A groan escaped him as she closed her fingers around him, a long heartfelt sound of desire and need. He gave up the last of his control to her ministrations as she put her mouth on him.

Her cherry-red lips caressed his length until they met her fingers fisted at his base. Then she looked at him with a gaze drunk on her own power over him. He almost came, hanging on only with the knowledge that it was too fast, that he'd rob her of something she badly needed. Her tongue swirling back up, she sucked the tip.

He pushed his fingers through her silky hair, begging her without words. This time she moaned and clutched his hips, taking him deeper, holding nothing back. Soft delicious sounds in her throat that vibrated against his nerve endings.

"You're so beautiful." The sight of him sliding inside her warmth, then his flesh reappearing, wet with her, the tip of her tongue as she drank from him. He lost himself in sight, sound and sensation, gave voice to it low in his throat.

"Take me to heaven, Simone. Please. Please." She'd cried out her joy for him last night. He would do no less for her now.

His muscles bunched beneath her touch, a fire built in his belly, then shot low and wide. His hips thrust, filling her. He closed his eyes, grit his teeth until he exploded in light and sound.

He called out her name, cried out to God and gave her his essence. She took everything he had, everything he was, keeping him inside until his spirit floated back and reentered his body.

He'd wrapped her hair around his hands. She'd left marks on his body where she'd clutched him. He cupped her face. She nuzzled against him.

Pulling her up, he pressed her against him, whispering in her hair. "Thank you."

She burrowed into his chest. "You shouted."

"Hell, yes." He'd do it again, shout out in pleasure and exultation. "Nothing you could ever do to me, and nothing I could ever do to you is shameful or embarrassing. Nothing."

She burrowed deeper and shuddered. Pushing her back a fraction, he tilted her face until she was forced to look at him. "Don't take that away from yourself. Or from me."

He was ready to battle the red stain on her cheeks. Instead, she glowed, her eyes, her moist lips still with lipstick amazingly intact. "That was the most incredible thing a man ever let me do."

"Let you?" He smoothed back the hair he'd disheveled. "I begged you."

She rose on tiptoe to throw her arms around his neck. "I'm special."

He squeezed her tight. "You don't even know the half of it."

SIMONE LOOKED DOWN at his head as he gathered the scrolls of her story, tossing the ribbons aside, ordering them, then rolling them all backward to force them flat.

What had they just done? It was much more than sex, more than taking him in her mouth. Brax wanted them all to hear. Not some guy triumph thing, as he'd laid the homecoming queen in his backseat.

He'd wanted *her*. He'd needed *her*. He'd come inside *her*.

"It's all about me," she whispered to herself.

He turned, flopped on the bed, his belt buckle flapping, then gave her a shit-eating grin. "Yeah. It's all about you."

She had the feeling there wasn't an exhibitionist bone in his body. Yet he'd cried out for her. He didn't care that anyone heard.

He fluttered the pages at her. "I'll take these with me to go over them more fully. You gonna be all right with Mommie—your mother?"

She snorted. In spite of Ariana. Maybe *because* of Ariana. "I'm going with you."

"Not."

She braced her hands on his shoulders and climbed onto his lap. "For sure."

"It's dangerous."

"You think Carl's killer is skulking around the scene of the crime?"

"They always come back."

She rubbed noses with him. "You're afraid my fantasy will be your undoing, and you'll have to have me six times on the way up there."

"You're already my undoing. I let you blow me while your mother was sitting out in the living room. And I've got a feeling trailer doors are very thin."

They were. Little better than wallpaper. She nibbled his lip. "Yeah. You let me blow you."

It was crass. It was crude. It was exhilarating. What she'd done. Sex play. Love talk. She'd never been comfortable with any of it. Except on paper. Always inadequate. Always wondering about the performance. But not with Brax.

"And you were so easy," she said.

"You were too damn good. I couldn't help myself. Think your mother will understand?"

She should have been horrified at what they'd done. At least a little embarrassed.

Instead, she still tasted him, still felt the throb of him in her mouth, the bite of his fingers against her scalp at the moment he filled her, his wholly animal cry that lifted her above herself.

Her mother would understand all right. Brax had staked a claim. He'd drawn a line in the sand. Shouted his emotions to the world with an "Ah, God" and an "oh Jesus" as if he were really saying, "Your daughter is the most beautiful perfect creature I've ever touched or wanted and I'm damn well going to let you know. Take that, Ariana Chandler."

"Let me go with you, Brax." She wasn't silly enough to think that what he'd done for her was love. But it was equally as important. And she wouldn't willingly let Brax leave her side until the day his vacation ended.

How many days were left?

He bunched her hair in his hand and pulled her head back. "Sweetheart, I—"

She put her hand over his mouth. "I'm going with you. We're going to figure out who killed Carl. We're going to save Maggie." She put her lips to his, a hair's

breadth away, as he'd done to her. "You don't have to do it all alone."

He searched her face, then seemed to find his answer. "All right. But you'll need better shoes than that." He pointed to her sandals. "And we sure can't leave this room with your lipstick still in place. It'll look like I made up all that noise for nothing." He took her mouth, stroked her lips, then dived deep. She tasted him all over again, his heat, his tang. Then he sucked her lower lip into his mouth and devoured her remaining cherry lipstick.

BRAX OPENED THE DOOR and guided Simone before him, then stepped out, buckling his belt as he turned in the hallway. Like the proverbial pin drop in a silent cathedral, the unmistakable clank of metal filled the trailer from one end to the other.

He wondered at the wisdom of his blatant display. He could have done up his belt while Simone changed her shoes. Ariana would find the belt exhibition distasteful. Simone would know it meant he wasn't ashamed, not of being with her, not for being loud and crude about how damn good she made him feel. What was between them was far beyond the physical. Simone needed a statement and making a statement required drama.

And it required further cementing action. He tucked his fingers beneath Simone's hair, kneading her nape. "From now on, you can only wear yellow. It makes you glow," he said, once again loud enough to fill the entire trailer. Then he turned her head with a gentle brush of his fingers along her jaw and kissed her, reveling in the warmth of her mouth, the zest of their lovemaking and the pulse beating wildly at her throat.

He was damn sure Ariana Chandler had never before been at a loss for words.

Simone had struggled to build her own foundation, and he wouldn't let anyone, especially not her own mother, tear it from beneath her.

Judge Della Montrose blinked, slowly, like an owl.

Simone fanned herself with the sheaf of papers. "We're going out for a while."

"Simone! You cannot leave me alone." Crumpled silk filled her mother's fisted hand.

"I'll be back. MOTHER." Simone's teeth snapped on the title.

"But—"

"We're going for a hike, Mrs. Chandler. A long hike. In the hills. We've got things to discuss." Brax paused long enough to suggest to Ariana that talking wasn't all they'd be doing.

Academy Award-winning Ariana Chandler blinked as owlishly as Della.

Simone slapped Brax's arm with twenty pages of pure fantasy. "Stop that," she hissed, then spoiled the effect by giggling.

Just as quickly, her smile faded. He knew the moment she remembered why they were going up there. Because Carl was dead. Murdered. You wanted to forget, you tried to forget, but as soon as you *did* forget, guilt slammed home like a battering ram.

It was like the first time he'd laughed after his dad died. When he realized he was laughing with his old man only days in the grave.

Simone turned soberly to her mother. "Kingston and Jackie will entertain you."

"They're gone. Kingston looked nearly apoplectic

and begged Jackie to accompany him. He practically dragged her out of here by her hair. I'm sure he wanted to save her from corruption."

Right. Brax had a feeling Kingston Hightower dragged the pretty Jackie out by the hair for a very different reason. There was something between those two. Furtive looks, sideways glances. A smile just between the two. He'd been in their presence perhaps all of ten minutes, but their byplay had set off his radar.

Ariana wouldn't have let them go if she'd had even an inkling.

"I would have rushed out with them, but—" she glanced at Della "—we have a guest." Her how-could-you look stabbed Simone.

He wondered if Ariana's sanctimonious, holier-than-thou attitude was a calculated method of belittling Simone.

He suspected the answer was yes.

Della jumped to her feet, tripped on a buckled bit of shag, then scuttled sideways, like a crab, to the front door. "Thanks for the coffee. Think about what I said. We'll talk later. Bye." The screen door slammed behind her.

"If you leave with him, Simone..."

Ariana's unfinished threat hung in the air. Brax prayed Simone would take up the gauntlet, at the same time fearing it. Neither woman would win, both of them would lose, and nothing would ever be the same.

Simone wasn't ready for that confrontation.

He also realized he wanted to be there for her when she was, whenever and wherever the time came.

CHAPTER TWENTY

"THIS IS IT. This is the cave. Just like Carl described it."
Simone flapped page twenty beneath his nose, pointing.

"Yeah. Looks like it is." After two hours of hard
walking and two bottles of water, they'd made it.

Glancing over his shoulder for the umpteenth time,
Brax couldn't shake the bad feeling. He noticed nothing out of the ordinary on the way up, but he couldn't
throw off the itch between his shoulder blades.

Carl's fantasy had been a map all right. Every landmark he'd requested Simone to use matched the long
trek exactly. The story ended with the words, "And
then he took her inside to bestow his final gift."

When he'd first read it, Brax had imagined the gift
was of the physical variety. Something sexual that he'd
planned for the woman of his dreams. Be it Maggie or
somebody else. A spectacular ending that only Carl
himself could write.

Now, Brax considered that something of an entirely
different nature lay inside.

Simone, like a child on a treasure hunt, skipped several steps into the gaping mouth of the cave. "Come on.
Let's find out what's in here."

"Bad idea." Brax wasn't given to flights of fancy,

but had often relied on instincts which had saved his life in times gone by. "We'll come back later with backup."

A gun wouldn't be a bad addition to the party. The nape of his neck prickled. He threw another wary glance over his shoulder. Nothing. The path lay empty until it twisted behind a rock outcropping.

When he turned back, Simone was gone.

Shit.

"It's dark in here." Her voice, disembodied, echoed off the walls and came at him in multiples of sound. "I can't see a thing. Bring the flashlight."

He'd retrieved it from the 4Runner's glove box before they left.

"Dammit. Get back out here, Simone."

"Come in and find me." She laughed, the sound floating out.

He clicked the light on, then followed the beam, locating Simone in the middle of a large, dank cavern.

"Let's see, let's see." She practically bounced in her tennies.

He sprayed the walls and ceiling with the flashlight beam. The roof rose thirty feet or so above their heads and the cave extended perhaps fifty in each direction. It wasn't large and it didn't appear to harbor any small offshoots leading to other attached caverns. A dank, musty, earthy smell and cool moist air wafted over him.

At least there weren't any bats. And no bat guano. Is that what Carl had wanted to prove to Maggie? That spelunking didn't necessarily mean bats?

"Well, this is sort of disappointing." Simone slapped her hands on her hips. "It doesn't even lead anywhere. All that build up for...not much."

Brax had to admit to being mystified, as well. Why twenty pages of mounting tension for so little payoff?

He moved the beam more slowly along the walls, wondering if he'd missed something the first time. Like a crime scene, it required a thorough going-over, and more than once.

Simone's warm hand grazed his arm. "Why do the walls sparkle like that? It's sort of eerie, isn't it?"

The walls sparkled, even as he moved the light away, almost as if they absorbed it for a few seconds after the beam hit.

"Brax. Is that," she gasped, then added, "gold?"

Almost as if he'd been expecting them, he heard the soft footfalls as a shadow passed over the cave's entrance.

"Yes, Simone, it's gold."

Filling the small cavern, bouncing from wall to wall, he almost didn't recognize the voice. Then he knew.

"Simone, you should have listened to your lover and stayed outside," Della Montrose said without a single inflection. "Everything would have been fine. Brax, please put the flashlight on the ground. I can't have you shining it in my eyes and trying to blind me."

If not for Simone, he would have done just that, shone the beam in the judge's eyes, then thrown himself at her in the brief moments it would take for her eyes to adjust.

Della had her own flashlight beam as well as the gun in her hand fixed on Simone. Jesus Christ. His heart beat loudly in his ears. But he couldn't afford the slightest miscalculation.

He hated giving up his only weapon, but attempting hand-to-hand combat when she had a gun on Simone was the worst of a bunch of bad choices.

"Put it down, Brax."

He squatted close to the ground, then let the flashlight slide off his fingers. It rolled a few feet in the direction opposite to where Simone stood.

"I knew there'd be trouble when the two of you said you were taking a hike. Taking a hike, my butt. I knew you'd end up here. Somehow, some way, you'd end up here."

Shit. He'd been so busy showing off his prowess to Mommie Dearest that he hadn't given a thought to what he'd revealed. He'd surrendered Simone to a killer through his own idiocy.

"Della, it's gold. Carl found gold." Simone didn't seem to get it. With Della standing behind the beam, maybe she hadn't seen the gun.

"Carl found the gold months ago. Three months to be exact."

About the time Carl starting acting funny and dribbling money out of the checking account.

Brax shuffled his feet, moving imperceptibly farther from Simone, circling round and closer to Della's right side. Her gun hand.

"Why didn't he tell anybody?" Simone sounded slightly bewildered but not yet afraid.

"He told me," Della said. "I was helping him stake a legal claim."

"Gee, that was awfully magnanimous of you."

"Sometimes, Simone, I really wonder about you. You can't be that dumb." Della sighed, the sound shushing around the cavern like the flutter of bat wings.

SIMONE WAS STUPID for having blundered into the cavern in the first place, but not so stupid she didn't real-

ize Della had killed Carl. Because of the gold, she'd lured him or followed him up the fantasy trail and pushed him over the edge. Della. Della did it all. Simone wanted to curl into a ball and plug her ears.

The only thing stopping her was Brax. She couldn't shut down and leave him all alone with Della. Della would kill him, and that was worse than anything. Brax needed her help.

Simone tried to keep the tremble out of her voice. "Was he going to cut you in on the gold in exchange for your help?"

She'd keep up the stupid questions, hold Della's attention, take it off Brax for as long as she could. With soft stealthy movements, he separated them so that Della couldn't easily take them both out at once.

"I wouldn't make him do that. I didn't give a flying fuck about the gold. I only made him give me money for filing fees so he'd think I was actually making the claim. I've still got it all, didn't use a dime." Affront hardened Della's voice. It was okay to be a murderer, but she didn't want anyone to think she was a thief?

Brax had inched away another few feet. In minutes, he'd be flanking Della.

"That's far enough, Braxton. You move one more inch, and I'll blow your sweetheart's head off."

Brax stopped, his fists clenching, unclenching. "You shoot her, Judge, and you die."

"May I remind you that I have the gun? I can shoot you both."

"I'll take you down before you even blink. And you won't die pretty."

Darn it, he was baiting Della. This wasn't happen-

ing. It wasn't real. Simone couldn't think straight. But she would not let Della harm a hair on his head.

Her only weapon was her big mouth.

"But if you didn't want the gold, Della, why did you kill Carl?"

"I'll tell you why." A silhouette filled the entrance. A tall, lanky silhouette, and there was no mistaking the smarmy voice.

"I'm here to save the day, Simone. Your pretty little sheriff boy here failed miserably. Della, I've got a gun at your back, sweetheart." Jason wasn't holding a thing. Empty hands dangled at his sides. "You better give your own gun to the nice sheriff, Della. The jig is up."

"You blackmailing bastard." Della's jaw tensed. "I didn't kill Carl. You did."

"Right. That's why you're the one holding a gun on my sweet Simone here. The perfidy of women. Now you're not even going to admit throwing Carl to his death and parking his truck at the bottom of the trail." He nodded at Simone. "I saw her drop the truck off, you know."

"Shut up, Jason." Della snarled but didn't move.

Jason was bluffing; he didn't even have a gun. They were all going to die the moment Della figured that out. Simone started to breathe hard, harder, faster. Oh my God. *Please do not let me panic.*

"Oh, Della, you can't tell me what to do anymore. You can't hold anything over my head. I've got you. I even saw you wipe all the fingerprints off the steering wheel and door handles so that no one would know you'd been there. I was on my way to tell the good sheriff all about it just as I saw you sneaking off again to follow Simone."

Brax made a noise, a horrible choking sound as he leaned over, bracing his hands on his knees. He was having a heart attack or a stroke or something terrible. He was dying. He was…

My God, he was laughing.

"Stop it," Della shouted, her flashlight beam swinging. "Stop laughing at me."

Brax raised his head slightly, then went at it harder.

"Stop it." Della shrieked this time and swung the gun at him.

Oh my God, she was going to shoot him. She was going to shoot Brax.

He moved so fast Simone almost didn't see it in the wavering beam of Della's flashlight. He tucked, rolled and slammed into Della's knees. The gun flew wide and left, skidding across the dirt, the flashlight flew right, smashing against the wall, and Della screamed as her tailbone slammed against the cavern floor.

Brax jammed his knee against her windpipe.

"Get her gun, Simone. Now."

"No need, Simone. I've already got it."

Brax froze. Only his eyes moved, twin sparks of light in all that gloom. "You know, Lafoote, I really didn't think this day could get any worse."

"You obviously think I'm going to shoot you with it." Jason turned the gun back and forth in his hand, up, down, perusing it from every angle.

Della groaned and wriggled beneath Brax's choke hold. He reached down, touched her neck, and she stopped struggling, her head slumping with a thud to the ground.

Vulcan death grip? It didn't matter as long as Brax

didn't have to worry about Della and Jason at the same time.

"Give me the gun, Jason." Simone held out her hand. He stood between them and the light of day outside the cave.

Between life and death. Della had been terrifying. Jason made Simone's blood run cold in her veins.

"He's an idiot, Simone, don't you see that? An inept fool. Della would have killed you if I hadn't ridden up on my white charger to rescue you."

"You're right, Jason. You saved me. I'm eternally grateful. I swear it."

In her peripheral vision, Brax's muscles bunched and readied. They made a good team, she did all the talking and snagged the villain's attention, while Brax plotted the action that would save them. All they needed was a little help from Above.

"He's a brawny caricature off some paper towel wrapper."

"He's a scurvy dog not worthy of licking my boots."

"You're playing with me." Lafoote's arm shot straight out, and his finger trembled on the trigger.

BRAX FELT her miscalculation in his bones. Simone had gone too far.

Lafoote went on, sniping and seething over his losses. "You haven't given me the time of day since I got here. Always lifting your nose in the air and walking away like I smell like bat guano."

"No. Carl smelled like bat guano. You always smelled like…" Obviously, her colorful phrases deserted her.

Dammit, he was trapped down on his knees on top

of Della. Think, man, think. There was a way out. There had to be. He would *not* let anyone hurt Simone.

Brax eased one knee up until he had a boot planted on the ground. "You can have the resort, Lafoote. Now that Della's out of the way, you've got it made, buddy."

"I'll back you," Simone added. "I promise."

"You're a liar, Simone. As soon as we're out of here, you'll revert to type and go for Macho Man here."

With the other foot and his hands on his knees, Brax readied himself like a springboard even as Lafoote sighted down the barrel. Their gazes met. Brax held, moving into perfect position.

"Please, Jason. Please. I'll do anything you want. Just don't—"

A shrieking, screaming flurry of body and motion hurtled through the air and slammed into Jason Lafoote's right side. "Youkilledhimyoukilledhimyoukilledhim." Jason and the screaming creature tumbled over and over several feet across the cavern.

Dammit, that was his sister in there. Apparently his mother hadn't even been able to contain her. Brax threw himself into the middle of the pile for the freaking gun before it went off and killed her.

A foot narrowly missed his groin. An elbow slammed into the side of his head. He groped, twisted, squeezed, wrenched and finally found cold hard metal. Thrusting his arm aloft, he held it in the air, then rolled right and out from beneath the writhing mass of his sister and Lafoote.

Jumping to his feet, he balanced into a crouch. The gun wasn't going to do a damn bit of good with his sister on top of the pile. "Maggie, I've got him. You can stop kicking him now."

Maggie screamed, a wrenching cry that tore at him almost as much as the sight of a gun pointed at Simone.

"Youkilledhimyoukilledhim." Maggie kept on kicking.

Until suddenly she was hauled off her feet by a shadow and clamped around the waist by a pair of strong arms.

"Maggie, honey," Sheriff Teesdale said so softly Brax almost couldn't hear over the dull throb of his pulse in his ear, "Let me and your brother take care of the whiny little bastard."

SIMONE DIED A LITTLE with every word of Della's confession. She wished the sheriff hadn't allowed her to stay. The only interrogation room had been lost to storage boxes years ago, and Sheriff Teesdale had no choice but to conduct the interview in the courtroom. Della's courtroom. As if she were already on trial.

She was. A trial put on by people she'd called friends. People who had loved her and trusted her. People who believed she loved them just as much.

Simone whimpered softly. Brax touched her hand, but she couldn't bear it. He'd almost died because she'd walked into the cave as if she hadn't a care in the world. With that gun quaking in Lafoote's hand, Brax's life had passed before her eyes. She couldn't say if the horrible man intended to kill Brax or if he'd been talking, talking, talking. God. She would never forget those awful moments.

Shaking off Brax's touch, she stuck her hands between her knees.

"I didn't mean to kill him," Della droned on for at least the fifteenth time. "Well, I did mean to, but I

didn't want to. If only he hadn't insisted on telling everyone about the gold. I couldn't let him do that."

Della didn't mean to, but she had. When Carl stopped on the path near the phallic rock, staring at it as if his mind were a million miles away, Della had whacked him twice with the end of her flashlight. Simone shuddered, wanting to bury her face in her hands. She knew in her heart of hearts that Carl had stopped to savor the fantasy. The one *she'd* written. Della seized the opportunity. After making sure he was dead, she'd pushed him over the edge, watching him tumble to the bottom. How long had Della stood, her heart in her throat, hoping and praying that his body took the full plunge? Afterward, she'd returned to town to sit beside Maggie at the tea party. In that awful cave, Simone hadn't thought about that. Now, she could think of nothing else. Della had actually sat beside her victim's wife and repeated over and over how Maggie would be better off without Carl. Somehow that was Della's worst crime. How she'd tried to justify herself by claiming Maggie was better off. She'd even brought Simone into the fray, going on over strawberry daiquiris about all the reasons she believed Carl was having an affair. All lies. *Cosmo,* for God's sake.

She'd betrayed Maggie. She'd betrayed them all.

Simone simply wanted to get away before she threw up.

"WELL, THAT WAS the cluster fuck of the century," Teesdale drawled. "S'cuse the language, Simone."

Simone nodded and gave the sheriff a halfhearted smile. She'd answered questions when she was asked, elaborated as necessary, but she'd closed in on herself.

Brax wanted to touch her, offer what little physical comfort he could, but she'd withdrawn from him behind halfhearted smiles.

He couldn't blame her. She'd gone through more life-threatening drama in half an hour than most people saw in a lifetime. Her trusted friend held her at gunpoint. Then everything had gone to hell in a handbasket back at the sheriff's department.

Della had started blubbering the minute Teesdale seated her at the defense table in the courtroom. Simone had slipped further into her own thoughts, her own darkness, as Della spilled her guts with all of them as witnesses. It wasn't a regulation interview, but then Goldstone wasn't a town that lived and breathed by the book. It was as unique as Teesdale, as complicated as Della Montrose's reasons for killing Carl, as soft in the underbelly as Simone herself.

The town would never be the same after the blow Della dealt it. Simone herself might never recover. And what of his sister? After the fray in the cave, he'd turned Maggie once again over to his mom's care. He still had to tell Maggie the villain in her husband's case was her best friend, not a skanky hotel mogul. Hell, after the number of meetings Carl had with Della over the gold, it was probably her perfume Maggie had smelled on him. The floozy turned out to be a murderer.

Maggie's world had gone to shit. And looking at Simone, so had hers.

"I'll take you home." Brax reached for her. She didn't so much withdraw as simply let her own hand lie unmoving in his.

"I can walk," she said.

"It's not…" He stopped. He'd been about to say it

wasn't safe. Della had stolen that. Simone's bleak gaze spoke eloquently of the loss of her haven.

He could have lost her in the cave. Now he'd surely lost her to the havoc Della had wreaked. He didn't have words to comfort her. He didn't have arms big enough to ease her ache. He'd prayed for the wisdom to help. He didn't suddenly find enlightenment now, any more than he'd found it for Maggie. He freaking didn't know how to make everything better.

"You're tired. I'll drive you." There was still Jason Lafoote to think of. She wasn't safe, even with the man behind bars for now.

"No. I'll walk." She didn't look at him as she rose from Teesdale's office chair.

He was about to insist. Teesdale interrupted. "We're done here for now, Simone. You can go. Walking in the fresh air, alone, will do you good. And you'll be perfectly safe." He looked pointedly at Brax as he spoke.

Alone. Brax feared that if he let her go, he'd never find her again in the emotional wasteland that lay between them.

But he would never learn the right words. He would never know the right thing to do.

So he let her go. Her dazzle smile would forever live in his memory. As would his abject failure to provide whatever the hell it was she really needed.

"Sit." Teesdale pointed.

Brax eased back into the chair.

"Let's review."

Review his life, his failures, his errors in judgment.

"You're laying it on a bit thick."

"What?" Brax hadn't said those things aloud.

"Give her time. Women need time. Then they come to their own conclusion even if it's the same one you told them over and over. Women are like that. They gotta think it's their own or it doesn't work."

Brax remembered saying virtually the same thing to Carl just a few short days ago.

"Thanks for the advice. Now let's talk about Della." Though Brax had already heard as much as he could stomach.

"The funny thing is, Della didn't need to be a lawyer to be the judge," Teesdale said.

Della had confessed to killing Carl over the gold strike for the reason she'd fought the resort. Whether they came to town for the gold or the resort, more people meant more scrutiny. She was afraid her secrets would come to light. But Teesdale's comment was still a mystery. "Come again?"

"In this county, the so-called judge is a justice of the peace and doesn't need to be a lawyer," the sheriff explained.

"Nobody would have cared that she'd been a show-girl and never graduated with a law degree from Harvard?" While most of Goldstone's residents appeared to be less than they were, Della was the only one who claimed to be more.

"Nope. And being mayor is only about residency."

"She killed Carl for nothing?" Brax suddenly felt tired and old.

"Yeah. Ironic, isn't it? She was afraid the media circus over a gold strike would eventually reveal she'd lied about her background. But she didn't have to lie in the first place. Last judge was some guy drove in on a Harley, the way I heard it. Before my time."

Jesus Christ. It almost didn't bear thinking about. "How are you going to charge Lafoote?"

"Well, now, that's a sticky issue. The blackmail thing doesn't work."

According to Della, Lafoote had blackmailed her into signing his licenses and permits after he saw her drive Carl's truck to the trailhead, then wipe it clean and throw away the keys. Together, they'd come up with the story that she'd reverse her opinion in order to provide a memorial statue for Carl. Lafoote, of course, denied the blackmail.

"It's he said, she said. And after confessing to killing Carl, her credibility sucks." Teesdale shook his head. "Why the hell she didn't make Carl drive up to the trailhead himself, I haven't figured out yet. She might have gotten away with it, if she had."

Brax leaned forward and tapped the recorder. "Tape 2. She wanted everyone to think he'd run away with another woman. So, she planned to keep his truck in her garage for a few weeks, then drive it into the desert and push it off some bluff so it wouldn't be found. Don't know how she figured she was going to get back home after dumping it." Brax puffed out a disgusted breath. "Course, when the chickens found him, she had to improvise. Lucky for her, the trailhead wasn't a far walk from her house."

Teesdale snorted. "The criminal mind. Musta really missed the good part when I got up for that doughnut. Sorry I didn't bring you one." Then he smiled a shit-eating grin. "Thank God I had a good small town sheriff holding down the fort in there."

Brax didn't comment that Teesdale should have stayed to handle the interview since he suspected a

doughnut wasn't the business the sheriff had taken care of. A man deserved privacy. Between them, they'd gotten what they needed out of Della.

"You know, women really make murder complicated," Teesdale went on. "She doesn't kill Carl because she wants the gold, she kills him because she doesn't want anyone to find out she isn't really a lawyer. Is that ass-backward or what? She could have stolen the gold or put her own name on the claim, or, for that matter, hightailed it out of town and started over somewhere else. But no, she creates this elaborate murder scheme."

"Women are deep, complicated creatures." Brax doubted he could ever truly understand them.

Teesdale stretched back in his chair and put his hands behind his head. "At any rate, Lafoote will hire some wily lawyer to get him out of any blackmail charge. His story is that he didn't understand the significance of what he saw Della doing until after you told him Carl had been murdered." He raised a skeptical brow. "In fact, he claims he was on his way to see me when he saw Della following you and Simone and thought he better see what was up."

Bullshit. "He was following Simone, not Della. I think the little weasel's been following Simone for a long time."

Teesdale spread his hands. "It was Stalking Light, if anything at all. Nothing we can prove."

Earlier, in her same flat monotone, Simone had confirmed a feeling of being watched a couple of times. But there were no threatening phone calls or messages, nothing about her trailer that appeared tampered with. In short, no hard evidence.

Dammit. Teesdale was right, even if Brax didn't like the fact. Lafoote had skirted the hairy edge on everything he'd done, and consequently, they couldn't get him conclusively on anything. "Fine. I'll give you that. But he threatened us both with a weapon. Assaulting a peace officer. I don't care what you get him on, just get him. He's got some weird obsession with Simone, and I don't want him out there threatening her."

Teesdale shook his head sadly. "Says he was about to hand the gun over when your sister jumped him."

"Bullshit."

"We have nothing substantial to hold him. I gotta let him go."

Dammit. Brax finally raised his hands in surrender. Maggie's war cry had ended any further incriminating crap that might have flowed out of the guy's mouth. Jesus Christ. If Simone hadn't had a gun pointed at her, the whole incident would have been laughable. Teesdale had followed Maggie, who'd followed Lafoote who'd followed Simone. Why they hadn't stumbled all over each other, he'd never know. God. The sheriff was right. It was a major cluster fuck.

"I'll make sure he doesn't get near Simone." Though Brax wasn't sure she'd let him near her even to provide protection.

"That's your job, buddy boy." Teesdale twirled a pencil stub on his blotter. "What are you going to do about Maggie?"

An ache started behind his eyeballs. Maggie's *friend* had planned Carl's demise from the moment he'd demanded she process the claim ASAP, right after his wife had threatened to Bobbitize him. Carl told Della

he had to show Maggie the gold before she left him. It was the only hope of saving his marriage. Brax would take that with him to his grave and hope to hell Maggie never found out. Jesus, Carl had simply wanted to show Maggie he wasn't a loser. With a million bucks in the bank, he'd still needed to prove something. After 1987's Black Monday stock crash, Carl lost his belief in himself. His current bank balance hadn't restored his self-confidence. Brax was pretty damn sure the gold wouldn't have, either.

They'd never know.

Della had bled Carl. She'd had him give her money for filing fees, recording fees, etc, though she claimed she still had the cash in her office desk at home. Teesdale would check that. When she couldn't think of another erroneous fee, she'd had Carl catalog his entire financial history, which explained the organization of his files and the listings in his spiral notebook. Della had conned him into believing he'd need to provide every detail when they finally submitted the filing papers. Was it stupidity on Carl's part or implicit trust in a woman he'd known for years? Freaking pathetic. Della had been stringing him along to cover her own ass.

That last night, when Della demanded three thousand dollars to complete the registration, cash she'd never dreamed Carl had access to—she hadn't even looked over the fiscal information he'd given her—he'd gotten the money to her the next morning. Concealing her shock, she took it, revised her plan, said she had to see the claim itself in order to verify it before, as a judge, she could sign off.

She'd killed him on the way up.

Brax couldn't tell Maggie all of it. It would kill her spirit to know exactly what Della had done, just as the truth had crushed Simone's.

If Maggie hadn't screamed at Carl, if they hadn't been fighting about sex and money. Maggie would drive herself crazy with all the *ifs,* and there was nothing he could do about it.

Except lie and hope she never heard the truth in the produce section at The Stockyard.

"Don't whitewash it, Braxton," Teesdale said, reading his mind. "Tell her the truth. She deserves it, and she's strong enough to take it. Never underestimate a woman's strength."

He didn't underestimate a woman's strength. He'd overestimated his own. And he didn't know where he'd find the extra reserves to do what he had to do.

CHAPTER TWENTY-ONE

MAGGIE SAT ON THE BED in her room, in the gloom, the blinds drawn against the heat of the endless day.

Brax picked up her limp hand, pressing his lips to the back of it. She hadn't spoken since he told her. The truth. All of it. From the gold to the fantasy, and finally what her friend Della had done to them all. "Maggie."

"I'm sorry, Tyler," she whispered.

Listening to her small childlike voice, his heart broke in half all over again. "Carl wouldn't want you to be sorry. None of this was your fault."

"I never thought he was a loser."

Nor had Brax implied it when he revealed the story piece by piece. He didn't give her verbatim every detail of Della's confession, but the woman had shed quite a bit of light on Carl's antipathy. Lafoote had hammered Carl with his "less than a zero nobody" theme in an attempt to sucker Carl into supporting the resort. His plan had been to reward Carl with a percentage of the hotel if he got Della to sign all the permits. The strategy backfired, creating a seething anger in Carl. As soon as Carl found the gold, he made his own plan to stick it to Lafoote. Whatever prosperity came to the town because of the gold, Carl intended to see that Lafoote didn't share in it.

Maggie had known Carl's insecurities, but she'd misjudged where the anxiety would take him. That didn't lay the blame at her feet. She couldn't have anticipated how Lafoote would use those insecurities and that Carl's lack of confidence would eventually lead to his death.

Maggie wiped a tear from her cheek before Brax could reach up to catch it. "I can't believe he had Simone write me a fantasy."

"He loved you. He was willing to do anything to make things right again."

"I wouldn't really have hurt him."

"I know. He knows it, too." Wherever he was, Carl knew.

They hadn't said a thing about Della's betrayal. Brax had told her. Maggie had heard. Then they'd put it away.

"I didn't mean to scare Mom by sneaking out."

"I thought you promised me you'd stay put."

She shrugged helplessly. "I said I wouldn't leave while you were sleeping."

He could have given her a hard time, but what was the point? With all his questions, he was the one who put the idea of Jason Lafoote in her mind in the first place. "You weren't thinking straight, honey."

Mom had called 911, and Teesdale had started an immediate search. No idiot, he'd assumed Maggie would head up the trail to see where Carl had died. The spot was a magnet. Jesus, they'd had a posse on their tail the whole time.

Yep, the cluster fuck of the century. He closed his eyes. Jesus. He'd almost lost Simone.

"Tyler, it wasn't your fault."

"Don't start trying to look after me, Maggie. I'm looking after you." The way he should have done from the moment he arrived. If he'd read the signs, Carl wouldn't be dead.

She stared at him. "You look like me when I see myself in the mirror. You think if you'd done this or you hadn't done that, none of this would have happened."

"Yeah, that's what I think." If he'd listened to his gut, Simone wouldn't have walked into that cave, either. But, as Simone said, hindsight only worked in hindsight.

"That's the way I think, too," Maggie said. "I shouldn't have said all those awful things to Carl that night."

If she saw that it was wrong for him to heap the blame on himself, then maybe she could see it was wrong for her, too. "We both should have done things differently. But we didn't."

"I should have told him he'd earned that money and he deserved to spend it without having to account to me."

He should have told Simone he loved her before he let her walk out of Teesdale's office. "I should have made Carl tell me how he was going to prove to everyone he wasn't a failure."

She cocked her head at him. "He told you he was a failure?"

"That was the gist." The night they'd driven home from The Dartboard. So many things he should have figured out that night.

"I never called him a failure. I never thought he was."

Maggie pulled open the drawer of the nightstand

and shuffled things around. Holding her hand out, the ring glittered on her palm, as if it somehow found what little light there was in the room and let itself be worshipped by it.

"Isn't it the most beautiful thing you've ever seen?" Maggie whispered reverently.

It was just a ring. Brax wasn't partial to jewelry. But it did glitter, a large diamond in the center flagged by smaller stones around the band. "It's beautiful."

"Carl found it in one of the outhouses."

The famous outhouse diamond. "Why keep it in a drawer?"

"I wanted to wait until he found a diamond necklace to match. I guess we were both waiting for something better to come along. Carl and his gold, and me and a diamond necklace."

"Start wearing it now, Maggie."

She shook her head. "It's too late for Carl."

"It's not too late for you. Put it on."

She slipped it on next to her wedding band. "We got married so quickly, we never even bought an engagement ring."

"This one will work."

She squeezed her eyes shut and leaned against his shoulder. "I miss him so much, Tyler. I made so many mistakes, and I can never take them back."

He held her hand in his. "There'll always be mistakes we can't take back." He'd made plenty of his own over the years. "But you have to let them go and start over for yourself. It wasn't your fault he fell. You didn't push him."

She didn't say anything.

"Look at me." He lifted her chin. "He loved you. Wear the ring and remember that."

"I'll try, Tyler. I really will." She sniffed, and sucked in her breath, holding back her tears.

The coming days and months would be hard on her, but he'd remind her how much Carl loved her every time she needed him to. She and Carl had both made mistakes, taken each other for granted once too often. There would be no second chance for them, and Maggie would mourn that as much as she would mourn Carl.

Brax couldn't say the right thing to cleanse Maggie's pain. He would never be able to. The only things he could provide were an ear to listen when she needed to talk and open arms to hold her while she cried.

Hallelujah. He'd finally figured out the big secret. After years of searching, it all came down to those two simple things. They were all any man could offer. Maybe they were all a woman needed. He planned on giving both to Simone. For the rest of her life, if she'd let him.

"Go ahead and cry your eyes out, honey. I'm right here to hold you." He held Maggie tight while she cried, never once begging her to stop.

"WHERE ON EARTH have you been, Simone? We've been frantic."

Her mother didn't look frantic. In fact, she looked fresh as a daisy in a silk Chinese print and perfectly painted red lips. Her silk print clashed with the orange tufts of Simone's thrift store sofa. Jackie huddled in a ball in the opposite corner of the couch, her chin on her knees, her eyes wide.

Kingston nursed a steaming cup of coffee and stared at Simone with worry. "You all right, honey?"

"I took a walk." She hadn't come straight home. She'd wandered Goldstone streets, the same ones she'd already traversed. No one had stopped to ask about Della or Carl. Nor had anyone accosted her. She was safe.

But she hadn't felt safe. The times she'd felt something in the shadows, Jason had probably been outside her home, watching her. She'd locked the darn screen, too, but he'd found a way to invade her territory.

Jason wasn't the worst. He'd never been a friend. He'd never been anything. Della was the one who'd ripped away her security.

Safety was an illusion. Maybe her sense of home was an illusion, too. Maybe Goldstone had never been home at all, but nothing more than a place she'd run away to.

"You should have called," her mother snapped, rising off the couch.

"I did call. I told you it would take a while."

"You look tired, honey." Kingston came close, as if he'd put a comforting arm around her. Simone jerked away, then was unable to look him in the face. "Why don't you take a nap?" he finished.

Simone just wanted to go to bed and sleep forever.

"She cannot go to sleep, Kingston. We are leaving. Jackie, start packing our bags. We're getting out of this horrible place. And Simone, you're coming with us."

Going with her mother? Ariana had saved the declaration along with the packing to create her dramatic moment. Her mother so loved her drama. Leaving with her almost seemed like a relief.

"I never should have let you follow your own mind and come here. I knew it would end in disaster." Ariana fluttered about, her fingers tapping her dress, her arms, her chin.

All that movement made Simone dizzy.

"Ariana, calm down."

"I won't calm down. She should have listened to me, Kingston. She ignores everything I say. And look what happened. She almost got herself killed in godforsaken gnatsville."

"It was a cave, Mother." She couldn't even manage the capital letters.

Her mother snapped her fingers. "Jackie, did you hear me? Start packing. And don't forget my toiletries in the bathroom."

"Don't snap your fingers at Jackie."

She flew at Kingston, stopping before she actually smacked him in the face. "It's the only way they hear. They don't listen. They don't take my advice. I won't have it, do you hear? I know what's best for them."

Her mother then whirled on her, stabbing the air with a long, manicured nail. "You're coming home. And you're taking that job with Ambrose. I won't hear another word about it."

"She never wanted the job with Ambrose. Can't you get that through your head?" Kingston slashed a hand through the air.

"Then why didn't she come right out and say she didn't want it? I would have found her something else. But she never even said what she wanted. She never says what she wants."

No, Simone never had. She'd hidden all her wants and needs from her mother for fear they'd be trampled

beneath more important needs. Ariana's needs. Simone had been hiding her own needs for so long, she wasn't even sure what they were anymore.

"Then let her tell you what she wants," Kingston said. "And listen to her this time."

Think. What do you really want? Safety. Security. Home. Della had taken those things away.

"I always listen," Ariana went on. "I know what's best, that's all. Why, she's a child. Look what happened in Silicon Valley. She failed."

Stop talking about me as if I weren't here. I can speak for myself. Yet she didn't say a word. Her mother was right. She hadn't done well on her own. Not well at all.

"She didn't fail. Her customer base went away. It wasn't failure." Kingston pushed Ariana back with the force of his rising voice. What had suddenly gotten into him?

"She ran out of money. Even her fiancé couldn't take it."

Andrew couldn't take her excessive and exuberant screaming during lovemaking, that's why he'd dumped her. Her business failure had been an excuse.

"That boy was a wimp. That's why he didn't stick around."

Ariana ignored Kingston, continuing with her rant. "If she'd taken my advice, she'd be married by now."

"Maybe she didn't want to marry him because you picked him out for her."

Maybe she hadn't wanted to marry Andrew. Maybe. Simone didn't know. She'd never known. That was the problem.

"I know what's best for her. I'm her mother."

Kingston didn't kowtow. He went at Ariana. "You decide what she wants because you can't stand not having control. You decide what they both want. They're adults. Let them make their own decisions."

"How dare you, Kingston? May I remind you that you work for me? You are not part of this family. And you can be fired."

"Stop it." Simone shouted. She actually shouted at her mother. It was the only time Ariana had ever shut up when Simone spoke. "Do you want to know what I want? Do you really?"

"Of course, dear," her mother said finally. "Tell us. We'll help you get it." But Simone knew there was a hook.

What did she really want? To stop letting what other people wanted be her guiding light.

"I want to buy my furniture at the Salvation Army and my clothes at the Goodwill."

It was so quiet, she could hear a fly buzzing in the corner.

Della's betrayal had ripped something away from her, safety, security, and yes, her sense of home. But Della couldn't take that away unless Simone herself let it all go. Goldstone wasn't The Emerald City or Munchkinland. It wasn't even Kansas. It was people who cared about her and most of them were still right here.

Della could never take that away from her. Neither could Ariana.

Something powerful and wonderful rose up within Simone.

"I want a lot of things," she said, her voice clear and strong. "I want to live in a trailer or a house or whatever I choose wherever I choose to buy it. And I want

you to say you like it even if you hate it. I want you to visit, and I don't want you to bring your fumigator."

Her mother's eyes widened and a glob of mascara stuck to her upper eyelid.

"I want to make pots of money writing erotica on the Internet. Because I'm good at it. Very, very good at it. And I like writing it."

"You write porn on the Internet?" Her mother looked close to expiring, her eyes wide and wild. A deep wrinkle marred her pristine forehead, and crow's-feet sprouted at the corners of her eyes.

"And I don't want you to ever call it porn, because it's classy and it's well written."

"But dear—"

"And I never ever want to own a pair of Barry Manilow shoes."

Ariana Chandler gasped. "Not Barry Manilows, you silly girl. Manolo Blahniks." Rolling her eyes heavenward, she added, "I cannot believe you came from my loins."

"And you know what else, MOTHER? I don't want you to ever send me size zero clothing again. I never want to fit into size zero clothing. Not ever. I want to have breasts and hips, and I want you to tell me I'm beautiful that way."

"Of course, you're beautiful."

Just words. Her mother was so good with meaningless words. Simone didn't bother rebuking her. "And I want to wear blue underwear with white pants no matter how bad you say it looks."

Someone applauded. A slow, steady clap.

Brax held the screen door open with his shoulder and applauded.

She stopped breathing and her heart suddenly stilled in her chest.

"Is there anything else you want, Simone?" Brax looked at her as if she were the only person in the room. The only woman in the world. The door slammed as he stepped through and stood before her to whisper, "Tell me your heart's desire."

She hadn't screamed with pleasure because her exuberance embarrassed Andrew. She'd run away from her Silicon Valley career because her mother called her a failure. She'd loved everyone in Goldstone because they hadn't cared about her failures. Then she'd been about to throw away everything important to her because Della Montrose had betrayed them all.

She'd never fought for anything in her life. She'd always given up at someone else's whim. Not this time. She would not throw away this chance because she was afraid Brax would reject her heart's desire. If she did, then she deserved to crawl home after her mother with her tail between her legs.

"I know exactly what I want," she started.

He put his fingers to her lips before she could get the next word out, then traced them with the pad of his thumb. "My turn." He leaned in close, his heady male scent surrounding her. "I've loved your smile since the first moment I saw it." He took his hand away to brush his lips to hers. "I love the skulls on your license plate and the bumper sticker on your truck. I love your pluck and your courage." Then he whispered against her ear, for her alone. "I love the way you scream when I make you come."

Oh. Oh. He loved her exuberance and excess.

Still for her ears only, he added, "And I especially love the way you told your mother to go to hell."

He *knew*. He knew how hard that was. How long she'd dreamed of it, but never had the courage to even admit she'd wanted to.

He tucked a stray lock behind her ear, then stroked her cheek. "I died a thousand deaths when I thought you'd be hurt up there today. I've made a lot of mistakes, probably half of them since I came to Goldstone. But this is one mistake I won't make. I won't leave here without telling you that I love you."

He loved her. He really honest-to-God loved her. "So what's your heart's desire?" she whispered.

Clasping his hands at the small of her back, he held her close and met her gaze, his eyes a deep true blue. "That you'll come home to Cottonmouth with me. Home, Simone. I want to be your home wherever you are."

His face blurred through a sheen of tears. She lost her voice. Home. With that one word, he proved he knew everything that was important to her.

"I think I'm going to vomit. Kingston, get me a paper bag. Quickly."

Simone didn't care if her mother threw up all over the orange shag. "Does your house have a foundation, Brax?" she asked.

"Hell, yes, even made it through the last earthquake without a crack." He leaned his forehead against hers. "But can you leave Goldstone?"

She would always love Mr. Doodle and Whitey and Sheriff Teesdale and Maggie and Chloe and the chickens, and she would never leave that love behind like a forgotten memory. Home wasn't a place. It was a feel-

ing. It was where you were warm and cherished. It was where you were accepted for exactly who you were instead of what someone else thought you should be. A person could have more than one home. In fact, the more, the better.

"Goldstone will always be in my heart, Brax, but I want to come home with you."

He sighed, then cupped her face in one big hand. "Aren't you forgetting one big thing?"

What? Maybe, "I love you?"

"Yeah. That's it."

She hugged him. "I love you, I love you, I love you." Then she jumped back. "Oh my God, I forgot to ask about Maggie. Is she okay?"

"There's another thing I love about you that I forgot to mention."

She cocked her head. "What's that?"

"The way you care about your friends." He stroked her cheek. "Maggie's gonna be fine. It'll be hard, but we'll see her through." Then he squeezed the breath out of her with a tight hug. "God, I love you."

"Kingston, where *is* that vomit bag?"

Simone turned her head.

Her mother fanned herself dramatically. "And Jackie, are you done packing?" she called. "We simply have to get out of here. Simone has lost her mind."

Thump. The trailer vibrated beneath their feet. Jackie stood in the hallway, Ariana's suitcases dumped on the floor beside her. "Your bags are packed."

"Where are yours?" Ariana huffed. "I specifically told you to pack your bags."

Jackie tipped her chin, and a small smile creased her mouth. "I'm not going."

Ariana's mouth opened and closed, then finally, "What do you mean you're not going?"

"I'm not going back home with you. If Simone's going to Cottonmouth, then I'm going to ask her if she'll let me stay in her trailer for a while."

"Of course, you can stay in the trailer," Simone said, her heart bursting. For Jackie. For herself. For the warmth of Brax's arm around her shoulders and his body next to hers.

"She cannot," Ariana stated.

"I can. And I will. MOTHER, go home."

Ariana stared. Her perfectly applied cosmetics started to crack. Then she found her voice. "You two ungrateful…after everything I've done…I can't believe I could raise daughters who would treat their mother…Kingston, we're leaving. Get my bags."

Kingston didn't move. "I thought I was fired."

"I said you could be fired. I didn't actually fire you. Now drive me home."

Jackie took a step closer to Kingston. "He isn't going home with you, MOTHER."

Ariana gaped, then recovered herself. She would never be silent for long. "Whatever do you mean, Jackie? Of course, Kingston's driving me home."

Jackie shook her head slowly. "He's staying here with me."

Ariana stared down her nose. "Why on earth would he stay with you?"

"Because he loves me." Jackie smiled and looked at Kingston with the brightest gaze, brighter than anything Simone had ever seen up on the movie screen.

Oh my God. Kingston and Jackie?

"And we're going to get married," Jackie added.

Ariana laughed. "Kingston, do you know anything about this child's delusions?"

Kingston put his arm around Jackie and tucked her close to his side. "As a matter of fact, I do. I was actually present last night when I asked her to marry me."

Ariana snorted. "This is a joke, right?"

"I've been in love with Jackie for a long time." Kingston looked down at Jackie with something far more than the fond gaze Simone was used to. "She only figured out how much she adores me a few months ago." Then he turned back to his so-called employer. "We don't feel like wasting any more time before getting married."

Ariana's jaw dropped. She'd hate the expression if she saw it in the mirror. "That's perverted. You're old enough to be her father."

Jackie leaned on Kingston's shoulder. "You can't say anything that will ruin this for us, MOTHER."

"He's deserting me for you. He's always got to attach himself to a star. He's nothing without it." She threw out her arm in Kingston's direction. "He's not even much of a man."

Jackie turned her face up adoringly. "I assure you, he's very much a man."

After a quick nuzzle to Simone's ear, Brax crossed the short distance and picked up the two forgotten bags. "I'll carry these out to the car for you, Mrs. Chandler."

"It's Miss. Miss Chandler." Ariana refused to be anybody's anything, even somebody's wife.

"If you hurry," Brax said, "you can make it to Las Vegas before it gets dark. Stay at the Venetian. I've heard the rooms are luxurious. You won't even need your fumigator."

Ariana looked at her daughters. Then she looked at her manager. She didn't even bother looking at Brax. Finally, she lifted her head regally. Then exited the small trailer.

Silence reigned for exactly three seconds. "Shit, the keys." Kingston dug in his pocket.

Simone took Jackie's hand in hers and smiled all the way from her heart. "I'm very, very happy for you both. Now give me the keys, Kingston, and I'll take them to her." Her last hurrah.

Her mother did not lower herself to acknowledge either the man who carried her bags or the woman who offered the keys, even if it was her daughter. She did not say goodbye. Nor did she leave them a tip.

"I didn't even know she knew how to drive," Simone murmured as Brax hugged her.

Together, they watched the car disappear around the corner.

Brax rubbed his nose in her hair. "You know, my mother's gonna love you as much as I do."

She slapped her hands to her cheeks. "Oh my God, I forgot. I'm going to have to meet your mother." But she could do anything if she put her mind to it. Especially with Brax at her side. "You're right," she murmured, letting a smile grow. "She's going to love me. And I'm going to love her."

EPILOGUE

CREPE PAPER STREAMERS looped the tables set along the back wall. Paper tablecloths festooned with flowers hung almost to the floor. Helium balloons had been set free to drift lazily along the ceiling while cardboard angels floated across the white walls. The aroma of freshly perked coffee wafted to every corner.

The dining hall of Our Manor of the Ladies was decorated more for a party than a wake. Brax didn't think Maggie—or Carl—would be unhappy with that.

"I made three trifles. Carl loved my trifle. Maggie always took home the center piece for him, where all the sherry soaks into the ladyfingers." Rowena dug out a large portion of whipped cream, bananas and sherry-laced cake. Then her smile suddenly drooped. "She is all right, isn't she?"

Brax had escorted Maggie, his mother and Simone to the funeral while Rockie the gigolo opted to stay at home. After the service, Brax drove them to the Manor, where they'd all piled into the home's small ladies' room. They were still there, as far as he knew.

All right? No. Maggie wouldn't be all right for a long time. But she had her mother, her brother and her future sister-in-law to help her through.

"She's going home with my mother for a while," he told Rowena. "Then she'll come to Cottonmouth. We'll take care of her."

Handing the plate to him along with a flower-flocked napkin and a plastic fork, Rowena gasped. "I didn't make the trifle that last time. I baked the scones instead. Maybe that's what went wrong. I always saved the last piece for Carl."

Brax didn't say that Carl was already dead before the last tea party. Nothing could have helped him then. "I'm sure he's enjoying this one from above. Just keep remembering that."

The little woman beamed. "You're right. Can't spoil the mood with crappy regrets. Carl would have wanted us to remember him with happy thoughts. Right, girls?" Rowena called across the room.

Standing like a welcoming committee at the door, Nonnie, Divine and Agnes tucked into their own plates of trifle.

"That boy always did love a party," Agnes intoned.

"So, we're giving him a proper send-off," Divine added.

"Do you know he used to dress up every year as Santa Claus and bring us gifts?" Rowena asked. "He always brought me lavender perfume." She savored a bite of trifle. "I never did tell him I hate lavender." Her small nose wrinkled. "Smells like bug repellant." She quickly covered her mouth with a dainty hand. "Oh, you don't think he heard, do you?" she whispered, then raised her voice. "Carl, I love lavender. It's my fa-

vorite. Always made the men gather round like tom-cats." She batted almost nonexistent eyelashes, then her features drooped once more. "I am so going to miss that boy. Whatever will we do next Christmas?"

Brax threw a glance at Teesdale standing between a tall woman with fading red hair and a young lady sporting enchanting dimples at the corners of her mouth. His wife and daughter. His pride and joy. His beloved Goldstone roots.

"Santa would never desert such lovely ladies as yourselves." He'd toss a hint at Teesdale before he left, though he was sure the sheriff would think of it on his own come Christmas.

"Oh look, the chickens." Rowena bounced and bubbled. "Yoo-hoo, girls, get some trifle before the whipped cream gets soggy."

The chickens had attended Carl's graveside draped in black. Without their distinguishing colors, Brax couldn't tell them apart. Of course, necklines plunged to reveal too much cleavage and matching skirts barely covered their rumps. Chloe had said Carl wouldn't have it any other way. Maggie had hugged each of them with trembling arms.

"Mumsy, did you make any tarts?"

Brax raised an eyebrow and mouthed *Mumsy* with a question mark at the end.

Rowena rose on her tiptoes and whispered to his shoulder, which was all she could reach. "I give them pointers. So they sort of think of me as their mumsy."

Brax didn't ask what kind of pointers.

"I made tarts, of course, but they won't be coming

out until all the trifle is gone." She raised a snowy white brow at Brax. "Except for the last piece."

The chickens surrounded him then, pecking his cheeks with tiny kisses, then swiping at the lipstick prints left behind.

"Ooh, we can't let Simone see the evidence. She'll rip my lips right off my face and stuff them up my—"

"Chocolate. Behave yourself."

"Yes, Mumsy." But she smiled and simpered and batted her eyelashes at him.

Chocolate, of course. The thirstiest among the bloodthirsty.

"We were going to give you a bachelor party." Peppermint, maybe, smiled lasciviously.

"But Rowena and Chloe said it would be in bad taste." Cotton Candy, perhaps, batted her eyelashes.

"Do you think it's in bad taste, Brax?" Caramel, the only remaining choice, seductively bit her lower lip.

"It would be an honor, ladies. But Simone's planned my bachelor party."

"The bride-to-be can't plan the bachelor party. It just isn't done."

He liked Simone's plans. In fact, he loved Simone's plans. She was going to show him *The Wizard of Oz.* Because they'd missed most of it the first time, and they still had a bet. Simone threatened to make him watch the whole thing, but he had a few plans of his own.

Then Chocolate did an odd thing. She wiped the lipstick from her mouth on her flowery napkin, rose up on the toes of her spike-heeled shoes, and kissed his

cheek gently. "We already bought a robot," she whispered.

Peppermint-Maybe followed suit, wiping clean her burgundy lips, and planting a kiss in exactly the same spot as the Chocolate kiss. "For the first baby," she said.

"And we're going to learn to put the robot together ourselves." Cotton-Candy-Perhaps.

Caramel-Definitely. "We've already started practicing. I even know which is the Allen wrench."

His heart swelled, with the image of Simone carrying his child and the sweetness of the chickens. "Thank you, ladies."

Rowena set her plate down, wiped at a mysterious moisture in her eyes, then clapped her hands. "Girls, go and put your lipstick back on now. You look positively naked."

The chickens filed out just as Doodle scampered in. Followed by…damn. The stately woman entering on his heels was nothing less than a goddess. She had the ageless features and magnificent beauty of Sophia Loren. Her hair, a brilliant blend of silver shot through with black, piled elegantly on top of her head, tiny wisps falling in curls about her forehead and temples.

This was Mrs. Doodle?

"She was a beauty queen in her younger days." Rowena then dropped her voice to a whisper. "But we won't mention how long ago that was."

It didn't matter how many years, the woman was gorgeous. Somehow, he knew Simone would retain that same ethereal quality.

"She dotes on Doodle."

And had Simone write little snippets. Perhaps snippets were the secret to a happy marriage and a long life. He'd have to think up a few for Simone to write for him. One for each day of the week.

Mrs. Doodle stopped to speak with the sheriff's wife, but Doodle scurried to Brax's side.

"Son, son, it was a glorious service, wasn't it?" Doodle clasped both Brax's hands in his bony ones. "They buried Carl right next to Wyatt Earp."

"Ya don't say?"

"Well, they dug Wyatt up in the twenties and carted him off to Tombstone, but the ambience is still there. And free, too."

Brax hadn't forgotten about the free plot when he made arrangements for Carl, though Maggie had picked out the spot itself and the style of headstone. She had yet to decide on the inscription.

"How's my Maggie girl?"

Brax smiled. His sister had so many people to care about her. "With all of you to look after her, Mr. Doodle, she's going to be just fine."

"Well, shit, ain't that the nicest darn thing anybody ever said. Whitey wanted to come, but his editor called about that change he wanted to make to the dedication."

"A change to the dedication?"

"Yeah, his new book. He's gonna dedicate it to Carl. But there was some rigmarole he had to go through because the book had almost gone to print or something. Don't know the technical terms. But I'm supposed to tell Maggie. Thought she came over here with you."

"She did. She's powdering her nose." And pulling herself together. Maggie was strong. She'd make it.

Brax watched as Teesdale separated himself from his ladies and Doodle's wife and made his way over.

"Braxton, got something to tell you."

Mr. Doodle cupped his ear. "We're waiting with bated breath, Sheriff."

Teesdale looked down. "That's why I'm telling Braxton here, Doodle, so you can make sure everyone else hears it, too."

"Do tell, Sheriff."

Gossip had buzzed from one corner of town to the other in the four days since the arrest. Every detail of the how and why of Carl's demise had been bandied about and dissected. But no one, not one person had mentioned Della Montrose's name. They'd simply referred to her as the judge. It was as if she were dead to them.

Brax didn't expect her name to be on Teesdale's lips now.

"Lafoote's skipped town."

Good thing or bad thing, Brax couldn't be sure, but his gut tensed. "Where to?"

"Who the hell cares? He left on the morning bus."

"What happened to that fancy car of his?" Doodle asked.

"Repo Man in the middle of the night. I think our Lafoote has a few creditors he didn't tell us about. Seems he was only the front man. He didn't put up the money for the hotel. Now he's skipped town before they find him."

"Sounds a little too good to be true, Teesdale."

"Maybe. But most of the time, things too good to be true do happen in Goldstone."

Even as she lost something precious, Maggie had found friends who loved her. "Yeah. I think you're right."

Simone had found her courage. Brax had found Simone. All good things happened in Goldstone.

She entered then, in a black suit she'd found on a Goodwill rack on fifty-percent-off Tuesday. It was some designer brand a rich woman in Scottsdale probably got tired of. Simone always found bargains at the Goodwill. They didn't carry size zero.

Her mother was probably still hyperventilating over it.

Mom and Maggie followed, also in black. They resembled a wedding procession. A beginning rather than an ending.

Maggie accepted the hugs and the kisses and the tears, then made a beeline straight for the table.

"Elwood Teesdale, I think you have something to tell me, don't you." It wasn't a question.

A hush fell, waiting for Teesdale's answer. Brax felt a hand slip through his arm and a warm body press to his side. He smelled her, the citrus of shampoo and the tang of woman. His woman. Simone.

Teesdale rolled his shoulders forward and hunched. "Shit, Maggie. Who the hell told you?"

"Everybody. Why am I the last to know?"

"I didn't want you to know at all."

"Maggie, honey, what are you talking about?" Enid Braxton put her arm around her daughter. Simone touched Maggie's arm.

"Tell them about the gold, Elwood," Maggie insisted. "The chickens told you, didn't they?"

Maggie lifted her chin, keeping her secret.

Until Chloe suddenly shoved through the crowd. "I told her. She's got a right to know, Elwood. Best coming from a friend."

His face fell in a hangdog expression. "I didn't want to upset you, Maggie." Teesdale's attitude was contradictory in view of the fact that back in his office he'd told Brax that Maggie was strong enough to handle the truth. Guess it just depended on who was the bearer of bad news.

All the bluster and anger dropped away from Maggie's face. "I know you worried, Elwood. You thought I'd break down and say that everything was a waste, a mistake, then I'd put a pillow over my face and try to suffocate myself."

"Well, not quite that."

"I'll be okay." She tugged on his arm. "Tell them, Elwood."

Teesdale looked at her, his lips pressed together, then he raised his voice. "Went back and looked at that gold. No claim was filed, but it was Maggie's no matter what anyone said."

"And?" Maggie pushed.

"It wasn't gold, sweetheart. It wasn't gold at all."

Simone gripped Brax's arm. Squeezed. She knew as well as he did what was about to come. Brax put his arm out to catch Maggie if she fell.

"What was it, Elwood?"

"Aw, Maggie, you know it was Fool's Gold."

She rubbed her lips together, then suddenly looked to Brax, a shimmer in her eyes. "It wasn't Fool's Gold. It was Carl's gold. And he got it for me." Her lips trembled.

Brax tugged her closer, into the circle of his arms that included Simone and his mother. His family. "Yeah, honey, he got it for you because he loved you. The man was no fool."

The place erupted around them. Hoots and hollers and shouts and cheers. Like something you'd hear at The Dartboard. But this was Goldstone. When they loved, they shouted. When they mourned, they sent a man off with a smile and a piece of trifle.

Rowena handed Carl's trifle center cut to Maggie with great ceremony. "Saved his favorite part, dear." Maggie kissed the little woman's weathered cheek, then started kissing all the other cheeks turned her way.

"She's going to be all right, isn't she?" Simone whispered in his ear.

"Yeah." Then he turned and pulled her close, melting with her into the corner of the room. "We're all going to take good care of her. Especially Mom."

"I know. Your mom's great." She leaned back to look at him. "Did I insult her? I mean, when you first meet someone, you're supposed to tell them they're beautiful or something. Not, 'gee, you look just like a mom.'"

The antithesis of Ariana.

He laughed. Simone would always make him laugh. "She knew it was the biggest compliment anyone ever gave her." Sobering, he said, "Your mother will come around eventually."

She sighed. "No. She won't. She's never going to accept me just the way I am. But I'm okay with that." Stroking his cheek with a finger, she added, "I really am," as if his doubt showed on his face.

He'd make damn sure she was okay. That was his new duty, and he relished it. Sliding his hand down to the small of her back, he pulled her close once more. "Say it."

She knew exactly what he wanted. "I can't say it here. You know what happens every time I say it."

"Please. It's been a hard day." He did his best imitation of a pout.

It worked. "All right," she said. "But you *cannot* touch me till later."

"When later?"

"Later later."

"You gonna get rid of your sister and Kingston for the evening?" He waggled his eyebrows.

"I'll send them down to Flood's End for one of Mr. Doodle's new Lava Flows. Jackie's still sort of nervous about meeting new people, so it'll be good for her to get out. Especially with Kingston to take care of her."

"She's a movie star. How can she be nervous?"

Simone shrugged. "She's shy. You know, she's always had my mother to run interference."

Shy? Hard to believe, but it was probably why Jackie had decided not to come to Carl's memorial. Too many people she didn't know.

"Make it a pitcher of Lava Flows." So Jacqueline Chandler would have plenty of time to get used to Goldstone's residents. And Brax would have plenty of

time alone with Simone. He tipped his head back to look at her. "I've got a very serious question."

She smiled his favorite dazzle smile. "Ooh, I love important questions."

"Do you want me to read that planet book before we get married?"

"What planet book?"

"You know, the one where you're a planet, and I'm a planet, and it tells us how to…" He stopped. "The how-to planet book."

"You mean the one where I'm from Venus and you're from Mars?" She laughed softly. "Let's save that for later. Right now, I've got enough evidence that you know exactly 'how to.'"

He breathed a sigh of relief. "Now say it."

They communicated perfectly. She leaned back as far as his arms would allow, looped as they were behind her back. Putting a finger in the center of his chest, she dipped her lashes, drawing it out, driving him crazy.

"Now," he whispered.

"Don't *make* me bring out the flying monkeys." Then she poked him in the chest.

He slumped against the wall, pulling him with her. "Promise you'll say that every day for the rest of our lives."

"I promise," she whispered as solemnly as if it were a wedding vow.

He closed his eyes. "I feel a fantasy coming on." Then he looked at her, waggling his eyebrows. "Want to write one?"

"Well, I do know the perfect hero to write about."

He pulled her close for a sweet kiss. "I think we're going to have to do a lot of research to get it just right."

He couldn't wait to get her home. Home was anywhere as long as Simone was with him.

"Now," he murmured in her ear. "You piqued my investigative curiosity the other day. Tell me more about blue underwear and white pants."

Simone smiled. Brax was dazzled. He always would be.

Dear Reader,

Have you ever visited a town and simply fallen in love with its people and its atmosphere? That's what happened to me when my husband and I visited his brother in a small Nevada town. The eclectic citizens treated me with kindness and generosity, and I couldn't wait to write a story featuring their unique qualities. I did give the town the fictitious name of Goldstone and changed a few other things to suit the needs of the story I wanted to write, but I couldn't find a better place for Sheriff Tyler Braxton to meet his match in the lovely Simone Chandler. Yes, I fell in love with Brax when I was writing *Sex and the Serial Killer*, and I just had to find him the perfect woman. I hope you love Goldstone, as well as Brax and Simone's story in *Fool's Gold*, as much as I loved writing it.

Enjoy!

Jennifer Skully

THIS QUIZ IS FOR THE GUYS!

1. When looking to get away from the daily grind of the big-city rat race you:

   A) Take a vacation.
   B) Quit your job.
          or
   C) Quit your job and move to a small Arizona town.

2. If you've discovered that the most gorgeous woman in Goldstone, Arizona, turns out to write erotica on the Internet, you decide:

   A) She's a woman of mystery (what's hotter than that?).
   B) She's a potential home wrecker (if the way the men in Goldstone look at her means anything).
          or
   C) No way she's the kind of woman who would have an affair with your overweight, balding brother-in-law, Carl! Or be a murderer!

If you picked A or B, then immediately check your judgment meter. But if you chose C for both questions, then welcome to Goldstone, where you'll find yourself embroiled in murder, Internet erotica and the wacky, wonderful and often misunderstood world of outhouse excavation, and learn that the real thing shines far more brightly than *Fool's Gold!*